IRONSFORK

IRONSFORK

R. Lee Fryar

Copyright © 2022 R. Lee Fryar

All rights reserved. No part of this publication may be reproduced, distributed, or transmitted in any form or by any means, including photocopying, recording, or other electronic or mechanical methods, without the prior written permission of the publisher, except in the case of brief quotations embodied in critical reviews and certain other noncommercial uses permitted by copyright law. For permission requests, write to the publisher, addressed "Attention: Permissions Coordinator," at the address below.

ISBN: 979-8-88-785006-1 (Paperback)
ISBN: 979-8-88-785008-5 (Hardcover)

Library of Congress Control Number: 2022947532

Any references to historical events, real people, or real places are used fictitiously. Names, characters, and places are products of the author's imagination.

Book design by Allison Chernutan.

Printed in the United States of America.

First printing edition 2022.

emily@fracturedmirrorpublishing.com
Fractured Mirror Publishing
Knoxville, Tennessee

www.fracturedmirrorpublishing.com

To Mel,
who stuck with me through every iteration,
every draft, and every setback.
This one is for you.

TRIGGER WARNING

THIS BOOK CONTAINS SCENES
INVOLVING SUICIDE, PHYSICAL
ABUSE, AND SEXUAL ABUSE.

THE DRAGON'S LAMENT

When I opened my eyes, I saw darkness—
Blind to all but the fire in my heart.
Flame consumed, me bones and all, in the womb of my mother earth,
Devoured the blood and body of my father magic,
And so I was born, dead before I lived.
The world was my teacher and taught me well.
These are the gifts of my teacher.
The wind, my voice
The water, my song,
The earth, my mind
The fire, my soul.
God formed me in the image of a warrior.
My world created a man of sacred words.
My folk?
Who are my folk?
I have no mountain.
No clan will claim me.
The fire owns me, whole and soul.
I can never be anything but what it made me.
Mother, hold me.
Father, remember me.
God preserve me.
As I was born is this how I die?
Dead before I live?

DWYN ARDOCHE
Seidoche dhu Riordiin Wytkyf, Nations, Washington

DRAGON AT THE GATE

Dwyn was a Southerner first, a Dragon second. When his time came, he went south.

In general, he stayed the hell away from other dwarves and dwarf mountains. It was safer that way. But whenever his sickness grabbed him by the bones and ripped him apart by the sinews, he became a child again, weeping for Tennessee, his dead grandfather, the clan who would never claim him. He might be a damned Dragon, but he was all dwarf when it came to dying. He wanted to go home.

Colorado to Arkansas in a night, and he was tired, sick, and far from the mountains that bred him. He gagged on the cinders tickling the back of his throat. More and more often, the fire took him this way, no real warning, just waking up in a pool of lava, hot from the bones out, with a headache hammering his skull into powder and setting off the tell-tale explosive vomiting of recrudescence. How long did he have before the fire devoured him? A day? Maybe not half that.

"God under the earth." He slapped his hands on the steering wheel and the sparks flew upward. He wouldn't make it. It would have to be here. Still, he hesitated, smoking blood melting down his forearms, and wondered whether he had time to turn around. Rain pattered on the roof as he leaned back and stared at the scorched fabric overhead, debating.

It wasn't that he didn't like what he saw. Surrounded by taller mountains, this little hill would wring the clouds out like a sodden rag. Weather mattered. He'd set the woods on fire in Yosemite once. Dwarf necromancers from every mountain descended on his hiding place and he'd barely escaped. He damned well didn't plan on making that mistake again. If he drove on, would he find any place more secluded than this? He'd not seen a single vehicle since he'd run out of blacktop, and the few buildings—trailers with the cinder blocks showing and derelict chicken houses— belonged to humans. Humans he could fool.

Goblins on the other hand...he glanced left at the stately rows of mature oak trees, all the same species, if not the same cloned tree, a goblin plantation if he ever saw one. He wanted no trouble with them. Elemental fire—raw, unrestrained, out-of-control as it always was at his time of recrudescence—was a crime against all magic. Dwarves would capture him and hold him for questioning. Bad enough. He wasn't going back to jail. But goblins shot first and they never asked questions. If it hadn't been for the rivn, he'd have been a mile deep on the right side already, putting distance between himself and the goblins before he torched the place. But there it stood, like an obnoxious panhandler outside his passenger side window, and he couldn't ignore it.

It stood four-feet high at the intersection, a square stack of round stones held together by magic, or at least, once it had been held together. The stump was submerged almost entirely beneath a red waterfall of Virginia creeper. He would have missed it if he hadn't pulled over to vomit, and when he found it, he stumbled back to his truck as frightened as if he'd discovered a mutilated corpse in the weeds. Ruined it might be, and centuries older than the road and the reservoir he could make out in the gray distance, but dwarf watchtowers never slept, even when they were down to their last stone and their mountains no more than a home for bats. Dwarves once lived here. Maybe they still did.

He burped brimstone, less disgusted with the taste than his own cowardice. He ought to drive up to look. If dwarves lived here, they'd have gated the road, surely. As for the rivn, he'd seen more than his fair share of them and dealt with the ancient magic clinging to them too. He gathered his guts to step out and see exactly what he was dealing with when he saw headlights, coming down the road toward him, dim and watery through the rain.

He reached behind him, grabbed his sword from the gun rack fused to the smoky glass, and hid it in the seat. Then he sucked in his breath along with his fire and waited.

A dump truck loomed out of the fog, and without signal or hesitation turned left, passing Dwyn's pickup where he sat, fighting fire. Chains swung back and forth as it bumped away with a full load of gravel. He craned his neck to get a better look at the driver—tanned skin, ballcap on top, no beard, not so much as a hint of magic about him. He was human.

He let out his fire with a sigh of relief. There was a quarry then, somewhere up there beyond the lake. Sometimes dwarves sold old mountains for the stone—curse the faithless folk who sold them—and humans weren't much of a threat in themselves. But if they found a naked dwarf burning in their wilderness, they might tell someone, and who they might tell made him nervous. He'd go up the road and see if he couldn't find a better spot to make his invasion.

"Come on now, you fucking piece of...come on, please... damn you..." The engine gasped to life as he fed it with an alternating current of begs and curses. He didn't have much time to find a spot to hide his truck, climb the mountain, and get on with the wretched business ahead—finding a safe place in which to pass nine days of hell.

Not that any place was ever truly safe, especially after he'd spoiled the aethr for miles around. When this was over, he'd best make himself scarce. He'd head east to Tennessee like he'd planned. Once he stopped smoking, he could pick up some work, get back on his feet. In Appalachia, there were wealthy mountains with big libraries, necromancers' libraries, and where there were libraries, there were books in need of the services only a Seidoche like Dwyn could provide. He had the credentials to recommend himself, even if the rest of him was less presentable. When this was over, he'd get a good bath in some pond, fight his beard into submission, braid himself up and see if he couldn't wash some of the stink out of his clothes.

He turned sharply onto a disused logging road, and the truck shuddered to a stop. He got out, belching cinders, and reached for his sword. It was a marvelous piece of ancient Southern craftsmanship, a heavy chestnut core with twin rows of black obsidian embedded on either side. A real Appalachian mh'uital—a warrior's weapon, and worth more than him, truth be told. He could have sold it for his keep many times, but there were things a dwarf wouldn't part with, although Dwyn had parted with much he'd have sworn on his bones he'd never sell. Himself, to start with.

In the back of the truck, tucked beneath the camper shell, all he loved in the world lay hidden in a box heavily protected by his best hexn: his writing box, his inks, the little paper he had left, a sack of ammunition he wouldn't get rid of although he'd pawned the gun years ago, and nine magical books. He'd take them with him if he could, but his soul was in those books. They would be safer here, protected from the inferno he would become. When this was over...

When this was over, he might be dead.

He touched the back of his left hand to his mouth, and the incendiary rune, the mark of his shame, felt hot. "Paloh mhu," he began, but the prayer stilled on his lips. His god wouldn't abandon him. He would survive.

He walked around his truck, writing the runes in blood over hood, doors, and camper shell, murmuring spells of illusion.

Tangles of sumac, blackberry brambles, and broomsedge appeared wherever his magic had taken effect. There were few warloche as good with illusions as he, and he took pride in how he'd made the rain drip off the branches of the piss-elm parked right in the driver's seat.

Then he glanced across the road, where remnants of a broken stone fence huddled miserably in drifts of sodden goldenrod and blown asters. Beyond it, overgrown pasture blended into an encroaching forest; the steady ranks of oak, hickory, maple, and pine climbed gradually up the mountainside. Gray outcrops scratched across a patina of tired autumn colors showed where a recrudescing Dragon might find a rocky spot in which to shelter. Ragged clouds draped the mountain, coy as any necromancer. It reminded him of Tennessee.

He balled his burning left hand into a fist. "Nine days. Nine days, and I'll be done, and I'll go…" He fell miserably silent.

Home. He had no home.

He trudged across the muddy road and squatted down in the ditch below the ruins of the wall, smoking as he dug through a clump of rank honeysuckle to get at the largest pile of rocks. He extracted one, then sat, back to the wall, shifting sword to shoulder with practiced ease. To an untrained eye there wasn't much to read, but beneath the golden shroud of lichen, he spotted lines never made by nature. Carefully, he singed the stone clean, and as he did, the fire flickered beneath the rune on the back of his hand, dancing to the echoes of elemental magic.

"Kiss my ass. Dh'Seitha. Appalachian, late Southern Kingdom, maybe. Shit." He tossed the stone back on the pile. That explained a few things, the rivn for one. This was an antebellum dwarf mountain, centuries old—probably not a bone left in it, and yet the protection felt as aggressive as an army of Southern warloche, copper-plated and swinging swords as dangerously lethal as the one he carried. He glanced up and down the road. The wall dipped in and out of existence as far as he could see.

Now what?

His body answered him. His stomach twisted, pain pulsed, and with a gasp he went down, vomiting in paroxysms. Damn his fire. Damn it to hell. It would have to be here. But maybe he could find a better place to cross. If he walked the road, he might follow the wall until he came to a place where the barrier had been completely broken, where the magic might have forgotten its charge to protect and defend the land. He stumbled upright.

Reeling like a drunk, he staggered forward, keeping an eye on the wall and his ear on the road, ready to bolt at the first sound of an engine. He wasn't sure how far his legs could carry him, and still the wall ran on, disappearing in places only to rebuff him with a spark when he set a boot near the buried footings.

What the hell? Fortifications this decayed should not be this alert. The irony wasn't lost on him. Old mountains, Southern mountains, where ancient Dragons once danced, made perfect hiding places for a modern dragon in need of a quiet place to die for a while. So much of their magic lay in tatters, not unlike his magic at the height of his recrudescence. He might hide from necromancers indefinitely, provided he could get across the old barrier wall. But if he didn't find a way in soon, he'd have to take his chances in the goblin plantation. He retched until he brought up blood.

Then he came to a curve and saw the oak.

It was more than half dead, leaning over the road, where the backslope drained a raw, red stain across the gray gravel. Its narrow fern-burdened limbs stretched helplessly toward the wall that defied him, a handful of broken stones remembering the strength of magic centuries gone. *Dh'Seitha.* Was there anything that could beat it for staying power?

There was one thing.

He glanced over his shoulder, looking back at the mist covered road. He didn't want to do it, not with so many dwarf mountains around, and not with the fire raging through him unchecked. He'd have to hope the necromantic signature of a tree dying was enough to cover his, that was all.

He scrambled up the side of the bank, bracing his feet sideways, hacking roots with his blade. It wouldn't be enough to simply kill the tree; it would suffer death with the patience of the earth. Make it hurt, and death would release its power. Pain is power—the first rule of necromancy, as true now as the day he'd first memorized it, *Seida Ethean*, twelfth page, first paragraph, two lines from the top. Blood ran down his arms in rivers as he took a fighting stance next to the tree, already pulling loose, the weight of the sodden branches dragging it down.

"He ethe!" Despite his nausea, insatiable hunger gripped him as magic flooded into his bones.

The oak shone with golden light. Leaves burst forth, spring-bright and alive. Even the ferns clinging to the rotting bark glowed a healthy green. Then the tree groaned. Death climbed from the base, through the trunk, and then rot reigned in the green ferns exploding in fiery death throws as the tree fell. The tearing, cracking sound stilled even the rain.

He jumped up on the crumbling remains of the trunk and ran, weaving through the branches cracking to the left and right as he passed. He leapt through the gap in the wall.

As he dropped out of the tree, Dwyn was already plotting his course to a ridge above the green line of pines he'd seen from the road. It was not in his line of sight now, although he knew where it should be. Head west, then turn to the east—that would bring him up behind it. With some luck, he'd find a comfortable cave for shelter. With better luck, he'd find ruins. But getting there was his first problem.

Pasture would have been easy, but here the saplings had grown so thick, he'd need to cut his way through. He drew his sword. He was leaving a trail any fool could follow, but he chopped anyway, wincing every time a sumac or winged elm smacked him in the face before combusting. Rain sluiced over him and the wind picked up, ripping autumn leaves from the trees, and dumped them all over his back. Every branch in front whipped him in the face, the ones behind grabbed at his shirt and canvas pants, ripping new holes where he hadn't already burned through. Vines about his feet tripped him, and whenever he fell, he found a carpet of thorns waiting. By the time he crashed into a canebrake an hour later, panting, he'd been flogged bloody.

He stopped and stared, horrified.

Where a river had been, a brown flood rolled through the woods. White foam curled around tree trunks; whole branches churned past on the froth. He could see the opposite bank, not fifteen feet away, but it might as well have been a mile. He was a small dwarf, barely three feet tall in his boots, and no swimmer, had he dared to set foot in the water.

"Fuck." The taste of bile on his lips gagged him. He had a few more hours at the most before the fire took him, tearing him apart, dissolving his magic and his flesh with it. He'd drop when that happened, delirium would take him hostage, and he would be helpless to do anything but lie there, burning in the pyre of his curse until someone followed his trail and found him or the river carried him off, whichever happened first. He sat down on the nearest fallen log with a miserable squelch.

Slowly, he eased one leg up and unlaced his worn, patched boot. He dumped a pint of steaming water out of it, and rubbed the blister on his heel where his sock used to be. His hand came away coated in blood. He started on the other boot. Everything had gone wrong for him this year. The hot summer that had forced him out of his usual haunts in The Cumberlands had been the start of it.

No. That wasn't the truth, and the faith constraining his lies wouldn't let him believe his own falsehoods for long. It had been wrong for nine damned years, ever since the rune, ever since...

Ever since Riordiin. He slammed his hand against his thigh angrily. *No. Not thinking about him—not right now.* Wearily, he gripped a handful of cane and pulled himself up. Upstream the river might narrow, and he could fell another tree.

But it didn't. The river lay in a wide valley before the mountain, never narrowing, but spilling out of its bed into a million new ones. He splashed across a minor tributary, cursing as the deceptive water came almost up to his waist, and clambered out on the other side, found another one, went down, hauled himself out, and then did it all over again. He was up to his knees struggling in muddy water when he came out of the forest and saw the bridge.

Like the fallen wall it was made of sandstone, but unlike the wall, the bridge had been maintained. Dh'Seitha script covered one column rising out of the murky torrent and the river rushed through two arches below the gray parapet. Glyphs were carved there, also a name in standard Runic, *Ironsfork*. A road of placed stone ran over the bridge. Dwyn could make out the faint shimmer of magic hovering above it. Large willow oaks bordered the road; their golden leaves lay scattered over the rain-darkened pavement as it curved, ascending a slope to where a set of massive doors loomed, cut into a face of stone as smooth as the page of a book. They frowned darkly down at him where he cowered.

Dwyn boiled water to the safety of a large willow, broken over at the bank. Behind it, a stand of young saplings grew, still clinging to their leaves. Into this he crept, a brown dwarf in a brown background, and he crouched there, simmering.

Nothing moved. Little trails of smoke and vapor drifted from his nostrils as he watched the doors. One minute. Two. Ten. Fire guttered through his matted beard, over his arms, dripping down like candle wax. He couldn't cross the bridge. He couldn't even risk crossing the road. The only way out of this mess was to go back the way he came and pray that the dwarves who lived here hadn't detected his magic the moment he crossed the wall. He gazed back helplessly at his route, filled with water, so much damned water. Wearily, he rose, dragging himself up by the willow wands.

Something dark fluttered above the bridge for a moment. A crow perhaps. No. A face.

A voice sounded like a thunderclap from the bank. "Morven, stay down!"

A heavy stick cracked Dwyn over his shoulders, knocking him face first into the river. For one terrifying eternity, the current grabbed him. He couldn't see. He couldn't find the bottom. Then his toes touched, he regained the shallows and came up steaming.

A tall dwarf woman was wading toward him. Her bright blue eyes were all he could see of her. The rest was swallowed by a yellow rain poncho that fell to her ankles. She carried a stav trained on him like a loaded gun.

"Come out of the water, Dragon. Slow, and I won't hurt you. Do anything stupid, and I'll blow your head off."

But he had his footing now, and he knew where the current was. He reached for his sword.

"Hands where I can see them!" Rain lashed her face and the hood flapped back, revealing a sleek helmet of red hair, standing up nervously in a ridge along the top of her skull.

She'd send him back to the capital, back to Nations, back to prison under the mountain where he'd die, bereft of magic, bereft of God. Slowly, he drew his sword. Breathing deeply, he widened his stance.

She backed up; her stav crackled with power. "Don't you do it!"

He lunged. He roared like a draugr of the underworld was trapped inside his soul. Fire exploded in all directions.

Up came her stav. Light grazed the left side of Dwyn's head— the hot sting of a paralyzer—but he rocketed out of the water and crashed into her, blazing. He caught a whiff of sweat, full of fear, and her blue eyes widened in terror as he raised his sword like a hammer. He brought the hilt down on her stav hand. She let go, screaming, and hit him over the back of his neck with her other hand. It would have flattened him if he hadn't kicked her knee first. Another howl of pain—she grabbed his shirt. It tore and he bolted.

Screams chased him as the dwarf from the bridge ran to help the one in the river, but he didn't look back. Fear whipped him raw, and he ran faster, expecting another blast of magic, a sudden pain, and the end of everything. Only after he had thrown himself in an overflowing tributary, been swept downstream, grabbed a tree, and crawled ashore, did he stop. He stood, shaking—looking, listening.

Thunder cracked overhead, and he jumped. God under the earth! Nine years a free dwarf, and he'd almost lost everything. He swiped at the burning gash on his temple. Hot blood dripped into his eye.

He hadn't won the fight, he knew that. He couldn't panic. Panic meant prison, and the eternal death that came with it. He needed to lose this blood trail, that was it. He would stay hidden long enough to let the pursuit move beyond him, and then make a run for the fence. But he didn't know how far away it was. Miles, maybe. He jammed his sword back in the sheath and ran.

He hurried through a low spot where the backwater had set up a temporary swamp, keeping one hand clamped over the cut as he hunted around for refuge. He found it in the shape of a tall pine with a thick canopy. Up he crawled as fast as he could, gripping the trunk with his knees and thighs. He wedged himself where a major limb met the trunk, and traced the runes for illusion on his chest with a shaky hand.

"Dh'ben, Paloh mhu, heshee mi, y seidr ti dan." He slumped forward in a cloud of damp smoke. Illusions for objects were easy; illusions for his person damned near broke his bones. They were too much like a lie. But if he'd done it right, anyone who looked up would see only gray branches and long green needles shivering in the rain. He'd better have done it right. He didn't have strength to do it again. Little gusts of wind and rain quested through the trees around him, the too-hard branch bit into his ass, and he threw up into his beard, rather than let anything fall to the ground where it might give him away.

He'd been such a fool. He'd assumed a quarry of men meant no dwarves, that an old wall meant no protection, no warloche, even if a few weak, magicless dwarves worked there. He should have turned around the moment he saw the rivn. Trespassing in his condition was bad enough. Attacking a warloche was worse. And she was no ordinary warloche. He knew the smell of necromantic magic. Ironsfork must be a big mountain in this region, a powerful mountain with many warloche. They would all be after him now.

When the sound of voices reached him, he shrank beneath his illusion, shaking.

"God under the earth," he whispered, "Paloh mhu, do not leave your Mn'Hesset defenseless. Remember my service. Remember that I—fuck." He couldn't go on. The sight of the necromancer took his hope away.

She'd discarded the raincoat. A dark green shirt stuck wetly to her arms and her chest, and she carried the stav in her left hand. Her face, red as her hair, looked singed from her forehead to her beardless chin. She cradled her injured hand against her middle as she limped through the backwater.

Behind her walked the dwarf Dwyn had glimpsed on the bridge. Gender wasn't always easy to tell from a distance, but the dwarf was so tall and the black hair so lustrous, she had to be female. Her beard wagged back and forth as she studied the water, looking for a sign of his passage—burned foliage, ashes, blood. Beside her trotted a white wolfhound.

Dwyn stiffened. He couldn't take his gaze from the dog. He'd put his illusions up against most necromancers, but he'd never been able to fool a dog for long. He flinched when it bayed and cast about for the scent of his magic.

"Stay back, Morven," the necromancer said. "Let her work."

The dark dwarf huffed. "You shouldn't have jumped him. I thought you wanted to find him, not scare him stupid."

The necromancer waded after the dog. "Eche, Kritha!"

The hound barked and retreated to the far side of the water.

"Did you see how fast he ran? Like a fucking deer. He could be at the fence already. Turn her loose, Nyssa. She'll run him off."

"I don't want him run off. I want him run down." The necromancer tapped her stav against an oak, pursed her lips, and moved to the next. "That Dragon will scorch magic from one end of the county to the other if we don't catch him."

The dog had finished her first sweep around the water.

"Kritha, welo!" Nyssa called. The dog sat, haunches quivering. "How do you know he's still in here?"

"He's not passed this point. I would know if he had." Nyssa's acidic gaze raked Dwyn's illusions. He cringed.

"Bullshit." But Morven sounded impressed.

"I know Dragons. There's a necromantic taint in their magic. I'd never miss it." She touched the pine. "I would—" She jerked her head up. "Kritha!"

A sharp crack, a shower of sparks, and Dwyn's illusion fractured. So did the branch. Yelling, he fell the first ten feet, reached out, got smacked by another branch, and then he landed almost on top of the necromancer. His splash, hot and full of steam, hit her in the face. She screamed.

He jumped up and ran. It was hopeless, yet he ran. His breath came in long ragged gasps, the dog howled almost at his heels, and then—merciful God—he emerged into pasture. Beyond, he saw the fence, a few piles of disconnected rocks and one broken rivn strangled in vines. He burst into a blaze of incontinent fire and flung himself into the boundary.

Explosions went off left and right as magic flung him sideways. He landed on his rear end in the mud, and the length of his sword catapulted him face first into the rubble. The rivn shattered. Rock blasted up, out, and around him in all directions. A stone struck his head, and mercifully, all memory ceased.

CHAPTER TWO

JUST PLAIN DWYN

Memories found him first. It always happened that way.

It was raining, a cold, quiet autumn rain smelling of snow, when Dwyn got off the bus and swiped his way into Nations like any other dwarf on his way to work. Other dwarves, most of them bundled up in their winter jackets and wearing snug scarves around their bearded necks gave him a wide berth as he stumped into the mountain, clapping his arms around himself as if he too, were cold. He wasn't. Recrudescence always left him a smoldering furnace when he finished. Still, appearances mattered.

He dragged into the Haneen Etheanoche shortly before noon. The heavy, iron hinges opened with less than a whisper as he let the massive oak door shut behind him.

"Morning," he said, glancing at the coats on the rack where he never needed to hang one.

Sorcha looked up from the circulation desk where she'd been checking in books. Her beard jutted out as she thrust her chin in his direction disapprovingly, like he'd been on a nine-day bender, not the nine days of hell he'd spent in a Nation's void cell. But her eyes glinted like gemstones and her teeth glittered in a fierce smile.

"Why aren't you dead, warloche?" she asked.

He grinned back at the joke, tired as he was. "Dammit, I knew I forgot to do something!"

She laughed, and so did he.

If there was one thing Sorcha and every other Seidoche in Nations knew about him, it was this: He never forgot anything. His memory had been enhanced with necromancy, honed by years of study to photographic brilliance. So he always remembered every moment in the void cell, dying flame by flame until unconsciousness released him. And he remembered recovery, too—waking to the stink of his body, his wretched fire magic, and the unhappy life waiting for him on the other side. But he remembered nothing in between.

It was the scariest part of being a Dragon.

The memory faded, leaving only the echoes of laughter and the scent of autumn rain. Dwyn swallowed, tasting blood, bile, smoke. Where was he? He couldn't remember.

Oh, God. He couldn't remember.

He clenched his hands into fists and fought for something beyond the memory of Sorcha and the library where he used to work. Aching, terrified, he struggled to cling to the bits of who he had been in the hope it would tell him who he was now. *Dwyn. Dwyn Ardoche. Seidoche to Riordiin Wytkyf. Friend to Sorcha Flintridge. I was someone. Once.*

Footsteps echoed in some vast chamber. A chair scraped across the floor with a bone-chilling sound.

"No change?" A heavy, growling male voice asked.

A female voice answered. "No. He's stirred once or twice. I wish I could clean him up. He smells like a pile of mildewed socks."

"Not long now. He's down to embers. He can clean himself up."

"After that, he'll need feeding. Look at him, Tully. He's nothing but bones and hair."

"Don't overdo it."

"I won't. Soup and bread, maybe. I'll take a break if you'll stay. I'm worn out waiting for him to wake up."

"Take your time."

More footsteps. A door swished, and shut with a soft click.

Motionless, Dwyn listened to his fire crackle and snap ominously in the magicless air. He was in a void cell. He didn't need to see the leaden barrier of bloodsmeldt set into the floor or the matching boundary above to know he was trapped. Everything hurt. Everything burned. Hot, rank urine snaked along his naked left side, crotch to elbow. Had they stripped him or had he incinerated his clothes? Sometimes that happened.

A sudden whiff of cigarette smoke stung his nostrils. He opened his eyes a slit. Boots thick with red clay paced beyond the lead line, a few feet away from where he lay.

"Might as well open them. I know you're awake." A dwarf stepped into Dwyn's firelight.

Had Dwyn glanced into a mirror sixty years into his future this face might have gazed back. There wasn't a half inch of difference between their heights. The dwarf's dark eyes skulked beneath a shelf of graying eyebrows, and his thick brown beard fell nearly to his waist, neatly braided. Smoke drifted from the cigarette he held between his fingers. "What's your name, warloche?" His voice rumbled like the dump truck on the gravel road.

Dwyn didn't answer.

"You don't remember?"

I'm trying, fuck you very much.

"Where are you from? Why are you here?" The questions drove at him like hard rain.

With a soft groan, he rolled over on his back. Overhead, a white sky showed through a shaft cut in the ceiling. Muddy water poured down the far wall of the room for many feet before a sluice funneled it away to places unknown. A grate gouged him in the small of his back—a drain. It might be big enough for his body if he pried it up. He dismissed the idea almost as he thought of it. Crawling around in the sewers of a strange mountain might be the worst plan his fevered mind had ever come up with.

"You plan to answer me sometime today, Dragon?"

"Fuck off," he whispered. Lying on his back bothered him. He shouldn't be able to do that, but even as he wondered why he felt so uneasy, he drifted off.

The first thing he did upon waking the second time was to vomit all over himself. He completely missed the drain. Hissing curses, he dragged himself clear, and rolled up to a sitting position.

No light came from the ceiling now, but a wicked yellow glow fell over the blue-black bloodsmeldt boundary, the wet sandstone floor, and his own dirty body. He squinted at the walls. Seidr lamps, run on magic alone.

He glanced around. It might have no electricity, but for a void cell, this was a palace. Twenty by twenty, or he missed his measure. The bench in the center might serve as a bed, and a half-wall in the corner screened a bath or a toilet. The public void cells he was forced to use at Nations were miserable six-foot diameter circles, circumscribed in bloodsmeldt, with a drain right in the center. A small dwarf could angle himself over the hole to purge from one end or the other as long as he was conscious, and Dwyn always tried to do so. Once delirium set in though, he was as hapless as anyone else. He always woke drenched in piss and shit and there he had to lie, reeking and miserable, until the Seidroche, dressed in their clean, white coats and masks, declared him fit to leave. No dwarf would touch an elemental while he was sick, and precious few would do it afterwards, not without hazard pay.

He rubbed his shoulder where the necromancer had struck him. She ought to be down soon to interrogate him, curse her bones. He felt stiff, bruised, and bereft...of what?

Then he knew. His sword was gone.

"Mh'Arda!" With a terrified cry, he bolted upright and crashed into the barrier. Showers of sparks flew as he cursed, furiously, but impotently. No Dragon born could break out of a void cell. In the end he fell, and knelt there, rocking back and forth.

The necromancer would pay for this. No one could confiscate a warloche's weapon without his consent, unless he attacked, and he had not attacked. He'd defended himself, yes. Any warloche would have done the same. But that defense would be as useless as his futile effort to escape.

"Mh'Arda." He curled up, sobbing into the stones. His sword was the only thing he had left of his family and the only link he had to his faith. Oh, God, he wished that he'd never come to this place! Miserably weak, he burned out beside the boundary.

No one came.

When he woke the third time, it was still dark, and the seidr lamps still oozed their yellow sick down the walls.

Mh'Arda. His chest swelled with anger but he didn't rage this time.

Instead he stood, swaying. He tried a step, didn't fall. Another. Not so good. He blundered sideways, fell, and smashed his head against the boundary. Pain bombarded him like the rocks of the rivn. "Fuck!" He thrashed away, on fire and furious. "Fucking, fucking hell—shit, dammit—"

"What on earth or under it are you trying to do to yourself?"

He saw the red hair first. "Leave me alone, deathsucker! You've hurt me enough."

"Quit thrashing. Let me help." Hands grabbed for him.

He shoved them away. "Help me? Give me back my fucking sword!"

"Your sword is safe," she said.

Dwyn scrambled away from her helplessly. "You'd no right to take it!"

"I can't give it back to you. I'm sorry."

He pressed his cheek to the floor, fists clenched in his hair. "Please."

"Look at me." It was an order, but a pleasant voice gave it. He looked.

It wasn't the necromancer. This woman was older, as old as the warloche he had seen on waking, but less gray. Her long hair and short beard were deep red, her eyes dark blue, and when she smiled, dimples creased her cheeks. "My name's Jullup. Tully said you were awake. I thought you might be hungry."

He turned stubbornly away from her. "I want my sword. It's all I have stomach for."

Jullup squatted next to him. "Yes, well, I believe that's why Nyssa felt it best to take it away from you. Now let's have you up."

He had no fight left. She lifted him easily, carried him to the stone bench and deposited him there, and went around the half wall. Water splashed into a tub, not quite masking a more pleasant, musical sound. Jullup was humming. When she returned and touched his shoulder, he roused.

"I don't need your help. I don't want it."

Jullup smiled. She looked so much like the necromancer, but her mouth was carved along softer lines. "What's your name, warloche?"

"Dwyn."

"Just plain Dwyn? No clan name? No mountain?"

He shook his head.

She smiled. "Well, just plain Dwyn, wants and needs are not the same. You need a bath, and food, and rest. You can either accept help, or you can be a fool." She held out her hand to him.

He smelled danger. But she had touched him. No one had touched him in years. He took her hand, and she pulled him to standing.

"Easy now, easy," she said, letting him lean on her as he stumbled toward the tub of cold water.

He was sweating lava by the time he got there. Jullup lowered him into the bath, and he shut his eyes as she poured the water over his head and worked soap into his matted hair. Then she cleaned the rest of him. He leaned against her, wet and shaking, while she scrubbed at the filth caked down the back of his legs. She was so gentle. It was like she knew how embarrassed he was by what she was cleaning, and wanted him to know it was all right, she didn't mind. Well, he minded. What anyone could gain by caring for a sick Dragon eluded him. There was a trick in this. Still, he felt he should say something.

"You are the fool, putting yourself in danger. I'm not quite through with this recrudescence, you know."

"Whatever happened to a simple 'thank you'?" Jullup laughed. "I'll have you out now." She was sweating as the steam billowed around her. She wrapped a thick rug around him. Ice kissed his skin.

"What is this?" He shuddered in ecstasy and buried his face in it up to his eyebrows. The last time he'd actually felt this cold, he'd been lucky enough to wake up from recrudescence in the middle of a mountain snowstorm. He'd done nothing for three days but roll in the drifts, wallowing in the pleasure of a full body icepack.

"A water blanket. Tully made it." Jullup guided him to the bench. "My mate is a Seidroche; he said it would be perfect for you."

A Seidroche? And here he'd thought she was a tompte, a working caste warloche, forced by birth and circumstance to do the dirty jobs in the mountain. But tompte did not mate with the upper caste sidhe.

"He was the one here earlier?" he asked hesitantly.

"No, that was Tully, my brother. My mate is Nolan. He'd be here, but he's working emergency at the hospital tonight. He'll see you in the morning. He's been here most of the week taking care of you, but once he was sure you would recover he left you to me. Are you hungry?"

His stomach growled.

"I'll be back." Jullup left the void cell and returned from the hallway carrying a basket. She sat down on the bench next to him and took out a thermos and a bowl. Hot, steaming, red broth ran out when she poured. The most appetizing smell reached Dwyn's nostrils. He grabbed the bowl with shaking hands, and drank, disregarding the spoon that slapped the side of his face before falling to the floor. All too soon it was gone. He smacked his lips, stared at the empty bowl in dizzy amazement, and then at Jullup. He held the bowl out desperately.

She filled it for him again and again, and he drank it down as fast as she could pour. He didn't have a notion what he'd eaten. It tasted of tomatoes, red peppers, green beans, roasted garlic, oregano, basil, and other herbs he didn't recognize—summer in a soup. A crusty loaf of brown bread followed, and he wolfed half of it down in three bites. He ate, and ate, and ate, and still he wanted more. He was mopping the dregs out of the bowl with the last bite of bread when he looked up and saw Jullup watching him.

He blushed. "I didn't mean to yank it out of your hands. It's just that's the best thing I've eaten in forever."

"It's only vegetable soup, but I'll tell Nikl you liked it. I asked him to send food fit for a convalescing Dragon, and this is what he gave me. Now, what about dessert?"

"You speak my language."

She laughed.

It was some time before Dwyn could say anything else; his mouth was too full of butternut pie. And there was coffee. It had been so long since he'd tasted a good cup of coffee. He felt almost alive now. He rolled the cup around in his hands and read the label. *Rich Mountain Kitchen.*

Jullup was packing the empty thermos and quart jar back in the basket. He couldn't believe he'd eaten it all and still felt empty. He clutched the cup protectively against his chest, and looked down at his body as if seeing it for the first time—the bloated stomach, wasted arms, trembling hands, and toothpick legs. When had he become these straps of flesh stretched over bones?

Jullup's voice filled with pity. "Why didn't you surrender when Nyssa asked you to? We would have helped you."

He pulled the water blanket around himself, less ashamed of his naked body than his naked emotions. "You wouldn't have helped me. You can't understand."

A spasm of pain twisted Jullup's face. "Tully is an elemental dwarf too, Dwyn. He's a Water Wight. I know what recrudescence is, and what it does to a dwarf."

He said nothing. He'd heard it before. Always said by the well-to-do, those folk who thought they understood the pain of all elementals because they watched their loved one pass their illness in the comfort of a private void cell, with a personal Seidroche tending to every pain, providing them with the best of care. There was a world of difference between a gold-plated Dragon with the protection of a mountain and a bankrupt incendiary like him.

"Ironsfork," he said, changing the subject before he could argue, "You live here. I thought the mountain abandoned. I would not have tried to pass my time here if I'd known," he added, not that the excuse would help him if they charged him with trespass.

"Not abandoned, no," Jullup said. She pursed her lips together, and he had a feeling she was choosing her words even more carefully than he'd chosen his. "It's just our family. But we own a gravel quarry, and we do well for ourselves."

"Tully is the chieftain?"

Jullup looked amused. "I suppose you could call him that, although I never have. Next you'll be asking if Nyssa is chief warloche. You don't sound like a Northerner, but you talk like one. Where are you from?"

"I've spent time at Nations. What should I call him then, if not Chieftain?"

"Warloche, like a normal dwarf, not some velvet-throat politician. Why were you at Nations? Were you part of the elemental colony?"

"Xanadu," he muttered.

"What?"

Dwyn straightened. The water blanket fell from his shoulders to huddle around his thighs. "It has a name. Xanadu."

"Like the poem?"

"You'd understand if you lived there." The wariness that had served him well for his years of wandering had returned. Jullup might be kind, but she was the chieftain's sister, and maybe the necromancer's mother, and he was alone and vulnerable.

"Did you live there long?" she asked.

"I worked at Nations," he hedged. "I was a Seidoche there."

"A librarian! You must have studied at Nations for years then—a certified man of the words."

He grimaced. He'd heard that pun too often for it to be funny anymore. Seid did mean 'word' in the magical language, but librarian didn't begin to cover the extent of his responsibilities as a 'man of words'.

"Where did you work?"

It could be worse. She could have asked *who* he'd worked for. He rubbed the rune on his left hand. "Dhu Haneen Etheanoche." He'd only ever been one kind of librarian, a necromancer's librarian.

Her eyebrows lifted. He shouldn't care, he should let her think he lied, he should do nothing. Abruptly, he grabbed the coffee cup, jabbed his finger on the paper and scorched a few runes below the embossed logo.

"It won't work in here, but outside the void you'll find it satisfactory." He rose and tossed the blanket on the bench and stalked across the void cell. Anger churned the soup in his middle, and he felt vaguely nauseous.

Jullup set the cup in the basket. "Have you worked since you left Nations?"

"Who would have me? No one wants a fucking Dragon in their library, do they?"

"No work? How did you pay for a void cell when it was your

time?" Jullup looked incredulous, then horrified. "You haven't been…Oh, Dwyn, not on your own! You've had no one to help you!"

"Everyone recrudesces alone," he snarled.

She stared at him in disbelief. "It's a wonder you didn't die years ago." She pulled a paper sack from the basket, suddenly businesslike. "Here are your clothes, washed and dried. You can get dressed when you're ready."

He didn't watch her leave. But when Jullup had gone he pulled his pants on, cinched his copper belt tight, and he forced himself to walk around the void cell several circuits until he was sure he wouldn't fall again. No doubt, he was in a bad situation. But if Jullup was a good representative of the folk who lived here, there was a chance he could find a way out of the shit he'd got himself into. In this backwater, a clever dwarf might buy his freedom if he kept his head about him. Unless they looked. Found out who he was. What he'd done.

Dwyn was pacing the cell nervously when full day peeped in through the skylight. It was time he heard from the chieftain and the necromancer. When the door opened, he retreated to the middle of the void, folded his arms across his chest, and waited.

Tully came in first. His boots were clean now, but he'd dressed plainly, jeans and a white shirt with a stain on the collar. A pack of cigarettes poked out of the front pocket of his jacket.

The necromancer looked as if she were headed to a council meeting: starched shirt, black pants, a black jacket that crested her hips like the hilt of a knife, and absurd black stilettoes. Her flaming red braid pulled at the nape of her neck so tightly her mouth looked stretched. Dwyn tried not to stare at her face. He'd heard of women who shaved their beards, but he'd never known one who actually did. She carried her stav awkwardly in her right hand. Both dwarves entered the void without hesitation. He'd have called them brave had Jullup not done the same.

Tully sat on the bench, fumbled in his pocket, took out a cigarette, and lit it. "Ready to talk today, warloche?"

"What do you want to know?" He'd been planning this all night, figuring the best way to pay his damages and be done.

"First," the necromancer said, "where is your vehicle? You're not from around here, and you didn't come here on foot."

He put on a contrite expression. "I parked it up a logging road. I'm sorry—I meant no harm, necromancer. I believed the land abandoned. I would never have stopped here otherwise."

"Which road?"

"My illusions will still be in place. I set them for my expected time. I'll be glad to take them off when you let me out of here."

"Which road?"

"My hexn are dangerous. It would be safer if I—"

"What number, warloche?" Tully put a stop to Dwyn's redirection.

"Three-o-six."

"Too close to Forankyf." Tully spoke aside to Nyssa. "We can't let them know—not until I talk to them."

"I'll set a locater; disarm his hexn. I'll leave the illusions if they are worth anything—"

"Chieftain," Dwyn said, doing his best to sound pleasant, "where is my sword?"

Tully raised his eyebrows, not at Dwyn, but at Nyssa.

Nyssa grimaced. "In my quarters. There it will stay until your trial. I contacted our regional council of necromancers at Whiterock, and informed them I had a dangerous Dragon in custody. They agreed with me."

Tully took a long draw on his cigarette. "You've caused quite the commotion, Dragon. That bunch of old crows at Whiterock won't waste two minutes cawing about me when I step out of line, but you've got them squawking mad. You'd think you'd killed someone. Someone important."

All the hunger that had begun to gnaw at Dwyn's stomach vanished. Of course they'd look. Just plain Dwyn. How many

Dwyns lived in the colony at Nations? How many Dwyns worked in the necromancer's hall? And how many Dwyns killed a necromancer—murdered him in his own home, a horrible sight, blood everywhere, and the body stuck up on a knife of stone like a shrike spears a bug. And the worst of it? They were friends. Partners in magic. Partners in bed. That's what Dragon sickness did to a dwarf.

"It was an accident," he whispered.

"Nine years ago, you were branded incendiary for killing the necromancer Riordiin Wytkyf," Nyssa said. "Was that an accident as well? An accident of justice?"

Dwyn stood rigid, impaled by anguish. He was burning alive, he was freezing to death, and this was not happening—he would not be destroyed again.

With sickening clarity, his perfectly trained memory bled the pictures of Riordiin hanging dead in the dark, blood gushing from his surprised mouth on a cold night, with an autumn wind rushing down the mountainside.

The image, brightened with fresh pain, sliced Dwyn's belly open and filled it with venomous sorrow. The present room faded away.

The void cells under Nations were not like the ones in the colony. These cells were built for eternity.

Dwyn knelt, head pressed against the stone. The only light there was his own, and it bled on the floor around him—puddled fire, puddled guilt. "It was my magic. I don't know how, but it was. But I didn't mean to kill him. He came at me with my own sword in the dark. I was afraid, Ehrlik!"

The gaunt, twisted face of his mentor Ehrlik loomed over him. "What the fuck does that mean—you didn't mean to kill him? Do you know what the council will say when they hear that?"

He knew what they would say. He only wanted Ehrlik to hear his confession, to somehow absolve him. Nothing would blunt his torment.

Ehrlik's thin face, illuminated with rage, tightened. "The necromancers won't believe a plea of self-defense. A Dragon like you—no name, no clan, no mountain—only your word against the reputation of a famous necromancer, the heir to the Northern Dragon's dynasty? They won't have it. They'll say it was murder, and you will rot under this mountain. Do you want that?"

He rose, shaking. "But I should pay—it was my fault—our fault—"

Ehrlik struck him.

Dwyn fell silent.

Ehrlik cupped Dwyn's bruised face in both hands. "One of us has to think here. One of us has to save your ass. You will say nothing. You will admit nothing. You will take the rune, and that's the end of it. By the earth, I could kill you for the mess you've made."

He was more than a mess now—he dripped his guilt all over the floor, a persistent flood of shameful fire. He had not meant to kill Riordiin. That had nothing to do with innocence. Nothing to do at all.

Ehrlik's voice echoed in his thoughts, sharp and angry. *Never show fear to an enemy, Dwyn. The necromancers of this court will gut you with it.*

He held up his left hand, shaking. "I—I took the rune. This is the end of it," he said. God knew, he'd paid the price for his sin, nine times over.

"Not if I press my claim. You'll stand trial for this crime, and all your crimes in the past, Dragon, if you are convicted of trespass here. Your incendiary state is now in question. You broke our defenses with illegal necromancy, a blatant disregard of our laws—"

Lava beaded up on his forehead like sweat. "I didn't know anyone lived here."

"Recrudescing on dwarf land when you know the harm you

do to aethr with your burning is a crime, as is attacking a necromancer—"

"I defended myself!"

"You set me on fire, you drew a blade on me, you ran—"
Nyssa numbered his offenses on her injured hand.

"You damned near killed me!" He touched the long cut on
his temple. "What was I supposed to do? Get on my knees and
beg for mercy?"

"You could have surrendered and come quietly." She stared
down at him, lips drawn back against her teeth.

Dwyn snorted flames. "What would that have gotten me?
The same damned thing. Trapped in a void room, imprisoned,
and my sword, the only thing I have of my family, stolen from
me by a thief!"

Nyssa raised her stav; he flinched—

"Enough." Tully wore a curious expression, something
between pity and envy. "Nyssa, go get his sword."

"Tully—"

"Do as I say."

Nyssa strong jaw worked as she glared at the chieftain. Then
she turned and swept out of the room, leaving the door open
behind her.

CHAPTER THREE

NEVER SEEN A DRAGON

"Thank you." Dwyn's *voice echoed in the silence left behind.*

Tully knocked ash from his cigarette onto the floor. "I'm giving it back because I know what it feels like, not having... options. But Nyssa and her coalition will deal with you. I won't stand in her way. I'm not too happy about my fence, you understand?"

So he *had* broken it. Why had it broken him, then? The rivn crashed in his mind, showering him with questions, but he kept them out of his voice. "I did what I had to do."

"Don't we all? Bear that in mind when it comes to your punishment and restitution."

"Restitution?" His racing heart slowed a pace.

"It's the South, Dragon. Every man has his price."

Dwyn licked his lips. It could be a trap. Tully was Jullup's brother. Nyssa might be his niece. Damn these Southern mountains. Everybody was related to everybody else. "I have no money, and there's little I own that I can afford to part with. But I could mend your fence. The wall was written with Dh'Seitha glyphs. I'm a Seidoche."

"I saw the cup."

"Arcane magic is my specialty." Dwyn pressed. "Will you take my work as payment? Truly, I mean no harm to you or your family." His bones twinged painfully at the half-truth. He'd had his fill of that necromancer.

"You're offering me a bribe?" Smoke curled through Tully's lips.

Dwyn waved his hand at the void cell. "I want to pay my debt. Your mountain has cared for me, and I am grateful."

Tully snapped the cigarette out of his mouth and ground it under his heel. "Not so much grateful as in trouble. Trespassing on top of murder is a nasty crack to be stuck in, Dragon. What do you really want?"

Flames crawled up and down his arms. "If there is a single rivn intact on your land, I can restore the magic. Better than before. Isn't that worth something to you?"

Tully smirked. "Question is whether it's worth enough to me to protect you from extradition, isn't it?"

The menacing click of heels echoed in the hallway.

Lava pooled around Dwyn's feet. "Nine years I've been free, warloche, as free as any elemental can be. I've never asked anyone for help. Why would they help me? Who cares for elemental dwarves? But you are like me, Wight. Please."

Tully's face hardened, but Dwyn raced on. "They branded me incendiary at my trial. They won't do it a second time, regardless of whether I meant harm or not, and I didn't. I stopped here because I needed shelter. I didn't mean to break your fence. If it comes down to a penalty, make it a civil matter—between you and me, Chieftain. I give you my word, I can repair your wall, and I will."

Nyssa walked through the door, carrying his sword. Her cold gaze flickered between him and Tully. "What has he been telling you?" she asked.

Tully snorted. "You were right. He's looking for a deal."

"Is he?" Nyssa gripped the sword hilt.

"I can't go back to Nations. I won't." If he dove at her, pushed her through the wall, and grabbed his sword, he could fight his way out. But where would he go? He didn't have a clue where he was in the mountain. He imagined a maze of tunnels and the difficulty of keeping his sense of direction in this strange place.

"We'll see about that at his trial." Nyssa shoved the sword into Dwyn's arms.

"I'll have something to say at it." Tully rose with a grunt. "He's got a fence to fix for me."

Nyssa's hair rose along the top of her skull. "Tully, no! He is my responsibility, not yours."

"I'm not interfering with you or your plans," Tully said. "But I'm paying for this little gamble of yours. I ought to get something out of it."

"I didn't want you involved!"

Tully touched Nyssa's shoulder. "You think I'd let you do this alone? Don't worry. He can't live up to his end of the bargain."

Nyssa glared at Dwyn. "I didn't want a civil penalty because I don't want him out on our land. He broke our boundary!"

"I'm not forgetting he did." Tully jammed his hands in his pockets and turned his back on Dwyn.

Nyssa huffed, but she took the lead, crossing the void line first to open it with her magic so Tully could stroll across. The door to the room shut on their continued argument. Only the tone lingered—the angry snapping voice of Nyssa and Tully's curt, gravelly replies.

Dwyn clasped his hands around the hilt of his sword. "Mh'Arda. Oh, Mh'Arda." It was as if he'd lost his left hand in a dream, only to wake and find he'd been wrong, and all was well. He bent and kissed the floor. "Dh'ben, Paloh mhu. Ti arde." His god couldn't hear him, not with his magic mewed in like this, but he would be remiss if he didn't give thanks.

He wasn't dead yet. He and Tully might be miles apart in nature but they were both elementals. They could understand each other.

The trip through the river had made a wreck of the copper filigree crisscrossing Mh'Arda's fire-blackened chestnut core. Dwyn dug grit out with his fingernails for the better part of an hour, cursing. His sword had been left in that sorry state while he'd been melting down, and he felt more than responsible. He polished the obsidian blades until they gleamed. He was unwrapping the leather binding from the hilt to rub it dry when the door opened again.

A dark head poked around the corner and then the rest of a dwarf appeared—the one he'd seen on the bridge. Eighteen to look at her. Maybe not that old. Her adult beard flowed proudly over her chin, but wisps of juvenile hair fluffed around her face where her braids failed to cage it. Yellow eyes set in a dark face, her hooked nose, and wary expression made Dwyn think of a fledgling crow. She edged from the door to the bloodsmeldt line of his cell carrying a large beechwood tray.

"I brought breakfast." She set the tray on the floor, and nudged it across with her foot. Coffee splashed on the plate piled high with a mound of scrambled eggs and fried mushrooms.

"Mom says eat it before it gets cold."

When he rose, she backed away nervously.

He set Mh'Arda down. "I couldn't hurt you if I wanted to."

She said nothing—just stared. Well, one rudeness deserved another. He picked up the tray and carried it back to the bench. Ignoring the fork, he shoveled food in with his fingers, and washed the bites down with great gulps of coffee. Halfway through the mountain of eggs, black hair moved into his field of vision. He swallowed and fixed the child with a stern look. She froze.

"What's the matter? You've never seen a Dragon?" he asked.

She shook her head.

He tipped the rest of the coffee back and drained the cup. "What did you expect?"

"I don't know. I thought you'd breathe fire or something."

"Kind of done with that for the moment."

"Are you really a librarian?"

"Seidoche," he corrected, wiping his mouth with the back of his hand.

"It's the same thing."

He belched. "Morven, isn't it? I heard the necromancer call you that. Is she your mother?"

"My cousin. Jullup is my rigah."

Interesting. He didn't hear that particular word very often, it was so childish, but then again, this was the South. "Then why don't you ask your father if a Seidroche and a doctor are the same thing? I'm not up to giving language lessons today. Is there any more coffee?"

"Do you have—do you have the book—the one, you know?" Pink tinged the gray skin beneath her deep-set eyes.

He knew exactly the one, but he'd see what she was up to first. "Care to give me a title? I've got thousands in me."

Pink turned to scarlet. "You probably lied. You probably aren't a Seidoche. You probably aren't anything." She turned to leave.

He cleared his throat before she could clear the threshold. "What does a magicless dwarf want with the *Seida*? You're not a warloche. The seidr lamps didn't spit a lick when you came in, knockr." He grinned. That should piss her off if he'd guessed her politics correctly. He'd made no mistake with her caste.

Morven's nostrils dilated. "I'm still a dwarf. I've a right to study magic, too." Her prickly beard fanned proud as a turkey's tail.

Oh, ho. He thought he knew what Tully meant when he said he was paying for Nyssa's gamble, but he'd like to have his guess confirmed. Unauthorized necromancy was always punished in the aethr-bankrupt South, and whatever penalty Nyssa cooked up for him, it might be something like this. A written book, like the *Seida Ethean* of Cheyloche Daffyd, all eight volumes, would be worth a small fortune.

He leaned back, spread his legs wide, and draped his arms over the bench. "Let me give you some advice, infant. First, if you want a Seidoche to recite a book for you, don't call him a liar. Second, don't ask him to break guild regulations before he's had his second cup of coffee. Third, necromancy is for necromancers, not knockr."

Her hair puffed all over her head. "I believe in the rights of all dwarves to magic. I believe in the right to the books. Knowledge for all. Magic for everyone."

She wanted a fire-breathing Dragon? He'd give her one. Fire arced from his hands, his neck, his back, and his open mouth in a display calculated to send her running. Morven squawked, and fluttered backwards as he shot flames almost to the ceiling. It dispersed in the void as he stalked to the edge and toed the bloodsmeldt. "Even for Dragons like me?"

Morven flattened herself against the far wall.

He settled his coals in order. "It's bullshit, that garbage about equal rights and equal magic. When someone promises you what you most want in the world, they lie with their bones, not just with their mouths. Necromancy is not shared."

Morven straightened slowly. "Nyssa said you used necromancy to get past the boundary. Someone must have shared it with you."

He laughed. "What I have, infant, I have honestly. Necromancy was born in my bones, like it was with your dear cousin. I'm not some common Seidwendr, stuffed to the gills by a necromancer who needed a proxy. I own it."

"It won't matter if you own it or not, Dragon. It's against the law to use necromancy in the South without permission."

"Well, that's a pain, isn't it?" He flipped his sword, gave an experimental thrust, and then slashed the air with savage speed. "Must be quite the hassle for your cousin to call her regional coalition every time she wants to kill a rat."

"She leads the coalition."

"I thought she walked like she had a law codex rammed up her ass."

Morven flushed. "They'll haul you up in front of everybody and read your penalty at Rich Mountain in a few days."

"Good. I'm not the patient type." He rotated the blade and set the fire-hardened tip on the floor. "So, what does your law-abiding cousin want? Fine new books to buy her way on the council at Nations? Or is she not that ambitious? Just head necromancer over all the Southern cantrevs?"

The seidr lamps flared to white-gold brilliance. Morven scuttled for the door. Dwyn blinked, half-blinded. When the red star-bursts and blue splotches faded, he saw the Seidroche standing in the doorway with a satchel over his shoulder.

Nolan was a giant of a male dwarf—almost as tall as his dark daughter. His iron gray beard poured down his chest almost to his waist, with just enough fiery strands to show that once his hair had been red, yet he didn't look any older than Jullup. His vitality showed in the brightness of his charcoal gray eyes. He stared impassively at the girl squirming beside the doorway.

"I thought you had a physics test this afternoon," he said.

"I was—he wanted—coffee—I was just going—"

"You should be studying. Or do you plan to work at the quarry for the rest of your life?"

Morven cast a murderous look at Dwyn as if *he'd* said it. She slipped through the narrow gap between her father and the door.

A blaze of gold and red flames engulfed Nolan as he crossed the line. "Put your sword down, Dragon. Let's see what kind of shape you're in."

Dwyn stared, transfixed by the fire dancing protectively from the Seidroche's gray crown to his shiny shoes. "You've got a Dragon's blessing," he said, awed.

Nolan didn't reply. He felt Dwyn's neck first before digging his fingers deeply into the hollow spaces of his shoulders. Dwyn sparked painfully as Nolan paused over an old fracture, long healed, but healed incorrectly.

"Your glands are swollen, but better than I expected for this point in your recrudescence. How is your head?" Big hands engulfed the mat over Dwyn's eyebrows, and swept the length of the wound.

"Hardly hurts." A Seidroche with a Dragon's blessing? The intimacy required for an elemental blessing wasn't something any warloche took lightly, even the boldest necromancers. Dragon fire, even when given in love, could alter magic in terrifying ways. Dwyn knew. He'd seen.

Nolan dipped into his jacket pocket and flipped out a thin lancet. Before Dwyn could jerk away, Nolan filleted the sensitive bloodletting skin of his left forearm. He hissed. The wound clotted quickly, bubbling and sizzling as his heat sealed it.

"Sit." Nolan took a silver blood scry from his bag. Dwyn had never seen one so small, not even in Riordiin's extensive collection. Dwyn had cataloged them all, from a golden Kibolean cruchis with obsidian inlay, to a modest Appalachian clay bowl with rude glyphs stamped around the rim—ages older, and worth far more. He itched to look at this one when the test was done. The runes around the edge must have been etched by a Seidoche with the hands of a child.

"Any vomiting?" Nolan asked, setting the scry on the bench.

"Not since yesterday when I woke up."

"Jullup has been overfeeding you." Nolan glanced at the empty plate as if he had an idea of how much had been on it.

"I got sick because I was hungry not because I ate. I'm *still* hungry." Dwyn huffed into his beard. There wasn't one Seidroche who didn't believe that the very best way to restore a Dragon after recrudescence was to starve him to health. He'd be willing to bet he'd not see another cup of coffee for a week.

Nolan ignored him. He poured a green liquid into the bowl, and added Dwyn's blood. For a moment it boiled and smoked on the surface with the smell of melted tar, then aggregated into specks like pepper in a vile soup. "Very good, little Dragon," Nolan murmured. "You recover quickly. A necessity, I think, for a man who has been befouling magic for nine years."

Dwyn picked at the clot on his arm, scraping a few cinders

loose. "Not intentionally. If you Seidroche would come up with a test to predict these little events, I'd be happy to drop by a mountain with a void chamber whenever my time came. I'm just sure everyone would love to keep a Dragon for free."

Nolan frowned. "You might have chosen a place with more natural void."

"I did the best I could. I stopped here."

"What of the other mountains you passed? Did you consider the harm you might do to them?"

"Why should I care for folk who have nothing to do with me?"

Nolan's mouth tightened.

"I didn't *intend* to hurt anyone," Dwyn added, irritated.

"I hope you don't have to prove it," Nolan said. "You're already the topic of discussion between our neighbors, goblin and dwarf alike. There's considerable interest in your trial."

"And when's that?"

"In a few days. You're not strong enough to take a g'hesh yet."

Dwyn's stomach flipped. He stammered before he could stop himself. "A g'hesh? There's no call to put me in chains! I gave Tully my word!"

"Why would any dwarf trust the word of a Dragon?"

"You did!" Dwyn blurted out. "You trusted the one who gave you that protection. You shared his blood. You shared his fire."

Nolan rubbed the small of his back like it pained him, but he smiled. "You're wasting your breath, Dragon. I've met incendiaries before. You'd have done better to stay in your colony when exemption gave you the chance."

"A chance to go insane in a void cell? A chance to die?"

Nolan stood, looming over Dwyn. "A chance to do the right thing and take your fire-ridden magic out of the general population. You're lucky Nyssa caught you before your burning began in earnest. I'd have signed your extradition papers with pleasure. My work is protecting the magic of each and every dwarf in these mountains, I take it seriously, and I don't care much for a Dragon who couldn't care less about folk who have nothing to do with him."

It felt like the jaws of a g'hesh had already clamped down on his spine. Dwyn didn't reply. A dreadful truth was dawning.

"I'd soften your rhetoric if I were you," Nolan said.

When the Seidroche left, the lamps went out. Dwyn sat on the bench in the twilit darkness of the cell, twisting his sword hilt anxiously. The sun filled all the square of the skylight now, but deep shadows lurked in the corners, and the buttery light didn't melt beyond the hard edge on the floor in front of him.

A few days until his trial, Nolan said. A few days to think about the last time he'd been on the receiving end of a penalty g'hesh. A few days to dwell on the pain, the torture in mind, body, and soul.

A different morning. A different mountain.

Dwyn stared blankly at a court room full of angry faces. He couldn't explain what he'd done, how he'd killed Riordiin. Five days and nights in the void cell under the mountain and he'd not been able to puzzle it out. The only thing he'd concluded was that Ehrlik was right. The truth was more dangerous than the lie he must tell.

But to tell a lie…

His hands sweated fire, his arms sweated blood. He glanced nervously at Ehrlik, stone-faced at the necromancer's table.

"Stand, Seidwendr." The necromancer's sharp voice echoed through his memory.

He stood, shaking.

"Do you plead your exemption?"

If he didn't say it now, he never would. "I…I accept the verdict of this court. I am a danger to dwarves and dwarf society. I will wear the mark of a Dragon who has no control of himself or his fire." Nothing yet. Perhaps he was safe.

"That is not what I asked. It's a simple yes or no question.

Either you are incendiary or you aren't. You plead your exemption. Are you—and I charge you on your bones to answer truthfully—are you incendiary, Dragon?"

Ehrlik half rose in his chair.

Dwyn clasped his hands around his forearms, smoke billowing from beneath his clothes. He'd do it for Ehrlik. The punishment was fair. And maybe, maybe if his God was kind, it would kill him outright. "I am."

The g'hesh threw him to the ground. The incendiary rune should have been set on the back of his hand by a Seidroche, inked there under anesthesia. Instead, it was branded in his skin with fire, as his own magic took him at his word and found the lie. He writhed in agony, bones twisting as his own magic carried out his punishment, not his execution.

Charged by his bones. Condemned by them too.

Dwyn stumbled to the middle of the room, and stared down the drain. He took deep breaths through his nose as hope failed him, and despair filled the void.

He glanced at Mh'Arda propped against the bench—clean, shining, lethal—and threw up.

Dwyn saw no one but Nolan or Tully for the next three days. Tully never spoke. Nolan seldom stayed more than a few minutes after bringing him food and blankets. Dwyn was grateful for the blankets. He didn't need them for warmth, but padding the stone bench made sleeping easier. He slept as often as he could manage it—hopeless, dreamless sleep.

He missed his dreams. He could pray all he liked in the void, but God didn't hear him, and he couldn't hear God, not with his magic as trapped as he was. Some Mn'Hesset he was.

Sometimes, usually after a meal, he could pretend he would walk free after his ordeal. He would agree to a reasonable penalty, endure the g'hesh for the short duration it would take to fulfil it, and be on his way when it was done. But he knew that wasn't how it would go. Even if the penalty were reasonable, every promise he made now was twisted into that lie. G'hesh always hurt, but another one now would break him open, and if he weren't careful, he would scream out the truth in his agony. No. He couldn't and he wouldn't. He'd die first.

He wouldn't be the first high priest to kill himself rather than let his memories fall into darkness. Every memory that had belonged to the Mn'Hesset before him belonged to Dwyn, and he should long to follow in their footsteps, and he would—only—only the lie. That lie could be held against him for eternity. He couldn't die in the faith with an unfulfilled g'hesh tangled up in his magic.

But it had been nine years. The obligation that had restrained his hand through all the misery was almost at an end. He'd done his part for Ehrlik. He was no *common* Seidwendr after all.

Here he had to get up and walk until his fear settled into something he could manage. He'd have been grateful for some-thing—anything—to give him a sign.

None came.

On the day he walked out of Ironsfork, Dwyn was waking into a nightmare. He'd been stoic enough when Nyssa and Nolan came to escort him out of the void cell, walking him single file through corridors no more than five feet high and so narrow he couldn't imagine more than two dwarves could walk side by side. Floor to ceiling, the walls were covered in Dh'Seitha glyphs, a linguistic treasure trove, and he captured the images as he walked, storing them away in his memory automatically, anything to get his mind off what was to come. What if his timing were wrong? What if he died in vain? Hot dread stopped him cold in the doorway.

Nyssa jammed her stav in his back. He lurched forward.

If he could have done it then, he would have. But he didn't have his sword. Nyssa had it. She ushered him down the front steps behind Tully to where a gray crew cab pickup was parked below the front doors of the mountain and shoved him inside. His sword, she stowed in the floorboard.

Dwyn stared down at the thin blades of volcanic glass, swallowing hard. Mh'Arda was made to slash, to make the blood flow before death. He must cut his belly open first, and push through his diaphragm. He mentally recoiled from the sensation of cold obsidian slicing muscle. He shrank in the middle seat, slowed his breathing, and tried to think about the glyphs. The eagle—wind, strength, love. The heron—water, suspicion, blood. The buzzard—fire, protection, death. If he fell to the left, it would carry the blade up through his lungs and into his heart. Somewhere on this mountain, his memories were locked away in the books he'd written to preserve them. They should ignite immediately, they were so close to his heart—his work, his sword, and his blood, if he did right by God. *If.*

Tully drove. Jullup, sitting in the passenger side seat, flipped her mirror down and adjusted a moonstone earring as the bridge passed under them. "Will the goblins come?" she asked. "I've seen them patrolling the border every day I've driven through this week."

Nyssa spoke, almost in Dwyn's ear. "Midian will be there. I spoke to the Seitha, but she won't be happy until she hears the same thing from him."

"You told her we will mend the wall?" Tully glanced back at Nyssa.

"Yes, but she is impatient—she wants it fixed yesterday."

"Turn around, then. I'll get right on that," Dwyn murmured.

Nyssa jabbed the head of her stav under his ribcage, but Jullup turned around to look at him. Worry lines creased her forehead. "The goblins of Forankyf share the wall with us. They grow a kind of truffle under the oaks. It's quite rare. They depend on it, and if the aethr is contaminated—" She broke off and faced the front again. "Is Blackfork seeing to the surveys?"

Nolan answered Jullup. "Slowly, as I requested. With luck,

most of the fire-taint will be gone by the time they get to Forankyf. I expect Robyn will be at the hearing today."

"Couldn't keep her away," Tully grumbled. "She'll bring half her mountain to shout 'I told you so'."

"We should have left an hour ago. There won't be any parking near the haneen," Jullup said.

"We'll make it in plenty of time," Nolan said calmly.

Dwyn wondered how long that might be, how long he had left to think, when Tully turned right onto a road marked by two broken rivn.

Dwyn glanced at the relics, sure he'd been mistaken. "This is Rich Mountain?"

"Yes." Jullup turned to look at him again.

"Those glyphs. They are the same ones as I saw on your walls."

"At one time, all this was Ironsfork land," Jullup said. "Very long ago." She folded her hands in her lap.

Nyssa's stav dug into his side again.

He shut his eyes.

Paloh mhu, if today is the day I die, remember your Mn'Hesset. Remember my service.

After all his mistakes and all his failures, he was still Mn'Hesset, most beloved warrior.

Dear God, do not leave your high priest defenseless.

CHAPTER FOUR

BRIAR PATCH
JUSTICE

Jullup's fears were not groundless. The parking lots were packed, mostly with trucks muddy to the middle of their doors. Dwyn saw as many as five dwarves get out of one. All wore matching green jackets—tompte from a neighboring mountain, he supposed.

Tully turned left, passing beneath a vanguard of stunted oaks, all but stripped bare by the wind. Beyond the trees, heavy frost silvered the slopes of a lawn where a contingent of ten goblins marched together on a path winding toward the front gates of the mountain. They were uniformly dark-haired and gray-skinned with wispy beards and thin braids that writhed in the wind. One, taller than the others, with braids that trailed almost to the ground, waved. The others simply stopped on the path and stared.

Jullup glared at Tully.

He grunted. "Piss on them. I'll deal with it." He parked in a lot at the back of the mountain.

Nyssa got out first. She adjusted her suit, and picked up Dwyn's sword.

"I want it back."

"You'll get it when you're in the void, not before," Nyssa said. Water sloshed in his ears as he jumped down. Nyssa had bound him ankles to neck with Tully's water magic instead of traditional void chains so he'd pose less threat should he combust. Dwyn smoked and sweated miserably as the soupy magic boiled around him. He squelched forward when Nyssa prodded him, heading for a wall of exposed stone with a single iron door.

A tall red-haired dwarf bundled in a long black coat huddled against the wall, shaking with cold. He held a box full of paper cups in one hand and a single cup in the other.

"Nikl sent coffee." The dwarf handed the box to Jullup and then wrapped both hands around his cup. His teeth chattered when he spoke. "The heat is off again, here and at the school, Nyssa. Those Blackfork tompte should have fixed it last week. Talk to Robyn, will you? It's so cold in there, I came outside to warm up. What are you looking at?"

Dwyn jerked. He'd been staring at the cup in the dwarf's thin hand, but now he took in everything else—the intricately braided red beard, the slender hips and broad shoulders, the lean, balanced face, and those eyes, so blue a man might think the sky had been mislabeled. He'd seen his share of gorgeous men at Nations, but even there, he'd have worshipped this beauty.

"Lokey," Jullup scolded, and offered her cup to Dwyn.

Damn it, he was dying today and he'd have his coffee, but he wouldn't take it away from the only person who had shown him kindness. That pretty dwarf was a nisse, one step up from a tompte in caste but a staircase lower when it came to manners. In one fluid movement Dwyn grabbed Lokey's cup. He gulped a swallow, in case Lokey demanded it back.

Nyssa propelled him bodily through the door. Dwyn spilled most of the coffee down his shirt front.

"Thanks a lot," he grumbled.

"Walk." Nyssa jabbed him in the back.

Rich Mountain was a modern mountain—no seidr lamps

here, no glyphs. The corridor burrowed straight into gray sandstone, a uniform eight feet tall and eight feet wide. Wooden doors the color of early honey opened left and right onto offices or conference rooms. Dwarves in the hall stepped aside when Nyssa marched Dwyn by at stav-point.

The corridor emptied into a stark haneen, a large circular room with a fire pit on one side shaped to the contour of the wall. On the eastern side, a bank of narrow windows let in the late autumn sunlight over rows of common folding chairs, occupied by dwarves, goblins, and even a few humans.

Then he felt it, a cold so intense the water magic binding him shivered and cracked like ice. A memory from long ago haunted him—a harsh, breathy voice in his ear, a sour old face, dirty long hair, and even dirtier nails digging into his skin. He stopped, confused. Isolde was dead. But a similar magical gale whistled through his bones, pouring through every crack, and he blossomed into flame.

He looked up. Standing in the back where the midmorning sun shone brightest, white as clouds on a summer's day, stood a Thunderer. He looked right at Dwyn and a flicker of faint sympathy crept across his shockingly pale face.

"Who is he? The white dwarf?" Dwyn wouldn't say Thunderer, even if he thought it. He hated when folk called him by his elemental label, whether it was the insulting word Dragon in the south or the polite, but no less derogatory, Ardoche in the north.

Nyssa didn't answer. She thrust him across a bloodsmeldt line into a four-by-four penalty box. A high-backed granite bench crowded the space, and Dwyn stood face to chest with Nyssa, with nowhere to go.

"Sit," she said.

"My sword first, warloche, or I'll call you thief in front of your coalition and all your folk."

She thrust Mh'Arda into his arms. "Now, sit."

"I'm fixing to." He fussed with the straps on the scabbard.

"But I'll be pinned to that tombstone as soon as I do and I might as well get comfortable."

"Nyssa?" A warloche sporting a scant black beard and a bald head approached, and Nyssa left the void. Dwyn gripped the hilt of his sword before he sat. Tentatively, he tried to stand. Nothing doing. The bench had a death grip on his ass.

"Northslope wants his students to stay for the penalty. He said that you said they could."

"I said no." Nyssa glared around the room. "This is no circus, for all the clowns here."

"What did you expect? Old Asa raised them on legends of the Southern Dragon. It's simple curiosity. None of them have ever seen one." The bald warloche glanced at Dwyn. Dwyn stared insolently back.

Nyssa pursed her lips. "I'm glad I had the bench turned. Where's Neil?"

"With Rachet. He's understandably nervous about the Dragon."

"Go get him and Rachet too. The sooner this is over the happier I will be."

Nyssa stamped across the floor to a stage in front of the fire-wall. A long table stood askew in the center. The meeting drum with its worn cover sat next to the table. The dwarf manning it leaned over and spat a thin stream of tobacco juice into an empty coffee cup. This was no circus. It was a freak show, and Dwyn was the star attraction.

He eased Mh'Arda partially out of the sheath. The sword slid cleanly, unaffected by the hexn gluing him to the seat. When his time came, he'd be ready. Easier in mind, he sat back, and watched the Thunderer.

It never failed to amaze Dwyn that ordinary warloche were terrified by a Dragon sneezing, but they seldom noticed a Thunderer until he farted lightning in a room. Wind elementals were just as dangerous as Dragons in Dwyn's opinion—tidal waves of magical chaos, and this one was no different. The big fellow breathed magic in and out like a bellows. No wonder the room felt as cold as a cadaver freezer. And white! Scandinavian white. His silver hair shone like the moon in a sky of brown, red, gold, and black dwarves, gray goblins, and hairless humans. Leukistic dwarves were rare, even at Nations, but in the South, a white dwarf was the mythical unicorn in the briar patch.

Then lean, red Lokey appeared in the doorway, and the white dwarf grinned. The Thunderer's smile left huge crevices in his cheeks, deeper on the right than the left. *Like Ehrlik. Just like Ehrlik.*

Lokey's long, red hair swept close to the white dwarf's face. They kissed. The sudden surge of affection Dwyn felt was so incongruous with the torment simmering inside of him, he wanted to cry. Ehrlik was a friend like that, a dwarf who loved him when he didn't deserve it, and he'd thrown it away. His knuckles cracked as he hugged the hilt of Mh'Arda a little tighter.

The drum's call to order began. Chairs squeaked and folk grumbled as the late bumped the knees of the early with the best seats.

Two warloche joined Nyssa at the table. One was the seedy-looking dwarf who had intercepted her earlier. The other was an old man so bent he couldn't possibly be any taller standing than he was sitting. His thin gray face lay sandwiched between layers of heavy, gray hair braided into dirty ropes. He wore robes, putting him out of date by three hundred years. Southern necromancers—with the exception of Nyssa, Dwyn wouldn't have tipped his head respectfully to any of them.

Nyssa rose. "Necromancers, folk of the mountains, I charge this Dragon with the use of criminal trespass. By means of unauthorized necromancy and elemental magic, he entered Ironsfork without consent of my chieftain, Tully Irons He attacked me when I defended my mountain and then fled. He inflicted injury, and he destroyed property. The Seidroche Nolan Irons has found he intended to pass his recrudescence in the lands belonging to Ironsfork."

An angry buzz from the crowd let Dwyn know how much they hated him.

"How do you answer, Dragon?" The bald necromancer asked.

"In essence, she speaks the truth," Dwyn said. He gave Nyssa full credit for 'unauthorized'. He would have protested at unlawful.

"You meant to harm our mountains?"

"No—not intentionally."

"Necromancy is restricted in the south to trained necromancers only."

Dwyn ground his teeth, choosing his words carefully. "I've been trained in necromancy. My work demands it."

Nyssa bent toward the bald warloche. "Trained as a necromancer's Seidoche, Jack, not a necromancer."

"I've seen that fence," the old warloche said. "Seems to me you could have hopped the wall if you were a little taller, Dragon."

Everyone laughed.

Dwyn had to raise his voice to be heard. "I wonder at the depth of your training, warloche, when you question the power of old magic in old stone. That fence has forgotten less in five centuries than you have in the half-century you've been alive." Bitter anger seethed through his magic, and fire crept down his sides like lava. If only he'd remembered that himself, he wouldn't be up to his neck in shit right now.

The haneen went utterly silent.

"You were a Seidoche?" Jack asked.

"Am."

"But you don't work for any mountain?"

Dwyn held up his left hand. "Where the hell would I find a mountain? It's hard enough getting repair work."

"But you *have* found work from time to time, Dragon. A Seidoche commands a reasonable salary for his skill if he's certified as you claim to be. Could you not pay your way into a void room?"

Oh, that was clever, moving him from a position of need to a position of convenience. Dwyn fought back a snarl. "The last time I worked was six years ago. No, I couldn't pay my way into a void room."

"Could not or would not, Dragon?" the old dwarf asked. His hands splayed out on the table in front of him, curling and relaxing spasmodically like mating spiders. He was probably a political Conservator to judge by those robes, equal parts dwarf fundamentalism and morning piss.

"My name is Dwyn, not Dragon. Ask my captor if I had a coin to my name. I'm sure more than my person got searched."

"Rachet means that for a man with no options, the quality of your sword seems an odd discrepancy," Jack said. "How did you come by it? Did you steal it?"

Dwyn combusted; he popped and crackled like a crowning wildfire. Behind him, the crowd rumbled uneasily.

"I do not steal! Mh'Arda is mine." He pointed at a little girl clutching a stuffed animal in the row of seats behind him. "I was no older than she when my grandfather put this sword into my hands." Images flooded in, hurting him in their brightness— sitting on the bank of a creek, cutting his finger on the black blade, his grandfather, all sour smell and equally sour face telling him to be careful, just because it belonged in the family didn't mean it wouldn't cut him.

Jack leaned forward, and the front of his frayed sports coat parted, revealing a strange sight—a solid gold Christian cross on the breast of a necromancer. "And what would your grandfather think of you clinging to the treasure he entrusted to you? You might have used it to buy safety for yourself and others."

God under the earth! He despised dwarves like this one: warloche who abandoned their culture, who forgot the worship of the dead in their pursuit of human virtues, who put their faith in human gods. He put all the hatred he felt for heretics into his reply. "My grandfather is dead. His bones were broken by those who hated him as they hated me. Why? Because he wouldn't cast me off when I was a child. I would not dishonor his memory by selling this sword for your safety, warloche, no more than I would sell it for mine."

For once, his trouble seemed less important than the tears elemental dwarves wept for the families who had sent them to Xanadu. "I was born a Dragon! I cannot help what I am. You asked me if I meant to harm your mountains. How could I do more harm to you than has been done to every elemental in courts like this one? We are punished for what we cannot help. We are exiled for what we cannot prevent. All I wanted was to pass my time in a place where I would do as little damage as possible."

"Then you are aware of the danger you create at your recrudescence?" Rachet smiled, or at least his prunish face shortened and swelled around his mouth.

"I said as *little* damage as possible," Dwyn said.

"You speak of what you cannot help," Jack said. "You are also aware of the exemption for elementals like yourself, those who find themselves in trouble for magical crimes they can't prevent."

"Yes." He shifted uncomfortably against the bench, but he could no more find a position that didn't hurt his ass any more than he could find one that didn't hurt his chances. Nine years ago, that exemption bought his freedom. Now it would buy him a ticket to Nations and a slow death underground.

"Do you claim that exemption?"

"No."

The crowd vibrated like a disturbed beehive.

Jack cleared his throat and the room quieted. "This is not the time or place to be an activist, Dragon. You are already branded incendiary, and we must challenge you."

Dwyn rapped out the law like Ehrlik had sung it out for him years ago in front of the necromancers' court at Nations. "A regional council may challenge an elemental exemption, but they cannot overturn a previous decision without first assembling a full moot of nine at the start of a new legislative term, and holding a new hearing at which the elemental must be present. This hearing must be held before the new moot no sooner than six months and no later than two years after the charges against the elemental are stated. Codex seventy-six, page four-hundred-eight, paragraph ten, lines three through eight. Amendment sought and won by Byrd Oxfire before the six-hundred-eighty-ninth council of necromancers assembled at Nations and approved by the cantrev council of Catskills in the same year." He folded his arms over his chest. "Yeah. You can challenge me."

He all but cried at the irony. Exemption was meant to protect any elemental who did wrong by the law with no hope of remembering what he had done or why. To plead exemption, and take the rune that came with it, assumed dementia, the fate of all elemental dwarves at the end of their lives. But the amendment had been written to keep an elemental from being penalized for taking exemption, not for refusing it. Dwyn had never expected to use this law again, certainly not in the reverse. A chill of understanding passed through him. The first time had been a lie. Now the truth would set him free.

"Then you subject yourself to cantrev law." Nyssa's face was expressionless.

Ratchet's lips curled back over his yellowed teeth. "This is absurd. This Dragon is not one of us. He's an abomination of magic, not a dwarf at all. What rights should he have? Extradite him to Nations and be done with him."

Jack glanced at Dwyn, and then at Nyssa. "He's a northerner. Will cantrev law apply?"

Dwyn answered. "I was born in the South. I was bred in the South. You will penalize me as a Southerner." He clenched the hilt of his sword.

Jack sat back in his chair, clasping his cross in both hands. A troubled frown settled into his beard.

Nyssa's smile was as dangerous as a drawn handgun. "I will accept this."

"Rachet is right. He's Nation's problem, not ours," Jack protested.

"Nations can have him when I'm done with him. In the meantime, I can use him."

"In the meantime?" Jack leaned toward Nyssa. "My land backs up to Ironsfork. You think I want his magic leaking onto my mountain while you take your pound of flesh?"

Dwyn strained to hear as the three necromancers conferred.

"Enseitha!" Nyssa snapped the one-word silencer.

Dwyn sat back. Behind him, the haneen echoed with noise. Confusion swirled around him as he sank into himself. Blessed nothingness would be a comfort, and his god would protect his memories for the next Mn'Hesset. There would be pain, but that too would be a comfort in its way. He owed that.

Something touched his ankle and he looked down.

"Hi." It was the girl from the front row. She stared up at him from beneath the bench with large turquoise eyes. A thistle of blond hair retreated for a moment, and then with a short squeak, the entire girl appeared, squirming past his legs. She rose, dusting her hands on her pink shirt.

Dwyn froze, gripping his sword hilt. He stared up the necromancer's table for help, but they three of them had their heads together, arguing, if the angry faces and furious gestures meant anything.

"I'm Una." The girl wedged herself between his arm and his sword, and looked up with a curiously pleased expression on her velveteen face. "It's cold in here. You're very warm, though." Una burrowed into him.

"Get away from me!" His fire was at the breaking point. The last thing he wanted to do was hurt a child when he combusted.

"Una! Come back here!" A dwarf woman emerged from behind the bench, beckoning furiously. She was very pretty, nutmeg toned, with freckles, but her big brown eyes opened wide in terror. She hesitated, teetering on the bloodsmeldt line, and then she jumped across it as if plunging into a pit of snakes. She grabbed Una.

Una's shriek funneled right into Dwyn's ear. At the necromancers' table, both Nyssa and Rachet looked up.

Una braced her arms against the bench on one side and Dwyn's chest on the other, bucking and kicking as she was pulled out of the crevice. "No! I want to stay with him. He's warm!" She reached for Dwyn's beard but found something else.

"No!" Dwyn gasped.

Too late. Una seized the hilt of Mh'Arda, and the sister, or whoever she was, had a good grip on the girl's middle. Dwyn reached. He got the scabbard. Una got the sword. For one strange, clear moment, razors of obsidian bit deeply into his own hands. He gasped.

Una dropped the sword. It clattered on the floor just past the bloodsmelt line. As suddenly as she'd screamed, she fell silent. She stared at him, blood staining the wrists of her pink sweatshirt. Then she was gone, and the door closed, cutting off her renewed wails.

The necromancers jabbered inaudibly. Rachet pointed at Dwyn, and at the doorway behind him. Nyssa sneered at Rachet. Jack stood up and yelled at Nyssa—all in complete silence—but the dwarves in the haneen were yelling over one another. Submerged in a river of sound, Dwyn could not make the fire return to his body. His sword lay beyond the line, out of reach. Even if he broke free, he couldn't move fast enough to get to the blade and plunge it into his belly before the necromancers floored him. Damn them. Damn the child. Damn everything that had brought him here. He'd damn his own God if he dared.

He didn't lift his head when Jack spoke.

"As the lone dissenter in this coalition, I can't allow you to pass so quickly over your exemption. You have been ill. You admit the hardship you suffer for your nature. Why deny yourself the protection you are entitled to by right?"

"I do not choose to take exemption." Heavy now. Sandbags on his tongue. Pound of flesh, Jack said, and Morven had hinted at something like it. It would have been better to have impaled himself in the void rather than die in magical bondage.

Defiance built up in him, bonfire hot. He would reach his sword. It wasn't that far away. He wasn't done fighting—by God, he wasn't.

CHAPTER FIVE

THE DRAGON'S CURSE

Nyssa condemned him.

"Since you refuse to take the exemption granted by Nations, you assume responsibility according to cantrev law. You injured not only our mountain, but all mountains in our region. Your recompense will reflect what you owe us and our community. To Tully Irons, and Ironsfork, you will forfeit your freedom until the wall is repaired. You will complete the task, or pay for its completion."

Dwyn strained against the bench. Flames sparked from every part of his body. He only had one chance to go for his sword, and if he didn't show some anger, Nyssa would suspect a trick.

"For the use of illegal necromancy, you will render up your entire necromancer's library, written, to myself. The time for your recompense will be six months. You will be bound to this penalty with a g'hesh. Your magic will make your prison. Should you fail, you will be extradited immediately to Nations and your magic can dig your grave."

She rose, as did most of the room.

Torrents of fire ripped skyward as Dwyn thrashed in an epic

display. Behind him, people yelled, but the hexn on the bench held firm. He slammed his hands down against the armrests, defeated, and slumped forward. He kept one eye fixed on his sword.

Up at the table Rachet conferred with a plump blonde dwarf. Nyssa was still arguing with Jack.

"You ask the impossible," Jack said. "A whole necromancer's library scribed in six months? He'd need ten years to make a start. If you bind him to this penalty, you destroy him. He can't fulfil it. Did you not listen to his testimony? He admitted his hardship—he trespassed out of need—for the love of mercy, grant him exemption!"

Nyssa didn't even glance at Jack. Instead, her gaze bored into Dwyn, and he blazed hotter than before. "Tell me, Dragon, is it or is it not my right to pass judgment on a man who willfully destroys magic? A man who knows he is dangerous? A man who has killed with his nature?"

He didn't answer. He *had* no answer for a necromancer who killed men this way. His hand itched for his blade. If he'd been the incendiary Dragon he was supposed to be, there would be two deaths here today, not one.

"Nyssa—" Jack began again.

"He can refuse the penalty and claim exemption at any time before the g'hesh is cast—I've not stopped his mouth. Let that be mercy enough," Nyssa said.

By now, only the necromancers and the chieftains of the surrounding mountains remained for the penalty. The white dwarf had lingered at the door with Lokey, but they'd slipped out while Jack and Nyssa argued. No one else remained, or so Dwyn thought. Then he saw Nolan slip back in through the door. The big dwarf closed it behind him.

Dwyn grimaced. He hadn't expected to deal with the doctor. He'd just have to make his first cut lethal.

Rachet pulled his robes tight around his body. His own chieftain, the heavy-faced dwarf with a blond beard, looked nervous.

He glanced furtively at Tully, who stood near the necromancers' table, apart from the others.

"Send him away and be done with it," a thin stem of a woman wearing a green jacket said in a harsh tone. "If we can be rid of him, then get rid of him."

"Under cantrev law, I can't extradite him, Robyn, not unless he fails his penalty. Six months is the shortest time limit I could apply," Nyssa said. "Would you prefer I do nothing to restrain him in the interim?"

The blond chieftain's mouth twisted. "A Dragon? On our mountain? Niklis bad enough."

"Our mountain will never see him, Neil. We will only house the Dragon's work so we will have rights to it." But it was Tully Rachet glared at, not Nyssa. Tully stuffed his hands in his pockets and glared back.

"But will it be safe?" Neil didn't seem to take much comfort in the words of his necromancer.

"Nothing about this is safe," Jack said, "and it goes against my conscience, Nyssa. He's incendiary. For the love of God, forgive his debt! Then you can send him to Nations right away."

"It's my mountain. It's my right to demand a penalty. I've been fair enough, and we'll all profit by it," Nyssa said.

"*My* mountain," Tully rumbled softly.

"Profit? Profit from the wreck of a man's life—Nyssa!"

"I will take the g'hesh on myself. You'll have nothing to condemn yourself for, Jack."

Jack spread his hands wide. "Tully, you can't agree with this. Surely you of all people should show mercy."

Tully picked in his shirt pocket where his cigarettes were. "Jack, we both know why you don't like this, and your goddamn conscience isn't half of it. Shut up."

The top of Jack's bald head darkened as he flushed. "And that cursed fence isn't half of why you do."

"I didn't ask you to be my confessor, Chieftain," Tully said, spitting around his cigarette. "He wrecked himself on Ironsfork land, and that's where I'll have him bound until he's paid the price. Damn *your* land, Jack Sharpe. I'll have back what's mine."

That fucking sadist. Tully's civil penalty was included in the g'hesh. Dwyn's anger bubbled over, spilled into his magic, and kindled his temper. "I trusted you, Wight," he said, softly. "I thought to find fairness."

"There you're wrong, Dragon," Tully said. "I'm not a fool."

"You said you would consider my work repayment for my debt!"

"So I did, Dragon. Now I'm sure of getting my money's worth out of you."

Nyssa's rounded cheeks set, she threw her shoulders back. She marched from the table and crossed the bloodsmeldt line. Dwyn stared up at her. He wanted to kill her—he felt that as strongly as the rush of flame in his veins. But death was a gift of God, rightly bestowed by God, and she didn't deserve it. He drew in his flame, preparing his heart for the final time. He'd measured the distance from the bench to his sword a hundred times while the necromancers argued.

She grasped his elbows. Her arms—red and hairy on the back, but pink as roses on the soft underside—glistened wetly. His arms were already bloody with anticipation. She'd have to bring him out to place the g'hesh. He couldn't be bound in a void. He wrapped his fingers around her elbows, and the bench released him.

Today is the day I die, Paloh mhu.
Remember your Mn'Hesset.

Firelight streamed from the rune on Dwyn's left hand and branded Nyssa's cheek as she lifted him up.

Remember my service.
Remember I gave my life willingly.

He stepped across the line, and threw himself toward his sword, yanking Nyssa down in a conflagration as he fought. She tugged up on his arms, but not before he got a hand free. Blood sprayed his face—scalding hot. She screamed as he redirected the shower, catching her in the eyes. He hopped and jerked across the floor, dragging Nyssa with him. His foot struck the hilt of Mh'Arda once, twice.

"No. You. Don't!" Nyssa kicked. The sword skittered away.

No. No. The room was crashing around Dwyn. Someone grabbed him from behind. He jammed his head back and smacked into a solid, unyielding wall of muscle. The doctor's arms were as strong as tree roots. Nyssa panted, inches from his face. Her hair had come loose from her braid, tracing a bloody line across her forehead. She grabbed Dwyn's free hand—the one he was whipping about his head as he tried to hit Nolan—and pressed both arms against his.

"By my word, by my blood, by my bone, I bind you, Dwyn Ardoche, to the penalty imposed by this court—"

He punched. His knuckles cracked against her teeth. Too late. He went down in flames, screaming.

Nolan dropped him. Even the Seidroche's protection was not enough against the fire ripping through Dwyn from the inside. The g'hesh seized him with fangs and claws and shook him to pieces. This thing, this horrible thing—it was a monster, and it would pull him apart at the seams of his soul.

"Meda! Meda!" Fireworks burst in his skull, smoke strangled him, fire ate him out like a corpse. His bones creaked and groaned in the storm of magic beating him senseless. "Ata ti hacharda! Hacharda! N'mhu Dwyn! Mhu seid! Mhu seidr! Mhu cheyl!"

Nyssa sank to her knees clutching her chest, her mouth open in a wail that pierced Dwyn's eardrums.

"Ata ti hacharda!"

Someone yelled for help. Tully pinned Dwyn face down on the floor. He twisted, showering the Wight in sparks and embers. Tully slammed Dwyn's head into the stone.

"Hold him down," Nolan said.

"Nyssa?" All the gravel was gone from Tully's voice. Terror filled it.

"Damn it, Tully, I said hold him!" Nolan jerked his pants down. A needle stung his hip and was withdrawn suddenly.

"He's too hot, he's melting down." The needle skittered away to the corner, dancing and sparking across the stone. A naked syringe plunged upward between his straining legs. Dwyn bucked, liquid steamed inside him, and then it was over. The bright, iridescent explosions behind his eyes slowed to splashes of color oozing over his retinas.

Ata ti hacharda. Forever, I curse you. By my name, by my word, by my blood, by my bone. By my God, you will pay for what you have done to me. You will pay.

"Nyssa?"

"I'm fine—a shock—the recoil—I should have expected—"

"Nolan, help her!"

Nolan's thumbs flicked in front of Dwyn's frozen eyes and probed gently around his orbits. "A minute—"

"Leave him," Tully snarled. "I hope he dies."

Nolan's sedative did nothing for Dwyn's pain. It did paralyze him. He was as rigid as a stake when Tully and Nolan heaved him into the back seat of the truck. He didn't see where Nyssa went. Nolan drove. Tully sat on the passenger's side. And Jullup—

Jullup cradled his head in her lap the whole way back. Talked to him. Stroked his forehead like she cared.

Dwyn lost consciousness for a while. He knew because he didn't remember how he got from Rich Mountain to Ironsfork. He'd left the cursed courtroom with the full light of a white sun baking his unblinking eyes. At some point, he'd managed to close them, because when he opened them again, it was dark. All the sunlight had drained away from the skylight above him, and seidr lamps flickered dully on the damp walls, and over the sticky cauldron of gore he'd brewed in his purging.

He was back in the void cell. They'd dumped him in the tub, possibly to cool him. He squinted balefully at Jullup sitting in a chair outside the void cell with a concerned frown on her face before sinking under the water completely. He'd have stayed there forever, only *ata ti hacharda*. He emerged, bobbing in a froth of crimson surrounding him. He was a mass of welts where the g'hesh had beaten him raw. Part of the pain had ebbed with his bleeding, but the g'hesh was there, even if he couldn't feel it in the magicless peace of the void.

He glanced at Jullup again. A deep crevice had formed between her eyebrows. He'd not forgotten that it was she who asked his name, and that he owed at least some part of this misery to her prying questions but ...

"Will you help me?"

She was there before he finished asking. She supported him as he stumbled to the bench. "Lie down—" Her red hair, streaked with gray, brushed his cheek as she hovered. "Rest. You'll be all right." She put the cooling blanket over him.

He dragged it wearily over his head and lay shivering beneath it. She was right about that. He would recover. He had no choice. The g'hesh bound him to that penalty, and death had lost its power to save him. When he recovered, he *would* fix that fence. He'd fix them all. But for now, he was helpless. Much good it had done him to swear revenge. He couldn't even think up the beginnings of a plan tonight.

Footsteps crossed the room, but didn't come into the void.

"How is he?" Nolan asked.

"How do you think he is?" Jullup whispered. "Look at the bathwater! Bled like a knife cut his throat."

"I didn't know this would happen."

"You knew something would happen or you wouldn't have brought a tranquilizer."

"There was no harm being prepared; Dragons seldom go quietly to a g'hesh. I thought he would take exemption. Stubborn fool."

"You blame him."

"Yes, I do blame him. He might have ended his days in the colony, where he belongs. All laws aside, if he wasn't incendiary then, he's incendiary now. He's as wasted as I've ever seen an elemental that still had his mind about him."

"If it had been Tully in that courtroom, would you send him to the colony?"

Nolan snorted. "You know I wouldn't. He's family—"

"You have told me how much it meant to your Dragon, having you to comfort him, to remind him who he was when he couldn't remember anymore. Nolan, this man has no one!"

"You don't know that. He lived there once. He may have friends at Nations, who can—"

"If he had friends who cared, would they have let him suffer like this? If so, may the God of the Dead close the gates to them! May they rot in their graves!"

Silence. Dwyn thought both dwarves had walked out to continue their quarrel in the hallway. He peeped out from beneath the blanket.

Jullup stood at the edge of the void, arms folded over her chest. A fierce red light shimmered as her fire protection, a gift from her mate, writhed against the barrier. Nolan stood on the other side, equally bright, but diminished somehow in the glare of her fury.

"I want him upstairs. He's not dangerous, he's not recrudescing anymore. I don't want him lying down here where I can't help him."

"Not dangerous? Jullup, that little Dragon killed a man, horrifically, he tried to kill himself, he damned well might have killed Nyssa if we'd not been there—"

Jullup's jaw jutted forward aggressively, beard bristling. "He's a dwarf, even if he's a prisoner, and I will take care of his needs."

"Nyssa won't like—"

"Since when do you or I answer to my niece? You can back me up, Nolan, or you can say I did it on my own, but from now on, he's not going to be treated like garbage."

"Tomorrow, perhaps—"

"No. Tonight. He can stay in our quarters. I'll manage on my own. I don't need your help."

Nolan sighed. "Yes, you do. He's hot enough to burn you in this state. I'll carry him."

Nolan lifted Dwyn easily, blanket and all. Dwyn tried to relax during the crossing, but once free of the void, his mutilated magic stabbed through his muscle down to the bone. Pain rebounded, arcing up his back, exploding in his skull. He screamed, thrashing in Nolan's arms. "It hurts! It hurts!"

Nolan turned to go back to the void, but Jullup cupped Dwyn's face in her hands. Dark indigo eyes regarded him through the slashes of red, green and yellow that painted his vision with nightmarish rainbows. "Lie still. Please, Dwyn. Don't fight."

He swallowed hard, trembling as the electrical shocks of his raw nerves pierced his flesh. But he didn't fight. There wasn't any fight left in him. By the time Nolan laid him in a bed somewhere in the upper reaches of the mountain, Dwyn was in so much pain, he was near to fainting.

After the darkness of the void room, a seidr lamp shining down in his face blinded him. Dwyn blinked the spots away. He lay inert, a corpse on a slab, with the pungent odor of herbs wafting around him.

"Where do you want me?" Nolan asked.

"Go to work. I don't need you here," Jullup replied.

Shadow and light danced on the walls as Jullup lit candles. A warm, honeyed fragrance began to fill the space.

"I'm not comfortable leaving you alone with him."

"Tell Tully he's here if it makes you feel better." Jullup bent over. A copper chain spilled through her fingers. Tiny yellow globules glimmered as they clicked together.

"Jullup." Nolan's voice rose slightly at the end of her name.

"Or Nyssa. I don't care. You've done what you could for him. Now let me do my job."

Nolan growled low in his throat. He loomed over Dwyn briefly. "You do as she says, Dragon, or I'll hear about it, and you won't like what I do."

Dwyn caught a glimpse of some large room, with Nolan's broad back silhouetted against the light before the door shut with an airy thump.

Candlelight illuminated a low red ceiling as Jullup dragged the chain over his body, chanting. "Ti mikhave. Ti eseithe. Ono ti dh'tardi se bene."

The amber soothed his bruised body; the chant salved his tender magic. The copper rings chimed, and the beads clicked softly in cadence. *You are made safe. You are made whole. All that is wrong will be well.*

"You are…" A healer, an Arohnoche, not a Seidroche like Nolan, who would bleed an elemental dry for the sake of saving others. "Te mhu bena," he gasped. "Paloh tu bena." Blessed numbness began to dull his pain.

"Rest." Jullup rolled her sleeves up to her elbows, and poured a tincture into a stone basin. The soapy, sweet odor of mayapple flowers filled the air.

He cried when she touched him at first, but she whispered, "Se bene, Dwyn." Her fingers skated gently over his beaten flesh. He drifted, lulled by the smells, Jullup's hands, and the deadening effect of her magic until he didn't know where waking ended and dreams began.

He had been here before.

Four black walls, covered in runes. Fire blazing all around him. The smoke he breathed was the breath of fear.

There was a dwarf in the fire with him, a Dragon. He was dead. His eyes were open, and he stared blindly ahead. They were so empty, those eyes, but a face was reflected in them. A grinning skull, silvered, seamed with a red more crimson than the flames, and his own eyes were torches of hatred…

A tomb. He was in a tomb.

He screamed in terror. A thin, bitter wail sounded in his ears, and he lifted his hands to look at them. They were the bones of an infant, black as jet, hard as diamonds.

Still trapped in the shroud, Dwyn clawed to free himself. He thrashed. He hammered his ancient fists against the wall, and tore free of the fire swaddling him.

A thud, painfully real, jarred him awake. He gasped, sucking his fire in. An extraordinarily white light all but blinded him. The bedsheet, torn and burning, went out as his terror faded and the room from last night slowly came into focus. He was alone.

No, not alone. A tail attached to the back of a fat calico cat vanished over the end of the bed. It ran off with a peculiar hopping motion.

He'd been dreaming about the tomb again. The images were so familiar, and yet he knew he'd never been in that place, not in any life he'd known as Mn'Hesset. He sat up, rubbing his arms, and his hands slipped in oil. No wonder he'd caught the sheets on fire. He touched the welts on the back of his neck, the pattern of bruises on his chest. They barely hurt now.

He stood. Still disoriented, he took a few experimental steps, swaying, and stood in the doorway, elbows braced against the stone.

A cavernous room sprawled before him. It was a bedroom, but larger than most homes at Nations. A canopied bed flanked a wardrobe as big as a closet. In a corner, a white desk overflowed with paperbacks. In the middle of the room, a round table proudly displayed wooden boxes full of polished stones, glass jars of crushed herbs, a live geranium in a clay pot, sundry towels, a hairbrush, and one high-heeled black pump. Red sandstone walls basked in the sunlight streaming in through a sliding glass door.

Beyond the door, light fell on a stone patio in curious square blocks. Patterns of dark circles crossed the squares, spinning or swinging for a moment, and then stood still. Dwyn thought the door would be locked, but when he set his hand on it, he fell sideways when it slid. He stepped outside.

A lush jungle must have grown here all summer, judging from the number of pots grouped around every post of an arbor. Hanging baskets dangled on chains from the overhead beams. Ghosts of petunias, moss roses, and nasturtiums rattled when the wind blew, and all the baskets swayed and spun like tops.

A gazing pool, black with rotting water lilies, marked the limit of the patio. The stone bench beside it offered a place to rest, and Dwyn sat, tired even after the short walk. Mist rose where the river flowed toward the reservoir, but another white cloud spiraled some distance west of the lake. He squinted. It was thicker than smoke.

A crunching noise came from below, and Jullup appeared, carrying a five-gallon bucket in one hand, and a set of loppers in the other. She came up the stairs, swinging the bucket. It was full of neatly cut green twigs.

"Sassafras wands," she explained, before he asked. "Cut this time of year before the sap freezes, they are quite good."

"For healing?"

"For that, and other things. These are for Nikl. Twenty warloche are coming to Rich Mountain tomorrow for the Metalmages conference, and they always want a trout bake. Nikl cooks the fish on green sassafras twigs over the firepit. I told him I'd cull him some if he'd cook for me. I need to get some good food into you. I could feel every bone in your back last night." Her gaze traversed him from the crown of his head to his bare legs.

He flushed. "I didn't see my clothes," he said, by way of explanation.

"They're in the wash. I'll see if something of Lokey's will fit you. Come inside for breakfast?" She held out her hand.

He shook his head. "I want some air."

"Then I'll bring you some toast and coffee out here, but it won't be good coffee, I'm afraid."

"Can't be worse than what I make." He tried a smile.

Jullup laughed. "I'll remind you that you said that." She left the loppers, but took her bucket inside. The wind scooped scattered leaves from the corners of the patio and tossed them skyward. Dwyn hugged himself, hunting around in his magic, digging for the splinter. He flinched as the g'hesh needled him. It would dive deeper into his bones the more he resisted his penalty, and he would have to appease it soon. He'd promised a library and a fence, and his magic would hold him to both.

What good did it do him to curse Nyssa and her mountain when his own bones held him hostage? But curses were not g'hesh. G'hesh had to be obeyed, whether a man was able to fulfill them or not. Curses took ability into account. If he could vow revenge, there must be a way.

He picked up an escaped leaf and held it until it burned to ashes in his palm. No more charging ahead without a scheme and trying to make it work. He would study this mountain first— make a plan. Jullup could be a treasure trove of information, provided he asked the right questions.

He was mulling over this when Jullup returned with half a loaf of bread made into burnt toast, saturated with honey. He set about clearing the plate as soon as she handed it to him. He washed down the first bite with coffee. Oh, God, she had not lied. He licked his lips and bared his teeth.

"I warned you."

"So you did." He coughed. He nodded in the direction of the smoke. "Is that the quarry?"

"Yes," Jullup said. "No blasting yet, or we'd be hearing it."

"You said it was just your family who lived here. Who works the quarry then?"

"Humans work for us."

"Humans?"

"Yes. I don't suppose you went through the town, but that's where we hire from." Jullup got up, dusting off her jeans. "Now, finish eating, and after that, I want you to bathe. Then I need to do something about that haystack on your head. Let me see your arms."

He held them out for inspection.

She shook her head. "You heal as fast as a child. How old are you?"

"Thirty-five."

She smiled all over her face. "Why, you'll be of age this Dh'Morda!"

He blushed. "It doesn't mean anything. Not for me."

"No?" Jullup smiled. "Well, I still think it's an excuse for cake." She relieved him of the empty plate and still full cup. "The bath is to the left of the room you stayed in last night. Shut the door—The Mollycat will be in your bed if you don't." She opened the sliding door. "I never thought I'd use that room again. Morven slept in it when she was a baby." She walked off, humming.

CHAPTER SIX

HOSPITALITY

For nine years, Dwyn had not cared whether he worked or died.
He took care of the only things that mattered—himself and his
soul. With no other compulsions, he hid beneath the Cumberlands each winter, deep in the oldest caverns of Heldasa where
no dwarves lived. He fed his stomach on the fruit of the land,
and his magic on the bones of the dead, and he was free—alone,
hungry, and homeless, but free. God under the earth, he must
be free again.

He stared at his gaunt face in the fogged glass of the bathroom mirror and touched the umber bruise on the side of his
face. Blood pooled in dark puddles beneath his flame-reddened
eyes.

Another day. Another mirror.

Ehrlik, hissing in sympathy, pressed a red washcloth filled
with ice over Dwyn's left eye, for all the good it did. The ice
melted on contact.

"I can't go back to Rivnkyf," Dwyn mumbled through cracked

lips. The pain in his face was nothing compared to the pain in his heart. "Next time he'll kill me."

"But you will go back. You must." Ehrlik rubbed Dwyn's shoulders, and Dwyn leaned into the embrace for love, and wished for understanding.

"Don't make me," he said.

"I don't need to." Ehrlik kissed his ear. "The g'hesh will make you."

And Dwyn cried, because it was true. He could never ignore the compulsion, the drive to fulfill his obligation, to ease the building chemical hunger. He was bound by his bones to serve the Dragon necromancer, and bound by his heart to love him. And the next time, Riordiin didn't kill him.

He killed Riordiin.

Dwyn groaned, and sank down over the sink on his elbows, sick to his soul. There was only one way to undo a g'hesh permanently. Kill the one who cast it.

He ground his teeth and glared angrily at the miserable, haunted face that stared back at him. Jullup had been kind. She cared about him. Less than twenty-four hours since the g'hesh had beaten him into submission, and already he was questioning his resolve.

"Illusions," he muttered. "They're damned illusions—her kindness and caring." He threw the towel at the dangerous man in the mirror and walked out, steaming.

He found the clothes Jullup had promised lying on the bed. The worn shirt smelled like cherries, and something else, something alcoholic, but he was too tired to puzzle it out, and too unhappy to care. He pulled the shirt on, the pants up, crawled into the bed, and lay there. He didn't bother to button up.

When Jullup came for him, she carried a bottle in one hand and the second cousin to her loppers in the other. She snapped the blades together suggestively. "Up, and into the kitchen."

"No." He didn't move.

She lowered the shears. "It's a mess, Dwyn. Hair grows back."

"Don't cut it."

Jullup stared down at him shrewdly. "Am I correct in thinking if I cut your hair with that machete you carry, you wouldn't even accept that compromise, hesset?"

It was a peculiarity of his faith that he couldn't say, couldn't tell her she'd guessed his religion, but he was relieved.

Jullup rolled her eyes. "It's not like I haven't met a Knight of the Dead before. And I won't say anything!" She added as he opened his mouth to deny it. "I won't cut it. But you will come to the kitchen, I'm going to comb your mats out, and I don't want to hear so much as a yelp out of you when it hurts."

She helped him walk the long, dimly lit hall he'd been carried through the night before, muttering under her breath. "You zealots—can't worship the dead like a normal warloche, no, you have to drag the poor old God of the Dead into it, like he hears your prayers."

Dwyn didn't bother to correct her—he worshiped the dead as well as any warloche, even better than most, and the truth of his prayers showed in his body. He healed as only an appointed servant of God could heal, but faith or no faith, he'd purged a lot of blood in the last day and a half. He was panting by the time he reached the kitchen.

Dwarf quarters seldom had kitchens—most private mountains employed chefs and cooks to feed their people. At one time, this room had probably been an assembly hall for whoever occupied Ironsfork in the distant past. Now a large range shared the same wall as a refrigerator, and a sink filled with dirty dishes spanned the gap. Dingy cabinets squeezed the countertops too tightly between them. A stack of textbooks occupied one end of the oak table, the middle was taken up with laundry, and on the other, the remains of breakfast for three people had not yet been cleared. He straddled the chair Jullup pulled out for him, and embraced the sturdy top rail, shaking with exhaustion.

"When was the last time you braided this?" Jullup worked oil gently through his hair with her fingers.

"Eight years ago."

"What was the occasion?"

"An interview—motherfucker!"

Jullup dug her comb into his tangle and pulled. "I said I didn't want to hear it."

He bubbled frothy curses under his breath. After an eternity of yanking, Jullup presented him with a kitten of hair. "How did you put up with this? It had to itch." She dumped more oil into the bleedingly raw scrape she'd gouged on top of his head. "So, what happened then?"

He half turned in the chair, gasping. "Fucking hell—what happened when?"

"At your interview."

"The chieftain threw a chair at me. Dammit!"

"Threw a chair—why?"

God be merciful, she'd stopped combing for a moment. He flexed his left hand against the upright suggestively. "Why do you think?"

"Oh, ho!" she crowed. "You tried to find a mountain for yourself, didn't you? You're not quite so independent as you seem."

He grunted. "It was a promise I made my grandfather on his death bed. It wasn't any use. Folk don't like Dragons. And I don't much like—fuck!" He gripped the spindles and hung on as she started in again. For the love of earth, must she tug all his hair out by the roots? Witch hazel and licorice perfumed him as the oil warmed. He wished he'd said nothing to her about that foolish old man and his equally foolish promise. She would pry—drag her questions through his heart like that damned comb.

"You got on well enough with folk at Nations. Do you still have friends there?" Jullup pushed almost two feet of dark brown, oil-slathered hair over his shoulder.

He tensed. It was not an idle question. He remembered every

word that passed between Nolan and Jullup in the void room perfectly. It was not his nature to forget. He was far too accomplished a Seidoche.

Ehrlik, beloved Ehrlik. He might still be there, if he hadn't gone back to Norway like he'd planned to do. His old friend Sorcha was probably head Seidoche of Nations, given her ambition, only he couldn't call her friend now, not after she'd abandoned him.

He chose his words carefully. "My friends don't know I'm alive." For their sake, he was glad it was true.

"You have no other family?"

"None that claim me."

"That's hard, not having family."

He nodded politely, but inside he was a yell of pain. His grandfather and he had never agreed on anything once Dwyn had been old enough to argue. Always disappointed, always angry, always demanding—Dwyn had never been able to please him. When his grandfather died, he danced for the dead, sealed the house as a tomb, and left the grumpy old man at peace for the first and the last time. It should have been over. It wasn't.

A year later, he'd returned. Bitter sadness accompanied the images etched in his mind: the broken tomb door, crushed and blackened bones, and the neighboring goblin mountain still reeking smoke from the savage burning he enacted with his curse. *Ata ti hacharda* wasn't an idle threat.

He cleared his throat. If Jullup wanted to talk about family, he could do that. "That boy, Lokey, is he your son? Does he live here still?"

"Yes, but he's away more often than I'd like. He designs security software, and has clients all over these mountains. And don't you call him boy," she scolded. "He's not that much younger than you—thirty-two this Dh'Morda—and he's been running his own business for ten years now, at a profit. He'll have a nice little horde to give to his mountain when he comes of age, like you, and takes a mate."

Dwyn stared up at her, more embarrassed than he'd been when she'd looked his naked erection over with a practiced eye. Of age. Of all the foolishness. What the hell did it matter if he was legally old enough to give his life and wealth to a mountain for a family? His life was worth nothing. He had no wealth. He'd lost the only family he ever had, and he'd never have one of his own. Dh'Morda, indeed. But an odd sense of foreboding stirred him and set the oil sizzling on his skin.

It *was* early in the season yet, but he could feel it simmering inside—the mating urge, a strong desire to be with other dwarves, to seek out men and women both, although neither sex would have him for love or money. It was possible he wasn't entirely to blame for his foolishness in stopping here after all, but the thought gave him no comfort. The helplessness of instinct galled him far more than any error of judgement ever would.

Jullup ran her fingers through his hair. "You know, Dwyn, you're not a bad-looking dwarf when you clean up. I'll bring your pants when they're dry. Lokey's are too big for you. He's quite tall for a man, at least I think so. Takes after Nolan, not me, thankfully." She handed him the comb. "Now, the beard is your affair, and after that, I want you to lie down and rest today. Nyssa's orders."

Her name was throwing water on a grease fire. "I can't rest! You've tortured me enough; now let me do something to ease my suffering." He stood and almost fell. He grabbed the table for support and swayed, dripping burning oil on the floor.

She stepped back, eyes wide.

Shit. He'd not meant to frighten her. He needed her. He knew that as much as he knew he'd fall on his face if he tried to walk back to the bedroom on his own. "I'm sorry. You've never had a g'hesh. There's a need. When I fulfil the terms of my agreement, I feel—" He stopped. It sickened him, that g'hesh working its insidious way into his magic, triggering his weaknesses—his hunger for respect, his endless thirst to be needed, his eternal quest to matter. "There's a chemical component. I must work. I get no relief otherwise."

"I am sorry, Dwyn, but I do have my orders."

"And I have mine." He didn't take his gaze from Jullup's face. She sighed. "What do you need? Can I get it for you?"

"I need my tools—my paper, my pens, my ink, my glasses. They're in my truck."

"Tully had it towed. It's in the quarry yard."

"Can we go there?"

"Oh, Dwyn, I don't know—"

"I'm bound neck to ankle with this g'hesh. How far would I get if I ran?" He sank into the chair.

"That isn't what I meant," Jullup said, touching his shoulder. "I'm not sure how far you're allowed outside of the mountain. I don't want you hurt."

He didn't know what to think of that. But he knew what to say. "I'll take the risk."

"Dwyn."

"If I feel anything, you know I won't be silent."

She drew in a deep breath through her nose. "All right. I'll take you, but after you sleep, and after lunch."

He opened his mouth to protest, but Jullup stopped him. "No! One more word, and I won't take you anywhere. I may bend Nyssa's orders, but I won't go against my own judgment."

"If we go now, I can rest all afternoon—"

"Do you want to go or not?"

He clamped his lips shut.

"Good. Now finish your beard and go to bed."

It didn't hurt as much as he feared. The oil had worked its way down the sides of his face, through the sweeping sideburns joining the hair around his mouth and his chin. But he was so tired after he finished, he didn't move when Jullup stole into the room and covered him with the cooling blanket so he would sleep.

No dreams disturbed him.

Jullup's car was as dirty as Dwyn's truck was rusty. He got in, noting the torn leather seats, the sagging fabric of the roof, the mud slick in the floorboards, and wondered why she drove a wreck. Tully should have any number of decent, used trucks if he was rich enough to own a quarry.

Jullup's jaw tightened as she glanced side to side before turning onto the road. "When we get there, you don't stir a step until I say. And stay close," she said.

Dwyn didn't reply, but when Jullup looked at him anxiously, he shook his head. "There's no pain."

Rest and food had done wonders. While he'd slept, the chef Jullup had spoken of dropped by, picked up his bucket of sassafras wands, and left the refrigerator packed with soups, roasted meat, vegetables, and a salad that made a meal all by itself, it was so full of mushrooms and cooked duck.

"Does this road go back to the highway?" Far to the right, where the field ended in a green hedge of cedar trees, he thought he could make out a broken rivn.

"No, this is just our driveway. It joins the quarry road."

To Dwyn's left, the pasture stretched toward a sheer rock bluff, but stopped short where a vast brown hole gaped. Weeds grew thickly around it, brushy tents huddling together around the shocks of red broomsedge that glowed like campfires across a shale-strewn beach. The wreck of a long shed lay shoaled in a reef of blackberry brambles.

"What is that?" He'd never seen a place so desolate, so unattended, so completely perfect for hiding. If he'd been bolder, and come up the quarry road, he might have turned in here, parked in the shed, climbed that cliff with all the regular steps cut in it, and disappeared. He frowned. No, it wouldn't have been that easy. But it sure looked that way from this side of the g'hesh.

"The quarry. Well, forty-odd years ago it was. My father worked this site."

"It was a big place."

"Ironsfork wasn't always a small mountain." Jullup stopped at the intersection where the driveway met a well-tended gravel road. She waited while a loaded dump truck passed, and then turned left. "Remember what I said. Don't you go anywhere without me," she said tersely, rounding a spur of rock covered in dried grass and spindly stalks of mullein. The quarry gaped before them.

It looked like the face of the mountain had been cut away with an ax in great, uneven chunks. Nothing grew where the raw rock was exposed. A few scrubby post oaks clung to the edge of the pit, coated in dust, desperate and dying. Below, equipment lumbered across gravel roads raised in a bloody plain. Great heaps of rocks dotted the edges of this forbidding landscape, neat and orderly arrangements of what once had been the body of a mountain. In the archipelago, loaders dumped the viscera and bones into a machine. Conveyor belts ferried it in all directions. Dwyn licked his lips as his stomach churned. He glanced at Jullup, half-expecting to see the same disgust on her face. This was her mountain, cut open and bleeding.

But Jullup calmly pointed to a peninsula jutting into the scarlet sea. "There's the office. I don't see Tully's truck. He'll be in the pit." She put the car into lower gear and crept along the road on the rim, making for the prominence where a gray building kept watch over the carnage below.

Dwyn hunkered down in his seat, but even through the rolled-up windows he heard the high-pitched keening cry of magic being ripped apart, torn, and dissected.

"Funny how with Tully the water runs all the time, but there's still no end to the dust," Jullup said.

Dwyn slipped further down into the floorboard, jamming his ears mentally against the endless scream. He knew this sound all too well.

In his second year as a Seidoche, he'd been invited to a dissection in the necromancers' laboratories at Nations. They were making a g'uise, a skin of magic that a necromancer might wear to give him extra protection against magical attacks in a battle. There were no battles anymore. It was a completely pointless exercise, so of course he went. Arcane magic was, after all, his specialty.

Small as he was, they'd let him stand in front, closest to the table. He wasn't doing well. He'd been sweating from the first incision, and by the time the intestines and liver were out, he was distinctly queasy.

"You all right?" Sorcha stamped on his heels. "You keep leaning back on me."

"Sorry," he said.

"I can't believe they really did this," Sorcha whispered. "I mean, think about it. No proper waste disposal systems, no running water, no proper medicine—I mean, if they opened a plague victim, game over." She folded her arms and rested them on top of his head.

"They did it all the same," he said, swallowing hard. "It's magic from the Southern Kingdom, from the time of Dragons— I've—" A wave of nausea swamped him. "I've seen...pictures." He wasn't about to explain that those pictures were swarming him now, images not from the walls of abandoned dwarf mansions, but as if he stood at the table himself.

"Well, that tracks. Those people were weird."

"Yes. Yes—" He gulped down surging flames. Not *at* the table. *On* the table. The eyes of the corpse stared out at Dwyn from the silver mirror in the ceiling, begging him to intervene, to stop the desecration of magic before it destroyed him. Then the lips of the dead man moved and spoke to him in clear, Southern Seid. *You are like me.*

"Fuck!" Dwyn tumbled backwards.

"Get a grip, dammit, Dwyn, if you puke on me—"

One of the necromancers lifted the heart out of the chest

cavity, and dropped it like a great, jellied clot into the large, ornately decorated heart-jar of leaded crystal.

Dwyn screamed with the corpse. He flung himself past Sorcha, slammed shoulder first into the door and fainted, drowned in the noise of a million voices crying for vengeance.

He woke, not to roars of anguish, but roars of laughter. The necromancers had thrown him up on a nearby metal table to recover, and someone—probably Sorcha—had stuck his sword in a trashcan for a joke. He'd been shaken for days. He would never be rid of that sense of sacrilege, of wrongness, and brutality. But he'd not thought about it—until now.

He glanced back at the pit behind him. There wasn't a thing about this place that should remind him of that dissection. What the hell was going on with his head today? He rubbed his temples, agitated. That damned dream with the tomb, and now this. Sorcha's words came back to him. *Get a grip.* Get what he came for, and get the hell out of this horrible place.

Oh, he'd get his writing things, yes, but it was his soul he'd come for. He needed to reclaim the books if he was going to escape. He'd hide them in Jullup's quarters with an illusion until he was ready to make his bid for freedom.

On top of the hill, a metal building squatted in the middle of a chain-link pen. Around the shed, broken hulks of vehicles returned their rust to the soil. Dwyn spotted his truck, off by itself. Tully had taken precautions. It sat up to its axles in muddy water.

"Wait for me." Jullup stopped outside the gate and got out.

He watched her fumble with the chain on the gates, muttering various spells, hunting through a list for a particular combination she knew, but seldom needed. When Jullup motioned to him, he jumped out of the car, determined to ignore any more hallucinations, but he shrank when his boots touched the gravel.

Bones. So many bones. They littered the ground, and he crunched over them as he walked.

A polished silver truck, parked close to the screener, pulled away, maneuvering ponderously through the pools of water toward them. A gust of wind, cold and laden with rain, touched him. He pushed Jullup aside and ran.

"Dwyn? What is it?"

He splashed through the moat around his truck, grabbed the cracked glass and yanked the back of the camper shell open. He didn't drop the tail gate, but went over the back and landed with a thud.

Torn illusions fluttered above a massacre. "Fuck! Fuck, fuck, fuck!" He fumbled through the wreckage, tossing papers, empty bottles, torn clothing beyond mending, worn boots. Sticky, failed magic coated his hands as he dug frantically through the wooden chest that once held everything he owned.

"No!" He rocked back and forth on his heels, hands clasped around the back of his neck. They were gone. They were gone! And only one person could have taken them. The necromancer.

The sound of an engine brought Dwyn to his senses. He crouched, teeth clenched, breathing hard, and thinking harder. Get what he'd come for. Show Jullup he could be trusted. Only if she trusted him, would he have the freedom to hunt for his missing books. They would be at the mountain. They must be.

Quickly, he piled together as much paper as he could scavenge, seized a plain walnut box and opened it. Bottles of ink clicked together with a reassuring sound. One or two pens rolled around in the bottom. He jammed the lid shut. He was climbing out in a purposeful way when Tully barged through the open gate.

"What is this?"

"Dwyn needed his writing equipment." Jullup sounded calm, but her hackles stood up from the crown of her head to the back of her neck. Somewhere in Dwyn's seething fear, an unpleasant bubble of guilt popped. He'd gotten Jullup in trouble.

Tully rumbled like a storm on the horizon. "It's not enough you go against Nyssa and Nolan, you ignore me too?"

"He hasn't left the mountain. This is *still* Ironsfork, or what's left of it." Jullup's voice became a snarl.

"Take him back. Now. You hear me?" Colors raced over Tully's skin in a furious display—copper, rust, and green—as his water magic rose in a sudden, wet roar.

Jullup backed up, putting herself between her brother and Dwyn, crouched beside his truck. "He's under a g'hesh, Tully—"

"You think he didn't know you'd bite on that?"

Dwyn's fire crackled loudly in the breeze gusting from Tully's magic. Slowly, Jullup glanced over her shoulder at Dwyn.

Tully spat on the ground. "Get him out of here." He turned, and walked away, fists jammed in his pockets.

Dwyn peeked around Jullup's back at the retreating chieftain. Tully backed his truck around, wheels grinding. A human woman with short black hair sat in Tully's passenger seat. She pointed through the window and laughed.

Jullup's angry face didn't pair well with her smile. "Did you get what you needed?"

He worked his way carefully around the truth. "Enough."

Jullup said nothing as she drove back up the mountain. Her eyes were on the road, but she wasn't watching it. Dwyn hugged his writing box against his chest like a shield.

"I'm sorry," he said when the silence became toxic. "I didn't know I'd make so much trouble for you."

She gripped the steering wheel tightly. "I should have insisted we stay at home. Nyssa could have brought you what you needed."

"I...I needed to see, for myself."

She sighed. "I thought that might be it. Dwyn, whatever you may think of Nyssa, whatever she took from you, she will keep it safe."

That was true. Nyssa would not harm his books. She would know better. They crackled with necromancy. Still, perhaps she would not keep them. Journals she would think them the writings of a man not always in his right mind.

"Jullup, may I ask you something? The quarry. You said it was what was left of Ironsfork. What did you mean?"

Jullup slowed down. Two deer, both doe, leapt across the road in front of the car. "Back in my father's day, a hundred families lived at Ironsfork. Some of them were good friends of mine. When my brother Sullivan died—suddenly—Tully took over the management. The site had to be moved. I'm sorry—I don't like to talk about it Dwyn."

His bones chilled. "Then the quarry is—"

"All that's left of my home. Yes."

He didn't say he was sorry. It wasn't enough, and there wasn't more he could say.

Jullup made Dwyn work at the kitchen table. "So I can see you don't do more than you should," she said.

He didn't argue, although he would have preferred the table in her quarters, and not only for privacy. He never liked to eat food on the same surface he worked on. Necromancy was nasty stuff. He'd clean up after he finished, but it would still feel like eating on a coffin box.

He opened his writing case. The ink bottles had tipped, but the seals held. Most of them were empty. When did he last buy ink? Two years ago. No, four. That tiny repair job at Nantahala. He still had a decent supply of the refillable cartridges he liked. His fellow Seidoche, like Sorcha, used disposables, but Dwyn preferred the sturdier metal kind that didn't melt in his hands. Cleaning them was a hassle, but for that he had—Dwyn pulled out the square glass bottle, about a liter in size, half-full. The clear liquid glistened as he tilted it. Kvasir, liquid forget. He wished it worked as well on him as it did on ink. He thumbed through his paper with a practiced hand, counting. He'd have to make more, but the lint was among the things missing from his truck.

He cursed softly, thinking again of his books. They'd withstood every test he'd put them through, and he was just as attached to them as he was to Mh'Arda. Filled with every illustration of the dreams that were his legacy as Mn'Hesset, they were the written record he would pass on when his own memory was gone and the fire claimed him. He must get them back.

"What will you work on?" Jullup passed by with a sack of potting soil and a sad-looking rubber tree in a pot.

"I believe I'll start with *Mhu Mordr*," he said.

"How seasonal," she said with a laugh. "You're quite the romantic."

"Hardly. Cheyloche Daffyd wasn't much of a romantic either, lucky for me. It's his shortest work." He filled his pen. "Where is Nyssa anyway?"

"The cantrev capital, Whiterock. Dh'Morda's business. Won't be back before Monday. I'll be on the patio if you need me." Jullup walked off.

A fucking weekend Nyssa would have made him wait. She'd be rolling in bed with whatever unfortunate necromancer she planned to mate with that year, while he seethed in captivity, stewing over the loss of his property, fretting about how on or under the earth he could scribe a library without paper or ink.

Ata ti hacharda. A tiny well of blood accumulated in the hollow of his right wrist. He touched the pen to his blood and began to write.

CHAPTER SEVEN

MENDING WALL

Dwyn squatted on top of a rivn, ten feet up, free-handing glyphs on a sheet of necromancer's grade linen stock, some of the last he had. The ancient writing had been all but effaced. He reconstructed each image in his mind before he set anything down. He had no room for error.

Three weeks had passed since his g'hesh, but although healed in body, he was far from healed in his magic. The damned thing clung to him worse than cobwebs, it tortured him when he should be sleeping, and worst of all, he'd not had a single dream since the one about the tomb. He sure could use some divine inspiration about now.

A gust of clean, cold, November wind rustled through the trees, sending a storm of leaves cascading over him as he flattened his paper on the stone and sketched a vulture glyph beside the fawn.

Nyssa paced through the ferns at the base of the stone column. Her dog prowled closer to the rivn. The wolfhound snarled whenever Dwyn shifted position, dusting her with a liberal coat of charred lichen. The ice in the air didn't bother him, not with his built-in furnace, but the necromancer and her dog must be damned near frozen by now. He smiled.

"Are you almost finished?" Nyssa glared up at him. She clutched a battered paper cup with four black runes scorched below the logo.

He leaned carefully over the edge of the tower. "Drinking after a Dragon? Aren't you scared?"

Nyssa raised the charmed cup in mock salute. "I'm just warming my hands." She poured the cup's contents on the ground, and tipped it upright again. The cup refilled itself with a suggestive gurgle and a tantalizing cloud of steam. Even on top of the rivn, he smelled the coffee he couldn't have.

"Why aren't you finished?" she asked.

He stood stiffly. "Do you need to piss or something?"

"You should be done by now, if you are half the Seidoche you claim to be. You should memorize the words in minutes, not hours, and translate back at the mountain."

He squatted down with a huff. "Oh, necromancer, you make me want to cover my eyes—your ignorance is showing. Dh'Seitha isn't words; it's pictures. What's more, this is incomplete. When these rivn were made, the warloche who lived here would have known to refresh this stone with blood on a regular basis. Rain's wreaked havoc on it since. There's practically nothing left."

Nyssa folded her arms over her chest. "Fascinating. Now, when will you be done?"

"I couldn't say."

"I haven't got all day."

"Funny, I was just thinking I wouldn't mind spending all day out here. Weather's sweet. Air's fresh. Company sucks, though."

"Shall I leave you with Kritha and check on you later tonight? It's supposed to rain."

He had his line—about preferring one bitch to another—but a flash of sunlight on metal attracted his attention. He counted four matching vehicles before the bend in the road hid them from view. *Goblins.* "Warloche, you have visitors."

Nyssa flinched like she'd been struck, but she turned, and strode down the hill confidently, red braid swaying against her dark jacket.

Dwyn tried to concentrate on his work, but his heart thudded angrily in his chest and his hands shook. The old wound in his shoulder throbbed. Concentration gone, he replayed a dark night of his boyhood—the gunshot, cold rain pouring down on his head, blood and fire pouring down his chest. He shoved the memory away before it consumed him. These goblins were all he needed to worry about now. When it came to escape, they would factor into his choice of a route off this damned mountain.

The goblins swarmed together on the road before one began to climb the slope where Nyssa waited. He waved, and Dwyn recognized the tall goblin from the trial. Today he wore his long black hair in a beaded pigtail. It gleamed in the winter sunlight. Nyssa shook his hand, and then the two of them approached the rivn.

They grew truffles, Jullup had said. But this goblin didn't appear to be a farmer. He looked more like an ambassador, a mouthpiece for his Seitha—infinitely worse. Dwyn stared hotly down at the slanted green eyes, bright with magic, the delicately pointed ears capped with tufts of silver hair, the young, gray face, and the distinctive goblin cross—a long line of white hair clearly visible between his open collar and the thin curtain of his wispy beard. Dwyn reached for his sword.

"Dwyn, come down," Nyssa said.

Be damned if he would. He turned his back on them both. The g'hesh closed around his windpipe like a wrestler's fingers. Needles of magic stabbed him through his neck. He stood, strangling, but he couldn't hold on to his sword and battle a closed throat at the same time, and he dropped Mh'Arda. It teetered precariously at his feet, then toppled over the edge. He let go of his throat and reached for the hilt, missed, and then he was falling. He twisted in the air, grabbed for the pillar like a panicked cat, and slid, dragged down by his ankles, belly against the stone.

His shirt came up around his ears—his paper, his pen, he'd lose all his work—he let go and dropped. He landed hard, stumbled backward, and crumpled at Nyssa's feet. Bubbles of rage frothed around his lips. He clawed holes in the moss as he scrambled toward the rivn where Mh'Arda was hung up in the sawbriars. Kill Nyssa and die—he didn't care who killed him afterwards.

Suddenly, he could breathe. Tears of helpless rage burned his eyes as he clutched his weapon, gulping life-giving air.

"That's good to see. The Seitha will be pleased," the goblin said.

"You've nothing to fear, Midian. He's under my control."

The young goblin's fungal musk stank in Dwyn's nostrils, assaulting him with memories that screamed and threw stones at a boy who had not yet learned to run.

"I didn't know you would be bringing the Dragon across our land today," Midian said.

"Tully contacted the Seitha yesterday, I believe," Nyssa said. She sounded as casual as the goblin, but her hair rose in the middle of her forehead.

"No, the Seitha would have told me." Midian glanced at the goblins ranged on the slope behind him, all armed with sharp hatchets at their waists and semi-automatic rifles across their backs. "Had I known, I would have brought more warloghe." He leaned forward, and in a quieter tone added, "The next time Tully does this, he's in trouble with my mother, not just me. Best you take the Dragon and leave, Nyssa. Until the fence is repaired, none of us will be easy."

Dwyn struggled to his knees. He pulled himself up on the rivn. "Since when does a goblin give orders on a dwarf's land?" Fury surged through him—hatred of Nyssa, hatred of the goblins, hatred of everything that had brought him to Ironsfork— curiously mixed with something altogether different, something he barely grasped deep inside his rage—the urge to fight.

Midian's fixed smile vanished. "You speak our language, Dragon. Who taught you?"

"Folk just like you with equally bad manners." Dwyn coughed on what remained of the g'hesh jammed in his throat.

"This is my home. I will protect it, whether you care for my manners or not."

Dwyn blazed like a torch, kindling the moss at his feet. The goblins on the hill fell back, jabbering to each other and crying out fearfully at the shape of him, burning like a Dragon of the old Southern Kingdom. Midian gasped.

Dwyn snorted sparks. "I don't think much of your Seitha, boy, if you're what protects her border." He took a step toward Midian, fire crawling down his forearms.

Nyssa looked confused. Dwyn realized, with a sudden surge of amusement, she hadn't understood a word of the conversation. Lived next to this rabble but didn't speak their bastard language? What was the world coming to? But when Midian raised his hatchet, and Dwyn raised his sword, she got the gist. Dwyn crashed to the ground.

"My apologies, Midian. We are leaving." Nyssa hoisted Dwyn by his belt, heedless of the flames spurting in all directions. Past the vanguard of goblins she marched him, strangling, and pushed him up into the truck. Kritha bounded over him into the back seat, growling.

"Ethe," Nyssa said, slamming the door.

He sagged in the seat, gasping.

Nyssa got in on the driver's side and savagely dug the key into the ignition. "What did you say to him?"

"I—my hearing—you—torture…"

She backed around, digging ruts into the soft ditch. "What did you say? Tell me, or I will choke you into ashes!"

"Wrong—him giving orders." He gagged. Give this necromancer a g'hesh and she would yank it every time he gave her the chance.

"This is not your home, Dragon. You have no business saying what's right or wrong."

He stared sullenly out the window at the goblin's forest,

massaging his throat. The mountain wall rolled by on Nyssa's side of the road. Dragons like him built that wall, and others like it throughout the South. They filled the stones with the furious power of wind, water, earth, and flame, and he would bet his left hand *they* never took shit off of goblins. But Nyssa was right. It wasn't his home. He wasn't sure why he'd said anything.

Maybe it was being up on the rivn, sketching glyphs in the cold autumn sunshine that reminded him of his old home in Tennessee. The goblins too—particularly that punk-ass Midian—reminded him of days he'd rather forget.

His grandfather's cracked voice beat his memory like the old man's belt had beaten his legs. *Stay away from the goblins. Say nothing when they hit you with stones. Do nothing when they steal from our bee-tree. On no account will you ever cross the river onto their land. Do you understand?*

"Do you understand?" Nyssa's sharp voice cut him open, and he jerked around, having heard what she said, but caught up in the splash of a river's icy waters around his crotch, the feel of a lead bullet melting into his blood, and the foolish desire that had driven him across that river.

"I heard you," he growled. "Since you don't plan on bringing me back up here, I might as well get to work with what I have." He rubbed the hollow place in his right shoulder. When this was done, and if he could manage it, he'd find a way to include those goblins as collateral damage. Burn up their forest on his way out, maybe. "If you're done choking me, I've got some questions I need answered."

Nyssa's knuckles turned rose-red as she gripped the steering wheel.

He took her silence as assent. "This rivn. I don't have enough paper to rewrite all the magic these stones will need. Where am I going to get it?" He coughed. Damn her. Every word felt like swallowing fish bones.

"Do you not make your own?"

"I can, when you see fit to restore my property to me. My lint was in my truck." He needed ink too, but he'd have to wait to see how the paper conundrum went before he mentioned it. Ink was pricey. Paper was expensive, but unless one was forced to choose between bread and paper, not a painful purchase. He went on. "In any case, I doubt Jullup will love me if I ruin her table, soaking it with blood and water. I need a better place to work. Jullup showed me an old kitchen off the hallway."

"The pipes are broken."

"Water problems aside, I liked it." He waited, more hopeful about this request. Jullup had already complained to Tully on his behalf. The abandoned room had the space he needed, a large, long table, and best of all, a heavy door. In a place like that, he might work on a plan of escape without a necromancer breathing down his neck.

"I'll consider it," Nyssa said. "But you will make paper—or buy it."

"I need necromancer's weight. Standard won't take my heat."

"Fourche Mountain could supply you. I'll tell Jack you're interested in their stock."

"Samples first, before you beggar yourself."

"I don't intend to beggar myself in any way," Nyssa said. "Our mountain is not obligated to pay for the materials needed for your recompense. You want to buy paper? Find something of your own to sell."

Automatically, he pulled his shirt down over his copper belt. Of all the ways of punishing a man, the catrev penalty system was the worst. If would force him into one kind of debt to repay another. He understood it—he was a Southerner after all. But he could not possibly make enough paper for the fence and continue to appease his g'hesh. He was done with *Mhu Mordre*, and had started Daffyd's *Principles of Necromancy*. If it came down to a choice between working on the book or the wall, he'd have to pick the book. It didn't do to leave necromantic works in an unfinished state. Like milk left out on a counter, incomplete necromancy soured in a hurry, and he'd be forced to burn what he'd written to save his own bones. Be damned if he would give any more to this mountain than he owed, though.

"Those goblins patrol your border, guns and all? Some rare mushroom, Jullup said. *Tuber lyonii*, maybe?" He glanced sideways to see if she was paying attention. The tightness of her jaw suggested she was. "It's been a while, but I remember when a robust truffle of that variety would fetch three or four thousand in a fair market. No wonder they want the wall fixed. Blocks out all the nasty necromancy reeking out of this hellhole."

Nyssa clenched the wheel. "Make your point, Dragon."

"You gave me a penalty. I made a promise to Tully, and you bound me to both with the same g'hesh. But I can't do both at the same time, not with the paper I have. It's in your best interest to loan me the money—"

"Make your own paper!"

"I can't make enough, dammit!" He sat back in the seat, tense and fuming. He slumped, arms clutched around himself as the spines of the g'hesh bit deeper into his magic. He'd lost his temper, and with it his advantage.

She let him have his glasses. And the roll of lint, his antique paper frames, and the lignyn glue.

"The linen binder," he said. "I'll take that." His throat felt tight but it wasn't the g'hesh. This was his life, open to dissection.

The paper frames leaning against the closed door of Nyssa's library were a gag gift from his friend Sorcha at a lavish Dh'Mordadan Ehrlik hosted for all three of them one November, all dwarves usually being born between Sm'hain at the end of October, and Dh'Morda in December. How he'd laughed. And Ehrlik had gotten so drunk he'd forgotten his dignity and sung a Nordic ballad for them in his fine, bass voice.

He winced when Nyssa picked up a worn, blackened wool blanket and tossed it aside. That had been his grandfather's. He'd considered leaving it with the body, but the dead didn't need comforting anymore, and he did.

He kept his face deliberately stiff, and did not look at the stack of leather-bound books on Nyssa's desk. They hid their secrets, obedient to his magic as he had taught them, so many years ago, oh, so many. He turned his spectacles over in his hands with careful nonchalance.

Nyssa handed him a coil of red thread. "Anything else?"

"My books," he said, as carelessly as his thick voice could manage.

She stared at him.

"They are mine. I made them."

"Then I will count them toward your penalty. That will give you some relief from the g'hesh, since you intend to work on the wall first." Nyssa picked one up and set it in her lap. "I've decided you may use the old kitchen for work. Jullup will provide the water from her quarters, and will unlock the door for you every morning, and open it for you in the evenings, and for meals. You may go now."

He gulped. He had to make her believe they were worthless—nothing he would die for. "But they're of no importance to you, they're—"

"N'maha." A huge chandelier overhead cast a pale silver light over soapstone shelves lining the walls, Nyssa's walnut desk, and the white carpet Dwyn avoided where he stood, dripping fire on the stones. "I'm not a fool, Dragon. Those books are necromantic. They stay here, in my library."

"They're not part of the penalty! The law—"

Nyssa stood. "The law requires a necromancer's books be lodged in an appropriate library, and that's where they'll stay."

"Give them to me!" He crumpled, crushed by bands of magic tightening from his neck to his knees.

"This is the third time today you've tested me." Nyssa released him with a wave of her hand. "Next time, I will not be so gentle."

He crawled away, bright as an escaped ember, and got to his feet near the door. She would regret this. He would make her regret it.

The door to the old kitchen stood open to darkness. He kicked it closed behind him. Something metal crashed to the floor followed by the sound of glass breaking. Arms full with the tools of his trade, he waited for the lamps to figure out a warloche was in the room. They spluttered, wet with long streams of stagnant water.

"N'maha, dammit!"

A few lamps managed a pallid green light. Most sparked and fizzled out when his hot fury met their cold magic.

He flowed into the room like lava. "Se hexa, se hexa; eshr seidri dynwithi." *Damn Nyssa. Damn her dead as these lamps.*

Umber shadows fled into gaping holes on the far wall, long empty freezers with their doors missing. Dwyn slammed his press and frames on the table; the clatter echoed. The ceiling was as high as the one in Nyssa's library, but no light came down the shafts yet. The sun was still on the eastern half of the mountain.

He set his bag of lint and the glue next to the double sink. His writing case lay on the zinc countertop. Someone must have brought it, either Nyssa or Jullup. It was open, so probably Nyssa. Grumbling, he went through his inks, brushes, and pens again. He found everything in order, even the lump of beeswax for his thread in the ornately carved soapstone box that Riordiin had given him years ago. He opened it. The hard, golden block smelled as sweet as spring.

He touched it gingerly, remembering.

A blow to his face, the first, but not the last. He hadn't seen it coming, although he knew—he knew—all Dragons lost their minds when the fire ate their memory, but he'd believed his control would be enough for them both.

"What are you doing?" Dwyn cried.

"You make me hurt you," Riordiin snapped. "How dare you say I don't keep this house in order? It's my home—not yours, Seidwendr!" He stormed out of the library, leaving Dwyn with a shattered lip and fractured confidence. God under the earth, how would he tell Ehrlik? This wasn't supposed to happen, not so soon.

Gently, he touched the hot swelling, trying to decide what to say. Nothing would prevent the dementia. Someday, the same thing would happen to him, and when it did, he'd have nothing—nothing unless he stuck to the plan. Ehrlik would say that, too.

Dwyn crept to the bedroom that night, quiet as a dream. He didn't mean to wake his lover, but when Dwyn slipped into the bed next to him, Riordiin growled a welcome, and folded him in an embrace before resuming his snores. Dwyn didn't sleep.

Then in the morning, the box. Dwyn had seen it in Riordiin's collection. It belonged to a Dragon of his clan, the enigmatic one, Cheyloche Rivnstone, uncle of the famous Cheyloche Daffyd.

Riordiin pressed it into Dwyn's hands. "Please forgive me. I don't know what came over me yesterday. Don't go. I'll be dead if you leave me now. Please." Soft, gentle, irresistible.

Forgive him? Dwyn would forget everything if he could. "I'm not leaving you, mh'arda."

Riordiin held Dwyn close. "Oh, beloved, my dearest one, I've given you so little for so much."

Dwyn stroked the delicate carved flowers and bees making love in them. "Don't say that. You've given me everything."

The bond wasn't what kept him with Riordiin. Love did.

Dwyn closed the lid.

"Paloh…" He stopped. Speaking into an emptiness as dark as his memories required all his faith. "My God, if you cannot forgive me, if I cannot die honorably, let me save my books— my memories, the ones you entrusted to me. Make a way. I am a fool, I've always been, but I am your Mn'Hesset, your most beloved, and I have served you since you touched me for the first time. Let me save them as I could not save him."

But prayer gave him no more comfort than kicking the door. He pulled the crumpled paper from his shirt, and sat at the table, recalling the last of the images from the end cap. He transcribed them with painstaking precision beside the others.

No room for error. No room left at all.

The better part of the morning Dwyn spent translating. He was impressed and also worried. It would be the challenge of his life, perpetrating a major illusion on magic older than the trees growing on the mountain. And he must do it if he wanted to control the wall when he finished. When the door opened hours later, Dwyn didn't even turn around, he was so absorbed in his work.

"Time to close up."

"A moment." He had his compass out, a rare thing for him, and it took all his concentration to keep the instrument steady in his right hand. He followed the progress left-handed, tracing over the light graphite marks with ink. A parsimonious stream of blood trickled down his forearm and over his thumb, where a groove in the pen drew fresh magic with his blood to mix with the ink.

"I have to leave." High heels clicked behind him.

He hesitated a second too long. The compass slipped. Blood and ink splattered the page.

"Fuck you!" He flung his compass down on the blotting rag in his box. "Go ahead. Choke me. Why don't you cut off my hands while you're at it? You've ruined this, just like you've ruined everything else!" He whirled around to face Nyssa, braced for punishment.

Jullup stood there, clutching her purse to her chest like a shield.

"Oh." He picked up the blotting rag, and pressed it over the smoking blood steaming on his arm. "I—I thought you were Nyssa."

"Be glad I wasn't." Jullup stared at him as if she'd never seen him before. "Are you all right?"

He scratched the back of his neck, burning with shame as he picked a pine needle out of his hair and dropped it, smoldering, on the floor. Dammit, he should have looked before he exploded.

"I have an errand to run. You have to stay in our quarters when I'm not around," Jullup said.

"I'm sorry—I—"

Jullup glanced at the table where the paper lay, smoking at the edges. "I hope it wasn't ruined."

"I can make another." He forced himself to smile.

"May I see? Before you burn it?" Jullup smiled back.

He stepped aside, and she approached, bent over, and studied it.

"It's beautiful. What's it supposed to be?"

"Nothing now. But it was meant to be a rivnstone, had I finished."

Jullup angled the page. "Will you engrave this picture on the stone?"

"Engrave glyphs? Hell, no!" He laughed. "No engraving. It's magic, not a tombstone."

"I assumed," Jullup said, waving her hand. "With everything carved on the doors, I thought—"

He snorted derisively. "None of that was carved. It was drawn—drawn out of the stone itself. Glyphs are the shape of magic made by the Southern Dragons. That's why they're so damned hard to interpret. It's not the words, it's the intent I have to find, draw it over again, then write it out in runic. It's not like carving at all."

"They *look* carved."

"To you, maybe, but to an educated eye, no. There're no chisel marks, no raised edges, no stone lost. Once the dwarves of this mountain cut your doors, some Wight spent blood and magic pulling those glyphs out of the stone. No tools. Just his magic and what he wanted the stone to say and do."

Jullup gave him a long, steady look.

"You think I'm pulling your leg?"

"I don't think—"

"I've been a Seidoche long enough to know my shit."

Jullup's mouth tightened. "It's time I locked this door and left." She thrust the page back in his direction.

"What?" He grabbed his writing box and scrambled after her. "What did I say? I didn't mean you were uneducated. I've studied this kind of magic for years: it began with the making of heart jars in Rigah Tarn and—"

"Maybe you should stop talking." She let him pass.

He could have kicked himself. Why hadn't he just burned it the moment he told her it was ruined? At the very least he could have held his tongue when she asked him to explain. He followed her meekly back to the Irons' quarters.

"Wait here." She stopped just inside the doorway. She pulled a slate key from her purse, and unlocked a door in the narrow hallway. He'd passed it a few times, but he thought it was a closet. Beyond the open door, a narrow set of stone steps led down to darkness.

Jullup touched the wall and a light flashed, the distant star of a seidr lamp. "This is where you'll be staying from now on. Go in. I'll bring you something to eat before I leave."

It looked like the entrance to a tomb. He didn't move as she swept past him. He was still standing there when Jullup returned with a sandwich on a plate and a glass of tea. "You'll have to eat this in the room—I promised Nikl I'd pick up the quail for dinner. That man! Duck would have been fine for a Dh'Mordadan supper." She descended the stairs, and he followed, hesitating on every step. At the bottom of the staircase, the seidr lamp spilled a golden patch on a heavy stone door with an iron ring in the middle. Jullup opened it with another key.

The room was bigger than the keyhole entrance suggested, and octagonal, like Nyssa's library, but the resemblance ended there. The library wallowed in sumptuous comfort, but everything about this room suggested a prison. Dim light fell from a single overhead seidr lamp. A cot crouched alone on one wall.

A battered writing desk had been foolishly oriented on another wall in attempted symmetry. It stood completely in shadow. He'd have to drag it to the center of the room to get any use out of it. An archway gaped in the back of the room.

It was a simple bathroom with shower stall in a corner, a sink, and a urinal—no door, not even a curtain. Bare, cold, and utilitarian, it had been designed for function and nothing more. He'd known it was coming. They wouldn't leave him where he had any kind of access to the outside of the mountain.

He returned to the main room. Jullup eyed him like a spider she'd like to squash as he made a circuit of the walls and sat on the cot. His legs dangled a foot above the floor.

"'Tully stayed here, when he first lived alone in this place. I've tried to make it nice," she said, purse in the defensive position again.

"Jullup, about what I said, it was a mistake. I only meant—"

She cut him off. "Eat your food. Then you might think about taking a shower—a cold one, to blunt your temper."

"I'm sorry—"

Jullup shut the door on his apology. The lock crunched, grinding stone on stone.

CHAPTER EIGHT

NIKL

They would expect him to try the door. He rattled it good. The lock was a standard tabah, two-way magic, controlled by a key. He might break the enchantment on his side, but he'd still be stuck, and if he made a real hash of it, he would fuse the lock. Supposing he broke free, where would he go? Nowhere. Not until he dealt with the g'hesh, and the fence had to come first before he killed Nyssa. He rubbed his throat. She was damned quick on that trigger. Caution was the prudent course. In the meantime, Jullup's suggestion seemed sensible. With what he'd been through today, he didn't smell any better than a fart.

After the shower, he set about the serious business of fire-proofing his room. He put his blood into it, anointing mattress, sheets, pillow, and pillowcase, and the single change of clothes Jullup had put on the desk—the old shirt that had belonged to Lokey and a pair of his pants, hemmed almost to the knee.

Dwyn stared at them, reddening. This wasn't Nations, where an explosive outburst from Riordiin's personal Seidoche was a guarantee he'd be left to work in peace. No wonder Ehrlik called him "the blunderkind", insisting he'd never met anyone so smart and so foolish at the same time. He needed Jullup and he'd called her stupid. Meanwhile, she'd done this and arranged a Dh'Mordadan dinner for him at the same time. Ehrlik had been too kind. He was the biggest idiot ever bred at Dh'Morda, a real stonehead of a dwarf.

He fingered the papers he'd placed carefully in his writing box—*Mhu Mordr*, finished and ready to be bound, if he'd had the leather for it. Jullup had called him a romantic. When she fetched him for dinner, he would apologize. He'd say something like he used to say to Riordiin whenever the necromancer raged at him, something like...

"I'm sorry. I was angry and didn't think. Can you forgive me?" When the door opened, the regret he'd been simmering in for the last three hours flooded into his words.

"You ought to be. She'll figure you out in the end." Tully emerged from the stairwell. The stink of the quarry came in with him. He snubbed out his cigarette on the wall. "How do you like it? Jullup did more for you than she ever did for me."

Anger blistered Dwyn's throat. "Your sister has been kind."

"Well, she's always been a poor judge of character. Nyssa said you wanted to talk to me?"

God under the earth, he was seething with hatred for this dwarf, his mountain, his evil necromancer, and now he had to beg. He hurried before he choked. "Chieftain, today I found out how much repairing the fence means to your neighbors. Much is missing from your wall, and I have to overwrite the rivn before I can restore the magic. I need paper. It's in your best interest to loan me the money—"

Tully flashed dangerously green as his water magic charged like a malignant well. "Shut up. I've already dealt with your shit today. I'm not in the mood for more. Seithe dichri mi, Ardoche. Understand? Nyssa may hold your g'hesh, but you pull any more stunts like you did today, you'll find a flood isn't any easier to breathe through than a g'hesh. Eta, warloche?" A cold blast of rain slapped Dwyn in the magic.

"Eta, Chieftain." He shuddered.

The impending storm rolled back under Tully's skin. "You've got ten minutes to shift yourself before the tabah resets if you want to eat tonight." His phone rang as he turned away.

Dwyn picked up his sword. "You want the fence done, Chieftain. Your necromancer wants it done. That goblin asshole wants it done. I want it done. Why hamstring me? We all want the same thing."

"Don't call me Chieftain. And that's my godson you just called asshole. Hello." Tully walked up the stairs. "He did what? You're shitting me. What does he want? Rupert. Who gives a rat's ass what Danny wants? He wants firing, that's what he wants. You don't know? Why the hell don't you know? Call him before you call me—no, it's not your fault, Sarah. I'll take care of it. Yeah. Love you."

The door began to close at the top of the stairs as Dwyn bounded up after Tully. He jammed his foot in it before it closed. Ten minutes might be ten seconds with that treacherous sonofabitch.

Sarah must be the woman he'd seen with Tully in the truck that day at the quarry. Disgust galvanized into revulsion as Dwyn's mind conjured images of the chieftain having sex with a human. So close to Dh'Morda too. He stepped into the hallway.

Someone, probably Jullup, had cleaned up the pine needles he'd tracked in. Tully had vanished. Voices came from the kitchen, but Jullup's wasn't among them. Dwyn heard Morven's snorting laughter, things sizzling on the stove, and something else—a sound he hadn't heard in years. Music. Someone was playing a piano, and not some child plunking keys, either. He'd heard less quality produced at Nations when he accompanied Ehrlik to the symphony on winter evenings, Riordiin not being fond of music or society. Dwyn followed it into the sitting room.

Jullup had straightened in here, too. The magazines reposed in a tall stack under the single mica lamp on the end table, and the newspapers had been stuffed into a basket near the television. The Mollycat was nesting in them. She spat when she saw Dwyn, slithered out, and squirted behind a leather armchair. She stayed there, growling as he passed. A door in the wall next to the couch stood ajar. The music prodded his magic, gently at first, then with a vigorous thrust that made him quiver.

He opened the door and the stairs took his feet. He followed the music, descending two staircases before emerging in a spacious room. Light dazzled him. He blinked, and stood frozen, enchanted by sound, paralyzed by beauty.

Lokey sat at a grand piano. Waves of sleek, red hair flowed around his shoulders as he leaned forward, playing. His slender fingers tumbled over the keys like lovers in bed. An intoxicating whiff of whiskey and cherries teased Dwyn's nostrils. He didn't mean to make any noise—he didn't want to disturb Lokey's playing—but he drew in the wonderful scent with insatiable hunger, devouring the elegant lines of the man making magic at the keyboard. His shoulders were an opera of movement, a glorious aria to grace. Could the rest of him be any less wonderful? Dwyn reached for the crotch of his pants. He'd not be happy until he found out.

Lokey stopped playing. He picked up a pen from the bench and marked the sheet on the music stand, completely unaware of Dwyn in the doorway. But Lokey was not alone in the room.

With a tremendous bark, Kritha charged out from under the piano. Dwyn didn't waste breath on a yell. He spun around and tore up the stairs. He slammed the door behind him, but it banged open again as he skidded into the hallway.

Kritha's jaws snapped behind his calf as he shoved a big dwarf out of his way, bounded up on the kitchen counter, and scrambled to the top of the refrigerator. He flattened himself against the wall, fire erupting in all directions.

Safe—no—Kritha's long legs appeared at the same time as her head. She bayed. All her white teeth flashed like sabers.

"Motherfucker!" His heart almost stopped.

"Kritha!" Morven called. Kritha dropped. She slunk across the floor.

"You can get down," Morven said. "She won't bite."

"Like hell she won't."

The dog sat next to Morven's chair, growling. Her blazing eyes never left Dwyn's face. His overlarge pants were sagging down to his knees, but he didn't dare move.

Morven sat again. "Stay up there then. Starve."

"Morven, put the damned dog out." The dwarf Dwyn had pushed out of his way looked up from rescuing a basket of mushrooms. He dumped them in a colander in the sink. It was the Thunderer.

Morven snorted and opened her book again. "You do it, prick."

"I'm working here," the dwarf grumbled, "not messing with shit I shouldn't be messing with. Shit that won't get me anywhere."

"You're an asshole, Nikl Fart." Morven smiled.

"And you're a bitch, beautiful." The white dwarf smirked. "Lokey!" He thundered so loud that the skylights rattled.

Lokey appeared as the echoes rolled away, pen in hand. "What the hell was that?"

Dwyn pulled his pants up, flushing fire.

The chef jerked his head at Dwyn. "Get rid of the big, bad dog so the little squirrel can get out of the tree."

Lokey took hold of Kritha's collar and dragged the unwilling animal out of the kitchen. Only when the sliding door shut did Dwyn jump down. He landed almost on his knees.

A meaty, white hand reached for him and pulled him up. "You okay?"

Dwyn shook so badly that the room trembled, but not the way his fire trembled when that storm surge of icy elemental wind hit his fire. Dwyn jerked his hand away.

"Easy," Nikl said. "Not like I could blow you out like a candle." Curious silver eyes glinted as they shifted from gray, to a startling white, then back to gray again. He was a huge dwarf, broad and plump as a cloud, but his grip belonged to a man who wrestled bears for a living.

"Didn't anyone ever tell you not to run from a dog?" Nikl grinned.

Ehrlik's smile. Oh, Nikl's mouth was wider, and his lips were pink and full, but they curved in at the right cheek making a glorious dimple there. Just like Ehrlik. Dwyn damped down his flame with effort. "You'd run if that thing jumped at you."

The Thunderer swelled pompously. "Do I look like I run from anything? Back off—you're too close."

Dwyn edged away.

Nikl sighed. "I didn't say *leave.* Just stay away from my range, that's all. Glad I set up where I did. If you'd stepped in my cooking instead of the mushrooms, I wouldn't be smiling. I'd be kicking your ass." He waved a hand at the counter.

Flanking the sink to the right, a little flock of silver ardchuk squatted on the counter, each trivet about six inches apart, all incubating a copper egg nestled under three legs. Flames crowned the surfaces of a few of the eggs, others glowed a warm orange. All the platforms were occupied by pots, pans, or skillets. But for the wonderful smells drifting through the air, Dwyn might have been in Riordiin's lab. Ardchuk were used to warm the various oils and liquids used in necromancy. He hadn't known they had a more mundane use. The controlling copper wand sprouted from the chef's back pocket when he stooped to check a dish cooking over a larger ardchuk perched in the oven.

"Do me a favor," Nikl said. "Pick through those mushrooms and toss the ones you squashed. Don't put them in the trash. I'll compost them."

"I didn't mean to—"

Nikl grunted. "No need to apologize, Dragon."

"My name is Dwyn."

"I know what your name is. I've been feeding you long enough—hey! Lokey! Lokey!" Nikl gouged in his pocket and brought out a wad of keys on a chain. He threw them at Lokey, back from putting the dog out. "Go upstairs and get the wine out of my truck, will you?"

Lokey caught the keys; the long tail whipped his legs with a discordant jangle.

"Don't drink it all on the way back if you can help it."

Lokey blushed redder than Dwyn thought a red dwarf could go. Morven let out a cackle. Lokey murdered her with a look and stalked away, long red hair draped over his shoulders like a veil of fire. *Damn.*

"Quit drooling," Nikl muttered. "He's not all that." He pointed to a hefty cutting board on the table. "Chop those shallots for me." He turned back to his ardchuk. "Don't mince," he added. "You do know how to use a knife—Goddamnit! Peel it! Peel it! Give me that!"

Nikl snatched the shallot and deftly shelled it. He threw it back at Dwyn. "Would have thought a man who had to hunt for his meals would know to take the skin off."

Flushing with embarrassment, Dwyn picked up the knife again, set it against the purple flesh and cut. The blade sliced through the shallot with a scalpel's precision—sharp and cold as the Thunderer, with a clean, white fir handle and hand-forged blade of bloodsmeldt.

Dwyn had the shallots drawn and quartered in no time at all. He was hesitating over the distinction between chop and mince when Nikl relieved him of both cutting board and knife. "I'll take those," he said, backhanding them into a hot skillet. The sharp onion odor was replaced by the buttery smell of frying.

Nikl nodded his approval. "Well, you didn't cut your own fingers off. Might have to hire you after all. Do those mushrooms for me. Slice, don't chop this time."

The basket of mushrooms took Dwyn only minutes to carve, but he used the time to study Nikl as he bustled around his ardchuk humming a breathy version of Lokey's piano piece.

Ehrlik had once taught Dwyn the names of all the major

European clans from Germany to the Netherlands, but he got to the end of the list without finding one that sounded right. He cleared his throat and did something he almost never had to do—ask. "I didn't get your full name. Phart?"

Nikl's chuckle sounded like wind rattling dried leaves together. "It's Phar. Morven's a tease."

"Where are you from?" Dwyn asked, covering his blunder with another question.

Nikl added the mushrooms to the shallots and tossed them a few times in the pan. "Oklahoma. You thought I was European, didn't you?"

"I did." No doubt Nikl was used to being placed by the color of his skin, but Dwyn's embarrassment turned into a smoky blush.

"I'm as southern as you are. What about you? Got a clan name?" Nikl removed the cover from the baking dish in the oven. A savory aroma billowed out. Mingled with the scent of the herbs and the frying mushrooms, the smell set Dwyn's mouth running.

"No," he said, licking his lips.

"Lucky you." Nikl snipped herb leaves into bits with shears and added them to the mushrooms. "No clan, no mountain, no responsibilities. You ought to be living it up, Dragon."

"Didn't work out so well for me, did it?"

"At least you don't have a family to ruin, do you?"

No, he didn't, but it stung. "I take it you do?"

Nikl's eyebrows arched. "Watch it, Dragon. Remember I feed you—Lokey, decant the Riesling for me, I need the Burgundy. Tell me you didn't shake it on the way down."

"I would never shake it." Lokey set a bottle of wine so red it looked black on the counter next to Nikl and filled a tall glass carafe with the white wine.

Nikl rolled his eyes at Dwyn. "He's a little pissed with me, isn't he?"

"Fuck you." Lokey didn't look up.

The Thunderer smirked. "I love you too, sweetheart."

Morven coughed a warning.

Jullup came in, shaking an umbrella. "Raining again. Who let the dog out?" She pulled a bottle from a shopping bag and handed it to Nikl. "Here. I got ice cream to go with the cake."

The chef didn't say a word when he poured the heavy cream into a new pan and fired up an ardchuk beneath it, but his shoulders went up about an inch and the hair on the top of his head lifted slightly.

"Where's Tully? I saw the basketball game was on." Jullup slung her purse over the back of a kitchen chair.

"Dumbass Danny took two loads of shit up to Mt. Ida," Morven said, eyes locked on her book. "Tully said he had to fix it with Rupert. Sarah called."

Jullup's smile vanished. "Did he say if he'd be back?"

Morven shrugged.

Jullup sighed. "Why that man hasn't been fired—"

"Danny or Rupert?" Morven turned the page.

"I guess it will just be the five of us, Nikl." Jullup frowned. "I'm sorry. I hope we won't put you out."

"No problem," Nikl said. "I figure the Dragon will eat enough for two."

Nikl made Dwyn sit next to him. "Folk like you and I, we need to stick together. Besides, you'd curdle my good pan sauce if you sat too close to it."

Everyone laughed, even Lokey. Nikl put the food on plates before bringing it to the table, as if the kitchen was as good as a feasting hall.

Jullup cleared her throat when Nikl sat. She raised her wine glass. "Tully's not here, so I'll do it. On behalf of our mountain, happy Dh'Mordadan. To those who have mated, may Dh'Morda bring blessed memories. For those who have yet to mate, grant them strong lust to make new life. The dead watch over us all."

Dwyn raised his glass. "The dead watch over us all," he intoned with the rest.

"Now can we eat before my good food gets cold?" Nikl said with a touch of irritation. Jullup laughed.

Nikl had been generous—two portions of quail, a pile of wine-glazed mushrooms, and a small mountain of roasted sunchokes sending forth pungent green waves of basil. When Nikl passed Dwyn a tureen of white sauce, he started to ladle it over everything like gravy, but the chef took charge.

He rapped Dwyn's knuckles with a fork. "That's for the quail. It's infused with sage. Use too much, you won't taste anything else." He dressed Dwyn's plate with a bare drizzle of the cream.

"Too much sage," Lokey said. He passed the tureen on to Jullup.

Dwyn cut one of the quail in half and shoved the whole piece in his mouth. He bit down, the bones crunched, the juices ran, and he was transported.

"What do you think?" Nikl whispered. "Too much sage?"

The purest compliment Dwyn could think of was to keep eating. Nikl half-closed his silver eyes and smiled.

No one talked at first. The only conversation wanted was the crunching of bones, the refilling of wine glasses, and the clink of silverware on stone plates. Long after everyone else finished, Dwyn ate on. The sunchokes came from some warm dream of a garden where nothing ever grew poorly, the mushrooms boasted the richness of the earth, and whatever Jullup said about duck, nothing could beat these quail for freshness. Nikl was a culinary genius.

Jullup was in a good mood after a few glasses of wine. She kept Nikl occupied with a barrage of questions as to the events on Rich Mountain. Nikl seemed just as cheerful, although his glass, like his plate, was half-empty. Morven had cleared her plate to make room for her books at the table. She was working out something on graph paper, but she looked up from time to time, listening. Lokey sat, quiet and remote at the far end of the table. He hadn't touched his wine. Dwyn was on his fourth glass, and already feeling the effects. He belched and pushed back from the table.

"That's my cue." Nikl got up with a grunt. "Where's Nyssa tonight, Jullup? I thought she might join us for dessert at least."

"She went to Wyvernholt to visit Tam."

Nikl laughed. "She's starting early. Is this the year she lands the big fish and brings him home?" Nikl ladled fruit from a glass bowl into scalloped serving dishes lined with a square of delicate white cake. He topped each with a dollop of yellow custard. No one mentioned ice cream.

"Tam will come for Dh'Morda," Jullup said.

Nikl rolled his eyes. "That's not what I meant." He set a dish in front of Jullup.

"Tam Wyvern will never leave his mountain," Jullup said. "He's happy as steward there, and his sister lets him run the place the way he wants. Why would he give up a good position for love? Nyssa wouldn't and neither would you."

"All is fair in love and war."

"But sensible folk know how to compromise." Jullup took a bite. "Oh, Nik! Can I expect this for Dh'Morda? I may skip Magazine this year and stay home."

Nikl laughed, obviously pleased with the reaction. "It's a bit of a production for a crowd. Now for a few intimate friends? I don't mind." He winked at Dwyn.

Lokey abruptly reached out, grabbed his wine glass, and gulped it.

"But Tam is coming?" Nikl said. "Neil's fuming about the cattle guard at the orchard. You know, the one I've been begging him to fix for the last six months? It finally took out his tire, so now it's a problem. The work will be Tam's, if Tully isn't interested."

"Tully doesn't have time for the forge these days. I'm sure Tam will do it, as long as Neil pays him, you feed him well, and everyone is impressed when he strips to his underwear to dance your Dh'Morda."

Nikl burst out laughing and Jullup joined him. Lokey snorted. A smile even drifted briefly across his face. But Morven scowled.

She hunched her shoulders and coiled protectively around her book.

Dwyn almost choked on sacrilege and sugared blackberries. "He dances the Dh'Morda?" It was the mating season and a man could be excused for losing his head to the hormones, but the Dh'Morda was first and foremost a dance for the dead. Dance it for love at the risk of your bones. And for a mountain that wasn't his? Outrageous.

"He says he does." Jullup shrugged. "So we say we believe him. It's more interesting that way. What about you, Dwyn?" She leaned forward on her elbows. "With a sword like yours, I expect you dance the J'hen at least."

He nodded reluctantly.

"What about the Dh'Ben?"

"When I have need of it." Of course, he could dance a blessing. He was Mn'Hesset. There was no one better qualified to dance it, or the Dh'Morda for that matter.

Lokey sneered. "What possible use is a Dh'Ben? A J'hen, I understand. It's an art or a sport, depending on who you ask. But a Dh'Ben is nothing but foolishness. Dance isn't magic."

The hair on the top of Dwyn's head rose in a ridge, his fire rose in his blood, but defense came from an unexpected direction.

"What do you know?" Morven snarled. "All your magic goes into computers now. You don't have a fucking clue what magic is about anymore. Dance is magic of the oldest kind. You will never understand it."

Lokey glared at her. "As if you ever could, knockr."

"Lokey." Jullup didn't raise her voice.

The floor screeched a protest when Lokey pushed back from the table. "It's true. Dance is no more magic than she's a warloche."

A reckless mood seized Dwyn, propagated by the wine and fueled by his own indignation at the idea of anything as heretical as dancing a Dh'Morda in front of anyone but God.

"Cheyloche Daffyd wouldn't agree with you, Lokey. Effective magic alters aethr. Dance alters aethr, if danced by a warloche trained in the art. Dance is magic. Whether it is of any use depends entirely on the skill of the warloche. Dhu seid, dhu seidr."

"*Principles of Magic*, yes, I've read it," Lokey said. "We're not hayseeds here, whatever you Nations-trained warloche think. He didn't say a word about dance."

Dwyn ran his finger around the top of the wine glass. A narrow band of fire danced along the rim as the vapors ignited. "What is the nature of magic? Order from chaos, seidr from aethr—you should understand this, warloche, you're a musician. If dance is not effective magic, it is because those who dance have forgotten the meaning."

Lokey brightened to autumn rust. He opened his mouth, as if he wanted to speak, but instead he reached for the wine and refilled his glass.

"Tam Wyvern would love you, Dwyn," Jullup said. "Don't you think so, Nik?"

Nikl had been frowning, but when Jullup spoke he smiled. "No doubt." The frown settled in place again.

"When he comes to visit, the two of you should talk. There's nothing he likes better than discussing traditional Southern magic. He claims he's got the Southern Dragon in his ancestry."

"Maybe I should have dropped by there instead of here." All his goodwill had vanished.

Jullup's smile became fixed.

"Be glad you didn't," Nikl said. "Tam's a reasonable steward when he's not playing king under the mountain, but he doesn't tolerate trespassers. Set one foot on his land and he'll carve you a new one where your pocketbook used to be. But Jullup's right. He'd like you. Probably let you off if you'd dance naked for him." Nikl's gaze lingered on Dwyn like a caress.

That crooked smile brought back memories that made him harden with desire. Damn Dh'Morda, damn the wine, and damn his own foolishness.

"I dance for no one," he said, staring stubbornly at the table-cloth.

"Now that's a pity," Nikl said softly.

"I love to see a man dance," Jullup said. "Jack Sharpe—that man could dance a J'hen to make you cry, it was so martial."

"What's he up to these days?" Nikl stretched his arms and shoulders. "I haven't seen him since the trial."

"Church, mostly. I'm not even sure he's celebrating Dh'Morda. He gets more Catholic every year."

"How does he justify that?" Dwyn couldn't keep the scorn out of his voice. He felt slightly sick—eating too much, maybe, drinking too much, certainly. Nine years of forced abstinence had left him vulnerable and he was an ugly drunk.

"Dancing a J'hen? I suppose he does it for the exercise—"

"No," he snarled. "The words Catholic and necromancer are incompatible. How are you justified when your entire existence is a sin?"

"Surely he has some routine to absolve him of the stain of being both a man of magic and a man of faith. Don't all religions provide some form of grace for their acolytes?"

Not all. Dwyn downed his wine.

"You're one of them, aren't you? A Knight of the Dead?" Lokey scoffed. "I thought your cult claimed to always tell the truth. Seems to me you're full of shit, hesset."

The dizzy, overwhelming sense of misery wasn't coming from the wine. It was conviction. He'd said too much and he would pay. He folded his hands around his wine glass. "I always speak the truth, warloche. If all you hear is shit, it's because that's all you *can* hear."

Dead silence.

Nikl coughed. "Well, this conversation's gone out of my depth. I worship no god but the almighty stomach, and I've got morning prayers at four tomorrow. It's bread day."

"Thank you, Nik. It was lovely."

"Always my pleasure. Happy Dh'Mordadan." Nikl kissed

Jullup's cheek as he passed.

No sooner did the door shut than Lokey slammed his chair backward. It toppled over with a crash. He stomped out of the room.

Jullup shut her eyes. "Morven, call Kritha and put her in her kennel."

Morven bolted.

Jullup's voice was soft. "Dwyn, I know you've had a hard day, but there was no reason to—"

He shoved his wine glass away. "I'm your prisoner, Jullup, not your guest. If I were a guest, I would apologize. But since this illusion of hospitality is over, I'd just as soon go to bed. I have work in the morning."

She let him go.

Dwyn lay awake for a long hour, fighting sleep, with his stomach roiling. He hadn't meant to snap. He hadn't meant to say anything at all.

He should have simply eaten the meal and pretended he'd never meant anything with his outburst—pretended it was release of the tension caused by his g'hesh, nothing more, nothing to do with the sudden, miserable understanding that Jullup, like everyone else on the mountain, would try to manipulate him into compliance, and that hurt him more than Nyssa's cruelty or Tully's indifference ever could.

He pulled the covers over his head and waited for condemnation to fall.

CHAPTER NINE

MN'HESSET

Draugr.
*There could be no other explanation for the way the dream drowned him
in an instant, chilling his bones.*

*Behind him, the Land of the Dead slept in eternal night. Vapors from the
river obscured the single gate he was charged as Mn'Hesset to protect. Around
him the apple trees stood, stark white ghosts, bathed in their own luminescence.
Here he was born, ages ago. Now, ages old, he must defend, or die.*

*He smelled the draugr before he saw it. The dank graveyard pall was
unmistakable. He'd love to hunt them to extinction, or failing that, chase
them all into the sunlit world to trouble the necromancers who created
them with their corrupted magic. But he was one warrior, and draugr
bred like a plague on the liminal border where waking ended and dreams
began.*

*Mn'Hesset flung himself into battle with a cry to wake the living. Five-
hundred years he'd been fighting these battles. Mh'Arda, the black blade
of the Mn'Hesset, shone with his wrath. Beautifully lethal, she belonged to
this land as much as he did. This was his true home, wherever his unworthy
body happened to be.*

In the river behind him, black swans massed to feed, singing their eerie dirge. Their ruby eyes glimmered, and they hissed, flapping their wings with excitement.

He was all fire when he met the draugr. Roaring his death cry, he slashed through the curtain of darkness where the hidden heart should be.

A sudden, solid wall of malignant magic met him head on and tossed him like a dead leaf in the wind. Trees fractured under the sheering weight of his magic as he crashed through the branches. He landed hard, and his arm broke with a sudden, shattering crack. He'd never known pain like this.

Stunned, he rose, coated in defeat and smashed apples.

Forever, as far as he knew, the Mn'Hesset of the Paloh Ethean had guarded the Land of the Dead. This was his life, the twilight world, forever, as far as he knew. He'd never lost a battle.

Trailing fire, he ran.

Broken arm wrapped around the back of his head, Mn'Hesset lay face up in a tangle of burning blankets, gasping. Steam poured down his body like fog on a mountain. The orchard—where was the orchard? He stared wildly around a strange room, surrounded by the sulfurous odor of rotten apples. Where was he? Who was he? *Oh, God. I can't remember. I am Mn'Hesset, most high Knight to the Paloh Ethean. I am that dead Dragon, bones in a tomb, a skull on fire. No, that isn't right.* Heart pounding, he lay still while waking untied his limbs.

Then he remembered and his flames went out. He was Dwyn, and this was Ironsfork, cursed place. His arm wasn't broken now, but it felt like someone had taken a hammer to his elbow. He moaned.

The mountain moaned with him.

Soft at first, the slow howl rose to a crescendo, vibrated like a full-throated choir, and then with a dull boom it reversed, sinking back into the stone. For a minute, he thought he was still dreaming, and the draugr would loom out of the night and attack him again.

Then a logical solution presented itself. The mountain was breathing. He'd simply not heard it before. Either he'd slept through it—unlikely—or he was hearing it for the first time because this space connected through ventilation shafts to deeper passages underground. As if in confirmation, the dying echo carried a scent of fresh night air, moist with rain. Dawn was still hours away.

A wet place on his pillow smelled of warm blood, and his whole left side ached where he'd crashed into the tree. He didn't bother to feel for the head wound. Like the arm, it had already healed. By morning, every bruise and every wound acquired in his nightly battles would be gone. A million thin scars lay invisible under the velvety brown hair that covered every inch of his body—proof, had he ever needed it, that his dreams were a reality that marked him from the bones out. But this one terrified him.

"Paloh mhu," he whispered, mouth dry with fear, "you have chosen a weak vessel for your Mn'Hesset, fractured when I was born. If you cannot forgive me, do not crush me entirely."

The prayer brought him no peace. He lay awake, listening to the mountain mutter to itself.

"I want to search for stones," Dwyn told Jullup over breakfast. "I'll make paper later today, but it will need time to dry. I'd like to stay busy in the meantime."

"Surely you don't need to look. The quarry can supply you." Jullup offered a bit of scrambled egg to Kritha.

Dwyn went carefully, remembering his fiasco from the night before. Signs of it were everywhere—Morven's books on the table, Lokey's abandoned jacket on a chair, Nikl's temporary range still occupying the counter. A disaster of dishes and wine glasses clustered around an epicenter of greasy dishwater. "I wish it was that easy."

"Why isn't it?" Jullup set her coffee cup down on the table. It was more than half full, and so was Dwyn's—truly dreadful stuff, with grounds floating in it. Nyssa hadn't given the charmed cup back to Jullup. Well, he could take some consolation knowing the magic would burn itself out in another day or two.

"Quarried stone won't hold magic. It's too fractured. When the elemental dwarves protected your mountain, they would have used nine whole stones for the rivn foundations: cut by nature and shaped by the water since they were Wights, judging by the number of heron glyphs around here. I may hunt for weeks before I find anything worth keeping, and if it doesn't stop raining soon, might take me a month." He gazed up at a gray river sheeting over the skylight.

"What will you do with them when you find them?"

"Sound them for old magic first, then fire them. If the rock is flawed, the whole thing blows up. It could take a while to get it right."

Jullup's knowing smile made the corners of her eyes crease upwards. "And you want me to intercede with Nyssa or Tully so you can go look by yourself."

"That's about the shape of it, yes."

"You know, Dwyn, I think I like you better when you're asking for help instead of trying to manipulate people into doing what you want because you think they're stupid."

He winced. He could tell her he'd been drunk at dinner. He could tell her he'd not meant it and she'd misunderstood him. Instead, he reached across the table and put his hand over hers. "God under the earth, I was an ass last night. I am *so* sorry. Nobody else cares what happens to me. But you—I know you'll do what you can for me. I'm sorry if that comes off as manipulation. I don't have anyone else to turn to."

She squeezed his hand. "I forgive you. But I don't think I can help you, not this time. You'll need to ask Nyssa first, but Tully will have the final say."

"They won't listen to me."

Jullup rose, and carried her plate and cup to the sink. "I know it's difficult, Dwyn. Nyssa is stubborn, more stubborn than my brother sometimes. But she is your best hope of a reprieve—whether it's this, or your penalty overall."

"There will be no reprieve." Dwyn gripped his coffee cup so tightly that the liquid boiled.

Jullup returned and sat across from him. Her eyebrows narrowed. "Can I tell you a story? I don't know if it will help, but it might, if you listen to me."

"I will listen to whatever you have to say." He knew this method of imparting information when a dwarf could not be direct—either because of a g'hesh, or an unwise promise made in haste. Ehrlik called it "the necromancers' dance" and it was a dance Dwyn understood. He'd danced it a time or two himself with Riordiin, but never with Ehrlik. There was nothing he could put by the master.

"When I was a girl, my father Jull took us out West for vacation every Beltan. One summer we went to the Gold City at Telluride. It was as much a tourist trap then as it is now. Tully and I were six. They gave us spades and turned us loose in a sandbox with ten other children. I was so happy every time I found a gold nugget. I ran to show Sullivan, our big brother. He was eighteen and bored out of his skull." Jullup laughed. "But Tully never quit, not for a minute. Whenever he found one, he'd put it in his pocket and keep going. He had so many rocks by the end of the dig, his pockets looked like a chipmunk's cheeks. He wailed when we had to leave. It never occurred to him that it wasn't real. Sullivan told us later, the skunk. Tully didn't say a word. He'd spent an hour scrubbing that worthless pyrite with his toothbrush, but he gathered it up, took it to the bathroom and flushed it. Plugged the fancy toilet. Dad whipped him for that."

She fell silent. The only sound was the soft patter of rain hitting the skylight.

Dwyn waited, impatient for the punchline, but Jullup said no more, only scratched between Kritha's ears.

"Do I look like fool's gold? Then why should he deny me the right to work? Let me fail. He'll get what he wants."

Jullup's deep gaze pierced him. "What's scarier, Dwyn? Being fooled, or finding out *you* are the fool? Tully can't fix the fence. You can."

Dwyn digested that. He remembered the anger in Jack Sharpe's voice when he spoke of reclaimed land and broken boundaries. Tully had been defiant then. But goblins were not dwarves, and Nyssa's hackles had stood on end when she spoke with the goblin, Midian. Fences mattered, and goblins and dwarves sometimes had very different ideas of where lines should be drawn.

Jullup smiled grimly, as if she'd seen his thoughts shift.

"Ironsfork and Forankyf look like good neighbors, Dwyn, but in Sullivan's time as chieftain, we had a land dispute. It didn't end well for anyone. Forankyf lost a lot of land. Sullivan almost lost the quarry in the legal mess—it killed him in the end."

"I'm sorry."

She acknowledged his sympathy with a nod. "Tully wants the fence fixed, but I guarantee he's been on the phone with the goblin Seitha every day since you arrived, trying to convince her he's not Sullivan. It was a perfectly good boundary before because it meant little or nothing in a magical sense. Now it will. And they already find their borders too confining."

"I'll trade them a g'hesh. See if they find *that* less confining." He couldn't keep the heat out of his voice.

Jullup sighed. "I am sorry. More and more I feel like Nolan is right, and you should have gone back to Nations and the safety of the elemental colony. This is no place for Dragons."

"It's better than Xanadu." The colony would be the least of his worries if they returned him to Nations.

"You must have hated it a great deal if this is better."

He forced a smile. "Well, the coffee is worse, but the food is great, and I like the lady of the mountain quite a lot."

Jullup slapped his hand playfully. "That's Dh'Morda talk, and I already have a mate." She grinned slyly. "By the way, how did you like Nikl?"

Dwyn shrugged. "He's friendly."

"He was unusually friendly last night. But then Lokey wasn't himself either. Dh'Morda is never easy on anyone. It strains things. They'll sort it out in the end, I suppose. Men usually do."

Dwyn hesitated. "Has Nikl lived here long?"

"Not long. He came to us from Tellico about five years ago— six this April. Tully offered him a place here. He wouldn't have it. Not enough scope for his talents. He said that to Tully's face, and Nyssa's."

"He lives at Rich Mountain?" He'd have no chance with Lokey if Nikl were a mountain man, not with the way that man could cook.

Jullup shifted uncomfortably in her chair, eyeing the catastrophe on the counter. "No. Neil listens to Rachet, and Rachet would not have a Thunderer. Nikl lives off-mountain."

That was a black mark for Ironsfork, then. When a chieftain offers a home to an elemental dwarf, and that dwarf would rather live off-mountain than put his hands and his magic at that mountain's disposal, that was saying something bleak about both chieftain and mountain. Dwyn stretched, immensely pleased. Lokey, a younger dwarf and not of age to mate this year, was probably fair game.

There was nothing like seduction, even an impossible one, to take his mind off his troubles, waking or dreaming. "I believe I'll transcribe for a while this morning. You'll tell me when Nyssa gets back?"

"Why don't you work in here instead of across the hall? The lighting will be better."

"I didn't think you liked me getting ink all over your table."

She smiled impishly. "To tell the truth, I missed you yesterday."

So Dwyn spent the morning writing in the kitchen while Jullup ground herbs in a mortar, perfuming the air with essences of angelica, goldenseal, and wild ginger. When she left to visit a client at Rich Mountain, she didn't lock him in his room.

Early in the afternoon, Nyssa returned. She hung her raincoat in the hallway before coming into the kitchen. Morven followed in stockinged feet, dripping. Kritha bounded up from the floor, barking, and thrashing her long tail. Over the cacophony Dwyn recited:

> *She carried the storm in her stav,*
> *The rain of war she brought*
> *To the gate where the Dragon brooded*
> *Full armed, with fury fraught—"*

"An apt translation," Nyssa said. "May I?"

Dwyn handed her the page and leaned back in the chair, balancing it on two legs. "I dare say he got tired of waiting. Historical evidence points to a siege—the Southern Dragon probably surrendered to keep his mountain from starving to death."

"What is it?" Morven leaned over Nyssa's shoulder.

"*Hennessy at the Gate.*" Nyssa said. "A curious choice—beginning with poetry."

Dwyn turned the page over when Morven angled around him. "I need to talk to you."

"I'm listening." Nyssa sat, and folded her hands on the table. She wore a curious ring on her right forefinger—a hideous thing with a hunk of jade gripped firmly in the golden jaws of a serpent. If that was a Dh'Morda gift, her mate had terrible taste.

Dwyn told her what he had told Jullup. Her response was what he expected.

"Not until I speak with Tully."

"If you continue to deny me the right to complete my civil penalty, I can and I will lodge a formal complaint with your regional council."

"You'll get nowhere."

"But Tully will get a black eye. Necromancers' penalties are one thing. You can deny me materials. You can deny me paper. You can deny me a chair to sit on. But even an elemental dwarf has the right to fulfill a civil penalty. Deny me that, and your chieftain runs afoul of the law. It's not my fault you tied the two together in a bow."

Nyssa stood. "Tully's busy."

"So long as you tell him I'm ready. I'd hate to put a fellow elemental in error. What would the neighbors think?"

Nyssa's mask-like smile never altered. "Kritha! Come." She sailed away, silk shirt rippling. Dwyn smiled grimly. Jullup had certainly not had *this* in mind when she told him her story, but he doubted she'd ever negotiated with a terrorist. He tucked the completed page into the stack to his right.

Morven hadn't moved. "I can read Seid, you know."

"Can you now?" He cleaned his pen nib.

"So let me read it," Morven said.

He chuckled. "I'd be no kind of Seidoche if I let you read incomplete work."

"You let Nyssa read it."

"Well, warloche look after their own bones, don't they?"

"All dwarves have the right to read."

Dwyn tossed the pen into his writing box. "Eighteen, aren't you?"

Morven's beard bristled. "Nineteen, this Dh'Morda."

"Here's another piece of advice for you, infant. Don't quote Rok Dahl until you've learned to sift his shit with logic. He's not a Seidoche. He's not even a necromancer, just an Earthshaker with an ax to grind."

"He's an elemental like you."

"Not at all like me. There are reasons that Seidoche—like me—take care of written magic. You couldn't begin to understand the danger."

"How can we when you assholes restrict everything?"

"If I had a dollar for every time I heard that, I wouldn't be broke." He closed his writing case.

"It's people like you who make people like Jenr Rok Dahl." Morven stalked away, leaving wet footprints behind.

Dwyn hid the new pages safely under illusions with the others in his room. Given what Morven had just said, he felt it prudent. That girl quoted Rok Dahl like a disciple.

The Earthshaker had quite a following at Nations, where it was safe to Worship a demagogue as long as he lived overseas and wasn't a force in politics. Dwyn had even read some of Rok Dahl's rants on the universal rights of dwarves, but he'd gotten past them with his reason unscathed. Morven had fallen hard. Even asked him for the *Seida*, like she had a purpose for it.

If he was a sensible Seidoche, he would figure out who put Morven up to that shit. He would speak to Nyssa and suggest he work a deal with whomever Morven reported to in her sleeper cell. Then he'd let Nyssa alert the regional librarian. Hello, fat reward. Goodbye, paper problem.

Dwyn sighed. The sad truth was, he'd quit being a sensible Seidoche a long time ago.

He picked up the five-gallon bucket Jullup had loaned him, his bag of lint, and the bottle of lignin he'd brought from the old kitchen earlier in the day. If he wet the pulp now, it could soak overnight before he filled the frames.

Dwyn knew the dog had gone with Nyssa to her quarters, but he came into the hallway wary as Jullup's cat, half-expecting Kritha to jump out at him. No one was there, but heavy bass pounded somewhere behind a closed door up the hallway. Morven was sulking.

Dwyn piled the dishes in the basin on the counter, shaking bits of cold food into the gray water as he drained it. Cursing, he pulled out trash bags, bottles of bug spray, and a moldy scrub brush from under the sink before he found soap and a soured dishcloth. He ground his teeth, balled up the rag, and began to scrub with it rather than take his chances with the nastier brush. He heard the door in the hallway close, although he never heard it open.

"Now there's a man I could love," Nikl said, swinging into the room. "Cleaning the kitchen." He sagged comfortably into a chair and opened the bag he was carrying. The spicy aroma of pumpkin and pepper filled the air as he popped the lid on a bowl. The chef tasted the soup with a plastic spoon, smacked his lips in approval, and took a box from the bag. He opened it with a satisfied expression. A hot sandwich steamed with beefy fragrance. Next, he took out a cup and the warm smell of coffee was added to the atmosphere.

A sharp bit of broken glass laid the end of Dwyn's thumb open. "Fuck!" He threw the rag into the sink. "He arda!" Fire scalded the basin, burning rag, soap, and mildew. He stepped back, snorting cinders.

"Hard day?" Nikl was smiling, but that familiar uplift on the right side of his mouth did nothing to improve Dwyn's temper.

"What are you doing here?" He drew the fire back into his body like retractable claws.

Nikl blinked. "Well, aren't *you* friendly. I ran into Jullup at Rich Mountain. She asked if I would feed you when I picked up my ardchuk. I said I would." He wagged the cup at Dwyn. "Come and eat before it gets cold."

"I'm a Dragon. Cold means nothing to me." Dwyn found the drain plug buried behind the wine glasses. He filled the basin half full and added handfuls of white lint. The water frothed as his hot blood oiled the surface.

Nikl sauntered over. The odors of flour, yeast, and salt mingled with cigarette smoke and electricity. "What the hell are you doing?"

"Making paper."

"I thought there were people who did that job for you, Sei-doche."

"People I can't afford to pay." Dwyn pushed lint beneath the water forcefully.

"Speaking of making things…" Nikl's whisper became con-spiratorial. "I know what you did. I don't know how you did it, but I know it was you. Yesterday morning I was standing next to the brewing machine when a pint of coffee disappeared. Sucked right down into the counter. Somebody's stealing. No necromantic signature Rachet could find. But I smelled a Dragon."

"Do me a favor," Dwyn said, shaking wet lint from his fingers. "Tomorrow, fill the pot with a cup of your best pond water. Top it off with mud for color. Your stealing problem will go away, and I'll be laughing fit to burst."

Nikl chuckled. "If it was you, you'd owe me five bucks, but since it's Nyssa, it'll be three. Rich Mountain employee discount."

"Hit her up for it and don't forget to duck."

Nikl's silver eyes sparkled with mirth. "You know, this isn't the first time someone's tried to steal from me. I've got hexn in my kitchen, plenty of them. They'll scald the beard off a man who takes something he didn't pay for. But you don't look singed to me."

Dwyn flared. "I didn't steal your damned coffee!"

Nikl didn't flinch, not even when fire grazed his cheek. "Was it a draw spell, like Rachet said?"

"Look, I made that fucking cup for Jullup. Nyssa stole it from her, like she steals everything else. I never even used it!"

"Quit being so damned prickly. I just wondered if you could make something like that permanent."

"I've never tried." Dwyn stepped back from the sink. "It's best to get rid of a cup after a few uses."

"Why?"

"First, dissolving necromancy doesn't agree with my stomach. Secondly, if I use a cup like that to hit a place too often, they figure it out and put the nasty on me."

"Their hexn pick it up?"

Dwyn snorted. "With my magic? Not a chance. But when people figure out coffee is going missing, they piss in the pot."

Nikl looked properly disgusted, but then he said, "But could you? Make it permanent."

"Why would I want to do that?"

Nikl rolled his eyes. "Hypothetically, my fire-breathing friend—could you?"

Dwyn sighed. "If I reinforced a ceramic cup against leaks—yes. And found a way to fuel it. Then set the expiration date, and decided how to dispose of the thing if it cracked—look, I'm busy." He began to knead the mass of paper dough in the sink.

Nikl leaned in closer. "What if I paid you?"

Dwyn stopped kneading.

"Neil offered us incentives this year if we cut down on our garbage. He's pushing for a refillable cup. Never mind that I compost every scrap that comes out of the kitchen. Never mind that the school wastes more paper in a week than we do in a month with disposable cups. I won't turn down money if they want to throw it at me. But if I try to make my staff wash two hundred extra cups a day, they'll mutiny. So, what do you say?"

Dwyn raised his hands, festooned with red-tinged lint. "Why me?"

"Rachet says draw spells aren't your average apple pie. He gave me a quote that more or less took away my appetite for the project. But when I saw what you did, I got to thinking maybe another man might do it for me."

"What makes you think I'll do it for you?"

"A lifetime supply of free coffee?"

Dwyn grinned. He couldn't help it.

Nikl laughed, reached out, and scooped Dwyn away from the sink in a bear hug. "I knew you would! Lokey said no, and Morven thought I was crazy, but I knew."

Dwyn gasped. Nikl was freezing, like meltwater on the hottest of summer days. It felt amazing. He wanted all that cold up against him, right now. He pushed back, hot and confused. "Not so fast. I'll tell you what I think and let you decide."

"Shoot." Nikl folded his arms over his chest.

"I assume you don't want to be tasked each time someone wants a cup of coffee with cream and sugar across the mountain."

"You can do that? Cream and sugar, and the coffee?"

"Of course. But that's not the point. Reinforcing the cup to stand a draw is only the first part of the challenge; the real difficulty is tying the spell to a permanent decomposition source—unless you want that magic sucking on you like a tick. I'm not getting bled for it."

Nikl choked. "Decomposition source?"

"Second rule of necromancy: Something must die."

"What did you use for Jullup's cup?"

"The same thing I use for the ones I make for myself—my gut. Plenty of things dying in there, and it's a simple matter to get rid of the toxins."

Nikl looked like he didn't know whether to laugh or gag. "Shit. You run it off shit."

"A couple of large septic tanks would be a good choice for a project of your scope." Dwyn wiped his bloody arms on a towel, irritated. Whether it was complex cascade spells or translating glyphs into runic, folk wanted it clean because necromancers made it *look* clean. He wanted to tell folk to open a tomb and look at the bones of the men and women who took death magic less seriously than he did. Go look at the broken skulls. See the hollow vertebrae crushed to powder from years of poisoning. See the rot, and then worship the twisted shape of magic forced into a form with no thought to function.

But the disgusted scowl on Nikl's face went away. "What about a compost pile?"

Dwyn leaned against the counter, impressed. "Now you're thinking like a Seidoche. But you're better off using your sewers. Your necromancer didn't lie; draw spells aren't average magic. Any break in the fuel and you get a terrific mess. A little kitchen compost pile won't handle something like two hundred cups every day."

Nikl grinned. "You haven't met *my* compost pile."

"If it's the idea of raw sewage you don't like—"

"Nothing like that. If I ask Rachet about sewers, he'd figure it out and charge me. He's the steward after all. The compost pile belongs to me, and I'll keep all the money in my kitchen if it kills me. But I'll have to see it to believe it." A distinct note of challenge rang in Nikl's voice.

"Bring me a cup. But I want payment in advance."

"How much?"

Dwyn scraped a strand of wet lint from underneath his fingernail. "A tuhn of twenty-one weight linen paper, necromancer grade, sewing edge left, a roll of doeskin leather, one pack of steel needles, and a min of black ink, onyx flask. Deal?"

Nikl whistled. "You don't come cheap, Dragon."

"I don't make cheap magic."

Nikl stared at him shrewdly.

Dwyn stared back, not budging an inch.

Nikl sighed. He stuck out his hand. "All right, Dragon. You've got a deal."

CHAPTER TEN

DH'MORDA

Two days after Nyssa put him off, Dwyn found Tully and Nolan waiting for him in the old kitchen.

"Morning?" He stopped in the doorway.

Nolan sat quietly at the end of the long zinc table, arms folded, but Tully stood, leaning forward, gripping the table with blunt, grimy fingers. Muddy water seeped from under his nails. "You're not to do business with a dwarf from another mountain without the permission of the chieftain." His skin flickered constantly: brown to green, green to blue, and blue to rust as his water magic seethed.

Dwyn clutched the fresh ream of paper Nikl had brought him as a squall of rain whipped his beard back. "You told me not to call you Chieftain. I remember that distinctly. I'm an independent dwarf, and I have an agreement with another independent dwarf. There's no law against that." He reached into his back pocket and held up his written contract. Nikl had laughed, but to Dwyn, verbal promises were broken promises in the mouth of a man with the power to break them. He wrote everything on a sheet of fresh, white paper and made Nikl sign.

"That can be revoked," Tully snapped.

"Then Neil will know," Nolan warned. "And if Nikl wants to proceed anyway, he'll have to countersign. Nikl is his employee."

"Nolan is right," Dwyn said. "The work lies between Nikl and myself, independent of Rich Mountain. For now."

"You threaten me?" Tully's display grew more violent. Puddles appeared around his boots.

"The law allows a prisoner to engage in contract labor while under debt. You said you didn't care about your regional council. Does your fellow chieftain feel the same way?"

"You were under contract to me first!"

Gusts of rain hissed and fizzed against Dwyn's flames, and the room steamed like summer. "The penalty states I'm to repair your wall or pay for it to be fixed. You're preventing me from working. I need stones for your wall—I told this to your necromancer. Has she said nothing about it to you?"

Tully's dirt-colored eyes turned green. "You may seek your stones, Dragon."

Dwyn bowed, but only Nolan acknowledged it. Tully brushed wetly past and splashed down the hall.

Thirty minutes later Dwyn walked through the doors of Ironsfork singing "I broke the bones of the dead, I stole the breath of the living" at the top of his voice. The *Triumph of Kelequah* belonged to him that day, and he sang it like his soul's anthem, but his elation didn't last long. Victory came with a price.

It came with Kritha.

The sky was a patchwork of gray on darker gray. Snow flurried around Dwyn as he followed the river west across the lowlands of Ironsfork. The Dh'Morda gift of December snowfall seemed unusually extravagant for the South. Three inches was enough to keep Jullup home—Lokey and Morven too. But Nyssa hadn't been daunted, and neither had Tully. They went to work as usual. Nolan didn't come home at all. He stayed overnight at the hospital where he was needed. Consequently, Jullup stomped around the house, frustrated. Dwyn left after breakfast, eager to get outside where the air was less frosty.

"Kritha, I see you."

She was hiding today. Red ears poked up over a hillock made by a snow-crushed cedar tree. A week she'd been dogging him, but today, he was trying something new. He took a lump of foil from his pocket and unwrapped it. The bloody steak glistened rawly between his fingers.

"Want a bite?" He tossed the meat.

Kritha slunk forward, stiff-legged and bristling.

"All yours. Good dog."

Kritha nosed his offering, raised her lips, and snarled. She cut through the snow-covered bushes at a gallop. A battalion of cardinals shot skyward, breaking formation as they passed up and over Dwyn.

Well, so much for that idea. He picked up the meat and clamped his fist around it, charring it into an ashy lump.

The day he had walked out of the gates singing, Kritha had come after him, yelling for blood. She grabbed him before he could swarm up a tree. He reached for the sword on his back, too terrified to think she might not kill him. Nyssa's protective shield all but bludgeoned him into submission. The g'hesh clamped down on his spine as strongly as Kritha's teeth held his leg, and he screamed for mercy, burning leaves and ferns beneath him to ashes. Kritha wasn't even singed. Above him, Kritha stood on the driveway that paralleled the long ridge of the mountain before intersecting with the quarry road. She was watching him. She watched him all the time.

He left the meat burning a hole in the snow beside the river and climbed up after her. The river was played out. A week of wading in water as cold as his fear, and he had a single workable stone to show for his efforts. A mountain as old and deep as Ironsfork should be richer in rock, but the mountain's back had been broken, first by war, then by the clan who maimed it. It was as bankrupt as he was.

What he wouldn't give for some solid chert nodules, or better yet, itzha, the black obsidian he used to dredge from the river in Xanadu. Not as wearing as flint or as durable as quartzite, but it took his fire like no other stone he'd ever found. Dwyn gathered all he could find, buried it behind his cinder-block house, and set vicious hexn to protect his horde. He'd always meant to take it with him when he left.

When he left, there had been no time.

Ehrlik had saved him. Practically carried him out of the void cell where he lay recovering after he destroyed the necromancer's council chamber when the g'hesh branded him incendiary. Packed him too—Dwyn lay prone on the bed, still feverish, too weak to stand, undoing hexn one by one so his only friend could collect the books he would not leave behind.

Ehrlik complained the whole time. *Dwyndoche, we need to leave now. We don't have time for your damned nonsense. I must get you out of the country. Don't you understand? I give you full marks for acting—no one doubts you are as incendiary as a volcano—but did you have to explode? There's no time for this, Dwyn, and you are oblivious.*

But he wasn't. He knew it was over—Ehrlik, Riordiin, everything. God under the earth, he missed them both, especially now at Dh'Morda, the time of the darkness. Aptly named, the mating season—life, death, love, hate, and all dark to him now.

Kritha splashed across a small watercourse, and as if sensing his intentions, flopped down on the opposite side to wait. Below the bank, fallen logs partially dammed the stream, forming a pool. Dwyn propped his sword against a twisted maple tree. No sense walking around smoking like a geyser in damp clothes. He'd steam himself dry after the dip.

He shucked his underwear on top of his jeans, noticing the scorch marks. One of these days, he'd drop his pants and find nothing but ash in the crotch. When the seams started to fall apart, the magic wasn't far behind. He eyed the pool with dislike.

In general, Dwyn regarded water with the fondness of an average cat. Riordiin had taught him the sensual pleasure of bathing with a friend, but he didn't like water over his head, and he loathed places where he couldn't see what was below him. He waded into the pool, feeling his way over the disgusting bottom barefoot.

He heard Morven coming before he saw her. "Morning," he said.

Kritha gave a sharp, happy bark.

"Nice day for a swim." Morven grabbed Kritha's wet muzzle and wrestled playfully with the dog.

He bent and groped the bottom for the rock he'd located painfully with his toes. "Where are you off to?"

"Forankyf." Morven showed him the rifle hanging on her shoulder. "Midian invited me. Like it? It's a gift."

"Well, stay out of trouble." He had it now—a stone well-rounded by water, smooth and hard. Water sluiced down his beard and hissed over his belly as he stood.

"That's rich, coming from you. What kind of trouble are you thinking of, warrrrloche?" She stretched the honorific as she scratched around Kritha's chin and jowls.

Quartzite, heavy and solid, and pinkish in hue. He wiped the mud on his hip. "How about a little advice. What number am I up to now, infant? Five or six? Watch yourself around goblins. Love makes them a damned treacherous lot."

"Where is that written?" Morven straightened and shifted her gun to her back.

"On the cold, hard stone of bitter experience." Dwyn sloshed to the bank and set the stone on his shirt while he pulled his pants on, buckling his belt under Morven's insolent stare.

"Nikl says you have the best ass he's ever seen on a skinny little dwarf."

He snorted. "Whose is he comparing it to? Lokey's?"

"How about I give you some advice, Dragon?" Morven folded her arms over her chest and stared at him sagely. "The man in the middle of a cock-fight gets spurred the most."

"Come up with that by yourself?"

"Old goblin proverb. Have fun swimming." She crossed the creek below him where the pool ended, tight-roping across the fallen trees.

"Have fun hunting," he said. He glanced at the pool, disappointed. Two worthy rocks out of an entire mountain—pathetic. Kritha shook snow out of her coat in his direction. The icy bits hissed as they evaporated and stuck to his bare body, speckling him red.

He should take his rock and go back to Ironsfork. The old quarry lay beyond the ridge, and the stone there would be worthless to him. He glanced over his shoulder. Morven was trudging off in the direction of the border with Forankyf. He spat in the snow, backed up, took a running leap, jumped the creek, and landed near the dog with a shower of sparks. She raised her lip at him and walked off, tracking west. He followed, carrying the stone wrapped in his shirt.

Hunting, my ass. He knew damned well what *that* was code for, and it made his skin creep. But he was one to talk. He'd been quite as careless at her age. He touched his shoulder where the bullet had shattered his collarbone. That was what Dh'Morda did to men and women. Jullup said Dh'Morda strained things. More like ripped them out, rearranged them, and destroyed all hope of joy.

At Nations, elemental dwarves were forbidden to mate outside the colony. That didn't bother Dwyn. He knew he was worthless in that regard—he had nothing to give a mate but heartbreak, and as for his fellow colonists, who the fuck wanted to mate with them? But the remainder of the law drove him almost out of his mind every damned year. He wasn't allowed to have sex outside of the colony during the mating season, not with anyone, not with everyone's magic in turmoil. Accidents might happen. So Dwyn paced the confines of Xanadu every Dh'Morda, angry, hating the world, hating himself, and hating the season. He couldn't satisfy the lust that shortening daylight had spawned in every dwarf since evolution drove them underground.

It was such foolishness, that law. The chances of him reproducing had always been infinitesimally small, even had he not been born a Dragon. And even if he could, he had no clan name to recommend him. But sex, pleasure, even love—he could have that, couldn't he? His body told him he could. He was starving for it, and Dh'Morda was an incessant strip-tease driving him wild with fantasies. Alone, he might have been able to endure it. But there, with thousands of dwarves nearby, all of them happy, bedding whomever they chose, and only him, alone and miserable, rubbing himself raw trying to ease his desires, it had been almost intolerable. When he got clear of Ironsfork, he promised himself he'd find a hole in his beloved Heldasa and never leave it again. He could do without the temptation that blinded him to all reason.

Blinded him physically, too. A wedge of stone tripped him and he fell sprawling. The air whooshed out in a gust of smoke and cinders. He got to his hands and knees, mouthing the curses he couldn't find breath for. And stayed there, awed.

What he'd tripped over was the base of a broken henr stone. The rest of the great slab of rock lay flat, fractured halfway down its length. The others stood in a ring that Kritha trotted through, leaving dark prints across the middle. The uneven stones stuck up black in the snow, giving the stone circle the look of rotten teeth jutting out of dead, white gums.

He got to his feet, as breathless as he'd been when he fell. Never had he seen an Eseitha hengh this far west.

All the broken temples where the Dragons danced were back east, in Appalachia mostly. There were a few in the Cumberlands to show that the Southern Empire had annexed those mountains into the forgotten civilization dwarves once built on the backs of their Dragon warlords. He hadn't known any were made after it fell.

Hands shaking, Dwyn singed the plants away from the rock,

revealing the glyphs—eagle, heron, vulture, crow. The language was mostly intact. He could read it as easily as he read standard Runic. *Here is the heart of the mountain. Touch softly, warloche. You'll feel the blood pulse under your hand.*

"Why isn't this a landmark? Why hasn't it been preserved? Are they all here?" He panted in his enthusiasm, counting. One henr, two, three—four. Yes. Four, although it was no more than a nub beneath the snow. Five, six, seven, eight at the edge of the cliff—the cliff that…

He gazed across the spectacular chasm where the ninth should have stood, an intact Eseitha hengh but for that damned gravel quarry. He looked back over his shoulder at the remaining stones, their grandeur broken not by northern necromancers but by their own folk. Who'd carved the henr out and ground it up for gravel? Jullup's father? The dead brother, Sullivan? Or Tully?

"They ought to have their heads broken." He stared at the hengh, aching. "They fined me everything I was for killing a man, but I never killed a mountain."

Snowflakes whirled in the air, kissed his lips, and stung his eyes as they melted. He shivered, hugging his arms around himself.

I dance for no one.

It had been years since the last time he danced the Dh'Morda, heartbroken and furious before the wreck of his grandfather's tomb. He had taken his revenge for that atrocity, but the Dh'Morda had come first: a blessing for a curse, love for hate, life for death. Slowly, he unstrapped Mh'Arda from his back. He was Mn'Hesset, and this death, forgotten and abandoned, needed blessing.

He loosed the frayed leather thelon that bound his braids and combed his hair out with his fingers. The brown cascade poured past the small of his back, ragged and unruly. He unbuckled his belt and stripped reverently, leaving everything on the far side of the hengh where it would not interfere with the magic he meant to make.

He stepped into the Eseitha hengh, naked.

Barefoot in the snow as he had been in the river, he felt the chill—not of the snow, but of the cold death he was about to bless. The icy wind tasted as bitter as the broken skull of his grandfather when he'd kissed the crushed mouth, weeping for the second death of his only family. He dashed the meltwater away from his eyes with an angry swipe.

He danced.

He circled the ring, sword in hand, but this was no J'hen, no battle dance, but a Dh'Morda, meant to undo the curse of magic wronged and death forgotten. His fire rose, and with it his spirit. He kicked the snow aside as he whirled through the ancient steps.

Ekehda mi. Receive me. The mountain was always feminine in magic—he knew better than to dance without first asking permission. He spiraled out from the center of the broken hengh, long hair whipping in his face as the wind danced with him. Blood mixed with his fire, dripped from his forearms, and splattered the ground. He'd danced like this for old Isolde, for his grandfather, and for Riordiin too, for all death so lonely, so abandoned, so like his life.

Ehona mhu. Take my strength. His breath fogged before his eyes as he spiraled in and raised his sword above his head. It struck with a sucking sound deep in the wet earth. He whirled away to complete the dance, weaving a web of blessing between the standing stones.

A bloody handprint stood out on the frosted stone wherever he touched, smoking with fire, pregnant with magic. Snow fell heavily now, veiling him in a mist of fire and water. He had not danced like this in years, but how had he forgotten this deep sense of longing and desperate passion? It seemed so new.

"Eseitha ti." *You are renewed.* Or had he said eseitha mi? He stared up at the cloud-blind sky while snowflakes melted on his skin and ran down his arms in bloody rivers.

His body trembled with a need he didn't have a name for, but the magic word for renewal fit like a well-worn shirt. Dh'Morda was the season of renewal, the apex of the cycle, where death met life at the bones and all things were created. He sagged over the crosstrees of Mh'Arda, impaled by weariness.

The circle is complete. We were born, you and I, of earth's bones and magic's blood. We lived while we worked—you for your mountain, I for my pride. We are dead, you and I—you by cruelty, I by my own foolishness. May you find your rest. You cannot be whole, but be at peace.

He lurched back to his clothes. During the dance, he hadn't noticed the hundred or so cuts on the soles of his feet. He must have danced on thorns.

Kritha advanced stiff-legged, and stuck her whiskery muzzle almost on his lips, showing all her teeth. She rumbled softly.

"I don't need any comments from you," he snarled back.

He'd had his J'hen mocked plenty of times at Nations. Folk quit laughing when he danced circles around warloche regarded as fair fighters with a blade. Nobody beat Dwyn with a sword in his hand. But there was no denying it—when he danced, he looked like a fool.

And the Dh'Morda was an ugly dance. He certainly felt an ugly man when he danced it. Something about being naked before nature and God made him aware of every personal flaw—body, soul and mind. His mind he was proud of. His soul he felt he could not help. But his body? There was an eyesore. Thin, weedy legs under a short belly and a long torso. Supple, but stringy arms, bony shoulders. Eyes too wide to be right. All brown. Not so much as a stripe or spot to break the monotonous color. When he danced, he was little more than a dirty grasshopper capering about in a religious frenzy.

Yet, he looked out over the lonely hengh, immersed in a sense of satisfied exhaustion.

Kritha prowled the ring suspiciously. She touched her nose to one of the broken stones, and backed away, barking.

"Shut up." He distributed his weight to the outside of his feet and picked up his stone.

Fat snowflakes fell thick as tears as he shuffled back to Ironsfork. Kritha kept slow pace beside him. She stopped to sniff every large tree, every snow-capped bush, and every black, exposed rock. Then she'd gallop past him, whining.

"What the hell are you on about?" The euphoria he'd felt during the dance faded with every painful step. He'd wasted time—time he could have worked at the mountain on his copying. Or he could have fired this latest stone, a necessary step on his path to eventual freedom. He slipped and went down in the wet.

The heavy coating of snow melted instantly, soaking him through.

Kritha galloped away from him toward the front doors of Ironsfork, barking all the way. He wobbled up the stairs behind her. The door swung open. Kritha slithered through the gap. With an angry squawk, Nyssa bumped into Dwyn, spinning him around in the entryway.

"Ugh!" Nyssa brushed her front where Dwyn's muddy imprint stained her white wool coat. "Why are you always wet? Why are you always dirty?"

"Why don't you watch where you're going?" He snapped, desperately bowlegged, keeping his weight on the edges of his feet.

Nyssa combed pine needles out of her loose hair in a fury. "Can't you do anything without wallowing in it?"

"You know, if you'd let your beard grow like a normal woman, you wouldn't need to clean that coat," he grumbled. "Where are you going anyway? It's snowing harder than ever."

"None of your—damned business." Nyssa yanked her scarf off. "You stink like the bottom half of a lake."

He did not. He smelled like rotten apples, vinegary rotten apples, and she smelled like...roses. Dark, red roses, a valley of beautiful roses, strong as wine, wicked as poison. His nostrils widened. "You're going to see that metalmage, Tam Wyvern, aren't you?"

"I said none of your business."

"When will you be back?"

"I'll have to change, and I'm already late." She turned and stalked through the doors. Most of the rose fragrance went into the mountain with her.

Dwyn followed it, dripping mud and flames. "What if I need you? What if I want to go down to the wall?"

"Talk to Tully." She pushed open a door in the hallway. It slammed shut when he reached it, cutting off her scent.

He balled his fist, struck the door, and leaned against it. His pulse throbbed. His head whirled. The blood pounded in him everywhere.

"God under the Earth!" He let go of the handle, furious with himself. *Damn Dh'Morda! Damn it to hell!*

He staggered away, sick to his soul.

CHAPTER ELEVEN

DRAGON DREAMS

"What on earth or under it did you do to yourself?" Jullup asked when Dwyn limped past the sitting room.

"I fell." He brushed the crisping leaves from his pants. "Where's Lokey? I don't hear the piano." He was on fire inside. He needed someone—anyone—to take his mind off what had just happened.

"Out with a friend who has a four-wheel drive. He won't be back tonight."

Dammit. Morven's advice notwithstanding, Dwyn wanted the comfort of a man. With the season's help, Lokey might not have found him so repellant. After all, Lokey had fallen for an elemental dwarf once.

"It's past lunch—where did you go?" Jullup set her book down on the end table and rose.

"West, to the old quarry and back."

"I thought you couldn't use quarried stone."

Before he could reply, Kritha charged through the open door, knocking him sideways.

"Dog!" Jullup went after her, scolding.

Dwyn took off his boots slowly, grateful to the dog for once. He could hear Jullup fussing in the laundry room as she toweled the wolfhound dry. He hobbled to the kitchen, took a container from the refrigerator, and dumped a cylinder of packed meat, carrots, onions, and potatoes on a plate. It melted into fragrant stew as he sat at the table.

"Which reminds me," Jullup called, "Do you want venison or chicken on Saturday? I've asked Nikl to bring enough food to last through the weekend. Tully will be here, but he eats when he wants, downstairs."

"Nikl's coming here?"

"Tomorrow. He said he had business with you," Jullup said. "Venison or chicken?"

"Chicken." He wouldn't be on his own. Kritha. The tabah controlled his door, and when it was open, he couldn't shut it. The dog never took her eyes off him, even when he took a piss. Glumly, he stabbed the fork into the steaming meat.

"Chicken." Jullup came into the kitchen, scratching on a notepad.

"Why do you let Morven go to Forankyf during Dh'Morda?"

Jullup stopped scribbling. "Frankly, I don't think it's any of your business," she said, but she didn't sound angry.

"It *is* my business. I have a fence to fix. If goblins come and go as they please, because there's mating between the mountains—"

Jullup laughed. "Morven is too young to mate."

"Not too young to make mistakes."

"Oh, don't tell me you've never fooled around with your friends. Morven and Midian have been close since they were children, and it's perfectly normal she should be with him at Dh'Morda. As for goblins coming and going whenever they please, Midian is the only goblin who crosses our borders regularly. He will not interfere with your fence."

"It's your fence, not mine."

Jullup sat down next to him. "Prejudice doesn't become you,

Dwyn. Doesn't it bother you when people judge you entirely by the rune on your hand? They don't consider you as a dwarf before they decide a Dragon is someone they would rather not get to know."

He spoke with his mouth full. "No. It saves me the trouble of enlightening them. You can't change my mind about goblins so don't try."

She looked affronted.

For a moment he thought he'd said too much. Then Jullup reached across and gently picked a charred leaf out of his hair. "You can't make me stop trying."

Her mating scent, honeysuckle sweet and potent, tantalized him. He drew it in through his mouth to taste it fully. Blood beaded on his inner forearms, and lustful warmth spread through his shoulders, blazed into his chest, and set his hair on fire. Clouds of his own cider-apple vinegar billowed around him—oh, not again!

Jullup's widening smile cut a canyon in her cheeks. She laughed.

He extinguished himself. "It's not funny!"

"No, I don't suppose so. Poor boy." She kissed the top of his head and took his empty plate.

"I meant nothing by it." God under the earth! He wasn't twenty—he should be able to repress a sex flush.

"I'm not so old I've forgotten what it's like to be young. What have you tried for it?"

"What do you mean?"

"What remedies have you used to damp down your ardor?"

Oh, God, now he burned all over. "I don't know what you're talking about."

"Unicorn root? Chaste tree tea? Hot chocolate with peppers?"

"Hot chocolate with...you're joking!" He turned around in his chair, aghast.

"Don't you Seidoche ever memorize a book of common sense?"

"Are the insults free or must I pay for them?"

Jullup retreated to the stove. "Chocolate and chili powder it is, then."

"I see I'm paying. No thanks." He stood, yelped, and crumpled.

"What's wrong?" Jullup's playful smile changed to a concerned frown. "Dwyn?"

He gripped the table, panting. "Nothing I can't fix."

"Dwyn, your feet are bleeding!"

"Nothing to bother about," he blustered.

Jullup knelt in front of him and yanked off his socks. She gasped. "How did you do this? Cut glass couldn't make a bigger mess."

"I'll fire them clean; I've done it before—"

Jullup huffed. "No, you won't. Stay here and I'll fix you, feet and all." She set a cup of dark cocoa in front of him and stirred in the chili powder. "You drink that, and I'll go mix a salve for your cuts."

Spicy fumes rippled up from the surface. "I breathe fire. I don't drink it."

"What chocolate inspires, the pepper devours. Go on." She disappeared down the hallway.

He could tiptoe to the sink and pour everything down the drain, but then he thought about his foolishness with Nyssa. He took a sip and coughed smoke for ten minutes. "You could do—a pretty business—in torture," he spluttered.

Jullup reappeared, mixing lotions together in a bowl. "Oh, you're a grown dwarf. Take your medicine."

"When should I expect to die?"

"Morven didn't fuss half as much as you do." She sat in the chair next to him, lifted his foot into her lap and massaged the salve into his wounds with capable hands. Jullup knew her shit as well as he knew his. He choked down the rest of the drink.

Dwyn wasn't sure he'd credit Jullup's folk remedy, but he finished *Hennessy* that afternoon, and started on the second half of Cheyloche Daffyd's *Principles*. His concentration was marred only by the number of times he had to limp to the bathroom and guzzle from the tap in a vain attempt to curb his burning thirst.

Dinner didn't do much for the heartburn either. Why did this always happen to him? No one else he'd ever known struggled with lust at Dh'Morda like he did. Only he slopped around like a drunk, making himself ridiculous. He tossed and turned in bed, waiting for the mountain to breathe, sure he would never sleep, but when the rush of air moaned through his room, he woke. He breathed with it—breathed fire through his teeth— and drifted into dreams.

Roses grew in the land of shadows, a thorny vale of them. Mn'Hesset ran, trailing flames, wounded and weary. He slunk beneath the brambles like a hare.

How they came to be, the wild roses with their blood-red blossoms overhanging every path in his personal wilderness, he never knew. He only knew they had to do with him. They grew nowhere else but here— the mountain home of the Mn'Hesset. Their musky sweetness suffused the damp air as he limped through the wild tangle toward a ruin: a truly ancient dwarf mountain, surrounded by decayed rivn. Fallen walls, broken corridors, and chambers sunk in shadows spoke of an origin as black as forgetfulness. The river of the dead took its source here, but he could not remember how, or why.

The draugr's rotting stench overpowered the roses, but he struggled on, tripped, and fell hard on his broken side beside the black stream.

The water reflected his face—a small white skull seamed with silver, the dull red glow of the dead eye sockets, stacked teeth in a gaping mouth. He clawed the water with splintered finger bones helplessly as the draugr pushed him under, crushing him to death. Water rushed in.

The world turned over like a sick lake.

He saw the mountain.

It was his mountain. It had always been his. But now it gaped like a chest wound, with the blackening heart open for the buzzards to eat. Smoke poured from his broken gates—screams, too. The dwarves inside were being slaughtered by the northern invaders. He'd not been Dragon enough to save them.

Through the haze he caught glimpses of the places he knew and loved—the West Lookout, where he'd received his blade from the Dragon before him, the Eagle's Keep, where his personal birds of prey were mewed at their molt, the Fern Walk where he courted his mate at Dh'Morda. He roared his anguish.

"Subdue him!" The necromancer called from the top of the column. At her command, six more necromancers hemmed him in with their death magic, chanting, weaving a chaos of magic he could not control. He fell to his knees, cursing.

This should never have been. He was the Southern Dragon, the protector of mountains, not the last wretched survivor of what had been the longest war. He should have died too, fallen as his Eseitha hengh fell on the ridge behind him, hewn down with the necromancers' strong magic. Nothing remained to him now but a solitary and endless quest for revenge.

Ata ti hacharda.

He swore it on his bones.

Freezing. Screaming. Thrashing. No paralysis saved Dwyn this time—he pitched out of bed, shrieking, landed on his elbows and knees and scrambled away, trailing burning sheets.

"No! No! Oh, God, no. Not this. Not again. No..." He collapsed, curling his arms around his head. Brilliant images of the dying mountain exploded in his mind, dying dwarves screamed underground in their tombs, and every terrified face became a burning skull, accusing him in a torrent of wild, strange voices.

You abandoned us, Dh'Rigahn! We were left to rot.

His feet cramped so badly he thought they would never release. "Oh, Paloh mhu—don't abandon me!" He didn't close his eyes although the tears burned. If he did, he'd see that smoking mountain again, and he'd never see anything else. It was welded to his memory like his soul's-blood had soldered it there.

"God under the earth!" He staggered to the washroom where he collapsed on the edge of the shower stall and vomited. Black ash. Never a good sign. He balled up on the stone floor, arms clamped tightly around himself.

He felt like he was a child again, sobbing on the floor of his home in Tennessee, tortured by the dreams of a Dragon and a mountain of voices that hated him. His grandfather rocked him where he sat, petting his hair through the flames, repeating his name—Dwyn, Dwyn, Dwyn—over and over. His grandfather didn't understand the nightmares, but at least Dwyn had the comfort of his touch. No one would comfort him here. If he'd needed further proof he was beyond redemption, he had it now.

Hot, sticky ash fell from his lips. "Paloh mhu, please. I am your Mn'Hesset. I was always yours. You said I would always be yours."

A Knight embraces death as a lover. He does not run. And he had run like a coward from the draugr in his nightmares. He ran from Ehrlik who would have helped him. But that wasn't the beginning of his running. Riordiin—he'd run from Riordiin.

The Dragon necromancer had ripped Mh'Arda from Dwyn's grasp as easily as he'd ripped his heart and mind out, a clear sign from God that he should have died then, but he ran, and called for help as he did. Help had come and doomed him to hell.

Dwyn clamped his eyes shut as the knife of black stone exploded out of the ground, full of his wrath, serrated like his hate, and Riordiin died on it, shrieking like the dwarves dying in their mountain. It was the hengh—dancing a Dh'Morda for the damned hengh—that led him down this path in his mind. He would go back, and he would dance a J'hen, a battle dance, and he would prove that he was Mn'Hesset, that he deserved a second chance. He'd repent everything.

His faith required he remember his dreams. His Dragon nature required he record them permanently in writing. But when Dwyn finally uncurled and limped back to his room, he crept beneath his singed sheets and buried himself. He would have to wait for dawn to turn the shadow of his sin into something less real before he found the courage to face it.

"You look awful. You sure you're up for this?" Nikl was all concern as he crouched down behind Dwyn. The old kitchen was host to an experiment this morning. Dwyn had turned the table over to create a makeshift bunker facing the sink.

"Have a little confidence in me." He knew he looked bad. Morning had not salvaged the bad night, although he lit the lamp around five and documented his dream as his faith demanded. It ought to have been cathartic. Instead, he threw up again, and came upstairs still nauseous. Didn't even have a caustic comment to throw at the dog when she barked at him as though she'd never seen him before in her life.

"I'd be more confident if the cup was on the counter and not in the sink."

"Take proper precautions. Third rule of necromancy— Morven, get down!"

There was a sound like a pot boiling over, then fragments of crockery, coffee, and smoke erupted skyward with a resounding crack. The seidr lamps on the walls buzzed like hornets.

Morven doubled over laughing.

Nikl picked up a shard gingerly. "Yeah…I don't think exploding coffee is a great selling point, Dragon."

"I'd pay." Morven wiped the tears from her eyes.

"Shut up." Nikl shoved a finger under Morven's nose.

"All right, all right!" Dwyn growled. "Cut the comments, and get me another cup."

"Just one?" Nikl snorted. "Good thing I brought a case. You know, Dragon, I want this done *before* Dh'Morda is over."

"I'll make my adjustments, Thunderer."

"Next time, I won't pay you in advance, that's what I'm saying."

"Get me a damned cup!"

"I'm going. Quit blowing sparks." Nikl's lopsided braids swung from side to side as he rolled out the door, muttering. He was dressed for work, but the flour on the back of his black pants suggested he'd already been. White handprints stretched tightly across his prominent ass.

Morven's lips smacked together as she kissed the air. "Like it?"

Dwyn snorted. "I wouldn't dream of trespassing on your turf." He scooped fragments of shattered crockery into an empty coffee can.

Morven rolled her eyes. "I can do better. Can you?"

"Did I ask your opinion, infant?"

"No, you were too busy drooling. What will you do with the ashes? Better not throw them in the trash." She leaned against the makeshift barricade, grinning.

"What ash there is will be septic safe when I'm done with it. I'll say this, though—you've got more sense than most dwarves twice your age asking a question like that. Dealt with the land-fill mafia, have you? What exactly does Tully let you do in that quarry?"

Morven tossed her braids. "Now you're hitting on me. The assholes at Whiterock won't let us recycle millings unless they sample the pile. Like Tully doesn't know his business."

"They're testing for elemental magic?" What a colossal waste of time in this part of the world. The rocks would be naturally full of it.

Morven shrugged. "I suppose. Half the time they won't let us sell to other dwarves."

"What does Tully do then?"

"The highway department is less picky." Morven leaned forward on her elbows. "Whiterock necromancers persecute us because Tully's like you—an elemental."

"It's more complicated than that." Dwyn stirred the ashes collecting in the bottom of the can with his finger.

"And we lowly magicless have to believe it because you say so."

Dwyn chuckled. Too much like him, that girl. He liked her for it.

"Six cups," Nikl said, coming in and banging a case on the counter. "Try not to break them all in one go."

Dwyn took one. "All I want is to test the magic under stress one more time. I don't want these things breaking, ever, even if someone throws one off a cliff. I'm almost done; I'll write the spell up for you this afternoon, and you can apply it whenever you like."

"Me?"

"Yes, you! Do I look like I'm getting out of this shit-hole any time soon? I'll be explicit in the directions."

"Shit-hole?" Morven glared at him.

Dwyn clamped his lips shut.

"You know what? Just fuck you. Nobody asked you to come here, Dragon." Morven stomped out and slammed the door behind her.

Nikl whistled. "Smooth, buddy, real smooth. I leave you alone to start something and you blow it all to hell before I can wish you joy."

"Me?" He gasped. "I thought you—I mean—at the dinner, you—"

Nikl winked. "I can do better. Can you?"

"Oh! Oh, rub it in." Dwyn stalked to the table with his coffee can and began to crumble loose mudstone over the ashes. "He nehelo, he mikhaven—you know, it's not nice to jab a man who can't get laid this time of year. He kiranen, he shelo…"

Nikl grinned and pulled a hand-rolled cigarette out of a leather tobacco wallet. "Morven's more your type than mine—sarcastic, smart, and as bitchy as her red-headed brother after a three-day bender." He offered the cigarette to Dwyn.

"I don't smoke. He siken, he ardo."

"A dragon who doesn't smoke. That's a first."

Dwyn wrinkled his nose at the strike of the lighter.

"Is Lokey your type?" Nikl asked with a puff of smoke.

"He dwynen." Dwyn didn't look up. "You don't know a thing about my type."

Nikl chuckled. "You ever grown tobacco? No, of course you haven't. Not with those smooth hands. It's a tompte's work—hard work. You wouldn't know a thing about that. But if a friend came along and wanted to share his smoke with you, be rude not to try a taste, wouldn't it?"

Abruptly Dwyn took the cigarette. It incinerated the instant it touched his lips. "I know your type. I'm not it."

Nikl laughed. "Not exactly subtle, are you?"

"You're the one playing in the metaphors, not me." Dwyn mixed blood with the powdered mudstone. Lokey. He'd think about Lokey. He'd be happy to bed that man, not looking for anything more than a good, solid fuck. But Nikl—Nikl with Ehrlik's tender smile—he couldn't go there.

Nikl's soft, smoky whisper drifted across Dwyn's cheek. "Have you ever seen someone—maybe across a crowded court-room—and said to yourself, if he said yes, I'd fuck him for a smile? I'm not afraid of you, Dragon."

Dwyn whipped around. He stared into the chef's lead-colored eyes. "Don't call me Dragon."

Nikl wrapped his hands around the back of Dwyn's head and kissed him—honey-sweet, salty, bitter with tobacco. Dwyn melted. Nikl's tongue slipped in, and Dwyn sucked hungrily. He groped between Nikl's legs, nearly frantic with desire.

Flat. Passive. Not going anywhere.

Dwyn broke away, breathing heavily, blood pounding ferociously in his ears. "Don't you...don't you dare play games with me—"

Nikl held out his hands in a placating way. "I'm not. Dwyn, calm down."

Dwyn backed into the table, shameful flames pouring from his crotch. He swept his hand across his erection, furious with himself. "Why'd you do that to me if you don't mean it?"

"I do, I do! I want you, buddy. It's just I...I'm mating this year."

The flames went out. He gaped. "Mating?"

Nikl grinned nervously. "Maybe I shouldn't—that's what you think?"

"No, no. You're damned lucky." Dwyn couldn't process it. He'd be thirty-six in a few more weeks, and he'd never come close to winning a mate. He glanced warily at Nikl. "You're shitting me."

Nikl ran a hand through his white hair. "Took me most of summer and all of fall to court her. She just now said yes. Her name is Rene. She's the potter. I don't want to screw this up." A delicate sunset suffused his cheeks. Dwyn wanted to kiss him again, but he didn't.

Nikl was right. Getting magic aligned for a successful mating took time, and raging Dragon protection thrust suddenly in that arrangement might mean disaster. Quite likely, Nikl had a position in the mountain riding on his success. A man who can get children is worth his keep. Dwyn would no sooner compromise a fellow elemental's chances any more than he'd shit on a book.

He hesitated. "Nikl, if you didn't mean it, it's all right—I understand." He wanted to make light of it, but a moment ago, he'd been ready to drop his pants and do it dry with Nikl right there. By the time Dh'Morda was over, Nikl would be a mountain man, if everything worked out. He wouldn't want a lovesick Dragon.

"Call me Nik." The chef cupped Dwyn's cheek in one hand—a breadmaker's hand—strong, rough to the touch. His other hand drifted down lower to where Dwyn waited, hard for him. Dwyn moaned softly, and settled against Nikl's chest like he belonged there.

"I mean it," Nikl said quietly, lips brushing Dwyn's open mouth. "I'm coming back for you when Dh'Morda is over, and I'm going to fuck you so wonderful it'll be worth the wait. Promise me, you'll be mine." He spoke with surprising passion. "Not his. Mine."

Dwyn kissed Nikl, long and deep. Chocolate and chili powder? Not worth a damn.

Dwyn spent most of the afternoon working with unquenchable energy. He wrote the spell for Nikl's two hundred cups on the fresh, cream-colored necromancer's paper Nikl had brought, burned the pages to ash, and canned them for Nikl to apply with a simple dishwasher load of soap. He had daylight left when he finished, and Jullup loaned him two steel buckets in which to fire his rivnstones. Both survived. They lay soaking in a mix of water and blood to prepare them for magic.

That evening, Dwyn carried the coffee can to his bathroom to dispose of the contents. All day long the ruined magic had mellowed in the cocktail of mud and blood until nothing remained but clay and fragmented memory. He turned on the tap, closed the drain, and let the water gurgle into the basin.

Nikl had kissed him.

The water boiled in the sink as he added the sludge. It hissed and floated briefly on the surface like an oil slick before breaking apart. Mist spiraled up and vanished into the ceiling. The protective spell he'd chanted earlier rang in his memory. *It is forgotten, it is made safe, it is disrupted, it is broken, it is diluted, it is burned...*

"He dwynen," he said. *It's as confused as I am. I want him, and I'm afraid of how much I want him. Damn Dh'Morda. I'm not thinking clearly.*

He jacked off in the shower, and stood, swaying in ecstatic relief while his fire-ruined semen flowed down the drain. Long-standing relationships often broke apart at Dh'Morda. Nikl was angry with Lokey now, but they'd both find their sanity around the first of January, the same as every other dwarf. Promises were worthless.

He knew. He had promised Riordiin.

Riordiin's embrace was all fire now. Dwyn lay in his arms, watching their joined flame dance on the ceiling in Riordiin's posh bedchamber at Rivenkyf. The clean scent of rosemary mingled horribly with cider as Dwyn rolled over, heat waves clouding his vision.

"I mean it. I wrapped up my affairs at work before I came. It's only a month and they won't need me anyway. I'm staying the whole Dh'Morda."

"No you won't." Riordiin sat up, wrapping his arms around himself. "You'll change your mind in a week and then you'll be gone."

Dwyn raised himself up on one elbow. "Love is all I want. What use have I for a mate?"

Riordiin smiled wanly. "You don't understand the urge yet. You're not of age. The closer you get, the more you'll feel as I do. Anyway," he said, sighing and lying down in a puff of cinders, "If you don't change your mind, your red-headed friend Sorcha will change it for you. Ehrlik tells me you court her as much as you court any man."

Dwyn laughed. "Sorcha? She'd sooner mate with a cockroach. And you need me."

"What I need doesn't matter." The acid in Riordiin's voice made Dwyn shiver. "Dh'Morda is always the same—every dwarf for himself, and misrule is the king of all. The real reason there is no legislative session in winter is to allow every disappointed woman, every dejected man, and every jilted lover time to reconsider putting a bullet in his own head or someone else's heart."

"I won't leave you." Dwyn kissed the sad, warm lips gently. "I promise."

Riordiin smiled. "You will. You're no different than the rest."

Dwyn dropped the soap. It sailed around the slippery floor and bubbled next to the drain. Memories. Always too bright. Always too intense. He'd give a great deal to forget ones that made him ache like this.

Nikl had kissed him. He would dwell on that.

The house was dark when he went upstairs. He'd bid Jullup and Nolan goodbye and good Dh'Morda when they left for Magazine around five. Lokey and Morven left for Rich Mountain shortly afterwards. It was quiet—too quiet. Where was Kritha? He stopped, hand on the refrigerator, and listened. A scratching sound came from Jullup's quarters.

Dwyn could never approach the sliding glass door without the floor rippling under his feet, courtesy of the tabah Nyssa had put on every door leading out of Ironsfork. Kritha was on the other side of it. When she saw him, she went mad, throwing herself at the door, barking. Dwyn jumped back involuntarily as she slammed into the glass.

Kritha clawed at the crack where the door would open, whining plaintively. He grinned then, showing all his teeth. Nikl's kiss and a night without the dog—damn, this was turning out to be the best birthday he'd ever had.

He was headed back to the kitchen to eat a meal in peace for once, when he heard a door open.

CHAPTER TWELVE

IN THE LIBRARY

Years spent hiding in abandoned mountains where any noise might signal peril had taught Dwyn the value of caution. When he heard a door open and saw a quick flash of light appear and disappear in the vicinity of the sitting room, he slipped down the dark hallway without a sound. He glanced into the den, expecting to find Tully sprawled on the couch, dirty boots propped on Jullup's favorite pillow, watching a basketball game with the volume muted, but the room was empty.

He tried the door leading to Lokey's music room. The tabah stung him when he touched the knob. He shook the pins and needles out of his hand, cursing, and returned to the entryway. His own door stood rigidly open. No shadows moved at the foot of the stairs, but he descended slowly, hair standing up from the top of his head clear down his spine. He found no one. With everyone gone for Dh'Morda, he hadn't bothered to dress after his shower. Hurriedly, he pulled on his pants and buckled his belt. Only one possibility remained. Someone was in the long passage joining the dining room and Nyssa's quarters by way of the library. His books were in that library.

His jaw tightened. Nyssa might be back from Whiterock, or she might not. Either way, he wasn't facing danger without his weapon. He grabbed his sword and padded upstairs, every muscle tight with trained wariness.

The sliding oak door to Nyssa's library stood ajar. The room was cavernously black, but a thin stream of moonlight bled through the gaps at the tops of the curtains.

"Enseitha." Dwyn muttered the silencer under his breath. Thin as a wire he might be, but even he couldn't slide through the opening without making some noise. He oozed into it, set his back on the stone, let the air out through his nose, and wriggled through the gap sideways.

Quickly, he ducked into the shelter of the nearest bookcase. Dwarves see well in the dark, and he recognized the shape clinging spider-like to the top of a rolling ladder. He heard the rasp of a book withdrawn, and the crackle of turning pages. He grimaced. Fear of God, then.

"N'maha!" His roar bounced off the walls. The chandelier overhead burst into golden flame.

"Fuck!" Morven slid down the ladder, feet flailing. She came to a sudden stop with a shriek—her chin struck a rung—she let go and fell the rest of the way. An avalanche of books cascaded over her.

"What the hell are you doing?" He gripped his sword, scalp prickling at the scent of old blood, pungent with magic. His gaze fell on the book in Morven's hand as she stumbled up, rubbing her rear end.

"You scared the hell out of me."

"I heard a door open."

Morven straightened. "I promised Nyssa I'd check on the library. Make sure you didn't sneak in while she was away."

"Don't lie to me, infant. I worked for necromancers. Now tell me the truth!" He blew up, bright and fiery.

Morven cringed. "Go to hell."

He stepped forward, flames billowing, smoke swirling.

She raised the book to throw it. He snapped his fingers. It sailed through the air and he grabbed it. "What were you doing in here?"

"I...I was borrowing—"

"You'll have to lie better for Nyssa when you explain this." Blood dripped from the book's pages.

Morven went gray with terror. "Oh, shit. Shit."

A dark haze of smoke billowed toward her. She screamed as the cloud of magic reached her ankles and coiled around them.

Maroon blood overflowed Dwyn's fingers in a sickening cascade. He shuddered as he traced runes on the cover. "He nehelo, he mikaven—"

"Stop it! You're hurting me!" The curse wound up Morven's legs, swallowed her knees, and gripped her hips. She brushed at it frantically. Her tawny eyes filled with tears.

"He kiranen, he shelo, he siken—" He chanted as steadily as if he stood in the great library of Rivnkyf, with all that ancient corruption belting him like debris in a tornado.

"Stop!" Morven jerked convulsively.

"He ardo!" he yelled. His spell circled Morven's head in a loop of fire and alighted vulture-like on her scalp. It dug long talons into her blood-covered hands.

"What are you doing?" she wailed.

A brilliant sunset glow savaged the smoke, ripping through it like a volcanic explosion. Morven screamed. Dwyn stumbled forward, overcome with nausea while his furious counter curse descended from Morven's shoulders in a cloud to deal with the paralyzer next in a fiery conflagration.

"What were you thinking?" he shouted. "Tearing a page in a necromancer's text! Who put you up to it? God under the earth! Didn't your school Seidoche ever teach you anything? Do you know what might have happened to you?" Criminally careless of Nyssa, putting a book like that where a kid could find it.

Sooty tears streamed down Morven's face as Dwyn's flames

subsided. She sank to the floor, moaning. "It hurts. It hurts."

He picked her up. "Let's get you out of here. No! Don't touch it. Leave the book to me. I'll take care of that shit."

She buried her face in his smoky hair, sobbing.

"Te mikhava, Morven," he said. "You're safe."

Dwyn made Morven shower in his quarters. He set his fire dancing on the water to destroy any residue from the decayed magic before it entered the sewer where anything might happen to it. He burned Morven's contaminated clothes in one of the metal buckets. Between the necromantic magic and his counter curse, they looked like they'd been eaten by acid. When Morven emerged from the shower, dripping and shaking, he wrapped his bedspread around her and steered her through the smoke to his bed.

"Let me see." He knelt on the floor, hissing sympathy. Her ankles had been blistered raw, and her black hair prickled over a thousand welts almost to her knees. "This could be a lot worse, but I'll grant it hurts like a sonofabitch. Run this over them." He unbuckled his belt with the obsidian set between the copper rings. "That's not your mother's crystal. I found it in an Appalachian chieftain's tomb, and he knew what he was about when he commissioned it. Not a hole in that man's bones anywhere."

She stared at him, but she took the belt and stroked her legs with it. "What if it doesn't help?"

"You imagine I survived all these years without learning a few things?" He opened his spectacle case and set the square-rimmed glasses on his nose. He thumbed through the book, testing the integrity of each page with a small obsidian disk set in plain steel, a seidskrid, the lazy Seidoche's favorite tool for finding errors in magic. Dwyn seldom used his unless he was in a hurry. He *was* hurrying.

"What would it have done to me?" Morven asked.

"You had a taste of it. Burned your skin off, didn't it?" What she imagined would be only marginally less terrifying than the truth. Dwyn found the first page of decaying magic and marked it with a protective splash of his own blood. Angry smoke billowed from the page.

Morven flinched.

"It can't hurt you now," Dwyn said. He, on the other hand, was oozing like an open wound. Written necromancy was potent stuff, beyond toxic when damaged.

"Nyssa will kill me," Morven moaned.

"This is her fault, not yours. She should learn to lock a door." But he looked Morven in the eye when he spoke, daring her to lie to him again. The tabah on his door was still active, which could only mean one thing.

She sighed and swept his belt carefully across her blistered heels. "Tully made Lokey take the key tonight. Lokey had plans. I told him if he'd give the key to me, I'd give it back to Tully so he'd be forced to stay and let Kritha out. Only, Tully isn't here. So long as Kritha doesn't crap her kennel, Mom won't know."

"Where is Tully?"

"I don't know."

He stared at her.

Morven's face darkened. "I can't tell you, all right? Mom likes you, and you like her. If she asks, you'll tell her the truth."

The human. Dwyn fought down his disgust.

Morven grimaced. Scabs crusted over the burns as the obsidian did for her what it did for him—healed. "This absolutely sucks eggs."

"Why did you do it? It was stupid—"

"Just shut up, okay! I know I'm stupid. Lokey tells me all the fucking time. I don't need to hear it from you."

"I didn't say *you* were stupid. I said what you *did* was stupid." He was relieved to hear the anger. She must be feeling better. When he'd helped her into the shower, she clung to him, sobbing like a baby. The shock had immobilized her almost as much as the paralyzer in the library. She didn't even protest when he pressed his bloody arms against the weeping lesions on her legs and ankles and whispered his Dragon's blessing, hoping it wouldn't prove too much for a knockr—he'd never had cause to protect a dwarf with no magic, someone so fragile.

"Why don't you tell me who put you up to it? Soothe your conscience, that would." He sealed another page.

"No."

"But there is someone."

"If I say yes, will you stop badgering me?"

"It's my business to ask."

"No, it's not!" She tossed his belt across the bed. "You may be a Seidoche, but you're not in charge of anything. I don't have to talk to you. Why am I talking to you?" She balled up in his covers, growling.

"Did this person tell you stealing magic is dangerous? That you could be seriously hurt?"

Muffled grunts issued from under the blanket, and he sighed. She was right. He wasn't in charge of anything, not anymore, although he felt compelled to recite the law to the letter concerning magicless dwarves and the prohibition against reading necromantic texts.

He cleared his throat. "Morven, will you tell me something? I promise, I won't ask about what you anarchists get up to. You're nineteen you said, this Dh'Morda. Why aren't you at college? You should never have been taught to read Seid, but you can. You could apply to Nations as a Seidwendr. Nyssa would write you a recommendation, I'm sure. I'll admit, having magic crammed in your bones won't be any fun, but with the right necromancer you could go far—"

Morven hurled the pillow at the wall. "And let them fuck me over like the rest of the world? No thanks."

Dwyn huffed. "Listen to me. It pays well. You could be rich, respected, and you would have what you want—magic—and a chance to use that magic on behalf of a necromancer you can trust, one who…" He almost choked on his words. God under

172 R. LEE FRYAR

the Earth, how he had betrayed that trust. "One who would take care of you, Morven, protect you always with his bones, and ensure you never came to any harm in his service. Someone you might even grow to love."

She snorted in derision. "Like I'd believe that shit. Even if I did, I couldn't do it now."

"Why not?"

"I got suspended."

"Why?"

"Because the system's fucked up—"

"Don't spout that anarchist shit at me!" He interrupted, less angry at her than at himself. She might not believe it, but he did. He'd tried with all his heart to uphold that beloved bond between necromancer and Seidwendr for Riordiin's sake, breaking every rule along the way too. "Why?" he demanded.

"We broke into the library. There were four of us, all magicless dwarves. We chained ourselves to the tables because they wouldn't let us study necromancy—"

"Morven!" He pounded his forehead in frustration.

"You're just like them! Exactly like them. Everyone knows there's a conspiracy between Seidoche and the necromancers. Jenr Rok Dahl says—"

"Fuck Rok Dahl! Have you learned nothing tonight? There are damned good reasons for those restrictions." He tapped his seidskrid on another lacerated page. "You have no protection in your body against this decay. Now, if you were a Seidwendr, your necromancer would protect you. He would bleed away your danger as he bled his, in payment for the strength your bones gave to him. He would save you—"

"And what about the rest of us?" she screamed. "We have no protection. No one cares. Ordinary warloche won't let us work any job smelling of magic—never mind we might be better at it, because we know how to work around the problems. They treat us like shit. They call us all knockr like we don't know it means slave. They keep us from learning Seid. They cage us in like wild animals, they call us worthless for they do not understand our worth, and when we cry out for justice, we are silenced. We're less than dwarves!"

Dwyn sat silent, stunned. He'd heard those words before. They were his.

He'd spoken them in front of a full necromancers' council long ago, on behalf of a friend, condemned, like so many other elementals, to a fate he didn't deserve. But Dwyn had been talking about elemental dwarves, not the magicless third of society that worked, loved, and died without the power to change their futures.

Morven was still speaking, but Dwyn's memories found a skinny young Dragon, all heat and long hair, blazing with self-righteous fury while every necromancer in the chamber looked down on him like he was a steaming pile of shit, all but one— the beautiful necromancer with hair the color of night who sat apart from the others. There were golden rings on Riordiin's long fingers, and his eyes were a deep, understanding blue, and the fire burned in him the same as it burned in Dwyn's blood. He forced the image away, shaken, and more than a little disturbed.

"I was the best student at Rich Mountain in mathematics," Morven went on angrily. "I wrote magical proofs at ten that were better than what the secondary students turned in to Cheyloche Northslope, and he wasn't the only one saying it. But when I went to Whiterock, they wouldn't let me take basic Differential Equations because knockr are too stupid to learn Seid. A Seidoche told me that."

"I hope you told him to go to hell," he murmured.

"She. And no, I didn't. There wasn't anything to say. There never is anything to say."

"Who taught you to read Seid? Your Seidoche here?"

"Tully taught me. We didn't have a Seidoche. Still don't."

God under the earth. What sort of backwater was this? The most rural mountains in Tennessee had a Seidoche. "Who tends your library, then?"

"Cheyloche Northslope used to; I guess he still does. We can't get a Seidoche. Mom says it's the never-ending cycle of don'ts—we don't have a Seidoche because we don't have the books; we don't have the books because we don't have a Seidoche."

"I see." He gripped the seidskrid so tightly the steel glowed red. This was why Tully put up with him; why Nyssa fought to keep him rather than extradite him immediately back to Nations. They would mine him like that damned quarry and when they had used him up, they would toss him to the pit and no one would call it anything but justice. Fierce hatred bubbled up in his breast.

He would have wept at the chance to build that library if they'd paid him a pittance; lived out of his truck, isolated himself, done whatever they demanded for a respectable job that would have seen him clear back to Tennessee. Who knew? Maybe he would have even returned yearly, to make repairs and visit friends like Nikl and Jullup. And at the end of his life, he might have spent his dying years happy in a place where Wights owned mountains and Thunderers mated at Dh'Morda. Everything blurred in front of him: the book, the papers, the desk, the seidskrid shaking in his hand.

Ata ti hacharda.

"Let's talk about this book." His voice was so calm he surprised himself.

"Can you fix it?" The blanket slipped off as Morven sat up, exposing her tabby striped legs.

"I can."

Her face glowed. "You're a life-saver, Dwyn."

"I said I *could* fix it. I didn't say I would."

"But—"

He pushed back from his desk. "I need a few promises from you, and some information. Do you know when Nyssa will be back?"

Morven had tensed when he spoke of promises; she relaxed

now. "Not until Monday, if then. Tam usually gives her his undivided attention for Dh'Morda." She rolled her eyes.

Dwyn ran his hand over the book's cover, leaving fiery tracks across the dark leather. Two days. That was doable. The book wasn't a complete loss. Fooling the library would take a little more time, and he meant to have a good look for his books while he was in there, too. "First thing—I want the key."

Morven opened her mouth to protest.

He held up his hand to stop her. "Not tonight. But I will need to unlock the library when I put the book back."

"I should do that."

"No, you shouldn't—for a number of reasons, but the pertinent one is a whole library of books that must be convinced we were never there. Or would you rather Nyssa found out?"

"I've been in there a hundred times, Dwyn. She's never said a thing."

"You think she doesn't know?" Dwyn stared steadily at her.

"Why doesn't she say something?"

"It isn't to protect you from your mother, if that's what you think."

She frowned.

"If Nyssa tells anyone about your little fascination with illegal necromancy, her necromancers are the first to find out. When necromancers form a coalition, they take a g'hesh—no secrets between them. It would ruin your chance of ever reapplying to Whiterock after your suspension. One year, am I right? That's the usual penalty. Gives a dwarf time to get her head straight."

Morven's frown deepened.

"What about your parents?"

"They'll be back Sunday night. Lokey—I doubt anyone will see him until the end of December."

"What about Tully?"

She shrugged. "He gave the key to Lokey. If he asks me, I'll say Lokey was too drunk to drive home. It happens often enough."

"When you get the key from the door, keep it. I'll tell you when I want it. Lock the library as if nothing happened. I want things to settle down before I go in there again. God only knows what all you triggered in there tonight."

She grayed again. *Good.* He wanted her afraid.

"But I want something more from you, something for my trouble, something you will do for me, and not ask why. You will do this when I ask you to, and you will speak of it to no one."

She pulled the blanket over her thighs, flushing. "I can't—"

"Hear me out. It's not a big thing I'm asking. I only want you to take that dog for a long walk on a leash, and I don't want to see her for a solid eight hours."

She looked confused. "Why?"

"No questions. For my work and my silence, this is my price."

She chewed her lower lip. "And you won't tell Nyssa or Mom."

"On my blood and bones, I will not."

She shifted uncomfortably. Dwyn resisted the urge to say more, to remind her he had saved her bones with his, that without his intervention she'd be lying on the floor in Nyssa's library with a paralyzer holding her captive while death magic raped her bones raw, but suddenly Morven looked up at him.

"I'll do it. I—" She smiled in a shy, winsome way, so like Jullup. "I trust you."

He turned back to his desk and picked up his whetstone. He began to sharpen the sickle edge of his seam ripper with slow, even strokes.

Morven joined him at the desk, blanket hitched over her shoulder like a toga. He breathed in her scent appreciatively—all chocolate, that girl, and no chili peppers. He hooked the tooth of the ripper under the seam. His fingers dripped gore as he tore the cover away thread by thread.

"What are you doing?"

"Removing the ruined sections. I'll sew it back together when I'm done."

"And Nyssa won't know?"

"Are you insulting my competence, infant?" He'd spent too many years restoring texts in worse condition than this poor book to doubt it. That was why Riordiin hired him as personal Seidoche in the first place—that, and his speech perhaps—

"When should I take Kritha?"

"Not soon. It goes without saying you'll keep her out of the way when I return the book, but as for our bargain, I'll let you know when it's time."

The toga slipped down around Morven's waist, and she put her hand on his shoulder, kneading it softly with her fingertips.

He tensed.

"Dwyn, if you can fix things like this, why don't you do it? I mean, for money?"

He'd had enough of questions that hurt too much to answer. "Why are you still here? Go let the dog in before she has a stroke trying to beat down the door."

CHAPTER THIRTEEN

THE STONES

A foul smoke twisted above the cremains as Dwyn dropped the last of the ruined pages on the pile of ashes that had been Morven's clothes. He coughed, spitting up a foul smoke of his own. His spleen tightened, pushing more blood into his veins— he was purging heavily. He groaned and picked up his belt from the end of the bed and buckled it around his waist. The suffering had better be worth it, that was all.

If only Morven hadn't torn the book, he might have caught her, paralyzed her on the spot, and had a leisurely hunt for his own books before wiping her memory clean. One quick se dwynen and she'd be none the worse or wiser for the experience.

He pulled a few fresh pages of necromancer's stock from his case. He would write the illusions for his books tonight and take them with him tomorrow. His real books he would hide in this room, cleverly cast as part of the floor. Once he had them back, they'd never leave his sight again.

Morven was still calling Kritha. She'd been at it for several minutes. The dog had probably run clear around the mountain hunting for a way in. She'd be all icicles by now. Warmed his heart just thinking about it. The sliding glass door banged open, long claws scraped stone, Morven shouted, and then the juggernaut blasted down the stairwell into his room, hair, jaws, and roar.

He didn't even get a chance to curse. Kritha yanked him out of the chair, and he fell hard, cracking his head on the floor. Sharp fangs glistened over his head, seeking his neck. He punched, caught her jaw, his knuckles raked her teeth. Her hot breath stank in his face; her eyes were hateful yellow flames inches from his. She snarled, twisted. His right hand tangled in the chain she wore around her neck, but he pounded away left-handed at her nose, her eyes, her ears, everywhere he could reach.

"Kritha, stop!" Morven yelled.

Kritha's fangs crunched. Blood spurted, staining her fur red. His palm opened up like a split biscuit. He screamed and rolled over, hand knotted under his body.

"Fuck!" He coiled around his injury.

"Kritha? Oh, Kritha," Morven wailed.

Eyes shut, ears flat, Kritha cringed and cried, flinching as unseen blows rained over her head, shoulders, and flanks. Morven wept over Kritha's shaking body, stroked the white fur, crying, "Kritha! You stupid dog—why?" She hugged the evil thing as if to insinuate herself between Kritha and the magic beating her raw.

Damn it, she'd gotten into the blood-rich skin of his wrist. He was bleeding a puddle into the area faster than he could clot. He needed to cauterize it. Oh, God, it would be as bad as being bitten again. Shaking, he clamped his right hand over his left and branded himself on one of the most sensitive parts of his body.

He must have passed out then. He wasn't sure if Kritha got up, or if Morven carried her off, but it seemed as if little time had passed before Morven was bending over him.

"Dwyn? Are you okay?"

"No, I'm not okay! That damned dog tried to kill me!"

"She wouldn't have—never." Morven was doing something to his hand. "You didn't have to hurt her like that."

He yelped when sticky material touched him. "Don't! The elastic will melt."

Morven dropped the bandage. "We have to do something! I think you need stitches."

"Thus speaks a Seidroche's daughter." He sat up, groaning.

"Kritha's still crying. I put her in her kennel, but she won't let me touch her. She won't even look at me."

"Yeah, well, a necromancer's g'hesh always sucks," he said. He hissed, picking off the melted plastic.

"What? You didn't do that? Then who—" Morven looked sick.

He laughed harshly. "You thought different?"

"She's Nyssa's pet!"

"Necromancers don't have pets." He stood. "They have creatures they can use—that's it."

"Dwyn, I think—"

"I can take care of myself." He stumbled to the bathroom. He ran the tap to convince her he was cleaning his wounds in the usual way, but instead he shivered on the toilet and burned the rest of his raw flesh thoroughly, gasping every time he touched the blackened puncture near his wrist. His hand would be a damned balloon by morning. He'd have to work right-handed, and he'd never been as ambidextrous as a Seidoche should be. Ehrlick always scolded him about that.

When he returned to the room, Morven was gone. He sat at his desk, trembling, and tried to write, but gave up around midnight. His fingers were swollen sausages, and the mistakes were making him sick. He went to bed bloody with purging and lay flat on his back, hand elevated above his head.

Kritha would have killed him. He'd been right thinking the dog had to go. It would be his throat next.

He shut his eyes. Teeth flashed in his mind, ripped through his beard, and blood sprayed across the face of his imagination. Then a draugr smashed him into a river of icy black water, where there was a mountain…

The Dragon had never been in a place like this.

The room was dark, black as the sacrificial pits where he'd slaughtered goblins who betrayed his mountain by siding with the necromancers. He lay face down in a circle circumscribed with lead, naked but for his flame, chained by his arms and his ankles to the floor. He struggled, trying to rise.

Chains rattled beside him. He turned his head, scraping his cheek against damp stone.

In a similar circle, he saw another dwarf—a Thunderer, yellow-gray in color, with grizzled hair. He humped up briefly like a raccoon, and flattened, hissing with pain.

"Who are you, Dh'Rigahn?" The Dragon asked.

The dwarf's voice was less than a whisper of the wind. "Dh'Rigahn? I don't know what that is anymore. Who am I? I am you or you are me. It doesn't matter."

The Dragon hadn't thought the necromancers took prisoners. Perhaps the Dh'Rigahn were not all dead. If he could find them, rally them to his banner...he yanked his chains in frustration. "What is this place?"

The Thunderer grinned. "Don't you know? It's your mountain, now. Don't you like it? Is it not beautiful to you?"

The Dragon scrambled forward as understanding dawned. The chains brought him to a stop, and he fell heavily on his chin.

"No!" His mountain was far away, in the green south, where wind, water, and stone loved him and spoke to him, where he gave his fire in perfect union with the land, and his Eseitha hengh cradled him as he made his bed with the mountain every Dh'Morda.

"I should spit on you, Dragon," the Thunderer said. "You promised to protect us all. I meant to hate you. But I am dying now. There's no hate left in me. I pity you."

The Dragon roared as the stone opened like a gaping mouth. The chains wound about his arms and dragged him into the earth's embrace. A terrific bang echoed in his ears as the mountain entombed him.

"Rigah, mi mikeve!" Covered in slime, a worm fresh from the earth, Dwyn flailed, tugging violently at the chains around his wrists. Voices broke through his waking like an echo of horror from his dream.

You promised to protect us all. You failed.

He tumbled out of bed, fell on his injured hand, and pain exploded into reality. He lay flat on the floor, grinding his teeth. Why had he called for his Rigah? He'd never known his mother. And what the hell was that noise?

He rolled over. His door was closed.

"Shit."

Nyssa was back. Morven had been wrong, and all was lost. But in the absolute quiet, Dwyn reclaimed himself. Someone was home, but he didn't know who, not yet, and he wouldn't until they came to see him. When they did, he'd better be ready. His wound gaped on a bloated landscape of cracked, purpling skin. He couldn't allow Nyssa to see it.

He bled afresh when he finished his illusions. He'd never been good at disguising his appearance, not even to hide his rune. His skin melted with the deception, and his flesh baked over the bones. He sat at his desk, but couldn't scribe. Everything hurt too much. He felt as helpless as that Dragon in the void cell.

The Dragon hadn't known that room but Dwyn did. He'd been there before.

It was Rivnkyf, Riordiin's ancestral home. The bloodsmeldt circles were unmistakable. The runic letters that shone so brightly in the dream were faded when he'd seen them nine years ago. He'd not resisted when the necromancers took him from his vigil at the foot of Riordiin's cross, but they hurled him into the void cell all the same. He hadn't blamed them. He'd killed the man he loved most in the world. He deserved it.

Did the Dragon deserve it?

The rune on his hand blazed volcanically hot. He gasped. Hopefully the pain would release him when he removed the illusion.

When Morven opened the door a few hours later, Dwyn was pacing the floor. She held her fingers to her lips in an unnecessary gesture—he had no intention of making a racket.

He swept past her onto the stairs, sword hanging loosely over his shoulder, carrying his belt in his right hand. "Who is it?" he whispered.

"It's Mom and Dad. What am I going to do?"

She'd do something stupid like confess if he didn't calm her down. "It will be fine. I want you to open the library door again. I'll jam the tabah. Then you can give the key back to your mother and tell her whatever you want. I don't want to hear it. As you said, I'd have to tell her the truth if she asked."

"How the hell do you jam a tabah? They're keyed!" Morven's bare feet slapped the stone as she ran through the hallway with him.

"Yes, and that's their weak spot." They were making too much noise. He hoped Jullup and her mate had closed the door on their Dh'Morda activities, but why should they? They'd locked him in. He was mildly surprised the spare key still worked with the master in operation—pure luck, he guessed, although what luck there was seemed to be turning sour in a hurry.

"Open it." He gestured at the sliding oak door.

Morven shook as she inserted the key and pulled. It didn't move. "What now?"

"Try it again, slowly. You opened my door with the key; this one will open too."

"What if it doesn't? Oh."

"Fine, that's enough." He thrust his belt in the track where the door would slide when it closed. About midway should do it. "Now, slide it back, but don't slam—fuck!"

"I didn't slam it!"

Dwyn pulled his smashed fingers out of the crack and squinted into the thin gap, panting. The copper repulsed the tabah, and the glittering obsidian reflected the magic perfectly. Suddenly the door crunched once, twice, with an angry shudder.

Behind him, twin bangs echoed as his door slammed shut, and presumably, so did the door to Jullup's room.

Morven jumped. "Shit!"

"Calm down. Sometimes they snap like that. Go get Kritha. She can go out with me."

Her voice was a squeak of panic. "What? Go out where?"

"Hurry!"

Dwyn was dancing with impatience by the front door when Morven reappeared, dragging the dog by her collar. Kritha looked almost as bad as Dwyn felt. Her head hung low and she limped sadly on all fours as she protested with unhappy whines.

"Asshole!" Morven spat at him. "You're going to just go off and leave me here?"

He huffed. "So you can say you let the dog out and thought I might want some fresh air. How else do you want to explain the doors?"

"What if Mom checks the library?"

"Keep her away from it."

"Morven?" Jullup's sleepy voice called down the hall. Morven shoved the dog through the door. Kritha bolted.

"Dwyn!"

He turned in the doorway. "I gave you my word. Now keep yours." He ran up the corridor.

Kritha was waiting for him in front of the great double doors, stiff as a statue. She lifted her lip.

His heart jumped into his mouth. "Get out of my way, bitch."

She growled.

"You can't, or you'd have killed me last night." He had to believe that. "If you hurt me again, what will she do to you?"

Kritha lunged, but not at him. She darted to one side; he bulled forward, pushed the door open, and passed through.

It was still dark, not yet six in the morning, and cold, but not as cold as the day he had danced in the Eseitha hengh. He stood on the top step, looking out over the muddy landscape. That's what he would do. He would go back and dance that J'hen. Morven needed time to make her explanations, and Jullup would want to know what he'd been doing while out.

"Kritha, are you coming?"

She growled. Her white mustache stuck out from behind the door.

"Stay then. I'm not waiting on you." He shrugged his sword into a more comfortable position and trotted down the stairs.

With a token snarl, Kritha galloped past, away from the doors and up the hill toward the road. He climbed after her, pulling himself up the slope right-handed, slipping and falling all the way.

Nearly all the snow had melted. Threadbare rags still clung to the shaded backslopes, but the road was clear. If he followed it and cut left before the old quarry, he might find the hengh before daybreak. But he thought of Tully, coming back from whatever unholy tryst he'd been keeping, and crossed the road instead. He disappeared into the pine woods on the other side.

Kritha trotted beside him, a silent white ghost floating in a gray fog. Dwyn breathed in the damp air, grateful for the cathedral peace. His hand didn't hurt as much now. He'd discarded the illusion as soon as he left the mountain. It still looked like raw meat, but at least it belonged to him again. Even Kritha seemed happier. Her tail waved gently as she lifted her nose and sniffed the spicy air. She went rigid, growled once, and tore off, leaving Dwyn behind as she raced for the ruin on top of the hill.

"Got over me quick enough, didn't you?" He hitched his pants up one-handed and followed her. Kritha barked, gleeful as a puppy. "What's got you so wound up?"

He found out soon enough. Kritha was digging industriously at the foot of the tallest henr stone, head down a tunnel, hind legs braced, throwing dirt in all directions as she burrowed. He snorted. She must have a rabbit. He'd have to listen to that yapping the whole time he danced.

He unsheathed his sword and rotated his right arm and his neck, limbering up. He took a few experimental jabs right-handed and grimaced. Practice was long overdue.

Kritha backed out of the hole, shook mud from her ears, and dove back in happily. He glared at her wiggling backside. "I'm warning you, dog, get underneath me, and I'll boot you down that hole."

He stepped into the hengh, staring down at a velvety carpet of plush moss, perplexed. He would have sworn he'd danced over sticks and stones.

Dawn cast the shadows out of the ring as he dropped into his fighting crouch, legs apart.

"Mhu kemher, ita!" His opponent materialized opposite him; an illusion of smoke and fire, twice his size and three times as wide. He charged. No bows, no fancy footwork for him—just a bloodcurdling roar before he clashed with his sparring partner. This was the way of J'hen—a battle against the self.

He forgot his pain. He forgot the g'hesh eating him up inside, his worry over what awaited him back at Ironsfork, the trouble that had landed him here, the dreams tormenting him. Breathing fire, he circled his kemher, left hand dangling uselessly at his side, holding Mh'Arda ready in his right. A plume of magic arced out of the shadow, narrowly missing him. He lashed out and scored a hit. Sparks showered the moss.

No longer was he Dwyn Dragon: and angry, impotent dwarf, afraid to live, terrified to die. He was Mn'Hesset, age-old Knight to the Paloh Ethean, powerful in darkness, dangerous in war.

His kemher drove him, chasing him, battering his defenses as he danced, slashing at hidden legs and arms. It fought like him, thought like him. He could admit a loss without a stain of regret, but he didn't want to, not now, not when he felt so glorious. A golden sweep sliced behind him as he ducked and opened a hole in the kemher. It showered him with bloody lava. He yelled his triumph. Then the world became a sulfurous fog of skunk.

Kritha reversed out of the hole, whining, and slammed into

Dwyn's legs. He pitched headfirst into his kemher, and the whole thing went off in a towering blast of smoke and embers.

He staggered out of the cloud. "You fucking bitch! God under the earth, I'll kill you when I can see you!" He flailed wildly and hit something with a wet smack. Through his burning tears he caught sight of a writhing animal, black and white and stinking. He slashed down again, and it quit moving. Kritha sailed by, dragging her face on the ground and howling.

Dwyn stared down at the dead skunk. The fur stirred in the morning breeze, carrying the pungent smell into his nostrils. He clumsily wiped his bloody sword on his shirt. "Fuck."

No one heard him unless he counted the dog rolling in the woods beyond the hengh, but he felt better, as if his too-human curse was the right apology for profaning this sacred place with death. Guilt filled him as the rich necromantic magic poured into his bones, flooded his arm, and surged into his wound. He trembled and held his hand up to the sunlight. The swelling vanished and the livid color dispersed, just like the wounds he received on behalf of his God in his dreams healed every morning, leaving only scars under his hair to remind him that he was Mn'Hesset.

He was *still* Mn'Hesset.

He knelt, tears streaming down his face. "Dh'ben. Paloh mhu, dh'ben. Arden mi, ti ardo, ti ardo." He kissed the red mud, sinking to his elbows in the damp earth that Kritha had churned up. Warm to the touch, it clung and sucked him down. His fingers touched something cold, round, hard, and unimaginably smooth. He pulled and it popped out of the earth with a squelch.

It was a quartzite stone, large, white, and egg-shaped. Thin gray veins spidered the surface, but the stone itself was sound. He put it to his ear and listened, but not a whisper of magic was left in it. An Eseitha stone.

He'd seen them before. Riordiin had a complete set—nine in all—but those were black, completely filled with a wild, dark magic that kept its secrets, no matter how many times Dwyn tried to peer inside. This one was empty, and the single most perfect thing he had ever seen. And his God had healed him here, at the moment of his deliverance.

His scalp prickled. It was a sign—favor for his repentance. He hugged the stone to his chest. The wind picked up, rippled through his hair, and all the pine trees whispered among themselves.

Dwyn started back for Ironsfork around noon. On his back, he carried precious cargo. He'd knotted the open end of his shirt, filled it to the neck with the smooth oval stones, and padded them with moss—his Eseitha stones—seven in all. He hadn't found the eighth or the ninth, but not for lack of trying. He'd torn up all the moss in his frantic hunt, but either the quarry had claimed them, or they had shattered when the ring had been destroyed.

Kritha whined miserably as she shuffled behind him.

"Suck it up. You didn't finish what you started so don't expect me to be sympathetic." Mired up to his armpits, he had almost as much moss in his beard as Kritha had in her fur. His fingernails bled, he reeked of skunk, the g'hesh roweled him, he'd been away too long, and there was much he had left to do and much more that might go wrong, but he slid laughing down the slope, inexplicably happy. Kritha headed immediately for the front door.

"Don't think so!" he said. "You stink worse than me, dog. Let's go around." He trotted across the driveway toward the bridge, and after a moment, Kritha followed him.

He followed a path paralleling the river, lined with a hedge of young sassafras trees, recently pruned. About a half-mile along, Dwyn found a gap and squeezed through. He thought it might lead up to the patio behind Jullup's quarters, but he was mistaken, and he cut across the forest until he reached a sandstone staircase. He started to climb, but voices drifted toward him. Dwyn glanced over his shoulder. Kritha was rolling in the leaves at the base of the hill.

"Did you ask her?" Nolan's voice carried down the hill.

"Of course not!" Jullup sounded irritated. "You don't ask a woman that question."

"She's my child, too."

Jullup sat on the stone wall above, long hair blowing in the wind. Her bare back was a red hourglass shining in the sunlight. "If you haven't noticed, Nolan, she's not a child anymore. She's nineteen."

"But if you don't ask, she won't tell you. She's too much like you, my beauty." Nolan was naked, too—leaning against one of the arbor posts. "Why don't you ask him then? You like him."

"Nolan—"

"What do you want me to do, Jullup? I confined him to his room except when you let him out like the dog, and he still found a way. He strains my tabah already; there's not a day he doesn't tamper with them. You had better enlist Nyssa and her g'hesh if you want him shackled."

"I don't want him shackled. I just…I didn't want Morven having sex with him."

"She may have come home to take care of Kritha this morning, like she says, and been with Midian all night."

Jullup shook her head stubbornly. "She was here. And Tully wasn't. I'm going to kill him."

"Nothing may have happened—"

"You didn't smell her. She's soaked in his applejack. And her legs were blistered to her knees. She says she stepped in the fire pit at Forankyf, but she wouldn't look me in the eye." She sighed. "He's dangerous, but she doesn't see that. All she sees is his necromancy. I don't want her thinking this way again. Wanting what she can't have."

"Let me talk to her," Nolan said.

Dwyn heard no more. Kritha bounded past him, barking. Jullup jumped up. "Kritha! No, no—no! Don't jump!"

"Skunk! Where the hell did she find a skunk—no, don't you touch me dog!"

"Sit, girl, for the love of earth and stone, sit!" Jullup scanned the woods.

Dwyn got up walking as if he'd bent over and had just straightened. "I don't suppose you have a hose up there? It got me, too."

"I'll get one from the shed," Nolan said.

"Oh, no, you don't," Jullup said. "You stay right here, and hold her until I find her leash. I'll get the hose." She vanished through the sliding glass door.

Dwyn hesitated. He could leave the stones hidden in a drift of leaves, and come back for them later. But he was never sure from day to day how much freedom he would have, and after what he'd overheard, he couldn't take chances. Best hold on to what he had, and never let go. He walked up the stairs, trying to look casual.

Nolan looked no less imposing naked than he did clothed, even bent over, holding Kritha by her collar.

"Not my fault," Dwyn said, setting his shirt down on the patio. Despite the moss packed around them, the stones clinked together like wine glasses.

"Where did she find it?"

"Near the old quarry. She was digging; next thing I know, we're skunked."

"What were you doing there?" Nolan's eyes gleamed faintly with Dragon fire.

Dwyn shrugged. "Danced a J'hen. Looked for stones."

"Jullup told me you couldn't use quarried stone."

"I'm not."

"What's in that, then?" Nolan nodded at Dwyn's makeshift sack.

Before Dwyn could answer, Jullup bustled out. She snapped a leash on Kritha. "You go take a shower, Nolan; you too Dwyn." She set a plastic bucket under the spigot and turned on the water. She dumped a brown bottle of peroxide in as the suds foamed over the top. "Don't touch anything Dwyn—Nolan, I need a towel, the ones in the laundry room—"

Dwyn took his stones and trotted in through the open door obediently. Nolan didn't follow him. Nevertheless, Dwyn washed the stones before he washed himself, and spent a half-hour disguising them as uniformly drab, gray quartzite before he got in the shower. While he was washing, Jullup walked in without knocking and handed him a bottle of black soap.

"What is this shit?"

"Charcoal and lavender. Morven is giving Kritha another bath. I'm going to the store for tomato juice."

The door banged as she left.

Dwyn applied the soap liberally to his legs. He wouldn't be able to talk to Morven without creating more conjecture, but he was pleased. She'd misdirected as well as any necromancer. He'd be sure to commend her for it.

CHAPTER FOURTEEN

THE GHOSTS OF WARLOCHES' PAST

Tomato juice didn't produce any improvement in Dwyn's odor. He assumed from the absence of Kritha at the dinner table, it hadn't done much for her either.

Nolan was gone. When Dwyn asked, Jullup was gruff. Babies didn't deliver themselves, and Nolan had gotten a call telling him one of his patients had to be induced on Saturday, instead of Monday, as planned.

"A little late for a dwarf, isn't it?" Dwyn asked.

"Morven was this late." Jullup stared down the table at her daughter.

Morven raised her physics book like a shield and scratched savagely at a sheet of graph paper, ignoring her lunch.

Dwyn ate his grilled cheese and drank the beef soup with a good appetite, but his stomach twisted every time Jullup or Morven glared at him. An old Dh'Morda myth told of a time when dwarves lived apart, and children were born male or female from the bones of the dead in the stony womb of Mother Mountain. The sexes never mingled except to wage war and the men always lost. Dwyn didn't blame them for retreating.

He was glad to vanish into his room when dinner ended and shut the door on Jullup's muttered questions, and Morven's snarling replies.

He removed the illusions from Nyssa's unfinished book, popped the cartridge out of his pen, and filled it with new ink. He couldn't believe Jullup thought he'd seduce her child, but— he squirmed uncomfortably—the de facto chieftain of Xanadu, Jodan the Earthshaker, used to brag every Dh'Morda about bedding his mate of the tender age of nineteen when he was a forty-year-old oil-worker in Alaska. He'd been in desperate need of a mountain to provide for him before his elemental nature ruined him entirely. Mating bought him that security. At twenty, Dwyn had been appalled. At thirty-six, he understood.

The door creaked. He caught a whiff of bittersweet chocolate. "Better you're not here, sweetheart," he said.

"Shut it. I'm still pissed." Morven slouched in.

"Where is she?"

"Giving Kritha another bath."

"I'll be done tonight." He tapped the pages on his desk.

"I don't have the key anymore, Dwyn, and they'll lock you in."

"Uh-oh. I wonder what I'll do about that?"

"You know you're a fucking asshole?"

"You're not the first person to notice," he said, glancing up. "Tabah may be cast on multiple doors, but the magic has a singular source. Wreck one, you wreck them all. This concludes your magic lesson for the day, dirchita mhu."

She rolled her eyes. "Where did you go?"

"To pray. Ah! Don't touch!" Morven had picked up one of his Eseitha stones. "Break one, you'll find me three just like it."

"I didn't like lying to Mom. She told me she'll pretty much kill me if I don't go with them to Magazine on Sunday." Her dark face darkened further.

He turned his chair around. "Why Magazine? Jullup said something about staying here at Dh'Morda, for Nikl's fabulous cooking."

194 R. LEE FRYAR

"It's the tallest mountain around here. Lots of dwarves mate there because it's deep. It's good to be deep, Dad says." She blushed.

"You should leave before Jullup comes to save you from my evil clutches."

Morven tossed the stone at him.

He caught it. "I'm proud of you, infant. You lied like a necromancer."

"You say that to all the girls?"

"Only the ones I truly admire. Now get."

He listened to her footsteps on the narrow stairway until the door closed. The tabah clicked ineffectually. He mentally thumbed through the pages left to scribe. He'd worked on tighter deadlines, but the consequences of missing this one would be dire.

He picked up the stone on his desk. In all his years of skulking in and under the mountains, he'd never found one that was anything but shards. It was going to break his heart to use these for the mean purpose of rivn stones. Would it have cracked if Morven had dropped it? He felt the answer was no, but he also felt he would have thrown himself to the ground to keep it from ever striking the floor. It looked as fragile as his hope, but weighed as much as his need. So much could still go wrong.

He'd have to hope Jullup and her mate would be too preoccupied with their own lust to notice their door might not close perfectly. If the tabah tried to reform again, cracking the doors open and shut as it had this morning, the house would come down around his ears. Nolan's tabah. Tabah were a necromancer's bread and butter; where had the good doctor learned them? There was more to that Seidroche than he'd thought.

Dwyn slipped out of his room around midnight. The more he considered opening the door and just walking out, the less he liked the idea. He picked the lock apart, spell by spell. The original tabah was there, still jammed, but Nolan had added something new and unsettling: an alarm, a clever combination of necromancy and fire magic. It was a fiddly thing to undo. By the time Dwyn crept up the stairs, he was sweating embers.

A whispered word extinguished the seidr lamp in the hall before it gave him away. He stepped forward in complete darkness and almost tripped on the cat. She hissed and ran into the sitting room, growling. Frantically he whispered a silencer, glancing toward the kitchen expecting Kritha to bark. No sound. He eased into the passage leading to Nyssa's quarters.

He stopped again at the library door, testing the magic for any changes but found only the tabah, still confused, bless that copper. He opened it, sliding it quietly along the track, and closed it just as gently. He left his belt behind, wedged tightly in the framing.

Nyssa's desk gleamed in the sudden flash of light from the chandelier. He quelled it with a word too, but he wanted no more magic than was needed to do this job. Morven might have waltzed in without a care, but Dwyn was not so cavalier. Damaging a book was an offense most libraries were not prepared to forgive. Retaliation could be venomous. He drew his sword.

Thock! A sound ripped the velvet silence.

He froze. One minute. Two. Nothing. His shoulders dropped.

Thock! Every muscle in his body jerked in a convulsive gathering of magic. He was set to run, but no rush of power followed, and no swirling paralyzer threw him to the floor.

Thock! This time he was looking for the source. He found it at the same time the sound clattered in his ears.

A clock sat on the mantelpiece above a triangular fireplace. In the darkness the dim shadow of a sphere whirled through the air in slowly shrinking orbits until: Thock! It struck a silver post and began to unwind again. Somewhere near the ceiling a flying pendulum sent the planet in motion. Three minutes later the sphere clattered against the opposite post.

A puff of smoke drifted from his nostrils as he exhaled. Only a necromancer would want something so impractical to mark the time in threes. The magical maintenance on the thing must be ridiculous.

He toured the room, sword up to ward off attack, but none came. No illusions. No hexn. No curses of any kind. A long time had passed since Dwyn had been in a place so singularly undefended. It made him nervous. By the time he finished his sweep of the room, he felt ready to bolt.

Do what has to be done. Find your books and get the fuck out. He let out a long smoky breath and pulled the repaired book out from beneath his shirt.

He scaled the shelves with the help of the ladder, and put Nyssa's book back. Then he picked up the ones Morven had knocked down, calling each one into his hand with a soft word of command. He patted them all into place. Like pieces in a jigsaw puzzle, he knew they were right by the way the books touched, and the magic oriented as connections were made.

He jumped down and pushed the ladder away from the spot, sliding it along the overhead track. His gaze slid wistfully over the fat rows of books, the polished shelves, the plush carpet, the opulent desk, the chandelier, that ludicrous clock.

He'd wanted this, a room just like this, at Rivnkyf with his own attached quarters and a private void room. He told himself he would have it one day, even while he starved in Xanadu, wondering if he'd ever be able to build the library with which to sell himself one day. He thought he would get it, even as he withered under Riordiin's ever-worsening dementia, wondering whether the necromancer would honor his promises or if the madness was more than bone-deep when their bargain was struck. And even when it was clear that it was, he continued to believe that if he worked hard enough, and delved dwarf society ruthlessly, one necromancer at a time, he'd be rewarded.

God under the earth. What a fool he'd been.

He shoved the ladder harder than he meant to. It skated left, squeaking on the track, and stopped at the end with a jangling thump. He glanced back at the door, but there was no need for fear. His silencer absorbed the noise.

He was wasting time.

He started with Nyssa's desk, pulling out the drawers carefully, but found only hanging file folders, arranged alphabetically, the usual array of writing implements, lists of phone numbers, and a notebook of passwords to judge by the encryption. No books. That left the shelves. He'd have to go through them, one book at a time.

"Fuck." Up high, down low, wherever he looked, he saw no titles on the spines, no identification whatsoever, and Nyssa, curse her, liked doe-brown leather as much as he did. All those hours he spent creating illusions for Riordiin's library at Rivnkyf, and this was the way to hide things—in plain sight.

By the time he'd searched the lower shelves, the darkness outside had lightened with the moon well west. He grabbed the ladder and began on the upper shelves. He wished he'd not been quite so aggressive with his protections. Hardly a recrudescence went by without his frantic reassessment and more layers of illusion to cover his precious books. The damned things were chameleons now. They'd never come to his hand if he called. Autonomy was the first magic he gave them, so they could never be stolen. He grabbed hold of a book, pulled open the jacket, and was stung.

He almost dropped it before he got a shield between himself and the magic in that ancient volume, but when they clashed, instant recognition overwhelmed him and the pain vanished. He knew this work by heart.

"*Seida?* Nyssa has the *Seida?* How? How did she get it?" He slid to the floor and opened it, heart pounding. "It is! It's original."

There were few copies of the *Seida Ethean* in existence, and at least one was behind fireproof glass in the Haneen Etheanoche. Dwyn put it there himself after he'd restored it, the priceless work of the Northern Dragon. The only other copy he knew of belonged to Riordiin, but that particular set was incomplete, with books missing.

Nyssa must have stolen them. Dwyn's jaw tightened.

"What are you doing in here?" Nyssa's voice rang out like a drum in his ears.

He spun around. Stupid, stupid silencer.

Nyssa's smile was still fading from her face. The dwarf with her looked like he'd just stopped laughing at a joke.

Even in his terror, Dwyn thought she seemed surprised. She had not known, had not returned to investigate an intrusion in her library; she didn't know why he was there. He could use that.

He blew up, fire-bright. "What have you done with my books?" He shook the volume of the *Seida* for emphasis.

"What did you do? Steal the key from Jullup?"

Her calm unnerved him. He hoped to make her angry. Now might be the perfect time to set the carpet on fire. That would account for the smoke stains still visible from the night before. He took a threatening step forward, dripping flame. "Where are they?"

The barrel of a Glock settled right under his nose. Dwyn stared, petrified. His right shoulder seemed to break all over again.

Nyssa's companion was not a tall dwarf, but he seemed bigger because of his enormous goldenness. From the wheat-colored mane that flowed smoothly into his beard, to the heavy bracelets on his wrists, to the handle of the Glock, he was covered in gold. Even his voice was molten. "It's loaded."

Nyssa yanked the book from Dwyn's hand. "*My* books are in the library of my choosing, and so, not your business at all."

The carpet ignited. "Wait, what—they're not here?" He'd never considered she might move his books without his permission. "You had no right, no, they're mine—you can't—"

Nyssa tapped the floor with the point of her shoe, and the fire went out. "Tam, go wake Tully. I need him."

"I don't want to leave you." Tam didn't lower the gun.

Fire writhed in anguished spirals around Dwyn's body. "By law, necromantic property claimed by one necromancer from another must be kept where the former can access it in case of emergency, in an approved facility. You can't take books like mine from one place to another without *my* permission."

"How dare you quote the law to me? You don't even obey the laws of common courtesy."

"You steal my books, your dog herds me like a fucking sheep, you choke me every chance you get. Courtesy? Where'd you get your definition, I'd like to know!"

"And what were you planning to do when you broke into my library? Read? I'm not a fool, Dragon." Nyssa laughed.

"Then it's a damned fine illusion you're putting on!" Dwyn kept a wary eye on the gun. He didn't carry a shield. They were tough to maintain, requiring constant necromancy, and he never even bothered with one when he fought. No denying it now—they had their uses. "Tell me where my books are!"

"I counted them toward your penalty, Dragon; I'll keep them where I want them. Remember your place."

"My place is with my books!"

"You forfeited your books."

"Not those. You stole them!"

"I am not a thief." Blue fire crackled in the air as her magic surged.

He pointed to the book in her hand. "You lie! That never belonged to you. I know where it came from."

"Tam, go get Tully, please."

"What'd you do? Bribe the women of the watch at Rivnkyf? Must have cost you plenty. You couldn't buy them with your body."

The g'hesh split his skull. He fell, grabbing the back of his head, clawing at the magic splintering his mind into kindling. Tortured images flashed before his eyes—the broken Eseitha hengh, running from Nyssa, the rivn exploding, an infant in a tomb, a valley of roses dark as old blood. The floor rose up out of a jumbled memory of chains pulling him into the earth, and he smashed face first into the stone. Blood sprayed from his nose. He couldn't scream. He couldn't swallow. He tried to rise, but went down on one side; his cheek puddled in the froth of blood and ashes pouring from his lips. *Ata ti hacharda.* But he could do nothing.

"What is going on?" Jullup appeared in the doorway, wrapped in a bath towel. Nolan bounded past her. He knelt, enveloped Dwyn's belly in his arms, and began to chant.

God under the earth. He could breathe again. He leaned into the Seidroche's touch, sucking air in frantic gulps.

Nolan heaved Dwyn onto his feet. "Tam, help me, we'll carry him to my quarters."

"No." Nyssa's blue eyes dilated in cold fury. "Take him to the void room."

"Nyssa."

"He's my responsibility, not yours, Nolan."

Dazed, still hunting air, Dwyn slumped between Nolan and Tam, too feeble to kick as they pulled him through the library door, up the hallway, and into the kitchen. Morven was there, standing beside the table. Her mouth hung open.

They passed his door. The Eseitha stones. He spat blood; the taste of hot iron mixed with sulfur. "No...no..."

Like the Dragon in his nightmares, they dragged him under the mountain.

When the elevator door opened, Tully loomed out of a doorway on the left. "What the hell is going on?"

"He got past my tabah," Nolan said. "Nyssa caught him in the library."

"Tam." Tully nodded a greeting. "I didn't expect you so early."

"Nyssa was persuasive. So, this is your Dragon?"

"You want him?" Tully said, glaring at Dwyn. "I'm about ready to cut my losses. Shoot him, and you can stuff him and put him in that collection of yours."

Tam dumped Dwyn in the void cell and stepped out, but

Nolan stayed. He checked Dwyn's pulse at the neck, pressed an ear against his chest, felt his smashed nose, but when Nolan tried to thumb his eyelids, Dwyn slapped at him, irritated. "Leave me alone."

"Why did you do it?" Nolan spoke so softly Dwyn was sure the question was meant to be answered in equal tone.

"I had nothing to lose."

"Is your life worth so little to you?" Nolan straightened.

"You took my freedom," Dwyn snapped back. "What's left of life after that?"

Nolan stared down at Dwyn, face as impassive as Nyssa's had been when she'd tortured him. "You deserve what you get, then." He turned to leave. His curtain of silver hair swung to one side, revealing the most fantastic tattoo.

The branches and leaves of a massive tree occupied almost every inch of Nolan's broad shoulders and upper arms. The trunk covered his spine all the way to the waistband of his pants, and it took little imagination to imagine the taproot curling suggestively between his buttocks, and the finer roots draping his thighs, trailing down his calves to his ankles. Birds and fantastic beasts cavorted in the branches. The moon rode the Seidroche's left shoulder, golden and full. The whole image burned with Dragon's fire.

"Who did that to you?" Dwyn stammered.

Nolan's eyes narrowed angrily. "None of your damned business." He brushed his hair over his back and left the cell.

Dwyn sat, stunned to silence. Nyssa had an original copy of the *Seida*. Now Nolan walked around with the Rivnstone crest on his back. Dwyn had never seen a magical tattoo so large. It must have hurt like a sonofabitch. Who had put it there?

"Is he all right?" Tully asked Nolan.

The doctor folded his arms. "For now. The g'hesh will reset and it will hurt when it does. His nose isn't broken, but he'll have a pair of shiners in the morning. Jullup can take care of him."

"I don't think I want her around him anymore."

"You tell her that, Tully. See how far you get. Where are you going to put him? He's run my limit of tabah."

"Nyssa and I worked it out a few days ago when you said he was picking at the locks. No tabah. We used my water magic. Let him drown in it if he wants."

"Tonight?"

"If you say he's okay. It's comfortable enough for the likes of him."

Angry words cracked through Dwyn's lips. "I'm not a dog that you can talk in front of me. I will fight you until I die. Mhu seid, mhu seidr."

"Bold thing to say if there were no void to keep it from binding you," Tully said.

"Let me out. I'll be happy to repeat it."

Nyssa walked through the open door, carrying Dwyn's belt in one hand and—his heart sank—her book in the other. She sounded tired. "Move everything downstairs but be careful. Heaven only knows what he's put hexn on."

"Do you need my help?" Tully asked.

"If you don't mind, Tully, I'd rather you stay while I talk to him. Tam, would you help Nolan? I'd be happier with a necromancer upstairs."

"Of course, mh'arda." Tam frilled his golden mane in pleasure.

Dwyn gagged and got to his feet.

Nyssa waited until the elevator began to ascend with a clanking noise before stepping over the line. "Morven told me what you did. What did she give you for your help?"

Dwyn bared his teeth. "I have nothing to say to you, necromancer."

Nyssa advanced, her red face purple with fury. She grabbed his beard and yanked his chin up by it. "What did you do? Did you force yourself on her?" She hurled Dwyn across the ring, and he stumbled, falling hard on one knee. Stunned, he scrambled backward across the floor as Nyssa advanced. She couldn't hurt him with magic in a void but she didn't need magic to beat him to death.

Tully leaned forward, pressing against the lead line like he wanted to join Nyssa in murder. "What the hell is this about?"

"Morven was in my library last night and there was an accident," Nyssa hissed.

"Hell." Tully started hunting for his cigarettes.

Nyssa's voice cracked. "If you've hurt her, I swear on my bones I will kill you, I will see you dead—"

Dwyn rallied the little courage he had left. He spat. "I am a Seidoche! I did my duty—I protected the defenseless! You can't say the same, necromancer. Your negligence almost killed her."

Nyssa thrust the book in his face, screaming. "What did you make her promise?"

"I asked her for eight hours!" He screamed back. "Eight hours away from your damned dog! That's all I wanted. And my books. I want...I want my books."

Silence. Nyssa stared at him.

"Is he telling the truth?" Tully said. "Morven could have died?"

Nyssa ignored Tully. She drew herself up, nostrils flaring. "Thank you."

"I don't want your thanks. I want my books."

Her face solidified. "The penalty first, and I may be inclined to give them back—"

Furious smoke billowed from his lips. "You killed me with that damned penalty! I want your word on your god-forsaken bones I get my books back! Now, not later! Out there." He jabbed a finger at the room beyond the void line. "Where it counts."

"I will give them back to you, but not yet. I need you too much, Dwyn."

She used his name. She spoke the truth. The unexpected conjunction of the two momentarily silenced him.

Nyssa paced toward the edge of the ring and stopped there,

back to him. "There is something else I will do, Dwyn, in token of my gratitude—if you will work for me, if you will stop fighting me, if you quit making me hurt you."

"Say that at my hearing, and I will tell everyone how you abused your power!"

"I will speak for you at that hearing." She held up the book. "If you work like this for me. If you complete your penalty, to the satisfaction of the mountain that charged it to you, your debt may be forgiven. I will speak in your favor. You have my word."

He spat. "Your word is worthless!"

She turned back to him. "I need not offer. I could send you to Nations tonight, for attempted theft. I'm giving you a choice."

He trembled with hatred. "This is no kind of choice."

Nyssa held out her hand to him. "It's the only one you have."

CHAPTER FIFTEEN

NEW QUARTERS

Once out of the void, Nyssa tried to pull her hand free, but Dwyn dug his fingernails into the soft underside of her arm. "Your word and blood, necromancer. You will speak for me."

"Mhu seid, mhu seidr," she said evenly.

That was too easy. He'd been had. The g'hesh tightened.

He screamed. This time he knew his bones would break. He dove toward the void, desperate to escape, hit the line hard, and crumpled against the boundary, writhing like a poisoned wasp.

"I'll get Nolan." Tully's voice washed over him.

"Give him a moment," Nyssa said. "He'll be all right."

Like hell he would. The horrible, horrible magic twisted. "Meda!" he cried, but there was no mercy. In the end he lay defeated, cold stone pressed against his burning cheek.

"Tully, take his other arm. He's unconscious. We'll carry him."

He wasn't, but he couldn't resist. Tully's wet mass of magic sloshed when Dwyn sagged against him. Voices bubbled like running water in his ears.

"I can't tell Jullup what happened. She'd kill me. Lokey said he was going to Rich Mountain with Morven. Please tell me she isn't hurt."

"No. She is upset—more with me than herself, I think." Nyssa sighed. "I must report her to Whiterock, but when I do, I'll have something to say about them promoting dangerous politics on their campus. I've no doubt the anarchist thugs she ran with there put her up to this."

"The Dragon didn't lie, then."

"No. She was fortunate he was there and knew what to do. And he was right—I should have left my illusions in place, but with everything locked, I didn't see the point. I didn't want to carry the stress in my magic, not at Dh'Morda."

"Honey, I wish you'd blame me. It's my fault. It's always been my fault."

He heard a great rush of water, footsteps clumped through his trance, and stars flashed above, blinding him. A wave of fear surged through him when they laid him in a tomb. They would seal him away, and no fire could burn him to life again. But instead of the leaden weight of stone and magic, he sank into a bed of feathers, and a light blanket was thrown over him. Thin, red fingers combed his hair out of his eyes and arrayed the copper belt around his head like a crown.

"Is that what he really wanted? Eight hours away from the dog?"

"I don't know what he really wanted. He's cunning. Riordiin would never have had him if he wasn't."

"He won't stop trying to escape."

"No."

"What will you do with him now?"

"Keep him busy. Keep him close. This would never have happened if I'd been here. I won't make that mistake again."

Dwyn sank into oblivion.

Rain lashed the Dragon in the Eseitha hengh. The reckoning had come at last, but he would delay it as long as he could—the hateful embrace of this cold, bloody mountain where his enemies drew their might from his malignancy.

He paced the outcrop, long hair trailing behind him like broken wings. The g'hesh reminded him every day of his captivity, but it was a less potent symbol of slavery than this dark ring of obsidian bastards he had sired with the mountain. In the end, he gave in. He could not afford to refuse, lest he lose his mind to the fire that forged him. He needed his mind for revenge.

Thunder crashed, and lightning illuminated the cage in which he stood, swaying, screaming curses at the hengh—conceived in his magic, brooded in his blood, and born in this unholy ground. He could no more deny them his strength than deny his paternity.

Once, the pain of this sickness was the tithe he bled for the embrace of his beloved mountain. Now, it was punishment for his infidelity.

He screamed into the wind. "Bleed me to death, harlot! Take from me what you will. One day, the spawn you get of me will go South again. Mhu seid, mhu seidr. My word and blood, I swear it!"

Groaning, he knelt, lowered his hands into the mud, and kissed the earth.

Dwyn couldn't stop. He was awake, but he couldn't stop. He bolted upright and ran. He was still running when something clubbed him on the back of the head and smashed him onto a wet floor, dank, and smelling of rain. The sound of splashing filled the room.

He stared blankly at the darkness, breathing hard, expecting lightning to crackle and torrents to pour where knives of black stone tore open a stormy sky and the Dragon raved. But nothing happened.

He stumbled up, and reeled across an open space until he struck a wall. Braced against the damp stone, he heaved. He had little in his stomach, just the blood he'd swallowed hours ago. Hours? It felt like centuries.

"N'maha?" His voice quavered fearfully. Slowly, light began to fill the space.

A hexagonal room revealed itself in golden degrees—slick, damp walls, a smooth floor, and a vaulted ceiling that reflected his words back to him. Far above, a hole of pre-dawn sky gleamed, pale blue and a world away. He touched the back of his head. His fingers came away bloody. He'd hit it on something. Where had he sprung from? He looked around, dizzy.

It was an alcove bed—a niche cut into the wall and lined with a simple mattress, not unlike the coffin-chambers at Riordiin's home in Rivnkyf where all the great family of Dragon necromancers lay buried. He must have smacked his skull on the low arch when he'd jumped. The seidr lamps cast a yellowish light on rumpled white sheets, a gray blanket, and his belt, coiled like a copperhead snake sunning on his pillow.

That place where the Dragon stood—Dwyn had seen it, seen it more than once, staring through a bank of glass windows in Riordiin's receiving room at a grassy, flat space overlooking a narrow valley filled with the ruins of a town.

"You come highly recommended, Seidoche," Riordiin said, flipping casually through Ehrlik's letter. Dwyn kept his distance from the Dragon's fire, feeling strangely jealous. How nice it must be to burn when he pleased, to never hold back the flames that frightened the rest of the world.

"I trust you found your rooms adequate?"

After Xanadu, Dwyn had found his rooms palatial. "Perfectly adequate."

"Rivnkyf is a quiet mountain," Riordiin said. "There is myself, my steward, and the few families of knockr who have served my clan through generations of Dragons. You'll miss the entertainment you are used to at Nations."

"There is work enough to occupy my time, and the mountain itself is a wonder. I could gladly spend hours exploring." Dwyn nodded to the large, grassy lawn on the side of the mountain. "You have a spectacular view from here."

Riordiin smiled and his bright eyes took on a deep, red cast. "I suppose the view of a graveyard could be considered spectacular."

"The town, you mean?"

"No, Dragon. That is *not* what I mean." Riordiin stood, folded the pages, clamped them in his fist, and burned them. Dwyn concealed a gasp. He'd fireproofed that paper, but Riordiin burned through it with ease. "You will find the library in disarray. I have not the time, nor the skill, to deal with the decay. You may find it surpasses your skill as well, Seidoche."

"Respectfully, I welcome the chance to prove you wrong," Dwyn said.

"Do you?" Riordiin raised his eyebrows. "You consider yourself equal to a dynasty of Dragon necromancers dating back to the Southern Kingdom?"

"No, warloche. I consider myself honored to serve their legend." He bowed.

Riordiin laughed, and the red left his eyes, making him look almost normal but for the flame leaping around him. "There are no legends here, Seidoche. It's all frighteningly real, unfortunately."

And he'd been right when he said the place was a graveyard— where dreams died, and men lost their minds with the pain. The Dragon screaming in the Eseitha hengh had been the first. The last died on that same ground, speared through the belly by a knife of stone.

"Hell." Dwyn rubbed the knot forming on the back of his head, massaging away the memories. Where the fuck was the sound of water coming from? Made him need to piss. He grabbed the belt from his bed, fumbled his way through an opening, and went hunting for a bathroom.

The next room was also hexagonal, but smaller than the bedchamber, and dominated by a stone table. Seidr lamps flickered on when he entered, shining on a polished gray sandstone surface shot through with veins of green and gold crystal. The walls on every side were lined with shelves. There were no chairs or benches on which to sit.

The sound of running water increased as he walked through a short corridor into a small, narrow kitchen. No furniture here either. A hole in the wall over a stone sink admitted a narrow stream of water—but not enough to make the noise he heard. Dwyn turned right into the entryway and jumped back, startled.

Where a door should have been, he faced a wall of dirty brown water. The ceiling rained into a puddle the same dingy color as the waterfall. He inched forward cautiously until his toes touched the puddle. The shock he got sent him hopping backward on one foot, cursing. The pool turned yellow, then green, and back to brown. Tully's water magic. *Asshole.*

Dwyn limped away. He'd piss in the sink if he couldn't find a better spot.

The kitchen had no stove, no hot-plate, nothing to suggest he was meant to use it. But he noticed something more important on this second pass—his writing box on the counter. His paper was stacked beside it along with his clothes. They had brought his things here last night, all but...

"My stones! Where are they?" He opened an upper cabinet door and slammed it when he found nothing. He yanked a lower door open, blowing frantic sparks as he swept the dark recesses with both hands. That warloche, Tam, Tully said he was a collector—he must have taken them. Then Dwyn's hand bumped against a metal bucket, and the contents chimed sweetly together. "Oh, oh!" he sobbed, dragging the bucket out of the cabinet and hugged it to his chest. "Dh'ben."

All nine were accounted for, seven Eseitha stones and the two rocks he'd taken from the river, illusions intact if a little battered. He spread them out on the bed and checked each stone for damage. Not so much as a scratch.

"Dh'ben," he sighed. Calmer now, he listened. The water sounded different here, loud, but not like the waterfall. He paced around the room with his ear pressed against the wall and soon enough, he found the hidden door.

The bathroom was as big as the bedroom. If not for the bathing pool in the middle, he might have danced a J'hen from one side to the other without feeling cramped. A short cascade filled the pool before spilling into a narrow trough, and beyond that a long sluice carried the water away. The entire room was open without a pretense of privacy—a hesset's room he decided, a guard chamber once upon a time.

He relieved himself in the sluice, stripped off his jeans and threw them upstream. How he hadn't shit himself when Nyssa punished him, he didn't know, but he'd let other glands go in his fright, and he smelled about as pleasant as overcooked cabbage. He didn't linger in the bath, though, and he steamed himself dry.

Back in the room, he covered the stones with the blanket. His illusions had shifted far more than he thought they should, as if the stones themselves were too slippery to hold an image false to their nature. Someone would come for him soon, and when they did, they needed to see a bucket full of stones, the same stones they had placed under the counter. But not these stones.

He trotted back to the kitchen, and rummaged through his writing case. "Ink, ink—where'd she put my ink?"

He found it—misplaced—and filled a pen. He rubbed the skin on the inside of his right forearm rapidly until it puffed and the blood welled up, and scribbled his illusions quickly, muttering over the words as they caught fire and burned like gunpowder. The air was chokingly dark when he finished, but the high ceiling in the bedroom acted like a chimney, drawing both smell and smoke away. He crumpled the first sheet of paper and studied the details. Oval, misshapen, gray, and dirty— it was a rock to look at. He picked it up, tossed it. The weight felt right.

He arranged the paper wads in the bucket, and put it under the counter. He carried his clothes back to the room, but he buried the real stones under the featherbed before he dressed. They would be safest there, disguised as part of the stone platform. None too soon, either. An interrupted splash told him someone had just come through the waterfall.

"Here to torture me again?" He cinched his belt around his middle as Nyssa walked in.

"Glad to see you up." She was back in business gray, wearing black stilettos a mile high. Her hair was pulled back in the usual red helmet, with the long tail of her braid sweeping over her shoulder and trailing to her waistline.

"Do you plan to feed me at some point?" He tossed his pillow carelessly in the corner of the bed. "You didn't even leave me a can or a can-opener."

"It's time for you to go to work. You can eat afterwards."

"The stones aren't ready."

"You will go to work with me. You'll have the school library at Rich Mountain all to yourself—a full eight hours, dog-free. Consider it payment of Morven's debt."

"Fuck you."

"Finish getting dressed." She turned and walked back to the kitchen.

If he went into the bathroom, he could seal the door. She'd not get in easily. But there was a chance, a small chance, that she had taken his books to Rich Mountain. Dwyn yanked his shirt over his head so hard he ripped a new hole under the arm, and he laced his boots skipping every other hook.

Nyssa waited for him in the entryway. "I won't turn it off, so if you don't want to get wet, stay close to me."

He scrambled almost on her heels, but he didn't slip under her protection in time. The waterfall caught him in the small of his back, and sluiced down the back of his pants.

"Motherfucker!" It was like being flogged with an electric fence. He crashed into Nyssa, jumped past, and bolted into the middle of the room, dancing in circles, sizzling and sparking erratically. Then he saw the waterfalls.

They poured down every wall in the enormous cavern. Like the one in front of his door, they vanished when they reached the ground. Coalescing brown puddles turned the floor into a chain of widely separated islands, linked by thin, dark bridges of naked rock.

Nyssa raised her voice. "There is no exit without an escort, either Tully or myself. You would collapse in seizures before you could pass through. Follow me."

His muscles moved like glaciers as he shuddered and twitched his way after her into the elevator. By the time he followed her through the upper hallway of Ironsfork and out to the parking lot at the top of the mountain, he felt frozen. A dove-gray sedan was the only vehicle there. Nyssa unrolled a towel and opened the passenger side door. He flopped in with a squelch before she could protect the seat. Treat him like a filthy dog, would she? He'd find a way to scorch that white leather.

Nyssa didn't yell. She didn't order him out. She closed the door for him, and walked around the front, folding the towel, and when she got in, she placed it between them, and set her purse safely by her side.

"When we get to Rich Mountain, Dragon," she said, backing out, "you will remain silent until we reach the library. This is not a place for you to spout off unwisely—"

He growled. "And here I'd planned a speech—The Atrocities of Necromancers: Southern Kingdom to Present. How about I start with the stranglehold you like so much?"

His tongue thickened. Barbed wire wrapped around his neck. "Go ahead. Prove me right."

The pressure vanished. Nyssa's mouth tightened.

"You want my cooperation, necromancer? Stop calling me Dragon. I trained eight years as a Seidoche, three of them with a necromancer far more powerful than you could ever hope to be, and he called me warloche." He folded his arms over his chest and stared out the window at the mist drifting up like volcanic vapors from the lake.

"Merit the word warloche, and I'll call you one." Nyssa turned onto the highway.

The fog thickened over the road as forest gave way to pastures and stone houses. Human houses, Dwyn thought, until he saw they were bermed, with only the fronts showing and the rest buried snuggly underground, tucked into the hillsides. Nyssa stopped to let a school bus sidle over. Two dwarf children were kicking a soccer ball in a front yard, but when the red lights flashed, both scampered to grab their backpacks. The bigger girl booted the ball hard, scoring a goal on the front door of the house, and both she and her smaller friend raised their arms and yelled. A thin goblin woman banged through the door and picked up the ball, lecturing both children even as they swung up into the bus and the door closed.

Dwyn squirmed uncomfortably. It did happen. A dwarf could lose his head entirely in the mating season, especially a young one. "Do they go to your school? The kobolds?"

Nyssa didn't spare the goblin woman a glance. "No, we're not in session for Dh'Morda. Kobolds go to the human school."

"Ah." He stared at the weedy front yards, the brown, bare spots where the occupants must park a car when they were home, and thought of Xanadu. Add a pile of garbage to each doorstep, and he could be looking at his old home.

He was glad when the dismal houses gave way to majestic oaks collecting mist in their branches. He hadn't thought he'd enjoy anything today, but when they drove over the dry, sunlit expanse of Rich Mountain, and all the mist rolled away, and the polished stone doors of the mountain home gleamed, his spirits rose inexplicably. He felt curiously excited, even eager to arrive. Then he registered the seductive smell of roses. Soon his peculiar odor of fermenting apples mingled horribly with Nyssa's mating scent. She lifted her lip, tasting his aroma, scowled, and rolled down her window.

Dwyn slid down in his seat, embarrassed. Cultural propriety dictated you didn't call a man out for smelling like a cider house any more than you complimented a woman for smelling like a garden of earthly delights, but he was heartily sick of this damned Dh'Morda.

Nyssa bypassed the main gate and turned onto a road following the contour of the summit. Ahead, an isolated spur of rock hung out into space like an unhappy fool making up his mind whether or not to jump. The morning sunlight glanced off windows, doors, and a set of steps leading up to the school from a graveled parking lot.

"Good God," he said, incredulous. "What do you do? Teach everyone in one room?"

"It's larger than it looks."

He'd concede it might be deeper, but he found it impossible to believe the rock could support more than a few select hallways and offices. It looked weak enough to fracture at any moment and open the worm-eaten space to the sky.

Nyssa parked in front, and he got out. Apart from the doors—standing open—the only welcoming feature of the place was a beautifully terraced garden that started at the edge of the parking lot and climbed the mountain adjacent. Every flowerbed showcased something bright—pansies, in every color from gold to black, blue kale, strangely shaped purple cabbages, red-leafed beets. The beds were mulched with straw. In the afternoons, the hillside would glow like gemstones on a bed of gold.

He followed Nyssa up the cracked steps. The ceiling was high in the entry, but beyond it dropped to five feet, and the walking space narrowed to three. He imagined the riot if there was a fire, and the children tried to pour out of this hallway. They would clog the pipe.

Most of the classrooms were deserted for Dh'Morda, but in one, an older dwarf scratched away at a stack of papers on his desk. Light glinted on the bald spot capping his long gray hair. When Dwyn followed Nyssa up the first set of stairs, he turned and saw the dwarf standing in the doorway of the room, watching.

In another small room, almost entirely taken up by computers, a boy with black hair and a quilly beard pecked resolutely at a keyboard. Like the teacher, he stopped and came to the door to look at them as they passed. Nyssa paid no attention, but this time Dwyn stared back. The boy ducked behind the doorway. The sound of typing did not resume.

Another few right turns brought them to the extent of the building. The sandstone walls were crumbling here, and wide cracks in the floor had been sealed with tarry-looking magic. Sudden light flooded the tunnel, and Dwyn blinked, momentarily blinded. On one wall, a long continuous window overlooked the blunted tops of trees that kissed the spur goodbye before marching away down the mountainside. It was an impressive view, but one that told a dismal story of decay.

There could not have been a worse place for a window. It was modern, a sure sign this part of the structure had already suffered catastrophic magic failures. The glass crackled with necromancy, but it was the only thing that didn't look ready for a wrecking ball. The windowless side was no better. A wretchedly utilitarian drinking fountain sagged between two doors, one closed, the other open to a closet. Its contents spilled on the floor: a mop bucket, piles of dirty rags, cans of paint. Nyssa's eyebrows knit together. She took a key from her purse, unlocked the closed door, and pushed it open.

An evil, graveyard air slithered out into the hallway. It got in Dwyn's nose and his mouth; he squinted, and was about to comment when he saw Nyssa glaring at him.

"Don't look at me. I didn't fart." He lifted his upper lip, drawing in the scent. Nyssa looked to the near wall, lined with overflowing trash bags, but Dwyn turned to the far end of the room, where a door stood open just beyond the circulation desk. He was sure he was right. Dh'Morda gave men the advantage over women when it came to differentiating smells in the mating season. He could clearly identify his own cidery musk, Nyssa's floral aroma, rancid paint, the musty odor of mold, the decomposing sealant leaking out of the cracks in the stone, composting garbage, and something else—something horrible.

It smelled remarkably like meat left out for a day in the July heat of a damp summer—dead, rotting, breeding maggots. He knew that odor. Nothing good ever made it.

"Go in." Nyssa took a small book from her purse and began to thumb through, a jet stylus gripped lightly between her index finger and thumb.

Dwyn slid past, hackles up.

It was a desperately small library. There were no books on any of the sandstone shelves, no ladders, no tables, no chairs. Sunlight sketched a golden scribble on the cracked flagstones through the dirty window in the wall, but the darkness Dwyn sensed was not something any light would cure. He jumped nervously when Nyssa's sharp voice cut the stillness.

"Talus!"

Dwyn turned around. The boy he had seen typing in the computer room shuffled into view. Furtive eyes looked everywhere but at Nyssa, and the feet scuffing the floor seemed to be dragged against his will.

Nyssa spoked down to him. "I told you to clean this up Sunday last week. It is now Sunday. Again."

The boy's voice was changing from a child's tenor to deep bass and it squeaked horribly. "I meant to, warloche, but I had an essay due. Cheyloche told me I could finish it over the holiday because of practice, but then Tanta Robyn wanted me to go to Magazine with the family, and Midian invited me to go duck hunting with him and Morven and—"

Nyssa's icy stare cut the boy off sharply.

"I'll do it. I'll do it now." Talus scuttled for the door. Paint cans clattered in the hallway as they turned over.

Nyssa turned to Dwyn. "You will work here today until five. In the room behind the desk, you'll find boxes of books which need repair. I want you to make a start on the worst of them. You'll find rippers, ink, and paper in the desk. Pens should be in the storage closet, and a seidskrid, if you need one."

Dwyn's hackles rose. "I was penalized to create a library, not repair a wreck of one!"

"Last night you promised me—"

"I agreed I would work—on my penalty. This is not my penalty." He glanced back at the storage room. The idea of spending an entire day in this mausoleum was unthinkable.

"I *am* counting this toward your penalty."

"I need my tools: my pens, my paper, my ink, and my glasses— how the hell am I supposed to write in this light without them?"

Nyssa folded her arms over her chest. "Maybe next time I tell you we're going to work, you'll be ready. If you need me, there's a phone in the back. Call the principal's desk." She turned to go.

"Do I at least get coffee?"

"Talus! After you take that paint out, go tell Nikl the Dragon wants breakfast." The door shut with a faint click behind her.

Dwyn rattled the door, more for confirmation than anything else. It was locked. No doubt she'd keyed it to open one way.

He faced the yawning pit in the back of the library and drew his sword.

CHAPTER SIXTEEN

WHERE THE
MONSTERS LIVE

No seidr lamps flared when Dwyn walked into the storage room.
A string dangled from a light bulb attached to the ceiling. He pulled
it. Nothing happened. He tapped the fixture with his sword.

"N'maha," he said doubtfully.

It shattered. He jumped backwards as glass rained down.

Ordinarily, Dwyn would have lit up like a candle. At Nations,
there were no seidr lamps in the library, only modern fluorescent
fixtures. The constant buzz gave him one hell of a headache. He
routinely turned them off whenever he worked in the stacks.
He'd draw up a chair to the transcription table and peruse the
texts for any degradation in magic, basking in his comfortable
self-sufficient light. Sorcha always said she knew he was working
whenever she saw his forge-fire leaking under the door. But
that was the Haneen Etheanoche—a proper library. In here,
there might be open ink bottles, or containers of Kvasir leaking
flammable gasses into the air. He didn't want to start the day
with a bang.

Something hairy ran over his foot. A tail flashed across the
top of his boot. A rat. *Wonderful.* He fumbled his way to an open

closet and poked around on the lower shelves. A mousetrap
snapped shy of his fingers, but he found no light bulbs.

"Fuck me." He set his sword down, hitched up his belt, and
tested his weight on the first shelf. It held. He dug through the
stacks of dusty paper, torn leather, and dirty spools of thread.
Books in the back. Trash in the back, more like. Damage by mice
or rats meant a complete rewrite and everything burned with
appropriate precautions.

He was about to give up when his hand closed on a package.
He jumped down, borrowed the chair from the miserable transcription desk, and angled it under the light. By standing on his
toes, he was just tall enough to unscrew the old bulb.

The library door opened and closed. Dwyn jumped down
from the chair. "Did you know you've got rats, necromancer?
And who knows what the hell else. I'm a Seidoche, not an
exterminator."

No answer.

"Necromancer?"

Thud. Thud. Thud. Someone—or something—was banging
on the circulation desk. A peculiar sucking and snorting sound
interrupted the percussion, and then the drumming began again.
Dwyn peered cautiously around the doorframe.

A child looked back.

She sat cross-legged on the floor, thumping the back of her
head on the walnut panels. A shocking tangle of blond hair
straggled over her puffy eyes—great teal-colored things that
were overlarge for her triangular face. Her upturned nose was
red. "Hello," she said in a hoarse voice. She suctioned mucus
with disgusting relish, drove one hand across her slimy mouth,
and wiped it on her pink shirt. In her other hand—

"Where did you get that? Give it to me!" Dwyn grabbed the
book.

She hung on, howling. "I found it. It's mine! Mine!"

"Let go of it—"

"No!"

But Dwyn had made his books of stern stuff. The leather heated in his hand like a branding iron, and the girl let go with a squeal. Hurt tears filled her eyes.

He thumbed through it rapidly, terrified, but everything was as he'd written it—his soul—pure necromancy, bright with passion, dark with magic, the last thing a child should be looking at. "Where did you find this?"

She pointed to the storage room. "In there. Where the monsters live."

"Fuck!" Dwyn blazed back to the closet, stuffing his book under his shirt. He tore into the lower shelf, ripped out a box, slammed it on the ground, and slit the rotting tape open with his sword. He dug through the contents frantically.

"What are you doing?" The girl had followed him.

"Get out of here, kid." He ripped open a second box.

She blinked. "Don't you remember my name? I'm Una."

As if he'd forget. The little brat had ruined his death. Algebra books. He threw one across the room. "Which shelf did you find it on?"

Una pointed to his sword. "Do you use that to kill the monsters?"

"Which shelf, dammit!"

"You should say please," Una said. "Teacher says to always say please."

"If please ever gets you what wasn't already coming to you, I'll give you a gold ring I haven't got. Which shelf?"

She looked confused. "The top one."

The top shelf contained several boxes, plastic and heavy. He didn't drop these, but lowered them carefully to the floor. Una perched on the desk, watching him. Mucus overflowed into the thin wispy goat's chin that was all children had for a beard.

"That's gross. Go blow your nose." He jerked his head toward the tiny water closet in the rear of the room.

Una shook her head. "I'm scared of the monsters."

"They're just rats."

"I'm not afraid of rats. Teacher has a rat. He's nice."

Dwyn popped the lid on the first box. It was filled with letters. They didn't smell horrible, but they weren't right either. He picked one up gingerly, scanned it, then dropped it back in the pile. He'd have to fire his own hands after touching that. "How'd you get in here, anyway?"

She rolled her eyes. "Through the door. It's my school. I go here."

"Not on holiday, you don't." He eyed the second of the plastic tubs. It was much bigger than the first—deeper too. It had a swollen look, like a boil full to bursting. Cautiously, he set the edge of his sword blade under the lid and cracked it open.

"Fucking hell!" He rocked backwards, overwhelmed by the stench.

Una's shoes clattered on the desk as she stood. "Monster," she quavered.

It was subtle—a shift in the air, a magical hint of decaying apples mingled with rotting flesh, and a dreamlike heaviness, and he was sinking, pushed underwater by a weight heavier than lead, darker than death. He scooped Una off the desk, tucked her under his arm, and ran.

He flung himself against the library door before he remembered that damned tabah. The crash jarred him sideways. He dropped Una and faced the storage room in his fighting stance, feet slightly apart, sword raised. Una landed on her feet like a kitten. She ducked into his shadow.

A strange shape flickered in and out of the glow of the overhead light, shivering beneath a milky caul of magic. A grotesque hulk of gray flesh rolled forward, heavy as lead and just as toxic.

"Monster!" Una flung her arms around Dwyn's waist, heedless of the flames. She shrieked when he burned her.

He grabbed her hand, roaring his protection. "Te arda, te bena! Shut up!"

She burrowed into his belly, sobbing.

"Te bena. Te mikhava," he said in a gentler tone. He should have been less ferocious. She was only a child. He'd been eighteen when he'd seen his first draugr and even as Mn'Hesset he'd pissed himself.

Ten feet tall and eyeless, they held no shape at their worst, were mountainous at their best, and always stank of the rot that bred them. Logically, he knew them for what they were: the offspring of corrupt magic spawned in error, gestated in forgetfulness. Metaphysically, they were beasts of terrifying proportions. And Una could see them! Remarkable. He could only name a handful of warloche with that kind of seidr-sight—Riordiin, his grandfather—and here was another.

Her voice shook. "Don't let it get me."

"I won't. Go sit over there," he pointed towards the window seat.

"No! I want to stay with you. It's only safe where you are!"

"Sit, or I'll make you!"

Una's custard-colored face hardened, but she slumped reluctantly to the window. Dwyn crept back to the door of the storage room.

The draugr rolled silently around the room, rooting through the filthy magic, scattering it everywhere. Had he more confidence, he might have rushed in and fought until it retreated into his dreams, where he could kill and dismember it properly. But he remembered the folly of the battle he had lost.

He drew the blunt tip of Mh'Arda slowly across the threshold. "He dwynen; mhu seid, mhu seidr, dwynen he. N'mhu Dwyn, Mn'Hesset." Superstitious, maybe, but he wanted his real name between himself and that thing. Magic was such dark water. The draugr might be fathoms deep or it might be lurking just below the surface, ready to pull him under.

Una peeped at him from around the nearest bookshelf.

"I told you to sit," he said.

"What did you do?"

"Confused it. It will leave. Eventually."

"What if it doesn't?"

The draugr bumbled against the line. The heavy head smashed

against his firebreak. Una grabbed Dwyn around the leg. Malevolent pits dilated where eyes should be, and then it lumbered away to splash through the corruption.

"It can't see you," he said.

"What is it?" Una tugged on one of his long braids.

"It's called a draugr."

"Mhu Paloh! Those aren't real!" Una laughed—a high-pitched, unhappy giggle.

"You ought to have your mouth washed out with soap," he said, offended.

"They're not real." Glued to his side, she stared at the draugr, upright now, head invisible in a floor above. Dirty genitals wobbled side to side. It squatted and drenched the boxes with rancid piss. The smell was horrific—something between rotten fish and raw sewage. Una's yellow skin paled to cream. Dwyn grabbed her shoulders and steered her back to the window seat.

She sat, twisting her hair between her hands, shaking. "They're not real. They're—not!"

He patted her knee. "Calm down. It's not going to get past my line, okay?" He wished that boy would get back. Children, unlike adults, had wide open bones. What he could bleed off in ten minutes, Una would harbor in her magic until she was old enough to purge. He unbuckled his belt, and draped it protectively over her round stomach.

"You want to tell me how long you've been seeing monsters here?"

She gulped. "Four. I think."

"Four what? Years?"

Una nodded.

"How old are you?"

"I'm six." She bit her lip, and a nervous look flitted across her face.

Not a chance. When draugr appeared, complete destruction wasn't far behind. The spur should have tumbled down the mountainside in that time. He stared directly into her turquoise eyes. "Tell me the truth!"

She frowned. "I did!"

Dwyn pulled out the book from under his shirt. "Where did you really get this?"

"I won't tell you! You're mean."

"Nyssa's office. Am I right?"

Una's lower lip stuck out a foot.

He sighed in relief. His other books would be there, not safe, but safer. He would demand Nyssa return them to Ironsfork. She'd see reason once she saw this mess. But this book—now that he had it, he wouldn't give it back.

He left Una sitting, and went to the circulation desk. He found six sheets of paper, liberally peppered with mouse droppings in one drawer, a ripper and a skein of thread in another, but nothing else. "Surely there's a pen in here." He slammed the drawer.

The copper belt clattered to the floor as Una left the window. She held up a purple marker. "I have a glitter pen."

He stared at it, incredulous, but it was better than nothing. He set Mh'Arda down on the surface in front of him. "Don't touch," he warned.

The first sheet of paper was no good to him, but the bottom sheets had been protected from all but gnawing. He seared the edges and laid them flat on the desk in front of him.

"What are you doing?"

"Nothing that concerns you. Go watch for that boy, Talus. When he comes in, don't let him shut the door."

She didn't leave, but hung onto the edge of the desk, watching him curiously. "Can you draw me a picture, like the ones in the book?"

"Did you or did you not hear me?"

She pouted, but went. She stood on her tiptoes and pressed her lips against the glass. Dwyn shuddered.

When he finished, he wiped the blood from the pen on his shirt before carrying it to where Una stood guard. "Where the hell is that kid? How long does it take to get a cup of coffee on this mountain?" Dwyn stalked back to the desk and took out the ripper and the thread.

"I can run the whole way to the kitchen," Una said, examining her pen with interest. "Nikl says I'm fast as a lizard." She slashed the pen back and forth like a sword.

Dwyn began to punch the holes in the pages with the point of the ripper.

"I see him! Talus!"

The boy crashed through the door, butt first. In one hand he carried a huge paper bag and what looked like a bucket of coffee in the other.

"Come in, Talus! We're fighting monsters," Una sang.

Dwyn roared over her, "Don't shut the door! For the love of earth, don't shut it!"

Talus froze, half-in, half-out of the doorway.

Dwyn relieved Talus of the coffee. "Take this girl with you and go get Nyssa. Hurry."

"Uh, she's in a meeting—"

"Then get her out of it. Tell her the Dragon is about to blow up the library." He grabbed Una by the seat of her pants and tossed her out the door. The g'hesh stabbed him through the wrists as he slammed the door behind the two children. He doubled over, wringing the thorns out of his hands.

Talus stared through the glass at him, gaping, but he hauled Una onto his back and ran up the hallway. Soon he was out of sight.

Dwyn went back to the desk. He sewed the papers together by pushing thread through the holes with the tip of the ripper as best he could. Damn that g'hesh. His fingers were all pins and needles. The liquid slop of unhappy death filtered into his bones from the back room as he cast his illusion. Dreadful stuff, but it did the job. Two identical books now lay in front of him. He shoved both under his shirt and checked his firebreak.

The draugr was drifting deeper into magic beyond his sight

distance. Seeing them like this was rare, even for him. Nine years had passed since he'd encountered one in the waking world. The last time had been at Nations.

He leaned against the doorframe, watching.

He'd watched it then, too. No one else in the room saw it—a filthy draugr wandering up and down the dais behind the necromancers arguing over whether they could try him for murder once they'd branded him incendiary. He wondered now as he'd wondered then if the sin of a man in one world always followed him into another.

For a moment, the faceless monster turned and looked at him as if it could see him. Then it winked out, a shadow disappearing into darkness.

When Nyssa came in, stamping the floor into submission, Dwyn was sitting on the circulation desk, sipping the giant cup of coffee. The wizened necromancer Rachet followed her, and behind him the round-faced, straw-headed warloche Dwyn recognized as Rachet's chieftain, Neil.

"How long has that been festering back there?" He slid down from the desk.

"What are you talking about?" Nyssa asked.

Una slipped in behind the group and started to skip across to Dwyn.

"Get her out of here," Dwyn said. He pointed at the chieftain. "Him too; he's no warloche."

"You can't order the chieftain to leave," Rachet said.

Dwyn curled his lip scornfully. "Fine. He can blame you when his balls rot off."

Nyssa broke in. "Una, go outside. Neil, would you take her? Rachet will call you if you're needed."

"A matter of the mountain matters to the chieftain. He should be here." Rachet's eyes narrowed maliciously. "Unless we now obey Ironsfork's Dragon as we obey her necromancer?"

Neil didn't leave. Wordlessly, Nyssa led the way to the storage room.

The weak overhead light cast unusually deep shadows around the boxes—puddles of piss that only Dwyn saw. But he wasn't the only one who smelled it. Nyssa put her hand over her mouth and nose, as did Neil.

Only Rachet stood defiant. "Did you bring us here to tell us the toilet is backed up?"

The lid still lay askew on the second box. Dwyn flipped it with the tip of his sword.

Nyssa's face became a raisin. Even Rachet pulled his jacket up around his long nose. His silver beard bobbed as he swallowed.

Once they had been books. But the magic had leaked out, leaving a dark, bloody tar in which rotting leather soaked and stank. Sluggish bubbles rose to the surface and popped as the corpses floated in the blood of their maker.

"What is it?" Neil stood in the open doorway, right on top of the firebreak. Una stood well behind it. Either she saw what was left of it, or she remembered where he'd drawn it. Smart girl.

"Dead man's blood," Dwyn said. "From the bouquet, I'd say fermented eight or nine years."

"Ten. Asa Black has been dead for ten years," Nyssa said.

"Well, he's not a vintage that's improved with age, I'll say that."

Nyssa dropped her hand. "This isn't a joke. It's serious."

"Oh, yeah." Dwyn nudged the box with his foot. The liquid sloshed, churning up a funeral stink. "So serious I'd say some necromancer needs firing if you ask me."

"It's dangerous?" Neil looked like he might faint.

"Melt your bones, this would." Dwyn stared at Rachet. "You know, somebody knew what they were doing when they stored this shit. Plastic tubs are useful to a point, but soak rot in them long enough, and the protection falls apart. Did you know that, necromancer?"

"Are there more?" Nyssa broke in with a shallow gasp.

"Several. I opened this one and stopped." He didn't mention the box with the letters.

Nyssa squared her shoulders. She seemed to be recovering from the shock. And she *was* shocked, or doing a damned good job faking it. "First, we must contain this. Rachet, take Neil and conclude the meeting. Don't say anything about this. We have no idea if there has been permanent damage—"

"Nooooo—the mountain is falling down, but you have no idea if there has been permanent damage."

Nyssa tightened her mouth instead of his g'hesh.

He smirked.

"Nyssa, the council must be told. We have to protect ourselves or Whiterock will shut us down," Ratchet said.

Nyssa's lofty tone never faltered. "Not until the regional Seidoche has been called, and I am in charge of when and how that happens. For now, we clean this up. We have better options than plastic bins."

Unlikely. But Dwyn was so pleased to see Nyssa squirming, he said nothing. When Nyssa reassured Neil that nothing would happen to him as a result of the poisonous soup that was probably chewing on his bones right now, Dwyn sat on the desk, swinging his legs, and said nothing. When she told Rachet she was sure the school would stay open and that the regional Seidoche could be bought, Dwyn drank his coffee, and said nothing. He hoped his appetite might come back in time to sample something from the bag Talus had dropped outside the door. Stroke of luck, there. He wouldn't dare eat anything that had been in this library.

Coffee—well, coffee was different. It burned the taint out of whatever it touched. He drank the stuff by the gallon when he worked in the library at Rivnkyf. Gave him a rotten stomach, but it was better than rotten bones. If Nyssa asked nicely, and if he was in a good mood, he might suggest she fill new plastic bins with it.

"Una? Nikl is making donuts this morning. Why don't you go?"

Nyssa asked, stroking Una's yellow topknot. "You don't want to miss out."

"I'm not hungry." Una sat below the circulation desk, doodling on her hand with her purple pen. The tip of her tongue stuck out in concentration.

"Please."

Una stared up at Dwyn and grinned. "If please ever gets you what you want, I'll give you a gold ring I haven't got."

Dwyn flinched. All children could throw their voices—those wonderfully flexible little vocal cords—but he didn't think he sounded quite so nasally.

"Go." All the honey vanished in Nyssa's voice.

Una bolted for the door. On her left hand she'd scrawled a reasonable replica of Dwyn's incendiary rune.

"We'll talk in my office."

Dwyn jumped down. "Frankly, I'd rather go back to Ironsfork and take a bath. I feel so dirty. You're protecting that dried-out tarantula, and I didn't say anything."

"Walk."

She marched him out of the crumbling library and back into solid mountain. But it wasn't safe. He could smell it here too—terminal rot, clouded by the odors of floor cleaner, beeswax, paper, glue, and old paint. He lifted the paper bag Nikl had sent and pressed his nose against it—blueberry muffins, fresh bread, tomatoes.

Shit. Something had spilled.

Compared to the garbage-pit of the library, Nyssa's office was as sterile as an operating room. Antiseptic whitewashed walls, minimalist shelves, and solid, sturdy furniture matched her composure as she walked behind her desk. She waved to indicate Dwyn should take a chair. He sat, and opened the bag. Tomato soup was everywhere.

Nyssa settled comfortably in her seat. "The first thing I think you must do is give me what is hidden beneath your shirt."

"The first thing I'm going to do is make sure nothing of mine stays in this cesspool," Dwyn said, digging through the sodden napkins. "Where are my books?"

Nyssa glanced toward the shelf and waved her hand. The illusion shifted. There they were, the last eight, nestled between a copy of *Practica Ethean* and a large bronze cruchis decorated with skulls and bones. He fought back a sigh of relief.

"They go back to Ironsfork. Your library I will accept as safe storage. I protest any other."

"Fair enough." Nyssa held out her hand.

He withdrew the fake from his shirt with plausible hesitation. Nyssa thumbed through it.

He flicked wet crumbs from his fingers. "So why?"

"Why what?"

"Rachet. He did it. I don't know how long that shit has been in your library, but it's been in those boxes a long time." He stabbed a piece of tomato-soaked muffin at her. "Moreover, those books were rotten when he put them there. No wonder he looks like he's a hundred and fifty years old."

"He *is* a hundred and fifty years old." Nyssa walked to the bookcase, and added the fake to the group of real books. "Clearly, you don't respect your elders."

"A dwarf may go from black to white with his century but that has nothing to do with whether or not I respect him. Nor should you, necromancer. It's your ass they'll eat."

Nyssa stroked the spine of the fake book gently. "You want to know why I didn't say anything to Neil about Rachet?"

"Since you're in the mood to confess—"

"I need him. Only a full local necromancer's coalition may challenge a regional Seidoche's opinion. Can I do that if I expel one of my own? Rachet's secret is safe with me. It's you I worry about."

"If you want to buy my silence, I'll have my books, thanks."

"Don't delude yourself." She walked back to her desk. "Your word has no value as it stands. But I do need something from you. To challenge Sorcha, I need a Seidoche—an interim one will do—one who can make recommendations—"

He dropped the muffin. "Sorcha? Sorcha who?"

"Sorcha Flintridge, our regional Seidoche. I must have a Seidoche who is qualified to evaluate..."

Although Dwyn registered every word, and could have repeated it verbatim if asked, Nyssa might as well have been babbling like an infant. *Sorcha Flintridge.* So she was still unmated. She always swore as soon as she found a mate, she wouldn't keep her knockr name longer than it took her to change it. He'd teased her about that every chance he got.

Sorcha's red hair gleamed in his firelit memory.

The last time he'd seen her, she'd been angry. Her voice cut him to bleeding.

"Listen to me, Dwyn. Nobody deserves to be treated this way. I don't care if he's the greatest Northern Dragon to ever crawl out of that damned mountain, you can't let him keep doing this. Necromancers don't get to abuse their Seidwendr. Tell Ehrlik!"

Dwyn pulled a couch pillow over his face, hiding his swollen nose, tear-filled eyes, and broken lip. "You don't understand. Riordiin needs me—"

Sorcha cupped his cheeks in her hands. "I don't care. Tell Ehrlik."

"I—I've already talked to Ehrlik. He says—" The words tangled on his tongue. It would absolutely be abuse if he left Riordiin now, when the dying Dragon needed him so much. "I gave my oath to stay with him, and that's the end of it."

Sorcha stamped her foot. "Have you lost every bit of common sense you ever had? You're not going back to Rivnkyf, Dwyn. I won't let you. I care about you too much."

He broke down, sobbing.

Sorcha wrapped her arms around his shaking shoulders.

In the end, he let her write his resignation because she

wouldn't let him leave her quarters without it. He'd burned it the next day, and went back to Riordiin, with Ehrlik's blessing.

Not Sorcha's.

And when he'd needed her help the most, she'd refused.

He pulled himself away from his memory, automatically rejecting Nyssa's first offer "No. I don't want one of my books, I don't want two. I want them all."

"I'd be prepared to negotiate with you on the rest."

He shook his head.

"Don't be difficult."

His pent-up anger spilled over. "Difficult? Do you have any idea of what you're dealing with? I've seen my fair share of necromancy gone putrid, and what I saw today scared me! Una, Talus too—Nolan should see them right away. And Ratchet, he put that garbage there—it's all up in his filthy magic."

"Other suggestions, warloche?"

He fell silent.

Nyssa's nostrils flared. "Very well. I will give you your books in payment—but not in advance."

"All."

"Yes. Including the one you have not given me that I am over-looking and don't know anything about."

He folded his arms across his chest. "This isn't penalty work. It's beyond what you tasked me to do."

"I tasked you to create a library, for me, for this school. Now I'm asking you to help me preserve it."

"There isn't anything to preserve! You'll be lucky if they don't fine the hell out of this mountain—*your* mountain, too—don't think they won't come after Ironsfork."

"So, help me. Help yourself."

He stared at her for a moment. "If I don't agree with you, I won't say I do. I won't lie to another Seidoche."

Nyssa smiled. "That's fair. I'll do the lying."

CHAPTER SEVENTEEN

DEAD MAN'S BLOOD

Nyssa left Dwyn locked in the library. He sat in the window seat waiting for her to return, watching dust motes swirl in the light—chaotic as his thoughts, adrift with distractions.

Would Sorcha have changed? He had. He wasn't the young, irrepressible dwarf who came to Nations so sure of his future, the dwarf she used to care about. He'd buried that boy long ago, buried him deep where his bones could turn to stone in peace.

His stomach lurched. Would she have news of Ehrlik? Was he still at Nations or had he gone back to Norway? He'd often threatened to go home when the politics of his adopted country turned against him. Dwyn was supposed to go with him.

Across the ocean, the political climate was better for Dragons with Jenr Rok Dahl hammering away for elemental rights. But when the time came, Dwyn couldn't go. He'd seen Riordiin transform from an aloof, sensitive man into a dangerously unpredictable Dragon. He'd be no different one day. What if he killed Ehrlik next? He couldn't stomach the thought.

At the time, he told himself he was going home to forget what had happened. Old Heldasa, his grandfather, quiet mornings spent on top of old rivn with sun on his back and wind in his hair—all that would help, as if he didn't know the sins of his past would haunt him wherever he went. Sometimes he imagined a draugr must live in his skull, so many rotten memories plagued him.

When Nyssa backed through the door carrying four new plastic tubs, Dwyn jumped up, glad to put his thoughts aside.

"About time," he grumbled. "Where's the coffee?"

"In the car," Nyssa said. "I paid too much for it."

"It didn't have to be good, just potable."

"Nikl doesn't make bad coffee," Nyssa said.

"I'll get it. I need the fresh air."

She hesitated. "It doesn't smell so bad now."

He shoved past her. "That's because you haven't been breathing it for the last thirty minutes."

The warloche who had been grading papers was gone. Either Nyssa had warned him, or he had left when the stench reached him. Maybe familiarity bred contempt in Nyssa's nostrils, but when Dwyn pushed through the front doors, he stopped on the steps for five minutes, sucking in gulps of cold, clean air.

"Don't help or anything." Nyssa wrestled a water cooler out of the back of her car.

"I'm coming." He trotted down the stairs to the car and took a handle. "I'll go backwards up the stairs since I'm shorter. We'll keep it level that way."

She grunted in reply. It was heavy and the liquid sloshed dangerously.

"When we finish with this," he said, "I need a couple cardboard boxes. Nice, sturdy ones."

"What on earth for?"

"Illusions to fool your nasty spider."

"I believe I can lock a door," Nyssa said in a lofty tone.

He snorted. "Humor me, necromancer. I'm doing your dirty work."

And for the most part, she did. She let him fill each new

plastic bin with coffee, and didn't argue when he laced it with fly agaric and not powdered rosemary. But she balked when he asked her to turn the old bins into the prepared ones.

"We'll put the old ones right into the new ones. You risk contamination your way."

"Hell, it's already in the air. It doesn't get more contaminated than—well, it can," he amended. "But we need to do this."

"The plastic will break when we lift it."

"Which it might if we nested them. Necromancer, you asked me to help, so you might as well listen to me, if you want to get out of what's coming to you because you didn't fix this."

"I didn't know about it." Nyssa set her hands on her hips. "I've been necromancer for the school for less than a year. The library was closed well before I took over when Rachet retired as principal so he could go back to teaching."

"And you didn't inspect every part of the building when you assumed authority? Tsk, tsk."

"Inspection was handed off to me when I got here. Make your point."

"My point is that the old boxes are old. The new ones are new. And they are *your* idea." He let it sink in for a moment. Either Nyssa was dense or abnormally conscientious. Most necromancers learned how to shift the blame around the time their adult beards came in.

When he took hold of the edge of the first tub, she grabbed the other side. "One, two, three—"

The contents landed in the fresh tub with a sound like vomit hitting the sides of a trashcan. Dwyn gagged, and turned away, burying his nose in his beard. Nyssa ran for the other room, covering her mouth and heaving. He picked up a broom, set it on fire, and pitchforked the last of the floaters under the brown-black liquid.

Then he joined her at the door where his firebreak had been. It might be his imagination, but he was sure the air smelled better here.

Nyssa leaned against the circulation desk, breathing shallowly, pale pink beneath her red hair.

"You need to sit down?" he asked.

"No," she snarled.

"I wouldn't mock you if you did. That's some fucking bad shit."

Sweat had loosened Nyssa's tight braids. She pushed the stray hairs back in place. "What does the coffee do? I know the principle ohn vogh, but I've never seen it used ohn cor, not even for bowel jars."

He raised his eyebrows. "Bit of a lab rat, were you?"

Nyssa smiled wanly. "I've done my time."

"Well, you wouldn't use it in a bowel jar, warloche. Coffee is too much of a dwynr. Magic falls apart in it. That's why it's useful here." He glanced over his shoulder at the storage room. "I want this shit so confused it can't find its way to the nearest asshole. Speaking of assholes, where are my boxes?"

"In a closet up the hall," she said. "And the agaric?"

He chuckled. "Confused, and happy about it."

Nyssa came with him and watched him pick through the recycling. He tossed an empty paper towel box aside, but he saved a sturdy paper case. "Two more like this, and we're in business."

She actually smiled. "Your mother must have had a strange sense of humor, naming you confusion."

He grunted. "My grandfather saddled me with it. Only joke he ever made. Borrow your pen?"

"Your father agreed?"

Dwyn sat, back to the wall, threw the box up in his lap and started to write. "No idea. I never knew him."

"Your grandfather told you nothing?"

"He told me to ask my damned questions to the rocks. Said they'd tell me more than he ever would. He went to the grave silent as the same." Dwyn signed the box with a flourish. "What do you think?" Without any warning, he threw it at Nyssa. It tipped over at her feet.

"Oh, God!" She jumped back, hand over her mouth.

R. LEE FRYAR

"Smells great, doesn't it?" For a moment even he saw the black sludge ooze across the floor and heard the splash and gurgle as the mess trickled out. He whisked the box up in both arms, and presented it to Nyssa.

"Check the weight. Feel right to you?"

She sagged. "Very...realistic."

"Remember where my name is? Look for it."

She did. Her shoulders relaxed.

He grinned. His real skill was back in the storage room, doing battle with draug magic, but he was damned proud of his illusions.

"But will it fool Rachet?" Nyssa asked.

"Oh, yes," Dwyn said. "That's the beauty of a good illusion. You see best what you want to see."

And did he ever. Nyssa called him warloche. Said she valued his skill. Said she respected him. He fell so hard, he might as well have been Rachet.

Dwyn finished the library with Nyssa, taking the rest of the morning to install a clever set of faux doors and walls around his illusions to keep the old necromancer out. He also set two more firebreaks in front of the library door and the window.

"For all the good they will do," he said. "But at least it looks like we're trying."

Nyssa watched him with her arms folded over her chest. "You've done this before?"

"Something like it." He hopped down from the window seat and watched the sheet of fire creep up like a curtain in reverse. "Rivnkyf was worse. That was like fighting a wildfire from the inside out. I'd better check the classrooms next."

He stayed busy for the rest of the afternoon, ferreting all over the school from attic to basement, firing any place on the walls, floors, and ceilings wherever he found a spot of decay seeping through.

They ate dinner out on the steps of the school together. Nikl sent a table's worth of food for him at Nyssa's request, and even better—he sent beer. Dwyn took a glass gratefully. He was already oozing blood in advance of the purge that would happen in earnest later—but then, so was Nyssa. She looked almost friendly with her braid loose, shirt untucked and sleeves rolled up. She'd kicked her heels off. They stood tall and proud on the step below her. The setting sun cast his overlong shadow against the building, twisting companionably against hers. They talked.

He talked anyway. He told her about his work at Rivnkyf, reclaiming and restoring Cheyloche Daffyd's lost manuscript, and doing his best to decipher the degraded material left behind by the Northern Dragon's uncle, Cheyloche Rivnstone.

"Now there was a real necromancer," he said, speaking around a mouthful of bread, bacon, and onions. "His kennings gave me fits, but what a mind. There's more finesse in his basic necromancy than there is in the whole council at Nations today."

Nyssa leaned back against the steps. She'd eaten less than a quarter of what he had, and pressed all the beer on him. "You admired the Rivnstones?"

"I admired them, yes. Made me think there might be hope for me—they were Dragons after all."

"Yet you did not pursue a necromancer's license for yourself. I'm surprised. When I was at Nations, promising students were coaxed into areas where their talents lay."

"Who says they didn't try?" He laughed.

"Someone should have enlightened you." Nyssa smiled.

"I'm not ashamed to be a Seidoche. You necromancers need us, more than ever. Everything is falling apart. Take Rivnkyf—the single most important treasury of necromantic works in the nation, and it was a trash-fire when I got there. If it wasn't for Riordiin, the council would have let that mountain rot. They haven't had a decent leader since Byrd Oxfire died—so Riordiin said, and he was right." Dwyn propped himself up on one elbow. "Did you know Cheyloche Daffyd wrote his journals in Southern Seid? Maybe one of the last necromancers to bother with it."

"*You* bother with it."

"My grandfather spoke it. I didn't even speak Northern until I went to Nations. Lucky for me, it's not a tough dialect."

Nyssa smiled and all her teeth glinted. "No wonder Riordiin found you irresistible. What an opportunity for any Seidoche: private librarian to a council necromancer. Only he made you so much more. What a horrible tragedy for you both, Seidwendr."

The suds in Dwyn's stomach turned to liquid dread.

The illusion was over.

Dwyn fired his book in the bathroom that night. He built a containment on the near side of the sluice: water on one side, fire on three sides, no escape. Leather and pages ignited with a touch; the angry tendrils of decaying magic fought his fire.

Ata ti hacharda, you ignorant fuck. Ata ti hacharda.

He tipped his head back and stared up at the ceiling, fuming. He'd seized on the fantasy she sold and wallowed in it like a filthy draugr. He'd like to blame his foolishness on Dh'Morda, but it wouldn't make him feel any better.

He was still burning with hatred when he folded the featherbed in half to hide his book beneath it. The Eseitha stones reflected his anger in their centers; red hearts beating beneath scar-white surfaces. He believed everything Cheyloche Rivnstone had ever written about them: The tears of Dragons, lightning glass, fossilized, crystalline echoes of what once was, and can never be again.

He picked one up, weighed it, weighed his heart. He'd spent a lot of blood already. He'd spend more as his body purged itself of the poison he'd slopped around in all day, poison he could use.

He shut his eyes. Nyssa smiled at him on the steps in front of the school, laughed at his jokes, called him warloche like she meant it. Then blood spurted from her lips, and she hung, dead in the dark, like Riordiin on the cross of his sin. Her head turned upward on the stake and her mouth opened, and spoke with a thousand voices. *You abandoned us, Dh'Rigahn. How could you?*

Dwyn gasped, and dropped the stone on the bed. Dammit, he was so tired he was dreaming where he stood.

Not tonight. Tomorrow. Tomorrow he would write the spells on paper, link them to the stones by glyphs, and bathe them all in his blood—turning the fluid magic of his mind into solid stone.

He lay down, terrified to dream, but when he finally slept, he slept unmolested.

Dwyn had no intention of being ready when Nyssa came for him. He seriously considered refusing to go with her. Better beaten than a fool. Nevertheless, he woke early, lay awake until his bladder forced him up, and lay down again. He feigned sleep until sleep overtook him, and when he woke hours later, the sun was burning a bright hole in the middle of his floor.

Something clattered, and a cabinet door closed with a thump. Warily, he rose, and padded quietly into the kitchen.

Jullup looked up. "Sleep 'till noon, you do. Where are your clothes?" Sacks of groceries cluttered the floor.

"Dirty." He'd left them in the upper sluice to wash.

"You can wear your new ones." Jullup nodded toward a sack on the counter.

"Where's Nyssa?"

"She went to Whiterock this morning. Go on. I want to see how they fit."

He opened the bag: Two pairs of blue jeans of a middle indigo color, three shirts, two of them pullovers, and one with buttons—he'd never wear that—underwear, socks, two beautiful copper thelon set with black tourmaline—no. He wasn't falling for this, not after yesterday. His gasps came hard and fast. He crushed the top of the bag into a tight roll, and hurled it at Jullup's feet.

"Dwyn! What's wrong?"

"Just—leave me the hell alone." He spun around and blundered back to the bathroom. He grabbed his wet clothes from the sluice and began to wring them out.

Jullup appeared in the doorway. "You don't like them?"

"I don't want anything from you—or her—or anyone!" Hot water splattered the bathing pool like angry rain. "I'm not going to be in debt to you, too!"

Jullup set the paper bag on the floor. "These are gifts, Dwyn," she said gently. "You owe me nothing."

She walked out, leaving him steaming.

Pants that didn't sag in the crotch, a shirt with no holes in it, and thick socks that cushioned his feet were all luxuries Dwyn had done without for years. He came to the kitchen, well-dressed, hair braided, and contrite.

"I—I'm sorry about that," he said.

"Don't apologize." Jullup said. "You're just hungry, I imagine."

"That doesn't excuse it." He took the cup of coffee and bowl of oatmeal Jullup offered. She'd been busy. He had a table now, folding chairs, even a tiny refrigerator complete with a cold block so it didn't need electricity. But something was missing. A noise.

"What happened to the waterfalls?" he asked.

"Tully took them down for me this morning so I could move in the furniture." Jullup glanced around the room as if measuring. "I have a sofa to fit that corner, but it's heavy. You'll have to help me with it."

"I really am sorry." He couldn't look at her.

"It's all right." The sadness in Jullup's voice hurt him. "Besides, I should be the one to apologize. Morven told me what you did for her the other night, and what you did not do." She flushed.

"I feel rather foolish."

She sat down at the table, wiping her hands on her jeans. "I wish it had never happened, Dwyn, but I'm glad she told me, otherwise you'd already be on your way to Nations. And Tully was no worse for going to a human university when Whiterock expelled him. Perhaps it's all for the best. We all pay for our mistakes, don't we?"

Dwyn flinched when she touched his hand.

"If you truly want me to leave you alone, I will."

"No…Jullup, can I go out this morning? I need a walk."

"If you don't mind company," she said. "I'll have to go with you."

He wouldn't have had it any other way.

A path ran along the lower reaches of the creek, paved with flag-stones, present, vanishing, and reappearing at intervals. Dwyn had followed it while searching for stones. He knew where it led. Kritha bounded ahead, but Jullup walked beside him, picking up sticks and throwing them into the woods.

"I really should do this more often." She stooped to pick up a branch almost as big around as her leg. Dwyn took an end, and helped her shift it. She stopped him before he could shove it into the woods. "No, leave it. Gives the snakes a place to go in the summer. Then I don't see them, and everyone's happy. Thank you for coming this way. I've been meaning to pay my respects to the dead this season, but Nolan is always away and Tully is busy."

"My pleasure." He smiled.

They stopped when they reached the solemn row of tombs cut into the rock wall. The vast majority of them were almost the same color as the stone, sealed long ago, but the one facing them looked much newer.

Dwyn knelt and pressed his forehead to the ground, saluting the dead as a Knight should. "Whom do I honor?"

"My brother, Sullivan," Jullup said quietly, kneeling beside him. "Dh'ben, Sullivan. Paloh ti mikave, e' tu Dh'Morda." He could use the familiar. The dead were all his family.

Jullup touched the ground with her forehead as Dwyn had, then rose, brushing dirt from her hair. "He died when Nyssa was five. She's very like her father."

Dwyn had already formed his opinion of whose blood ran in Nyssa's veins—more water than blood. He didn't wonder that Nyssa wouldn't own Tully publicly—no one would claim an elemental dwarf as father—but he was surprised Jullup didn't. But then he was a stranger here and supposed to be ignorant. He said nothing.

"He was a good man—devoted to duty, to his mountain. It mattered to him, like it does to Nyssa." Jullup took his hands in hers. "Dwyn, do you know why she insisted that she carry your g'hesh, and not Rachet, or Jack?"

"My trespass was here. You had the first right of restitution."

"The right, yes, but we debated whether or not to insist. Nolan and Tully said you should be sent to Nations right away. Nyssa said no. We needed a Seidoche to rebuild the library that was lost when Asa died. She would accept the responsibility that came with imprisoning a Dragon because she believed it was her duty, whatever the cost in magic. Tully could not dissuade her."

"What did you say?"

"Oh, I wanted to keep you from the start. You were so miserable."

His face grew hot. "You don't know—"

"—what it's like. You've said." Jullup shivered. She was wearing a sweater altogether too thin. Dwyn's rune glowed warmly through her fingers.

"A dwarf uses his hands, his heart, and his treasure to win his place in a mountain. You know how to use your hands and your heart, and you have the kind of treasure Nyssa can use. She is afraid of what the regional Seidoche will say and do, and terrified that you will sabotage her efforts."

"She told you about the school?"

Jullup nodded. "We own roughly three-quarters of Rich Mountain in debt. Some folk, like Rachet, have lobbied the council at Whiterock to force Tully to restructure things, to make it easier for Rich Mountain to pay their way free. It would be the death of that mountain, but they don't see it, all they see is Ironsfork making a mistake—Nyssa making a mistake—with you."

She stared into his eyes. "I'm going to tell you something, Dwyn, and you can use it however you like. If Nyssa fails, and the building is condemned, our recompense to Whiterock for the decontamination will include your penalty. Nyssa wrote it out last night. We will not need you then, and Whiterock will not want you."

"They would send me back to Nations." He wanted to curse.

Jullup drew him closer. "She means to threaten you into cooperating. Don't let her. Instead, be willing. Say you will help, that you will do everything in your power to save what we hold most dear, and then you will owe no one. She will owe you. Will you use your skill to help us? To help Nyssa?"

"Why?' He lit up, enraged. "She lied to me—"

"Because I want to see you free. I want you to walk out of Ironsfork a free dwarf, with nothing hurting you, or holding your better nature hostage. Whatever your past has been, you are a good man, Dwyn Dragon. I've had cause to be glad of it."

He shuddered. "I doubt Nyssa thinks she owes me anything."

Jullup flicked away a leaf the wind had lodged against his braid. "These thelon look good on you. Morven chose well. We all pay for our mistakes, Dwyn. Even Nyssa."

He bit his lip. "Only my word?"

"I trust you," Jullup said.

He shuddered. "I promise."

When Nyssa came that evening, Dwyn lay resting on the couch he'd helped Jullup move. He didn't sit up. "I've been thinking about the library. I want to set a tracer in there, give it a day and see where it seeps to."

Nyssa stopped in the entryway. "Well, you'll have to hurry. I talked to the regional Seidoche today and reported the situation."

"Yes, and attended to Morven's situation, I believe. Jullup told me. But Sorcha can't do anything for seventy-two hours. We have time to figure out if the school should close or just wall off the contaminated section."

"Seventy-two hours?"

"Technically, it's forty-eight now. But I wasn't there today, so—technically—I haven't had time to assess in my professional capacity. Yesterday I was just your prisoner. As your Seidoche, I have the right to find out how bad it really is before your regional librarian condemns it for smelling like a corpse."

"I stopped by on my way home. The odor is better."

"Don't be fooled. No one should be in there longer than they must."

"I told the teachers to clear out their classrooms to the front of the building."

He sat up. "Tell me they didn't take anything out."

"I'm not a fool. It's all still there."

"Then I'll check it tomorrow."

She looked uncomfortable. "I'm meeting Tam at Wyvernholt in the morning. In the afternoon, perhaps."

That snake. She cared nothing about the library, only that he failed.

"I finished *Principles*. Still needs binding, but Jullup took the cup spell up to Nikl. I expect he'll pay the rest of what he owes soon. Perhaps you'd care to inspect my work?"

He listened to the clack of her heels as she marched through the writing room, invaded his bedchamber, snooped about for a minute, and then walked out.

"Where is it?"

He smiled. "Where's what?"

"Your personal book."

He reached behind him, and held it up. "Some things I prefer to keep close. If you are going to Wyvernholt tomorrow, who is here with me?"

"Tully."

Dwyn nodded wearily toward the counter where nine stones, dark with inky blood, squatted in shadows less dark than themselves. "Good. Tell him his fence is ready."

CHAPTER EIGHTEEN

THE TIES
THAT BIND

Dwyn didn't love the rain, but drizzle usually didn't bother him.
Given his internal combustion, he could burn off the damp and
stay warm. But this was elemental weather. Sleet mixed with
freezing rain and soaked him through. It was like being thrown
in an ice-bath and told to boil it dry. He followed Tully through
the swampy margin of the lake, complaining.

"Are there any more rivn not in the water?" He shrugged off
a trailing weed caught around his ankle.

Tully sloshed ahead, hip deep in rotting cattails. "Not unless I
take you up on the Blackfork side. It's around here somewhere."

Dwyn stayed put. He didn't dare leave the shallows. He could
swim, meaning he could paddle with his head above water as
long as he didn't have far to go, but he didn't want to try it here.
The lake was muddy, the bottom strewn with broken bottles,
sharp sticks, and slippery rocks, and it was uncommonly cold.
Everything about it repulsed him.

Tully seemed cheerful enough. But he was wearing waders
and a wool sweater that looked like three sheep went into the
weaving of it. All that stood between Dwyn and the chill was

his threadbare jacket. The new shirts Jullup had given him were in the bucket he carried, protecting his precious Eseitha stones. He'd nestled them in fabric like fragile eggs he might break if he wasn't careful. Only one remained now. The rest he'd already set in the ground with his blessing, and his curse.

"Found it," Tully grunted.

"Where? I don't see."

"Kick out to your right. Wall's there."

Dwyn shuffled forward. Tully was stamping around in water no higher than his waist, but Dwyn didn't trust the depth. As far as he knew, a Wight could walk on water as easily as a Dragon might grab a fist full of coals to stir a fire. He cracked his knee on the low stone platform below the surface of the murky lake. "Shit!"

"Felt that?"

"Fuck you," Dwyn muttered. He splashed back to the shore where he'd left the bucket parked in a clump of sedge. He eased the last stone from its nest. So many layers of illusion shrouded it, even he had a hard time seeing past the gray mask of tumbled quartz to the Eseitha stone itself, black with the magic burned in its heart.

Nine spells for nine stones. He'd bled himself weak for them yesterday, sagging over the sink while they ate his magic and drank his hate.

Open the gate. Close it behind me. Protect me. Defend me. Attack my enemies. Avenge my wrongs. Renew my strength. Assist me in my escape. Confuse the hell out of these people determined to destroy me.

The dwynr stone would be the last to go in. All the others he had placed in the marshy ground with Tully standing well away, seemingly uninterested, although Dwyn knew both chieftain and necromancer would revisit every site, making sure he hadn't played them false.

They would find nothing amiss. Nyssa would walk this wall, and find what he'd promised: faithful stones, true to the meanings chased in the stone of the end cap on the intact rivn.

She would not see how he had twisted them to his advantage. The Eseitha made the best rivn stones he'd ever seen—hungry though, as insatiable as his bones. They took everything he gave them willingly, unlike the two river rocks he'd been forced to use. Most stubborn stuff he'd ever met. But it was done. With the wall under his control, all that remained was to break the g'hesh. Once his books were in his hands he didn't care if Nyssa wounded him to his death. He'd die properly—a free dwarf. God would not find him wanting.

But he stood up to his knees in the lake, hesitating. Everywhere else, from the intact rivn near Forankyf to the broken stub he'd done by the road, Dwyn had watched the stones sink slowly underground. When he placed this stone, the water would be well over his head.

"Need some help?" Tully lit a cigarette, sheltering his lighter from the drizzle.

Dwyn sucked in a nervous breath, let it out, sucked in again. "You know those things will kill you."

"I don't aim to live forever. What's wrong? Afraid of a little water, Dragon?"

Dwyn wasn't about to admit the truth. He debated: Sit down all at once and freeze immediately, or ease in inch by inch while the ice crept through his crotch, around his stomach, through his chest, his armpits, into his nose…

"Why cut it? How is a rivn in this part of the lake a problem? It's right on the shore."

"It didn't used to be. When I leased the land to the city for the reservoir, the channel ran through here. That rivn was the right height to take the bottom out of a boat."

"You let humans cut it?" Surely, he hadn't heard that right.

"No. *I* cut it, Dragon," Tully said. "Now, I took off a half-day of work for this, and it's nearly noon. Get it over with, will you?"

Something heavy and cold settled in Dwyn's chest. Cut it like it was a dead tree, a hazard, not a priceless relic of the time when the magical South still had some grandeur. Mud eddied around

Dwyn's legs like blood in the water. "*You* cut it?"

Tully sucked hard on his cigarette. "I did."

He flared. "Who died and gave you the right? Up north, if you defaced a historical artifact, they'd shove your ass so full of fines you wouldn't shit for a month."

Tully's flat voice turned poisonous. "This is the South, not Nations."

"It's our legacy as dwarves and you destroyed it." He clutched the Eseitha stone tightly.

"Ours?" Tully laughed. "Ours? You're a bigger fool than I took you for. When was the last time anyone called you warloche and meant it? Tell me that." Tully waded toward Dwyn, spawning whirlpools. "Where are your folk? What clan calls you son? My own parents took my family name away for being a Wight. They made my brother chieftain, and I was glad. I would finally be free. I hated them, I hated this place, I hated the quarry. Then he shot himself, Dragon. He left me his damned legacy and all the debt that came with it. And so I took my name back. I took what they stole from me. I remade this mountain, and I will do whatever the hell I want with it."

"No right gives a dwarf the authority to do what you did. Even a necromancer won't cut the heart out of a man the way you've cut the heart out of this mountain." The Eseitha stone was a magnet in his hands, pulling him forward, tugging him down. He braced his feet apart in the slippery mud, slid, and bumped his shins on the decapitated rivn.

"I did what I had to do. I saved this mountain. I saved myself. Just as you did when you killed your necromancer."

"That was an accident," he whispered. He stared at Tully, half-expecting to see Riordiin's face accusing him.

"Like hell it was. You're no more incendiary than I'm flooded. You knew what you did when you cut your ties to your old life. So did I."

"You saved nothing," Dwyn said, "and neither did I." Dizziness swamped him. He shifted the stone into his left hand and reached out with his right, groping for the top of the old rivn. He squatted, and the water embraced him.

When he opened his eyes, the world was green—all green— even the amputated rivn, cut clean a foot above the base. Tully's boots straddled the remains of the ruined wall, winding away into the lake across a murky leaf-strewn bottom. Dwyn set the stone at the base of the rivn and pressed it down firmly—a quick in and out and done. Then he tried to stand up. He couldn't.

His hand was stuck. He let go of the stone, but the ground clenched his wrist like a vice. He set his other hand at the base and pulled, and braced his feet, straining. But instead of break- ing free, he sank further in, pulled down, down, down by the weight of water, the weight of the earth.

He fought, he thrashed, he jerked his head violently upward. He could see the rain-dark sky, six inches away or less, but he couldn't get there. Hold on. Don't let the water in. Tully would see he was in trouble soon and rescue him. Just. Don't. Breathe. Air bubbles gurgled past his eyes.

He gasped unwillingly. Water flooded in, and his conscious- ness ebbed.

A warm wind, sweet and gentle, caressed Dwyn's naked body. He lay with his cheek pressed in mud, gasping. Air, blessed air, rushed into his starved lungs. Gratefully, he took the breath that had been stolen from him. He rose to his knees, covered in waterweed and frothy blood, the afterbirth of some terrible accident.

The breeze swept over him again, carrying scents he loved: mayapples blooming, sweet sassafras leaves crushed between a boy's fingers, the intoxi- cating fragrance of sourwood in the springtime. He squinted. The morning was as bright as May.

The last thing he remembered was the muddy bottom of the lake. Had he died? But if he had, torment awaited him in the underworld—dread judgement of his failures. He lay on a high mountaintop, surrounded by a towering ring of black stones. Huge trees grew nearby, bigger than any he'd ever seen, green and alive with birdsong. Submerged in deep peace, he couldn't be dreaming. Dreams tortured him. They confused the hell out of him these days. This—this was different.

"Where the hell am I?"

"You are home. Finally, you have come home." He answered himself, not aloud, but in his magic. It was ancient Southern Seid, as deep as the earth, and fierce as his fire, but there was a tenor in his voice he didn't recognize.

His skin crawled. "Who are you?"

"Don't be afraid, mh'arda." Voices. Not one, but many, joined together in a chorus. He reached for his sword but found nothing there. Panic seized him.

"Who are you? What do you want with me?" He thrashed, but the ground held him down.

"We want to love you. Will you love us?"

Pleasant warmth spread through his body, filling his lungs, his arms, his legs, his groin. Delicate pebbles kissed his lips, soil clung to his thighs, and he was hard in an instant.

"What's happening? I don't understand." His breathing became shallow as that strange magic breathed as one with him, excited, torrid with longing.

"You will understand when you love us, beloved. We must have you. We have waited so long to mate. You understand what it is to want, to need, to take, as we must. We can never let you go."

He struggled. "Why?"

"It is the bond, beloved. You offered your body to us and we gave you our soul. Now we are one, and we will never be apart. You promised."

"I promised you nothing! Nothing!" But his fury faded into an overwhelming desire to stay here, to love completely, and to never let go. How much of that longing was his? How much belonged to the strange magic fondling him? He didn't know. He began to fear he didn't care.

"Your life. Your love. Your strength."

His heart beat the truth in his chest. This was the kind of love he craved, the desperate kind he'd always been willing to die for—hard, passionate, and dangerous.

He kissed the earth until his mouth was full of mud. Sour, wet magic rushed in, redolent with a musty flavor of power so old it belonged to another world. He roared his passion, fire surged out of him with volcanic fervor, and he clawed the ground, his body ablaze with lust.

"Dragon!"

The mountain moved sensuously under him and the dark sky rained kisses over him. Who was calling? He couldn't leave. He wasn't done.

"Dragon!"

Somebody hit him, slapped his face. He couldn't breathe. They had said he would die, and he didn't care. Lips pressed against his, and a hand covered his eyes. He laughed. Riordiin was kissing him awake one morning at Rivnkyf, when they were new lovers, and their bed was all he thought of. A long beard brushed Dwyn's face.

Don't leave, beloved. You can never leave us. Silk sheets wrapped around Dwyn like water weeds, and he knew he was truly in love, and he was deliciously terrified. Only it wasn't Riordiin's voice.

"I'm sorry. I'm sorry I left. I'm sorry I killed you." Nothing came out of his mouth but bloody bubbles.

Lead filled his lungs, lead like a void. Old Isolde gazed at him with yellowed eyes as she died, with one long, clawed hand stretching toward him. *Remember us. Remember us, Dragon. Do not forget your promise.*

"Isolde?"

Then Riordiin came at him in the dark, and Dwyn cried out for help, and then a knife thrust out of the ground, split Riordiin in half, spiked his heart right out of his chest. Riordiin's twisted corpse dripped gore while Dwyn wept. "What have I done? What have I done? Forgive me."

The dead, dark eyes glassed over. Screams of anguish. It was still his voice, but the hatred in it paralyzed him with dread. Riordiin's dead mouth moved. *What have you done to us? What have you done, Dragon? You have betrayed us, necromancer's filth! We should have killed you!"*

He writhed. "Paloh mhu! Let me wake up. Oh, God, let me wake up." Voices. So many voices.

"Lokey, did you get hold of Nolan?"

"Fucking hell. What happened?"

"Help me with him."

"He's on fire."

"You've got your Dad's protection, hang on to him. I have to force the water out of him."

Chains gripped Dwyn by the wrists, and he tried to fight. Lips pressed against his lips, and suddenly—air. He wanted air. Yes. He gagged.

"Roll him over."

He saw the void cell at Nations again. Isolde spoke. "Get it out, Dragon. Water is not good for you."

He vomited, gasped, and opened his eyes.

He lay on his side in a wet clump of reeds. Black ashes, thick and tarry, spilled from his mouth. Rain blinded him. He blinked and saw the lake, gaping like a dark throat inches from his face. He yelled, but it came out as a hopeless gurgle. The lake wanted him dead. Some magic in it had dragged him down and tried to kill him.

"Easy." Someone gathered him up, someone with long, fragrant red hair. Jullup. Dwyn threw his arms around her and buried his face in a long, soft beard...not Jullup.

"Lokey." Dwyn clung to him, treasuring the warmth of life after his watery execution.

Tully squatted in front of him, eyes wide with concern or fear—Dwyn didn't know, and he didn't care. He wanted Lokey's arms. His soul was on fire, but in the cold flesh of his body he trembled with the need to be comforted.

"We need to take you back to Ironsfork," Tully said. "Do you understand?"

There was something he hadn't understood. Something he was supposed to understand. Something important. "What?" He spit blood and froth.

"You almost drowned." Tully yanked him up. "Problem with the g'hesh."

"I don't...understand." Dwyn grabbed the softer, yielding frame of Lokey on his other side.

"Neither do I, and that's the last time I do anything with you unless Nyssa's around. At least it's over."

Was it over? He thought so, but he didn't have the courage to look back at the lake.

He stumbled between Lokey and Tully, glad for their company. Before, whenever he was sick or hurt, Dwyn wished to be left alone. Not now.

Lokey pushed Dwyn into Tully's truck.

"Don't leave me," Dwyn cried, grabbing his arm. "Please."

Lokey's eyes were beyond blue. Briefly he touched Dwyn's knee. "It's okay."

The door closed with a clap of thunder, and Tully roared away. Dwyn banged his head on the window glass when a pothole tossed him sideways. Something peculiar had happened. He felt frozen, but desperately hot at the same time. He closed his eyes.

"Stay awake, you hear me?" Tully yelled.

Something with the g'hesh. That wasn't right. He must have been dreaming, but he always remembered his dreams. He barely remembered this one. There was a mountain. And a ring of stones. And...his head throbbed as he tried to reclaim his vision.

Tully and Lokey carried him into the mountain. Dwyn didn't know what he would do if they tried to take him through the waterfalls—scream and try to kill them both, maybe, anything to escape the miles of dirty water tumbling over him. He didn't care if he never drank another glass of water in his life. He never wanted to take a bath again. No water, ever again.

Tully slapped the waterfall in front of him, and it became a veil of fog shimmering harmlessly on either side of the doorway.

Dwyn began to cough in paroxysms when Tully and Lokey dropped him on the couch in his quarters.

"Undress him," Tully ordered. "I'll wait for Nolan topside. Wrap him up; get him warm."

"You're not going to leave me with him?"

"I need to call Jullup; she'll want to come back to take care of him. Go on. You love a naked man anytime."

"Fuck off." But Lokey gently took Dwyn's shirt, lifting up one arm at a time. "You're a hell of a lot of trouble, Dragon."

"I'm sorry." What was he sorry for? Something he had done, something stuck in his magic like the leaves in his hair.

Lokey pulled Dwyn's shoes off, then his pants. "Next time you drown, do it when I'm not around. I didn't plan on watching you cough all afternoon. I've got places to be. It's Dh'Morda after all."

Lokey left him, naked and shivering on the couch, but he came back quickly with the wool blanket from the bed. He tucked it around Dwyn. "I hope Dad hurries. He was in surgery when I called."

"I was afraid."

"Never liked that lake," Lokey said. "Even in summer, it's way too cold."

"There's something evil in it."

"You should know—you drank half of it."

Coughing rattled him; he spit up froth.

"Are you going to throw up?"

"No." He thought about how Nyssa had choked the air out of him with the g'hesh on the floor of her library. If she so much as constricted his throat one more time, he'd have no trouble killing her. He'd kill her bare-handed.

"You want a drink?"

"No water."

"I didn't say water." Lokey walked out the door where the waterfall was back to splashing and returned in a few minutes, holding a square bottle in his hand. "Tully's rotgut," he said, rummaging in the kitchen cabinet. "Is this the only glass you have?" He pulled out the one stoneware mug Jullup had left to go with Dwyn's one plate and his one set of silverware.

"Don't entertain much."

Lokey's laugh sounded like a perfect mating of Jullup's bird trill and Morven's bark.

The vodka was terrible stuff—fire and brimstone, just what Dwyn needed. His frozen body warmed with it, and the burn spread to his heart, his arms and his legs, not unlike what had happened when—he choked and handed the glass back to Lokey. The rim gleamed red where the blood on his lips had stained it. Lokey looked at him curiously, shrugged, and downed what was left in two gulps.

"You're not afraid of my blood?" Dwyn asked.

"Should I be?"

"Some people are."

"Some people are stupid." Like his laugh, Lokey's smile was summery, all sunshine and blue skies.

Dwyn wanted him to keep smiling. He hoped Lokey wouldn't leave. He needed Lokey to help him believe he wasn't dead in that terrible place where the water swallowed him whole and his magic ebbed away and rotted with the leaves at the bottom of the lake. He wanted to tell the nisse how much he loved to look at him, to listen to him, and how good he would feel if Lokey would undress and cuddle under the blanket with him.

"You. Your music…is beautiful."

"What do you know about music?" Lokey's face hardened.

What had he said? Something wrong. "Enchanted. Not easy… to do. You should…work…with music." But talking took his breath away. He panted, struggling against the fear that maybe he wouldn't keep breathing.

"I have my work. Music is my hobby."

"Why magic?"

"Because I can't help it," Lokey snapped. "Where's Nolan?" He paced the floor.

"You are as beautiful as your music."

Lokey reddened. "And you're an ass, like Nikl. Worse than Nikl. At least he has the decency to flatter a man instead of twisting a knife where it hurts."

"Don't want to hurt you. I want...to make love to you."

Lokey slammed the glass down in the sink.

Nolan hurried through the door, followed by Tully. "How is he?"

"Talking nonsense." Lokey glared at Dwyn and stomped out.

What had he said? *Don't leave. Please.*

"How long was he under?" Nolan listened to Dwyn's lungs and felt his pulse.

Don't leave us. You can never leave us.

"Not long. Two, three minutes. His hands were jammed under the rivn. Might have taken me another minute to pry him loose."

"I want him at the hospital, dammit." Nolan stared down at Dwyn. "He's all wet inside."

"I did the best I could," Tully said. "Did you call Jullup?"

"She's coming. Nyssa has her phone off, or she's too deep, but Jullup will find her." Nolan turned as if he meant to go.

"Don't leave...me." Dwyn coughed. Something horrible had happened in his magic, and he was undone.

"No one will leave you," Nolan said.

"I died. There was a mountain, and I promised. What did I promise?" He clutched Nolan's hand convulsively. "I don't know. I'm afraid of what I promised."

"What's he going on about?" Tully leaned in, and Dwyn jerked away from the odor of lake water, dead and stinking.

"He's disoriented."

"I promised. We said—I don't remember what we said."

Tully's eyebrows drew together. "Should we put him in the void room? If it's the g'hesh—"

Nolan shook his head. "No, it's not the g'hesh, but even if it was, he needs all his fire to dry out."

"You think he'll be sick?"

"He might end up with pneumonia, but let's hope he's Dragon enough to burn the filth out of his lungs."

"I promised," Dwyn whispered.

He should have died.

CHAPTER NINETEEN

LONELY, AFTER ALL

"He coughed all night," Jullup told Nolan the next morning. "Couldn't sleep, and he wouldn't eat."

"I'm not hungry." Dwyn wrapped his arms around himself. He was tired—exhausted, in fact—but he refused to sleep. He couldn't face dreaming. He couldn't go back to the mountain and listen to the dead sound in his own voice as he spoke of promises, wants and needs, or worse, relive in agonizing detail his moments in the lake with the ghosts of autumns past floating around him.

"The more he coughs, the less likely he'll end up with pneumonia." Nolan set his stethoscope on the table next to Jullup's coffee cup. "You need to eat, Dragon."

"I'll throw up."

"And then I want you up."

"I'm too tired."

"Moving makes your lungs work. I don't want you stagnating like the swamp you inhaled yesterday."

"I can't! Damn you—I can't." Flames spurted incontinently in all directions. Dwyn sank back in the couch cushions, too miserable to apologize.

Nolan and Jullup withdrew to the entryway.

"What did you use for him?" Nolan muttered.

Jullup folded her arms over her chest. "Amber and amethyst. I'd like to add hematite, but he's entirely too anxious right now. Tully had to take down all the waterfalls because he wouldn't stop crying. And he won't talk to me. Something is terribly wrong, and I don't know how to help him."

Nolan kissed Jullup's forehead. "He'll feel better once he moves around. And *you'll* feel better after some sleep."

"Someone has to stay with him. Where's Nyssa?"

"At Rich Mountain with the Seidoche," Nolan said. "I'll take over."

"You need your rest, too."

"I'll rest after I've got him up and eating. Don't you worry about us, mh'arda." Nolan stroked her cheek.

Mh'arda. The whispered word lingered like a bad dream. Dwyn balled up in the blanket, determined to never face the world, or his memories, again.

Not only did Nolan get him up, he chased Dwyn up and down the length of his quarters—entry to kitchen, into the bedroom, around it and back again. Every time Dwyn stopped to cough, Nolan pounded his chest like a drum. If he wheezed, Nolan clamped a mask over his nose and puffed in a spray that smelled like burnt garlic and tasted of metal. Only when Dwyn began to rant about doctors who killed elementals in the name of science, did Nolan let him sit, and fed him a warm broth that was more salt than soup.

"You spiked it with something, probably," Dwyn said.

"Stop fuming, little Dragon." Nolan wiped his sweaty face on a dish towel. "Drink that, go to your bed, and rest."

"I don't want my bed. I don't want to hear running water."

"Tough. I'm taking the couch where I can keep an ear on you," Nolan said.

It smelled like a coffin, his little alcove bed, and it stank like the lake. *He* stank like the lake. Dwyn allowed Nolan to cover his legs and his belly with the blanket, but not his chest. He didn't want anything near his face where it might smother him in his sleep. It had taken all his self-control not to whip the breathing machine out of Nolan's hands. He thought perhaps Nolan had known how frightened he was, because the doctor spoke kindly then, touched his back, and reminded him that he was strong, he was alive, and he was safe. But only one of those things was true.

He coughed and rolled onto his side, distinctly drugged. Some of his fear detached and floated away as he watched Nolan leaving the room.

The doctor's long braid hung squarely between his shoulders where the enormous tattoo lay hidden beneath his shirt. Something that large could be used as a permanent memory transfer...or perhaps a magic transfer. Was Nolan a Seidwendr for one of the Rivnstones at some point? Dwyn tried to run through the list, but it was no use. His mind continued to empty like a wastebasket as he struggled to stay awake.

Nolan had said Nyssa was at Rich Mountain with the Seidoche. Nine years later, Sorcha was still getting the jump on him. His thoughts blurred into an image of the school. He imagined himself running to the library, fire flowing like blood over the floors. The dim storage room presented itself, a draugr crashed through the wall, he drew his sword, and then everything turned an underwater shade of green. A dagger stabbed out of the earth and impaled him.

They drowned the Dragon. He lay in a shallow pit, his cheek puddled in froth pouring from his nostrils. He watched from the immortality of his flame as hooded necromancers moved through the shadows. The bells sewn on the hems of their robes chimed a funeral dirge.

This wasn't how he should die, gutted like a fish on a slab. When a Dragon died, he was supposed to become one with the mountain he loved, giving his flesh wholly in the way he'd always given his magic. His life. His love. His strength.

This mountain had betrayed even his most basic faith. Death was already beginning to rot him.

"It is almost over, Chieftain," a stooped necromancer said to a taller dwarf standing beside the burial pit. "We will seal him over once the bones are made and his fire contained."

"When it is finished, his curse—"

"—will be our strength," the necromancer finished.

The chieftain leaned over the funeral pit. His breastplate was as black as his hair, made of intricately fitted pieces of obsidian woven into a copper shirt. In the center, a silver tree embraced a mosaic moon of white gems. "Mellow him. The bones of my son must not stink of his carcass."

The necromancers surrounded the Dragon, pouring sweetly-scented water over him. Mud filled in his mouth.

Dwyn convulsed, gagging. He clawed at the gray shroud clinging to his face. "Meda!" He was drowning. They'd chained him to the bottom of the lake and his mouth was full of mud. He thrashed up stones, sticks, and leaves. He lashed out, and hit something soft and yielding. A muffled curse sounded in his ears.

"Calm down!"

"Meda!"

"Easy! Easy, buddy." Nikl yanked the blanket from Dwyn's face.

Dwyn sat up, grabbing Nikl in his panic. "Save me! Don't let them drown me, please. I don't want to die."

Nikl hugged him, rocking him back and forth. "It was just a bad dream. It's not real. You're safe here with me."

"Don't—don't let go. Don't leave me." In the desperate darkness, he could still hear the bells.

Not bells. A bell. He glanced around Nikl's arm. A ghost of a cat stood in the doorway. When Dwyn squinted to get a better look, it turned and ran into the next room, jingling down a corridor of light streaming from the kitchen.

"You," Dwyn whispered, gazing up at Nikl's round face. "You came."

"Told you I would, didn't I?" Nikl held him at arm's length. "Not dead yet? You look about half-way there."

Dwyn found his smile.

"Dinner's almost ready. I figured you'd be out for another half-hour at least, the way you were snoring."

"I'm not hungry."

Nikl laughed. "You'll eat. Got a sure cure for death here. A sniff of it would bring you back. Good for your blood, too."

"You sound like Nolan."

"Buddy, I've forgotten more about magical nutrition than Nolan ever knew. But you tell him I said that; I'll poison you." He stood, tall, wide, and confident. "Up on your feet. Got to eat to live."

Dwyn slid to the floor. His knees buckled. Nikl picked him up. *Damn.* The chef was all muscle under his bulk.

"Nolan said you'd be a little drunk but you'll be okay once I get some food in you." Nikl practically carried Dwyn to the kitchen. Once there, he deposited Dwyn in a chair and bustled to the counter. All his ardchuk were out, and skillets, pots, pans, knives, and cups spawned on every available surface. The rich, savory aroma of good things cooking perfumed the air.

Nikl stirred a pot briefly, sniffed it, and then ladled thick, maroon soup into a bowl. He dusted it lightly with pink salt and carried it proudly to the table. "Happy resurrection." He submerged a spoon reverently into the broth.

"What is it?"

"Borscht."

Dwyn scooped up a suspicious spoonful and tasted. He gagged and started coughing.

Nikl frowned. "I said eat it, don't breathe it."

"I don't like beets!"

"I don't care whether or not you like beets. Eat. It's good

for you." Nikl took a plate from a towering stack next to his portable range and slid a pancake on to it. He topped it with red sauce from another pan, garnished it with whipped cream, folded it over with the spatula, and brought it to the table. "I'll do you like I do the kids. You eat, you get dessert. You don't eat, *I* get dessert."

With a grumble, Dwyn picked up his spoon again.

It wasn't bad. In fact, if not for the beets...no, it wasn't bad, it was delicious. Dwyn tasted tomatoes and cabbage as much or more than the beets, and fresh dill—good, strong, earthy flavors, sweetened with dark honey. He would never have picked this out to eat—maybe if he was starving—but he finished every bite.

Nikl grinned. "Seconds?"

"Where the hell did you learn to cook like this?"

Nikl chuckled. "That's your magic singing out for what's good for it." He brought Dwyn a second bowl of the soup along with a slice of buttered rye bread. "Dip it in the soup if it bothers your throat," he said, but Dwyn didn't need any instruction there.

Dessert was a crepe with sour cherry sauce—absolute heaven with the sweetened cream. Nikl left Dwyn alone to eat it in rapturous silence and busied himself cleaning his pots and pans in the sink. The white cat twined between the chef's black pants, leaving scuds of hair behind.

"Your cat?" Dwyn asked.

"Hoped you wouldn't mind. Hungry are you, March?"

"March?"

"Short for Marchpane—almond paste, you know. I can't leave her home alone. She eats things. She stays in my office during the day and thinks impure thoughts about the birds in my garden." Nikl unwrapped a paper package, put the contents on a plate, and set it down.

"That's half a fish on there," Dwyn said, gesturing with his fork.

"We had grilled catfish for lunch, well, most of us did." Nikl scowled. "That red-headed Seidoche from Whiterock was there, along with a couple of necromancers to carry her train. They ate without complaining. She, on the other hand—" Nikl sat with a grunt of displeasure.

"Sorcha."

"You know her?"

"Nyssa knows her," Dwyn hedged.

"They should be best friends," Nikl said, "Never satisfied, either of them."

Dwyn laughed and promptly went into a spasm of coughing.

Nikl pushed a glass of water at him. "You know you have the creepiest laugh in the world, right?"

Dwyn hesitated, then picked it up and drank. "Did Sorcha say anything?"

"Besides 'my fish has too many bones in it'?" Nikl's eyes narrowed slyly. "Am I supposed to know why she's here or something like that? I'm not a mountain man, you know. I'm just hired help."

"Is that why you're here? Hired help?"

"You want me to leave?"

Dwyn spoke with his mouth full. "Hell, no."

"That's more like it."

"I only thought you'd be busy with Dh'Morda." He blushed.

Nikl snapped his fingers. "Which reminds me." He rummaged through the ten million pots and pans and brought out a cup, dandelion yellow, embossed with the green logo of Rich Mountain Kitchen. "Free coffee for life, as promised."

Dwyn flipped the cup over. A Dragon rune had been neatly worked into the clay.

"We sold out of the plain ones by noon yesterday, but I wanted yours to be special."

Dwyn touched the rim. Coffee surged in, bottom to top, hot and black, the way he liked it.

"There's my question and my answer," Nikl said. "I wondered about the range."

"I set it for the distances you gave me." He took a sip. God under the earth, now he knew he was alive.

When he opened his eyes, Nikl was smiling again, but there was something real in it this time; it wasn't that jaunty, superficial thing he'd been wearing.

"What?"

Nikl looked down. "Nothing—I'm just glad you're okay. The way Jullup talked, I figured you were on a ventilator down here."

"Then you *are* here to take care of me."

"Partly. You need taking care of, and between you and me— just us, mind—I'm not as busy with Dh'Morda as I'd like."

"I'm sorry."

Nikl waved a hand airily. "Can't say I'm surprised. Rene took pity on me, and I wish her the best of the season. She's the future of the place after all. One day her sack of a father will give his bones to the earth, and we'll have a real chieftain, one who doesn't let folk like Rachet run us into the ground."

Dwyn choked on his coffee. "Your mate is the chieftain's daughter?"

Nikl nodded. "Rene. Yes. Made that cup for you. She may be a tompte, but she's smart enough to kick me out of bed after a week. She's Nyssa's lover after all. She'll keep us lock-step with Ironsfork. That's how you survive around here."

Dwyn snorted in derision.

"So, what happened at the lake?" Nikl asked. "Jullup said maybe a seizure?"

"I don't want to talk about it."

"You probably don't remember much."

"Probably." He didn't want to think about it either. "You said partly—partly here to take care of me. What's the other part?"

Nikl folded his arms behind his head. "Okay—since you asked, I wanted to protect my claim. I heard there was a red-headed devil here yesterday trying to get the jump on me."

Dwyn couldn't help it. He laughed again. "Look, I wasn't in any kind of condition to fuck anyone yesterday."

Nikl engulfed Dwyn's left hand in his huge white mitten. "Oh, buddy. I didn't mean it like that. No. It's just—" His strange gray eyes turned misty and confused. "I didn't want you to forget I asked you first." A curious note of fear rang in his voice.

"You really want me that much?" Dwyn licked his lips nervously. He wasn't sure he liked Nikl's soul. It was too hungry, too much like his own.

"Yeah." Nikl twined his fingers through Dwyn's. "I'm lonely, and I think you're lonely too."

He wasn't lonely—not for Nikl. Lokey, maybe. Lokey was so beautiful just looking at him could make any man lonely. But Lokey would never have him, and Nikl was here. "There's something we need to do first. Are you okay with that?"

In answer Nikl laid both arms, soft side up, on the table facing Dwyn. Shell-pink skin glistened under his white hair.

"Now?"

Nikl rolled his eyes. "No...I thought I'd sit and gaze into your eyes for a few hours, have a glass of wine, talk about your problems—buddy, come on. I'm not afraid of your fire, you're not afraid of my storms, and we'll both die before we grow old." Blood flushed into Nikl's capillaries, turning the sensitive skin purple.

Dwyn gripped Nikl's elbows. The Thunderer's skin felt sticky, wet, and cold—wonderfully cold. Pleasure flooded Dwyn. He loved giving his Dragon's blessing. The flames that set him apart couldn't hurt someone the moment his fireproofing took effect. It was almost like belonging.

"Ata ti arde: ard d'tu dalo mi mhu seidr, mh'ardr, mhu benr. Forever I love you: from my fire I give my word, my heart, my blessing."

Nikl's pupils dilated. He gasped. "Ata ti arde: logowh d'tu dalo mi...y mhu...siedr, mh' ardr...oh...oh...oh."

"Nikl?"

"It's great, just—wow. Your magic is strong. Damn. It's so

strong." Nikl slumped forward onto their linked arms, slopping blood everywhere.

"Nikl?" Dwyn shook himself free.

The cat came over, licking her whiskers. She looked at Dwyn and opened her mouth in a soundless meow.

"Not my fault. I don't think." Nothing like this had happened before. Some people vomited. Riordiin and Sorcha had. Ehrlik only got dizzy. No one had ever fainted. Maybe Thunderers and Dragons didn't mix. Dwyn squeezed Nikl's cold hand anxiously.

A good ten minutes passed before Nikl stirred. "Where'd you learn to hit like that?"

"Sorry."

"Got to catch my breath." Nikl leaned back, and the white cat jumped up in his lap.

Dwyn carried his plate and cup to the sink. He turned off the ardchuk by touching them—they understood his fire perfectly. He glanced over his shoulder. "Are you—are you going to leave me?" he asked, hesitantly.

"No. No, buddy," Nikl whispered. "I'm here for you. I even took off tomorrow morning. Doesn't hurt to give the kitchen a chance to play while the boss is away. It's Dh'Morda after all."

"I didn't mean to hurt you."

"You didn't hurt me." Nikl stood with a grunt, displacing the cat. It hissed. "Be nice. It's his house."

"Hardly." Almost as he said it, Nikl's protection hit Dwyn like a wave. He pitched forward over the sink, heart thundering. If he moved, he thought he might fly apart. Nikl embraced him from behind, and Dwyn sank helplessly into that massive chest while Nikl's magic roared through him like a full-force gale. "Damn," he said weakly.

"Looks like you're not the only one who packs a punch. There's blood all over us, warloche. Let's clean up." Nikl kissed him.

Dwyn swore he could taste the sea.

Dwyn wouldn't get in, but Nikl plunged into the bathing pool up to his armpits before ducking completely under water. His white beard floated up first, and then he resurfaced, shaking ice pellets out of his ears. He pulled his thelon from the ends of his lopsided braids. "Water's cold, buddy. I could use a Dragon."

Dwyn shook his head. "No thanks." He'd consented to dangle his legs in the water. That was all. His heart thudded nervously.

Not like this was his first time, but it felt like it. It had been so long. What would Nikl think of him? He'd never been adept at making love. Ehrlik always said he blundered about the bedroom as badly as he blundered about life, all balls and no brains.

Nikl elbowed up next to Dwyn on the edge and grinned. "Come on in. I'm not going to let you drown."

"I'm fine right here. Not like I can't clean up." Dwyn scooped a handful of water and poured it over his legs.

Nikl set his hands on Dwyn's knees. "Allow me." He shouldered in, boldly pushing Dwyn's legs apart. His silver braids unraveled and streamed like seaweed over Dwyn's lap. Cool fingers climbed over Dwyn's cock with practiced skill.

"You mind?" Nikl's breath was as cold as snowfall.

In answer, Dwyn tangled his hands in Nikl's hair, inviting him in. With a sigh of contentment, Nikl's initiating kiss became a deep-throated gulp of desperate need.

Dwyn trembled as he kneaded Nikl's back. He'd needed this. Oh, how he'd needed it. His ears were full of the sounds of Nikl satisfying his lust, his hands were tangled in soft, slippery hair, and his gaze rivetted by the milky whiteness of the Thunderer's lightning-bright skin, flickering from silver to blue to gray.

Nikl came up for air. "Is that good?"

"Don't stop. Don't." Dwyn pulled Nikl in again.

With a laugh, Nikl grabbed Dwyn around the hips, pulling him closer to the edge, closer to bliss. All he knew was this moment, this pleasure. Nikl sucked him like he knew him, knew exactly what he wanted. There were no memories clouding Dwyn's mind, no old lovers haunting him, just cold wind and hot fire, what sex should be. Too much. Too quick. It would be over too soon. It was always over too soon. He gasped and spurted, thrusting forward.

And tumbled into the water. "God—" he went under, and came up spluttering. "—dammit! What'd you do that for?"

Nikl folded Dwyn into his arms, shaking with laughter.

"I ought to kill you!"

Undaunted, Nikl tipped Dwyn's head back and kissed him. He tasted dark, wild, wine-rich apples, still warm.

The bottom of the pool was solid under Dwyn's feet, but he couldn't stand. "I ought to kill you," he whispered.

"I told you, didn't I? I said I would fuck you so wonderful it would be worth the wait."

On the floor next to the pool Dwyn massaged Nikl by hand until he came. Nikl wouldn't let him do more, although Dwyn begged.

"I feel bad," Nikl said, sliding back into the bath with Dwyn when they were finished. "I was supposed to feed you and put you to sleep—Jullup's orders. I promised myself I wouldn't make love to you, but you're too damned hard to resist." He kissed the top of Dwyn's head.

"You did feed me," Dwyn protested. "And you knew I'd sleep better in your arms than any other way."

Nikl nuzzled Dwyn's neck. "You are so easy to please. You went off almost before I got hard."

"Can I help it when you suck me like that?" When was the last time he'd fucked or been fucked without trying to impress? Maybe never. It was common practice for dwarves to get to know a friend in bed this way, drinking their lust together like a companionable bottle of wine. But Dwyn had never had a friend, not unless he counted Ehrlik, and Ehrlik was his mentor first. Sex with him was always a test. It wasn't fun.

This had been fun—no strings attached, no love to screw

everything up. He nestled into Nikl's huge arms. The bath had grown comfortably warm, a mix of Nikl's natural ice and Dwyn's volcanic heat. He could easily fall asleep here.

Nikl stroked his hair tenderly. "I've worn you out."

"Well, you can carry me to bed, Nikl."

"Call me Nik. I like you, Dwyn," he said. "You're not pretty—not like Lokey—but your hands. Oh, God. I love your hands."

"Thank you."

Nikl laughed. "Thank you? What's that about? Come on, buddy—tell me I did you right. Tell me you loved that."

What could he say to a man who made him feel so good? He fell back on his old standby—his favorite poem from *Mhu Mordr.* "When I kissed you, beloved, you spoke of the pleasures of your bed, of yielding to our need. Admit me to your chamber. Drink from my fountain, and let me be drunk on your wine."

"Oh, yeah…talk dirty to me, buddy, talk dirty to me." Nikl ran his fingers through Dwyn's wet beard.

Dwyn rolled, twisting in Nikl's arms, and pushed Nikl's beard aside. He wanted all of Nikl against him for a kiss. His hand froze on a long pink stripe visible on Nikl's wet skin.

The goblin cross. Incomplete, it ran down his belly part-way, but didn't reach his limp dick, drowned underwater.

Dwyn's fire faded to a dull, frightened orange.

"What's wrong?" Nikl's eyes were soft as moths.

"You're…you're part-goblin."

Nikl let go of him. Lightning flickered under his skin. "You got a problem with that?"

Dwyn backed up. He stood waist deep in the water, colder now than it had been, as cold as the lake. "No—"

Nikl never raised his voice, but the fury of a hurricane filled it. "Can I help it if my asshole of a father bred me on a goblin?"

Dwyn's lungs tightened; he couldn't breathe. Riordiin's angry face loomed out of his memories, throwing punches. "Nikl— I'm sorry—I didn't mean—"

"Nik! I told you to call me Nik!"

"It surprised me, that's all!"

"I thought you wanted love. I guess I thought wrong. I thought you'd understand. You'd know what it's like, being hated for who you are. I've been hated most of my life because of this," he said, churning the water into whitecaps. "Now you're going to shun me because I'm a kobold? What the hell kind of racist are you?"

"Don't be angry—"

"You want me to leave? Get my goblin ass out of your clean water?" Nikl pulled himself onto the side.

Dwyn crept forward. "No, please, Nik. I want to have you, Nik, have all of you." He worked his way up from Nikl's feet to his crotch. If he could just get Nikl aroused he'd be safe—he'd done it so many times to save himself pain when Riordiin was angry.

Nikl slid into the water with a heavy splash. Dwyn jumped back, terrified.

"You're shaking. Why are you shaking?" Nikl cupped Dwyn's face in his big hands.

Dwyn flinched. "Please don't hit me—"

Nikl's face turned the color of chalk. "You thought I was going to hit you? Oh, God, Dwyn! No. I would never do that. No matter how angry I got, never." He pulled Dwyn close, and kissed the top of his head, rocking him gently. "Forgive me. I didn't know, sweetheart. I didn't know."

The chef's musky scent of yeast, honey, and cigarette smoke cloaked something familiar, a dangerous fragrance of decay that was stronger in necromancers like Ehrlik and Riordiin. Dwyn melted into the embrace.

"Please forgive me," Nikl whispered.

"I forgive you." Dwyn kissed Nikl's trembling lips.

Dwyn lay awake in bed for a long time. He felt much better. The food and the bath had helped. Or was it the elemental air breathing through his forge like a bellows?

He kissed Nikl, lying beautifully naked beside him. "It did surprise me, that's all. You'll have to forgive my foolishness."

Nikl grunted affectionately. "What a pig I am, huh? Tell you I love you and jump your ass the moment you get a little upset. You know what you ought to do? You ought to hit *me*. Hit me hard."

"But then you wouldn't make me breakfast in the morning."

Nikl laughed. "Oh, Dwyn." He combed Dwyn's hair with his fingers. "You asked if you could have all of me. Buddy, you had all of me the moment I saw you in that courtroom."

Dwyn settled in Nikl's arms. He couldn't reconcile his uneasiness with the feeling of peace and contentment holding sway over the moment, but perhaps it didn't matter. This was one night, not a lifetime, and it felt good to be with a man again, to twine his sensitive arms against equally sensitive flesh.

Nikl wasn't Lokey. But he was solid, and present, and Dwyn was lonely. Nikl had been right about that after all.

CHAPTER TWENTY

A LIE TOO
HARD TO SEE

"Ata ti ardam, Dh'Morda mordre, ti arcam he," Nikl sang. He
had the pitch of a jaybird.

Half-way through his second cup of coffee, Dwyn set aside
the page he was scribing. "You'll spoil your cooking," he called
into the kitchen.

"Listen to him," Nikl said, ostensibly to the cat, "Ungrateful
Dragon. And here I was singing him a serenade."

Dwyn left the writing room and strolled into the bacony
atmosphere of the kitchen. "When were you going to tell me
the truth?" He sat at the table, arms folded behind his head,
grinning. It was five in the morning, far earlier than he liked to
be awake, but waking to find Nikl wrapped around him, hard
and ready, was the kind of alarm clock he liked.

"Truth about what, sweetheart?"

"That's a very pretty European accent you have there."

Nikl gaped in mock outrage. "I told you no lie! I was born in
Oklahoma."

Dwyn chuckled. "When did you move to Europe?"

Nikl transferred a pair of eggs to a plate already loaded with a crepe and a thick slab of bacon. His face lit up like lightning on a horizon somewhere far away. "I was six."

"Your clan is Norwegian, then?"

Nikl snorted. "What clan?" He put a single egg on his plate and brought both to the table. "When I was nine, my magic came in. First thing I did was spawn a tornado. You know how that story ends. They threw me on the plane without telling anyone and sent me home. I waited two days in the Oklahoma City airport for my mother to come get me. Pissed her off. She cut me loose around fifteen to fend for myself. I haven't been home since." He dug into his egg savagely. "Dwyndoche, do you mind if we don't talk about my family? They give me indigestion."

Dwyn thrilled. Ehrlik used to whisper the diminutive in his ear in the darkness. *Dwyndoche, my little confusion, how sweet are you? You love so hard there's nothing left for me to do.*

"I figured you'd sleep," Nikl said. "Not many folk like getting up this early."

"You make it worth it." Dwyn put a forkful of fresh crepe and leftover cherries in his mouth and shut his eyes in ecstasy.

Nikl chuckled. "I could get off just watching you eat."

They did the dishes together after breakfast. Nikl scrubbed, breaking the ice from his knuckles every so often with a pained grimace. "Tell you what, Dwyn. How about I borrow Jullup's oven tonight and make us a peppercorn-crust tenderloin for dinner? I'll bake some bread at work this afternoon."

"Sounds delicious, but I'll be late getting back if Nyssa doesn't come soon to drag me by my chain to Rich Mountain." Dwyn reached over into Nikl's side and let the heat flow out of him until the soapy water began to steam. "Is that better?"

Nikl caressed Dwyn's hand. "You've no idea," he said. "You know, I've not had a hot bath since I was a kid? Not until last night. Everything about you is so warm, Dwyn."

"Dragon's prerogative," he said.

Nikl leaned over and kissed his cheek, so tenderly that Dwyn turned into it and opened his mouth, hoping for more, but tasted only bittersweet sadness on Nikl's lips.

"What is it?"

Nikl growled under his breath and plunged his arms up to his elbows in the soapy water. "Nothing—it's nothing. It's just, I hate it for you, being stuck. I've been stuck myself, but at least I could leave and get stuck somewhere else." He smiled ruefully. "But then I would never have met you, would I? You wouldn't have stopped here. You'd have been gone before the smoke settled."

Dwyn laughed.

Nikl winced as if he'd been hit. "I mean it, Dwyn. I'm glad I met you. I'm glad I got a chance to love you."

Those eyes—damn, he could get lost in those eyes if he wasn't careful. He smiled. "Me too." He flicked a soap bubble into Nikl's beard.

Nyssa came for him at ten. Dwyn was sewing the cover for *Mhu Mordr* when he heard Nikl go off like an angry tea kettle.

"So, you've finally come to check on him. I was beginning to think he's right—you really don't give a fuck whether he lives or dies."

"Is he ready to go?"

Dwyn knotted the thread, nipped it clean with his ripper, and set the sewn book aside. He packed up his writing case. He wouldn't be caught without his tools today.

"He damned near drowned, and you did nothing. You and Tully, you treat elementals like shit. You don't even give him more than a day to recover before you drag him off."

"You're working yourself up, Nikl Phar. I recommend you stop. Where is he? Still in bed?"

"I know people—people you'll have to listen to—"

"Take my advice, Thunderer." Nyssa's warning rang out harsh and cold. "You do yourself no favors interfering. He chose this way, and you chose yours. I can't think why you would risk what you've gained in our community for one night's pleasure—if it was pleasure, which I doubt, if he's as small there as he is everywhere else."

"I don't know what you're talking about." Nikl sounded out of breath.

"I can smell him all over you. Is he worth it? Would he risk the same for you? Now, is he awake, or is he sleeping?"

"Wide awake," Dwyn said, settling his glasses on his nose as he left the writing room, case tucked under his arm.

Nyssa stood just short of the entry, robed in her knee-length white wool coat, and armed with her stav. She had Nikl backed up against the counter, but when she saw Dwyn, she lowered her hand. "Where's your jacket? It's cold outside."

Dwyn shook flames over his arms.

Nyssa grimaced. She turned and disappeared into the entryway.

"Are you okay?" Dwyn asked. He touched Nikl's shoulder anxiously.

Nikl shivered. "Yeah. She just pisses me off. Even Rene says she can be a bitch sometimes."

"All the time as far as I'm concerned." Dwyn lowered his voice. "Nik, if it's bad for you to be around me, then don't. I'll understand."

In answer, Nikl pulled Dwyn close. His breath smelled coffee-sweet. "I'm always going to be here, as long as you need me." He closed his eyes and buried his nose in Dwyn's hair. "God, I could love you forever."

Dwyn froze. His passion burned out of control but his fear screamed at him to let go, to leave, before he did something he'd regret. He tangled his fingers in Nikl's beard, torn between kissing the man breathless or pushing him away. It would be easier to keep his distance if he didn't kiss him. But the salt-sea taste of him, the way the wind moved in Nikl's hair, the feel of those soft lips against his were too much. He tilted his head up and found Nikl's mouth.

It might have been five minutes or a year before he stumbled out of the eye of the storm. Dazed, he followed Nyssa under the waterfalls—up and running this morning—sure he'd fucked up.

"Sorcha is waiting for us," Nyssa said.

"At the library?" He clutched his writing box as the elevator rose.

"No. She called the council together this morning. We are summoned to the haneen. You will go with me and report—"

"We don't go."

"What do you mean we don't go?"

Dwyn strode ahead of Nyssa through the upper hallway, caught the door handle and pulled it open, ushering her through. "Exactly what I said." The ice in the air took his breath away. "Damn, you weren't kidding! It's freezing out here."

"It's not a good idea to insult a regional Seidoche by refusing to appear at a council meeting," Nyssa said, pulling her coat tightly around herself.

Dwyn's angry gust of smoke danced over the treetops. "Who's in charge here, you or Sorcha? I am *your* Seidoche. Be in charge, necromancer."

He sat in the passenger seat and set his box between them when Nyssa got in.

"You might be interested to know that Tully drained the lake down to expose the rivn. The current from the river still runs through that area when it's full. The base had eroded. You merely got your hands caught under it."

He shuddered. "I don't want to talk about it. Your fence is fixed and that's the end of my part."

"I must inspect your work, and you will be with me when I do."

"Might as well strangle me. I'm not going anywhere near that lake."

Nyssa smiled slightly. "There's no need for that. I will take you to the Blackfork side. No lake."

He grunted non-committedly. A few more days and he'd have no more necromancer. No more g'hesh. No more prison. No more Nikl.

Dammit, that hurt. He'd undoubtedly fucked up.

"I was concerned about you," Nyssa said, turning onto the Rich Mountain road.

He folded his arms over his chest. "I suppose it would look bad if a prisoner died because of your blatant neglect. I doubt that would go over well in an election for head of the regional council."

Nyssa's only response to his jab was a subtle smile. "How long have you known Sorcha Flintridge?"

Any other day, he'd have been furious at the direction of the conversation. Now anything was better than thinking about Nikl. "A while. I met her at Nations."

"Were you friends?"

"We've worked together."

Nyssa gripped the steering wheel with both hands and leaned forward. "She's been our regional Seidoche here for less than two years. I don't know much about her, only that she was the one who expelled Morven from school."

"Sorcha never suffered insults to her authority lightly."

"Yet you recommend we defy her."

"Absolutely. It puts her hackles up, and she doesn't think well when she's angry."

"That doesn't sound helpful."

He huffed. "Okay, necromancer, tell you what—let's not do it my way. Let's go to the meeting. Let her condemn your building in front of everybody where she knows she's all in the right. You can protest all you like. She won't budge. She's like you— she plays by the rules when they suit her game. But she doesn't have my experience with this kind of thing, and I'd like her to remember that."

He didn't think Nyssa would listen to him, but when they reached the split where the road divided, Nyssa turned right toward the school instead of the main mountain.

The wind blew harder here than at Ironsfork. Rich Mountain was taller, and the trees were too stunted to provide any protection against the gale. Nyssa buttoned her coat when she got out.

Dwyn spotted a necromancer's car—a black sedan with the logo of a white mountain plastered on the door. Runic letters spelled out the name, Whiterock. A few cars, well dusted with native dirt huddled together in one corner, but one, a Corvette, bright as a cardinal in the snow, sprawled over two spaces. Probably belonged to Sorcha. She'd always liked fast cars and fast money. Fast men, not so much.

The entryway was crowded with furniture, filing cabinets, chairs, bookshelves, and orderly rows of student's desks.

Dwyn kicked a chair leg anxiously. "This doesn't look like all of it."

"Cheyloche's classroom, Samara's." Nyssa pointed out each group. "Rachet would not empty his room."

Dwyn touched a child's desk. The top strata was a scribble of purple glitter—Una's desk. He jerked his fingers away, startled, and stuck both hands in his pockets.

"Nyssa, I finished the download, but I'll check it on my machine before I leave." Lokey balked in the hallway, clutching a thumb drive in one hand, and a slender tablet in the other. He stalked toward them, hackles up, red hair rippling over his shoulders. "Tell me, Dragon, is it necessary to haul me out at Dh'Morda to do your job? Don't they teach you Seidoche anything about technology? Or is it all old books and blood up there?"

Fire leaked around Dwyn's fingers. "Hardly," he squeaked. "But you wouldn't want me working around your computers. They won't take a Dragon's heat."

"Not my computers—they're all yours to destroy now."

"They may be fine," Dwyn argued. "They might not have caught the rot yet. I'll check the room now, if you like."

Lokey flipped the thumb drive in the air and caught it. "I have all I need right here. Go do your little song and dance routine.

I'm not sticking around for it."

"If we don't have to destroy the computers, I'd rather not," Nyssa said. "Lokey, go with him."

"Get Cheyloche to do it."

"But you're already here." Nyssa smiled.

"I'm going to Norfolk tonight."

"You have plenty of time. I'm going upstairs to check the tracer."

"You set one?" Dwyn was surprised.

"On your recommendation, Seidoche," Nyssa said.

"I'm not your donkey, Nyssa Irons," Lokey yelled as Nyssa walked away.

Nyssa turned, smirking. "No. You're my cousin, and I know why you're going to Norfolk and not to Magazine like you told Jullup this morning. Shall I tell her what you're up to?"

"Fuck you." Lokey shoved the thumb drive into his pocket. "Go on," he said to Dwyn. "I'll put this in my car and check it later, unless you have to sniff it first."

Dwyn said, "If it was bad, I'd have smelled it when I came in, ripped it out of your hand, and burned it at your feet already."

Lokey stalked off.

Dwyn used the time to go through the desks, the chairs, and the bookcases, burning anything with traces of decomposition. There was plenty of it. Una's desk was the first thing he torched. He was incinerating a shelf of encyclopedias when Lokey returned.

"A herd of people are headed this way," Lokey said. "I guess you're in trouble now."

"Show me your room. I'll likely clear it." He took off up the hall to the place where he'd seen the boy Talus working on the first day.

"It's not *my* room. I quit doing this shit-work when I graduated," Lokey said, but at least he was coming, and at a good pace.

"And left Ironsfork to study music," Dwyn said.

"Can't you ever leave things alone?"

"You did? I was only guessing," Dwyn said, slipping to the side when Lokey stormed past him.

"Why do you care?" Lokey unlocked the door to the computer room. "It's none of your damned business—" he slammed the door behind him "—what I do with my life."

Dwyn faced Lokey, furiously warm, nostrils full of Lokey's whiskey-rich scent. "Because your music is full of magic. It's your natural language, and I'm in love with language."

Lokey's hackles fell.

"See?" Dwyn said softly. "Old books and blood got something right about you, didn't he?" He stalked off through the room, lip raised, sucking in any odor that might indicate decay. "So why'd you quit?"

Lokey scowled. He leaned against the wall beside the door, glaring. Dwyn was sure he wasn't going to get an answer out of him, but finally Lokey said, "I didn't quit. I wasn't good enough."

"Who told you that?"

"The people who mattered. Do your job, Dragon, and quit telling me I'm not doing mine."

"Your words, not mine," Dwyn said, moving from station to station. He brushed the sensitive equipment, murmuring the revealer he'd been using for the desks. The computers were slow to answer him. Lokey was right. When it came down to it, he preferred old books and blood.

"Yeah? Well, I guess maybe I don't like starving when I could eat, and walking when I could drive. A second-rate musician isn't worth the piano he plays."

"Did they tell you that? The people you say mattered?"

"You flunk out at Carnegie and tell me it doesn't matter."

"So, test again," Dwyn said. "You could, you know. Who's holding your chain, Lokey Irons?"

The door in the entryway slammed and a hubbub ensued as a contingent of warloche threaded the barricade in the hallway. "Let me do the talking," he warned. Before Lokey could protest,

Dwyn flung the door open. And there she was.

Curly strawberry blond hair wiggled loose of her braids, as always, plotting further escape. Tawny eyes glittered, onyx-hard as ever. Her short beard twisted over her chin so playfully he could almost ignore the sharp white teeth between unsmiling pink lips. Sorcha hadn't changed one bit.

Then the fierce mouth curved upward at the corners. "Dwyn Ardoche," she said, extending her hand. "Why aren't you dead, warloche?"

His stomach somersaulted. "Dammit, I knew I forgot to do something."

"You'll miss your own funeral if you're not careful."

He glanced around Sorcha at the dwarves grouped behind her. "I beg your pardon, warloche, I heard about the meeting, but I asked if I could come here first. Nyssa is upstairs, checking a tracer. Lokey, thanks. I appreciate your help this morning."

Lokey stared at Dwyn like he had fire spurting from his ears. "My pleasure," he said, stiffly, but at least he didn't sabotage the act by rolling his eyes.

Dwyn turned back to Sorcha. "Have you been to the library yet? There are a few things I want your opinion on before decisions are made."

She didn't buy it and she didn't like it. But she couldn't refuse a request from another Seidoche, even a disgraced Dragon working off a penalty.

"I finished my assessment yesterday, Seidoche. Where were you?"

Drowned. "Sick," he said. "I hope you found my containment adequate?"

"Hardly. There were boxes filled with the most unbelievable things." Her lip curled.

Time to take her down a notch. "Oh, don't tell me my illusions fooled you."

"Fooled me?"

He scanned the group with Sorcha, grinding his teeth when

he saw the twisted face of Rachet in the back. He'd have to revise the damned things before Rachet got another crack at them.

"Morning, Seidoche." Nyssa came down the hallway. Cobwebs of broken magic trailed behind her. *Not good.* He needed to check that tracer for himself.

Nyssa's voice dripped apology. "I'm sorry we missed the meeting. My Seidoche insisted—"

"Yes, he explained," Sorcha said, tightlipped. "Well, since we are all here, I can only assume you'd rather hold the meeting in this stink."

"I'm perfectly comfortable with the containment Dwyn has provided. We count ourselves fortunate to employ the Seidoche entrusted with the restoration of the library at Rivnkyf."

It made sense. Nyssa wanted Sorcha to view her as competent, having utilized everything in her arsenal to deal with a problem that she should have dealt with long ago. Dwyn wished she'd thrown him to the floor with the g'hesh instead. How he hated her, hated that she was using him, hated that something in him still craved recognition. The sooner he got out of this damn place, the better off he'd be.

"This way, Seidoche." He shouldered Nyssa aside and blazed up the corridor. He took the stairs ahead of Sorcha, two at a time. "Won't take a half-hour."

"Dwyn. Stop. I want to talk to you."

At least she'd had the decency to wait until they were out of Nyssa's sight. He didn't stop walking. "You could have talked when it mattered."

Sorcha spoke in that softly disappointed voice she used whenever he'd done something, once again, to offend her. "This isn't any way to speak to a friend. I thought you were dead, Dwyn! You didn't write. You never called."

He yanked the library door open and rounded on her. "What reason would I have to think you cared? It's over. It's done. Go on thinking I died—that will be easier for us both."

"Oh, God." Sorcha gasped.

He sighed. It did look bad.

He had meant for Rachet to pick the illusions over, but it bothered him to see his work upset and scattered about. Scorches marked spots where the artificially created contamination had stained the floor. Necrophilia sometimes plagued old necromancers who found their bones growing weak, but the idea of Rachet dredging out baskets of fake corruption to nurse in the privacy of his home made Dwyn want to gag.

He jerked his head toward the back. "Nothing to worry about—the problem is back there." He lifted the illusion with a word. The fire-filled boxes burned brightly, dispelling shadows.

"Dwyn—"

"Leave it, will you. I spent nine years pretending it didn't matter. Come and look at this with me, and I can go on pretending." He led the way to the storage room.

The smell was markedly better. The coffee had helped the decomposition better than he'd hoped. Cockroaches scattered when he kicked one of the plastic tubs gently, but Sorcha didn't flinch. She made her inspection in silence while he leaned against the transcription desk, wrestling with emotions that choked him worse than any g'hesh. He'd be professional—that would help. He would not remember the endless flirting, his clumsy seductions, and how embarrassed he'd been when she left him before dawn at Dh'Morda after one bad night in his bed. He would not remember sobbing in her quarters, begging her to help him, to tell him what to do because he couldn't go on working for Riordiin, it would kill him—oh, how he loved the man, but it would kill him—

"I didn't abandon you, if that's what you think," Sorcha said quietly.

"I didn't say it."

She rolled her eyes. "What could I have done, Dwyn? Come down and held your hand in the void cell? Told you not to worry, that everything would be fine and nothing would happen to you? You killed him, Dwyn!"

288 R. LEE FRYAR

"It was an accident! You know I never would have hurt him if I could've helped it. I loved him, Sorcha."

Sorcha groaned. "You should never have gone back to Rivnkyf. I told you so."

Dwyn shot sparks to the ceiling. "Yes, you told me so! Must be wonderful you can say that, you told me so! Makes you feel better, does it? Does it help you sleep at night? I needed your help, not your fucking sympathy!"

Her nostrils flared. "You are such an asshole, Dwyn Ardoche. You asked me for help, I told you what to do, and you didn't do it. You screwed up, like you always do! So it's my fault you're hurting, my fault you killed a man, my fault you're working in this shit-hole, and not because you want to, because you're a prisoner—Dwyn, I'm not getting you out of this. You are not my problem anymore!"

"Fuck you." He kicked the desk chair over and blazed a trail back into the library.

"Nice to see you haven't changed!" she yelled after him.

He flopped down on the floor next to the empty boxes. Back in the storage room, Sorcha muttered to herself as she moved among the boxes, like a draugr bumping clumsily through his memories.

He fumbled through his illusions, gathering the boxes together, filling them all with fake sludge, fake misery, fake despair. No draugr would ever come to such a bait. The real stuff was needed, and it wasn't here now. But the draugr hadn't gone. The tattered magic Nyssa had tracked out of the attic was proof of that.

"Dwyn."

He stiffened. "Don't talk to me."

"You're in order back there. Good job."

"Thank you."

"Now, clear the smoke out of your ears so you can hear me, and so help me, if you interrupt, I will slap a silencer across your mouth you won't be able to peel off without taking half your beard with it."

He stared stubbornly up, silent.

"What good would it have done if I'd gone to the council and told everyone what I knew? That Riordiin raped you bloody whenever he felt like it? That he beat you senseless more than once? That you were terrified of him? Afraid that the next time—always a next time with you—that he'd kill you? What would they have done? You were his Seidwendr, Dwyn. They were looking for a reason to convict you of murder, incendiary or not!"

He opened his mouth, shut it.

"I could see it coming, even if Ehrlik didn't. He came to me after your trial and asked me to testify. I told him to go fuck himself. I didn't want your death on my conscience. I saved your damned life and you have the gall to say I abandoned you?"

He was bleeding to death. She had just ripped his heart out. Hate would grow there and not a thing in the world could heal the wound. Ehrlik had lied.

Ehrlik told him he'd asked Sorcha to speak at the trial, not afterwards. He said she wouldn't help because she was afraid— afraid for her career, tarred over by association with him. Or had *he* supplied the reason? God under the earth! Why were lies so hard to recognize when he couldn't lie to save his own soul?

Dwyn didn't mean to cry, but he wept, huddled against the cardboard boxes filled with illusions. He sobbed his heart out, and Sorcha had to hold him because he was broken, and no one could put him together again.

CHAPTER TWENTY-ONE

THE END
OF A LIFE

Dimly Dwyn became aware that Sorcha was guiding him to the window seat, holding his hand, saying something.

"I'm sorry. Maybe I was wrong, and one of those necromancers just needed to hear Riordiin was insane and you'd have gone free. It was self-defense, what you did. Ehrlik knew that and so did I."

He shook his head. "No. You were right, Sorcha. You were always right."

"You told me there was never any justice for elementals."

"There isn't." He sat, head against the window glass, replaying the aftermath of the trial, flailing for the truth. Memories crashed around him, breaking apart, cutting him.

Ehrlik wanted to take him away. He helped Dwyn pack and took him as far as Kibola, the Silver City, a hundred miles east of Nations and a world away from trouble. Dwyn didn't feel any better. He lay face-up on the silk-covered bed, weak from recrudescence and beaten raw by guilt.

Ehrlik sat next to him, facing him down like a prison warden. "I'm going back to Nations to straighten this out. You stay here. Until the paperwork is done, we can't leave the country."

"Ehrlik, I can't go with you."

"You'll do as I say. I can't believe it's come to this. I'll lose my job at Nations over this and all I've worked for. No. Don't cry, please don't cry."

Dwyn buried his face in Ehrlik's lap.

Ehrlik petted him until his tears were spent. "We're in this together, remember? Stay here and stay out of sight. I don't want to lose you. I love you and I'll always take care of you. Now kiss me."

Dwyn kissed Ehrlik like it was the last time because it was.

A day after Ehrlik left, Dwyn picked the tabah on the suite of posh rooms rented to Ehrlik, hitchhiked to the western edge of the mountains, and hopped a train going east before slowly making his way South.

He told himself he was ashamed. He couldn't live with the man he'd disappointed, and he believed it, even as he hid deep in the abandoned mansions of Appalachia, old Rigah Tarn, afraid to go home right away. Ehrlik knew he came from the Cumberlands, and he might...

"Come for me," he said aloud. Every muscle in his body tensed.

"My necromancers? Not likely. You should have seen the pair of them yesterday. Took one look at your boxes and bolted. I didn't exactly linger myself." Sorcha said, sitting beside him.

Dwyn jerked. He'd been miles away. Who was she talking about? Oh, yes, her necromancers from Whiterock, stewing in Nyssa's office over what should be done with a too-old building filled with too-strong poison.

"Are you all right?" Sorcha rubbed his shoulder. "You're thin, even for you. You were recrudescing, weren't you? That's how you ended up in this mess."

"More or less."

He couldn't tell Sorcha about what Ehrlik had said. He couldn't stand to hear her say "I told you so" again. But what if she still talked to Ehrlik? He'd mentored them both at one time. What if he kept up with the one student who could still make him proud? Dwyn chewed his knuckles.

"I don't blame you for taking a penalty over exemption. I wouldn't want to go to the colony. I still haven't recovered from the time you took me there. I couldn't believe people lived like that."

He cleared his throat. "Has he spoken to you? Since the trial?"

"Ehrlik? No. You were always the golden child. He's Seidoche over Nations now. He sent me the announcement four years ago. Looked as arrogant as ever."

Fire crackled through Dwyn's braids in the ensuing silence.

"I would help you, Dwyn, but there's not really anything I can do. Regional Seidoche don't have much authority outside of our area." Her narrowed eyes and grim mouth gave her a menacing expression, but her sympathy had always been fierce, as likely to wound as comfort.

He forced a smile. "No. You were right. I'm not your problem anymore."

The slits narrowed further. "Maybe you *have* changed."

"You can do one thing for me."

"Or not."

"Give Nyssa a fair hearing. The penalty is all that's standing between me and extradition. I don't want to go back to Nations, and Nyssa will bend the terms if I fix this situation. I could even go free." That last was a stretch. His bones complained.

Sorcha laughed. "You trust her. Are you out of your mind?"

Yes, and almost frantic to escape. He jerked his head in the direction of the storage room, and the rotten books swimming in the oblivion he'd created. "She let me go this far, didn't she?"

"Only because she expects you to fail, Dwyn."

"You think I don't know that?"

Sorcha folded her arms across her chest, leaning against the stone wall like she could hold it up if it fell. "What's fair in your book, Dwyn Ardoche? I could condemn the building today, and all of Whiterock would thank me. They've subsidized this school for half a century, and they're tired of it."

"You could." Dwyn's touch left scorch marks on the mouse-eaten fringe of the cushion as he fingered it. "I've already told Nyssa if you do, I'll be bound by guild oath to agree with you. But think about it. No contractor will take on the demolition. It will be just like Rivnkyf, festering and leaking for years, if it doesn't pour over into the main mountain. Imagine the disaster if that happens."

"Dwyn—"

"So let me take care of it. You'll get all the credit—wise decision-making, above and beyond your duty—you know that shit buys re-election." He waited anxiously.

She glared at him. Then she sighed, and lightly batted his head with the back of her hand. "Put your hair out. I'll see what I can do. But I promise you nothing. I owe you nothing. Where is this tracer Nyssa was checking?"

"She set it in the attic—"

"The attic? Dwyn!" Sorcha's face went crimson.

He held up his hands. "It's still a far cry from Rivnkyf—I was in the goddamned sewers chasing draug magic at one point."

"Give me your sword. I'm going to cut your head off. You're obviously not using it anymore."

"Sorcha—"

"I don't know why I let you do this to me! I feel sorry for you, and the moment I offer to help, you make me want to kill you!" She stamped her foot.

Once upon a time, he would have laughed and told her she was really in love with him, then curled his arms over his head while she beat him with whatever she was holding at the time. Not now.

"Sorcha. Please." He wanted to say so much more. He wanted to tell her how good it felt to have a friend restored to him, when he'd just lost the one who mattered most.

She rolled her eyes. "I'll look at it. But as far as this goes, I don't know you. We worked together, I knew you were involved with Rivnkyf, and that's all." She rose, brushing down her olive-colored suit, dusting her hands clean of his ashes.

"Sorcha, don't talk to Ehrlik."

She stared hard at him. "You don't trust him either."

He said nothing.

"I never understood why you trusted him in the first place."

"I had my reasons," he muttered.

"Probably something stupid like being in love with him."

If only that was all. The painful laugh that came out was a sob. There was nothing he could say that would explain, and nothing he could do that would make it right.

"Okay, I won't talk to Ehrlik. Now show me this tracer. I might as well see everything before I perjure myself."

Dwyn wouldn't leave the library until he was happy with his illusions. Rachet had heard him say the word, and a man who came looking for a lie would be almost impossible to fool. Sorcha tapped her foot impatiently, waiting for him to finish.

"Dare I ask why you're making a maze out of this place?" she asked as Dwyn wove the walls of the storage room out of magic and drew in the miserable little desk, the closet, the empty shelves, and the open bathroom door.

"You can. You know I won't lie."

She snorted. "Meaning you won't tell me anything. My God!"

"What is it?" He jumped, reaching for his sword. He felt so edgy now, it was hard not to see shadows stretching out to grab him. Even at his lowest moments of exile, he hadn't felt so hunted outside of dreams.

"She's let children in here!" Sorcha stormed for the door, but she was too late. Una burst in. Her face was a tragedy mask.

Dwyn whipped his sword out. "What's wrong? Where is it?" If the draugr was still there, he might catch it before anyone else detected it.

Una recoiled, tears streaming down her cheeks. "You killed him! You killed him!"

"Child, you must leave," Sorcha ordered. "This is no place for you—"

"Shut up!" Una snarled. Her voice dropped an octave. "You killed him," she whispered.

"What are you talking about?" Dwyn let his sword tip drop to the floor.

"Winston!" she wailed. "He was the best rat! And you killed him." Abruptly Una flung herself at Sorcha and buried her wet face in Sorcha's suede jacket.

Sorcha pushed Una away. "Winston?"

"Hell!" Dwyn stomped out of the library, a pillar of fire, and raged toward the entry where he'd left the furniture awaiting disposal, along with a glass aquarium containing one large, plump piebald rat—contaminated, of course, along with everything that had come from Samara's classroom.

A riot was in progress when Dwyn rounded the corner. Before he could speak, a short, black-haired dwarf jumped out of the argument and ripped into him.

"What do you mean by burning my file cabinet? My students drew these for me!" She shook a scorched manila folder in his face.

He backed up. "Who the fuck are you?"

Una ducked behind the woman. Fire leaking down Dwyn's front was usually a good deterrent, but now that the teacher had a student to protect, she surged after him, wild as a fighting hawk. Her eyes bulged, her hair stood up all over her head, and blood-red nails reached for him like claws. "How dare you talk to me that way!"

"This is why I said not to move things out of our rooms, Samara!" Rachet screeched. "I knew this would happen. I warned Nyssa—"

Sorcha tried, but reason shouted at the top of her lungs didn't have a placating effect. "Warloche, we have the right as Seidoche to destroy what we condemn without consulting anyone, least of all ordinary teachers without any training at all in—"

"I may not have much training," the bald teacher said, looking up from his blackened encyclopedias, "but these were almost new. I don't see why they couldn't have been decontaminated. A proper Seidoche would—"

"He's not a proper Seidoche, he's a Dragon, Northslope." Rachet waded through the clutter of burnt desks, pushing them aside as he came.

A ferocious roar filled Dwyn's ears, completely disconnected from the noise around him. It came from underground, surged into his feet, thrust upward through his legs, and pumped into his blood. He raised his sword as Rachet reached him. He meant to sheath it—or so he thought in the small sane part of his mind that wanted to retreat to the library and barricade the door. The angry Dragon blazing in his heart wanted to crack the old man over the head with the pommel stone. He hesitated.

Rachet's bony fist smashed into Dwyn's left eye. His glasses broke, and jammed sideways, cutting him. He stumbled backward, sat down on a scorched chair, and tipped over entirely when the legs gave way. His sword caught Rachet in the jaw, but it was only the horny tip of the blackened chestnut core the old necromancer felt, not the blades. He howled like Dwyn had stabbed him.

All the air whooshed out of Dwyn's lungs when he hit the floor. He couldn't move. He couldn't breathe. His legs were tangled up with the chair, but this time he was not helpless, chained under water. All he could think about was taking that burning chair and smashing it across Rachet's back.

Dwyn thrashed his way free, skin brightening to the color of hot coals. Rivers of lava crept down his chest, rolled down his arms and dripped from his fingers.

"What is going on?" Nyssa's calm words cut through the noise.

"He killed Winston!"

"Look what he did, Nyssa! My pictures, my pictures..."

"They aren't even old, and I don't smell anything—"

"Necromancer, you should not be letting a child anywhere near this place."

"Neil will hear about this! Your Dragon took his sword to me, I'll go to the council—"

What was left of the chair scraped the floor. Nyssa loomed over Dwyn.

"Are you going to choke me?" he gasped.

"Are you all right?" Nyssa extended her hand.

Dwyn rolled over, pushed himself up, and yanked off his shattered glasses. "Either you throw that bastard out, or so help me, I'll kick him down the stairs. I don't care if he is a hundred and fifty." He retrieved his sword, and leaned against the wall, one hand clapped over his eye, coughing. He'd generated a putrid smoke in his rage: fermented apples, sulfur, and swamp water.

Nyssa faced the screaming, yelling mass huddled among the desks. "Listen to me."

He didn't know how they heard. But had she placed a silencer, the quiet could not have been more absolute.

"I understand this is hard—far harder for you than it is for me. You are all so connected to this place. It must feel like the end of a life. But if we wish to save anything, we must be prepared to lose things that are dear to us. I promise you, as necromancer over this school, I will do whatever must be done to save it."

"He killed—"

"Te bene, Una. It will be well."

Whimpers followed Nyssa's statement, but no more sobs. Una allowed Samara to hug her.

"Neil." Rachet whimpered too. The chieftain had been standing in the entry way, flanked by the Whiterock necromancers, but he stepped forward and took the old man's hand.

"Rachet, please. Nyssa is doing the best she can—come with me."

"Necromancer?" Sorcha's clipped voice shattered the calm.
"You allow children into this contaminated area?"

"No, warloche, I do not." Nyssa's marble face didn't change
expression. "Have you finished your inspection?" She looked at
Dwyn.

"Just the tracer left," he said.

"I will await your report in my office. In the meantime, I will
see to the disposal of these...things." Nyssa's gaze roved over
the skeletal furniture to rest on a charred body curled up peace-
fully near its exercise wheel.

She didn't scold him. Didn't even threaten him. Dwyn fled to
the attic stairwell.

Sorcha muttered behind him as she climbed, "No, warloche,
I do not. Ugh. That woman. You'd think she shit roses to hear
her talk."

Sorcha dropped her own tracer in the attic while Dwyn
prowled the space, brushing cobwebs from stacks of desks,
old blackboards, a broken dissection table, and stacks of dusty
laboratory equipment. He noted, with growing anxiety, the odor
of decay. It was faint—nothing like the library—but present. He
pictured the draugr rolling around the loft, rattling windows in
the night.

"You were right. It's up here." Sorcha's voice echoed in
the stone rafters. She brushed her curls back from the worry
wrinkles on her forehead. "I never had your bones, Dwyn, but
even I can tell this is nasty." She rocked back on her heels, her
silver tracer vanishing into the floor beside Nyssa's delicate blue
threads.

He leaned against a support beam, cracked where age and
gravity were tearing the spur down. "I've dealt with worse."

"Did you kill it? The rat?"

"It seemed the kindest thing to do. It was already dying." Like
the building. Like the inside of him.

"Stupid of her, leaving the door unlocked where kids could
get in. I'll fine her satin ass for that."

Dwyn frowned. Nyssa hadn't unlocked the tabah. Rachet had. He'd done it to anger Dwyn, discredit Nyssa, and cause a distraction. What a damned ass.

"What about the classrooms on the lower floors?" Sorcha asked, standing.

"Look at them if you like, but I've already fired them."

She chuckled. "You should see your face. You're going to have quite a shiner. Years at Nations fighting every necromancer who stood up for a beating, and you get thrown over a chair by a centenarian."

He brushed her off. "That was swordplay. If I'd been fighting with my fists, I'd have looked like this all the time."

"He cares about the place, anyway." Sorcha flicked a cobweb from her fingers. "More than Nyssa does. Show me the sites you fired, and we'll call it done. I'll still have to recommend condemning it, Dwyn, but I'll leave it open-ended. I can't say you couldn't salvage it. They said Rivnkyf was a lost cause and you made them look like fools. That library, though? Walled off and sealed."

"Seems to me she cares."

"Why should she?" Sorcha led the way down the stairs. "She's been at this school less than a year, and not by election either, by appointment. The council at Whiterock practically pissed themselves when she said she would take the position."

"Why? I thought Ironsfork wasn't well liked up there."

Sorcha pushed open the stairwell door and held it for him. "Ironsfork has nothing to do with it. Nyssa was something big at Nations. I was told she used to be on the warloche council."

"Really?"

Sorcha shrugged. "I checked. I never found her. No Nyssa Irons."

Dwyn chewed his lip. Necromancers rarely, if ever, used their clan names at Nations. He might have been the only Seidoche who knew that Ehrlik Phaneugh was Ehrlik Valkgrim, and Riordiin Wytkyf used his mother's name in the same way Cheyloche Daffyd kept the name of Rivnstone clean for himself. Nyssa *had* been someone important at Nations—important enough to warrant the precious gift of original works by Cheyloche Daffyd. Not the common warloche council, then. Dwyn ran through the lists of necromancers in his mind, pausing whenever he came to a Nyssa on the role. None of them seemed a match.

His eye was swollen shut by the time he finished showing Sorcha the classrooms. The walls were black where he'd fired them, but they smelled as fresh as clean-cut granite. He sat next to Sorcha in Nyssa's office and remained quiet as she went through her spiel. Neil chewed his fingernails, and the bald Cheyloche Northslope, evidently standing in for the missing Rachet, rattled off costs like an adding machine. Dwyn sat silently, thinking over what Sorcha had said.

Ehrlik had lied about everything. Had Sorcha gone before the council after he'd already pled incendiary and said he'd been to her, crying out against Riordiin's abuse, his lie wouldn't have saved him. The abuse he'd suffered at Riordiin's hands was motive for murder, and they'd have charged him with it.

And what about the paperwork Ehrlik had gone to fix? He'd said he meant to take Dwyn to Norway with him. Had he gone back to Nations for that? Or was that when he asked Sorcha to condemn Dwyn as a liar and a killer before the warloche council?

Nyssa had once been on that council if Sorcha was right. Now Ehrlik was head of it. Had she already told him about Dwyn, trapped by a penalty g'hesh, ready for the taking?

Dwyn shut his eyes. His lungs ached from the smoke he'd generated in the fight, his face hurt from Rachet's blow, and his heart felt dead inside of him.

Ehrlik wanted him charged with murder. Ehrlik wanted him dead. He had to get out of here as soon as he could.

"Dwyn?"

He jerked. Nyssa had called his name three times.

"The decontamination of the furniture is complete, am I

correct? Neil can bring trucks in tomorrow?"

"If he wishes. It can be disposed of without further—" He began to cough.

"Landfills will charge more to handle dangerous material. It may be wiser to accept condemnation," Neil said. "It breaks my heart, but I don't see how we can afford the costs of repair, Nyssa."

"Demolition would cost twice as much in fees and permits," Nyssa said. "If we can save the building, we should try. For the teachers, if for no other reason. They are invested, as much in their magic as memories."

Cheyloche turned suspiciously toward Dwyn. "You actually decontaminated the library at Rivnkyf?"

Dwyn glared back through his one good eye. "Yes."

"Rivnkyf could afford it," Neil said. "We can't."

"Experience costs the most," Nyssa said, "and we get Dwyn's help at no cost to us at all. I'm counting it as part of his penalty."

"Rachet will oppose this—he wants no part of the Dragon's help," Neil said.

"I gathered that," Dwyn grunted.

"More than anyone else, Rachet wants this building saved. He'll listen to you, Neil, far better than he listens to me," Nyssa said. "You are his only family."

"You have more faith in me than I have in myself, Nyssa," Neil said, standing. "But I will do my best."

Dwyn huddled in his chair as Cheyloche followed Neil out of the office, leaving him with Nyssa and Sorcha.

CHAPTER TWENTY-TWO

WHERE DRAGONS DANCED

Sorcha had been quiet during the meeting, but the little uplift at the corner of her mouth was a smirk if Dwyn ever saw one.

"Will you stay with us at Ironsfork this evening?" Nyssa asked, rising. "I know Rich Mountain is honored to host you and your necromancers, but I understand Dwyn is a friend of yours. We would be glad to offer you hospitality."

Sorcha stood, straightening her jacket. "That's kind, but no thank you. I've seen all I need to see and made my recommendation. I'm bound for Whiterock tonight."

Nyssa shook hands with Sorcha. "Have a safe journey. We may meet again soon," she added.

When Sorcha left, first bowing in Nation's fashion to the necromancer, who did not so much as nod back, Dwyn tensed in his chair, braced for punishment.

But Nyssa only picked up her purse. "Are you ready to go home?"

"Where's that? But if you mean Ironsfork, I'm ready."

"I'll take you there, and then I too must go to Whiterock. I'll have to see if there are any funds to be had for restoration. It will come down to money. It usually does." Briefly, she caressed the surface of her desk as if she might not see it again.

"You expect them to condemn it," Dwyn said.

Nyssa locked the office door behind them as she escorted Dwyn into the hallway. "The mountain's vote is not yet taken. I have faith in Rene, if not in Neil. Rachet is like a grandfather to her. She can talk sense to him when no one else can." She paused to button her coat.

"Rachet's a fool. You can't talk sense into stupid."

"We are all fools at Dh'Morda, especially those who have lost a lover." Nyssa eased carefully through the cluttered hallway.

Dwyn followed, pushing things out of his way. "The old Seidoche who died, you mean?"

Nyssa waited for him on the other side of the debris field. "Rachet never mated, and he was devoted to Asa. He could have retired when I took over, but chose to teach instead. I think he couldn't stand to leave a place that meant so much to him."

Once outside, the frigid air hit Dwyn's burning lungs like a hammer. He doubled over coughing on the stairs. Nyssa waited patiently for him to finish.

"I do have one more request to make of you," she said.

"I'm not doing another damned thing until I get paid." He gagged on acidic phlegm.

"I'll give you your books as soon as we get to Ironsfork. Will that suit you, warloche?"

He flinched. First time the word had bothered him as much as Dragon. "What do you want, then?" He crushed gravel underfoot as he followed her to the car.

"Nothing you wouldn't agree to give me—your opinion. Whiterock will want odds with their risk. What are your honest thoughts—"

"I don't lie." He kicked a stone into a stand of ornamental grasses, sheared for winter.

"You were disturbingly quiet in the meeting."

"You said you'd do the lying."

"The truth, on your honor as a Seidoche."

Just shoot him in the goddamned ass—this fake respect bordered on cruel and unusual punishment. But she'd asked for it. "All right. It's draug. The rock has gone bad. The tracer showed it—and I was afraid it might. That building is splintered all to hell. I can get rid of the toxic shit, sure, but I can't rebuild a damned mountain out of broken bones. No one can." He buckled into the passenger seat.

"It's been a long time since I heard that word," Nyssa said, backing out of the parking lot.

"Cheyloche Daffyd used it in the *Seida*. That's good enough for me." He touched the puffy place under his eye. It hurt. His back hurt. His chest hurt. His heart hurt. Once Nyssa gave him his books, he was going to go below, hide them in his dungeon, eat the dinner the chef had promised, and spend the rest of the night soaking in whatever sympathy Nikl felt up to providing.

"Bad rock, you say."

He huffed. He shouldn't have to explain the concept to a Nations-trained necromancer. "When you get draug magic in a place like this—and I mean the really rotten shit, the kind that curdles your blood—it starts breeding on itself. It happens in ancient mountains like Rivnkyf, like every old mansion in the South, when new magic gets built on top of the old. No one remembers where or why things were made, stuff gets lost, and next thing you know your walls are falling down."

"Rich Mountain is not that old. The school was built less than a hundred years ago. This is not Ironsfork."

He snorted. "How do you explain the glyphs on those old rivn at the entryway, then? They're the same as the ones on your land. They built that school on top of an old dh'catha—a watchtower—and there's no doubt in my mind it belonged to Ironsfork back when decent dwarves lived in it. There's no telling how deep the roots go."

"You've been as deep as they go."

"Not deep enough. Something perked up in the last twenty-four hours. I could smell it, and I don't like it."

"It could still be the decay in the boxes."

"No. Given another week, you could use that shit to water the lawn. What I'm worried about is dangerously deep. I feel it."

"You feel it."

Nyssa couldn't have squeezed more contempt in those three words if she'd tried. Hatred surged through him. "Yes, I feel it."

She stared at him for a second before looking back at the road. "You feel," she said, placing a derisive emphasis on the word, "the contamination is deeper than you can measure. Therefore, you expect?"

"I don't know what to expect."

"At Rivnkyf—"

"At Rivnkyf, I had a necromancer worth his bones. He gave me what I needed when I asked for it. He didn't blow me off when I said I was concerned." At least not in the beginning.

"Riordiin, you mean?"

He didn't answer. Instead, he stared out the window at the dismal houses as they passed through Goblin Town. Smoked poured from every chimney, settling over the river opposite.

Ehrlik had lied. Lied about Sorcha, lied about loving him, lied about saving him. What other lies might he have told? Dwyn had believed everything Ehrlik had ever told him: about himself, about Riordiin, about just how a young, penniless Southerner might serve as the mind and magic for a dying Dragon of the North and live to tell the tale. From the moment Ehrlik had introduced him to Riordiin, he'd agreed with everything his mentor told him about the nature of Seidwendr, how dangerous it could be, and how between the two of them, they might save the man Dwyn first admired, and then loved. He should have known it was too good to be true, and yet he'd gone along with it, duped by the promise of security—a place at Rivnkyf for himself as a reward for his service, and Ehrlik to take care of him for the rest of his days. God under the earth, he'd been such a fool.

Nyssa hit a pothole turning into Ironsfork. He jerked upright from where he'd slumped, cheek pressed against the window glass. Dwelling on the past did no good—The present was the most important thing now. He couldn't risk Ehrlik finding out where he was. He must get Nyssa alone, kill her quick, and run away as soon as he got the chance.

The lake turned to gold as sunset gilded the smooth surface. Dwyn stiffened. He thought his heart had stopped—certainly the world had.

Before him, the mountain of Ironsfork glowed in the falling light, crowning crimson above the frozen trees. Where the mutilated rivn once skulked below the water, a polished tower of cut stone stood—black as the heart of a mountain, topped with a capstone, bleeding red in the dying sunlight. Stretching across the lake to the far edge, a wall of the same black stone marched resolutely toward the quarry, straight as a ruler, unbroken by the water, although Dwyn could still see the lake, hazy as a half-forgotten memory, existing on either side. The marshy bank had been transformed into a field of light. Cattails kindled like torches, sheltered beneath the protection of the towering rivn. And beside the lake's cold edge, where he'd all but died, there stood a ring of nine stones.

Not a one of them stood under ten feet in height. Obsidian dark and razor sharp, they cut the ground open, like the claws of some great animal reaching, straining to be free—an Eseitha hengh. And by the way the blood sang in his veins, he knew it was his.

He opened his mouth to scream, but Nyssa drove past them without a glance. She rocketed through the wall itself before he could even try for a shield to cover himself. The wall split around them, and closed behind as they passed, as if it wasn't there, had never existed, could never exist, did not exist. He was looking at the old boundary of Ironsfork, freshly written in stone and magic. But Nyssa didn't see it.

How could she not see? How could she not feel? His bones were throbbing in magical unison with the heartbeat of wild, passionate music. That rattled him far worse than the road bucking beneath him. He knew his own magic when he felt it, but what had he done? God under the earth, what had he done?

Nyssa was speaking—*pay attention, man, pay attention...*

"Wha—what?"

"I'll be back from Whiterock tomorrow afternoon. We'll check the wall when I return."

"Yes." He racked his mind for each glyph, and the Runic he'd overwritten them with. Open. Close. He'd used the rubbish quartzite stones for those simple commands. It was all they were good for. The empty Eseitha stones he'd used for everything important—protect, defend, confuse, attack, revenge, renew, and assist. But something had gone dreadfully wrong.

He glanced back at the hengh brooding on the landscape. It was an illusion, it had to be. But he'd be damned if he knew how he'd done it.

"Come to my library first, and I'll pay you your books."

The dwynr stone could account for the illusion, but that was one hell of an illusion. The strain should be breaking his bones, and yet he felt nothing.

"Get out."

He hadn't realized the car had stopped. Nyssa was holding the door open for him. He fumbled loose from his seat belt, and grabbed his sword, strapping it on half-way before he realized he'd only take it off inside. He hung it over his shoulder and followed Nyssa into the mountain.

He almost turned right into the elevator when Nyssa went left. With unnerving clarity, he realized this was not an entrance hall, and never had been. It was a mere access road. All the greatness of the forgotten mountain lay well below him, and he sensed myriad tunnels, empty and ruined, a broken body crushed into a coffin box and forgotten. He tripped over his own feet in the doorway.

"Dwyn?" Jullup sat at the table, a tray of crystals spread out in front of her. "What happened to you?"

Nothing. Everything. I don't know. Shit.

Jullup helped him up, dusted him off. "Who hit you?"

He touched his face, uncertain it belonged to him anymore, only it hurt, so it must.

Nyssa answered for him. "A misunderstanding. Nothing serious. I'm leaving for Whiterock tonight after I take care of business here."

"Everything went well today?"

"As well as expected, and no better," Nyssa said.

"Did they condemn it?" Morven spoke up from the bar where she was writing in a notebook.

Nyssa didn't answer Morven. "Wait here," she said to Dwyn. She vanished into the hall that led to her library.

"I'll mix you up some arnica, Dwyn," Jullup said, getting up and retreating to her quarters.

Morven grinned. "Which one of them hit you? Lokey or Nikl?"

The Eseitha hengh dug itself out of the ground and superimposed itself over her laughing face, and then the wall burst on Dwyn's vision, adamantine and forbidding. His resolve hardened. He had his books and his sword, and as long as that was all that mattered, he didn't care. He had to believe it was.

"Morven. Your promise."

The grin froze on her face.

He spoke quietly. "Tomorrow afternoon, I want my eight hours. You take the dog, like you promised."

"Here we are," Jullup said brightly, coming back. "Take five drops of this in a glass of wine before bed, and everything will be fine."

Nikl was not in Dwyn's quarters. All of his ardchuk sat out on the counter, but they were cold, and the place was dark. So much for promises.

Dwyn dropped his writing box on the kitchen table, but his books he took with him to the bedchamber. Nikl's white cat lay in the middle of the rumpled bed.

"Move your ass," he snapped.

The cat stared insolently at him. She jumped off only when he pulled up the featherbed, displacing her and exposing the platform where he'd once hidden the stones. He laid his books flat one at a time on the slab, smoothing the covers of each one as it assumed the hue of the dark stone as perfectly as a mirror. They were safe enough here for the night. For tomorrow, he'd need better concealment.

He chose one of his new shirts from the dirty pile on the floor and carried it with him to the kitchen. He picked the seams out with his ripper, turned the sleeves inside, and stitched it to the back of his old camouflage jacket, muttering illusions as he sewed. Drops of hot blood sizzled and smoked as he wove magic into the makeshift knapsack. He'd have to leave his writing case behind. If he succeeded, he'd be running the moment he passed the boundary, and he couldn't be weighed down with more than necessary.

The white cat writhed between his ankles. He glanced down. Animals didn't usually care for his company. Living with Nikl must have made her less wary of wild, elemental magic. "You're hungry?"

She bumped her jaw against his leg and meowed soundlessly.

He was hungry, too. Lunch he'd missed, and breakfast had been in another life. Peppercorn tenderloin and fresh baked bread clearly weren't happening tonight.

"Where the hell is he?" He followed the prancing cat to the refrigerator. How Nikl managed to cram it so full, he didn't know—it was like threading a needle to extract one package. He read the label—duck, brown rice, peas.

He snorted. "Cat eats better than most folk."

The block of food was frozen solid. He warmed the cube on a plate, thumb pressed against the stone. He ate most of it with his fingers, while the cat danced at his feet, glaring. "Wait your turn," he mumbled with his mouth full.

She thwacked her tail back and forth when he set the leftovers before her, nosed the bubbling, overcooked smear, laid her ears flat, growled, and bolted for the bedroom.

"Fine! Go hungry then." Dwyn yelled after her. He dropped the plate in the sink and slumped over the counter. He'd gone through every spell five times already, but again he ransacked his magic—language and method: everything from the collection of the stones to the way he returned them to the earth. Each image presented itself to him in perfect detail, until he arrived at the Eseitha hengh.

"They were inert. No magic beyond what I gave them." He ground his teeth. God under the earth, he needed to think and he couldn't. The day had thrown him over a chair as handily as Rachet.

He was still trying to think when Nikl came in hours later, although he'd dosed off once or twice. He lay on the deep side of the bed, jacket tucked safely under his pillow, listening to Nikl croon endearments to the cat.

"I'm awake," he said when Nikl tiptoed in.

Nikl groaned aloud. "I hoped you wouldn't wait up for me! Hell of a day—you know how it is at Dh'Morda. No sooner did I get dinner served then half of Blue Mountain shows up starving, and it's breakfast, lunch, and dinner all over again. I can't wait until this damned season is over. Then I can go back to my usual scheduled insanity."

Nikl stripped his shirt and sat down on the edge of the bed to untie his shoes. "My feet are killing me."

Dwyn turned his back on Nikl. "I thought we could fuck tonight."

"Only if you do all the work, buddy. I'm beat." Nikl crawled in next to him, and Dwyn slid into the furrow Nikl made when he lay down.

"In the morning, then."

"Hey? What is it?" Nikl massaged Dwyn's back, kneading him like bread. "You're so tense you're burning up. Did you eat? Can I make you something?"

"I ate."

"I heard about Rachet. You okay?"

"I'll live."

He tried not to flinch when Nikl pressed his nose into his hair. "Where have you been all my life, beautiful? You're not even mad at me for missing dinner. I love this. I love the way you smell, the way you feel. I want this—you and me forever—just like this. If I could find a way, I'd never let you go."

Dwyn shivered as Nikl held him close. He lay there until the Thunderer relaxed in sleep, still holding onto Dwyn like he'd save him if he could.

Only when Nikl began to snore, did Dwyn ease free. He pressed himself in the far corner, feeling under his pillow for his jacket. The tortured fabric caught his fingers.

Tomorrow would end it. No dream could be worse than the nightmare he was living in.

CHAPTER TWENTY-THREE

THE DRAGON'S BIRTHSONG

When the Dragon died, he dreamed in fire.

He didn't stay in the mud where they believed him extinguished. They left his body there, and sometimes he thought of it, and yearned for his mountain in the South and the glory of becoming one with the land he had loved and protected. It was not honorable to rot in unholy ground, but he bore the sting of the disgrace better dead than alive.

And there was his child.

The necromancers had taken a still-born baby and laid it in his tomb. A peace offering to him? A sacrifice to their dark god of death? He didn't know. He didn't care. It was his child.

Not the child he would have chosen, no. A living child would have taken his fire, his mind, and his soul, and remade him—warm with fresh blood, wide-eyed with life, full of the lust a young Dragon feels when he wakes to the world for the first time, and finds it good. These bones were as dead as his body, but if all this cursed mountain could give him was death, he would teach death how to live.

The Dragon curled around the infant. The plate bones of its fragile skull split open like a bad acorn, and the tiny fingers were no more than splinters, but he would make it strong. He had centuries to nurture these bones, to

*build the old on top of the new, to turn this corruption into new life. He'd
make Dragons of them all.*
He sang the birth hymn with all the magic that was in him.

*Let us dream, child,
Let us sleep the long death together.
As the mountain covers us,
We will speak bone to bone
And I will tell you our story:
The wind on the hill,
The water in the valley,
The strong earth of our home,
The fire in the stone.*

*Lest it be corrupt and wicked as the mountain that spawned it, he
named it in the language of the Dh'Rigahn, the language of power. Dwyn.
Confusion to my enemies.*
*Dwyn opened his eyes. He was in a tomb. Stone walls surrounded him on
four sides, a slab pressed over his face, and fire leapt around him. He clawed
at the wall of dark rock over his face and saw the bones of his own hands,
silhouetted small and black against the firelight.*

Dwyn slammed his fists into the wall. Pain exploded through
his knuckles.

"Easy! Easy, buddy!"

In his mind the song continued, not a single voice now, but
multitudes. He screamed and punched. Blood sprayed his face,
and a briny, salt-water odor filled his nostrils as lightning lit up
the darkness.

Nikl rolled out of the bed, cupping bloody hands around his
nose.

"Buried alive. They buried us alive!" Dwyn tore his beard,
fire twisting through his fingers. He was the Dragon, singing
his lullaby to the dead. He was the child, screaming in the cradle

of its grave. And still the song went on. A chorus of macabre voices sang it, jubilant as a morning full of birds.

"I think you broke my nose. Next time warn a man, will you? I'm bleeding all over the place."

"What is your blood to me? You think I care? They buried us alive." A sudden, choking rush of horror seized him as he thought of the long rows of tombs at Rivnkyf full of skeletal Dragons, all of them clawing helplessly at the rocks.

"Well, don't say you're sorry or anything. Might as well get up, Dragon. You pissed the bed."

"I'm sorry." This made the seventh time Dwyn had said it, but it seemed a necessary apology considering the flapjacks and honey.

"Don't mention it," Nikl said, also for the seventh time. He dabbed delicately at the tomato on his face with a bloody towel. "No wonder you're skinny as a skewer. You work off all your food thrashing at night."

"I'm sorry."

"Yeah, yeah, you said. Eat your breakfast."

Dwyn ate, but his stomach churned. The dream had lodged itself thorn-like into his waking mind.

After Nikl left for Rich Mountain, Dwyn stripped the sheets and tossed the linens and the sodden featherbed into the damp hallway. He put all nine of his books in his jacket, and eased it on, testing the weight. He groaned and heaved it off. In a fight with Nyssa it would be an impediment. He loosened the straps on Mh'Arda to fit over the bulk.

When Nyssa arrived, Dwyn sat working at the table in the writing room. The moment her hateful step sounded on the stone, his heart began to beat a furious rhythm, and he scarred the page with a river of ink. He crumpled it as she entered.

"Well?" His voice wasn't trembling at least, unlike the rest of him. But Nyssa wasn't looking at him, but at the wall, where the new illusions of his books rested prominently on one of the lower shelves.

The necromancer's bloodshot gaze followed his hand as he drew a second illusion over the first as if to hide them from her view.

"What happened at Whiterock?" He put his pen away in the box and closed the lid for the last time.

"Too early to say," Nyssa said. "I left the necromancers in deliberations. Are you ready to go?"

As he'd ever be. He picked up his jacket. The heavy books shifted ominously when he slid his sword over the top of them.

Nyssa paused beside the pile of linens in the hallway, wrinkling her nose. "Did Nikl's cat make a mess?"

"While I'm still alive?" He stopped short of the waterfall to wait for her, bouncing anxiously on his toes.

Nyssa stopped upstairs to talk to Jullup about the bedding. Dwyn paced near the elevator. He caught snatches of the conversation, but he wasn't listening.

The earthy scent of rain drifted down the hallway from an open door somewhere, but the proximity to the surface did nothing to dispel the weight of living stone beneath his feet, the eternal depths of hidden magic beating deep in the earth like a heart. The walls themselves might reach out to seize him. He blinked convulsively, trying to dispel the image of tiny fingers, lit by fire, scratching feebly at the walls of the tomb while Dragon song echoed in the burial chamber.

"Dwyn?"

His hand flew to his sword hilt, but it was only Jullup, smiling at him.

"Yes?"

"I asked if you wanted a raincoat."

He straightened. "No. I'd just burn it."

"Not one Tully enchanted, you wouldn't," Jullup said, handing him a heavy red one. "It's a long walk to the Blackfork line."

Nyssa had donned a poncho, buttercup yellow. Dwyn

recognized the scorch marks. He kept his back to the wall as the weight of the books shifted in response to his movement.

Jullup touched his eyebrow. "You look better this morning."

"I took what you gave me." But not internally. He'd put the flask in an upper cabinet where it could stay forever. He wouldn't be burdened by her kindness anymore.

"Put it on," Nyssa said impatiently.

"I thought we were driving," he said.

"A forest road goes to the property line," Nyssa said. "From there we follow the track up the west side of the mountain."

"Shall I hold your sword for you?" Jullup held out her hand.

Dwyn hesitated. "No. I'll—" He unbuckled his sword, and set it against the wall. The raincoat was too big for him. It fell all the way to his ankles.

"Where's Kritha?" Nyssa asked.

Dwyn paused in the middle of wrestling his illusion to incorporate the coat.

"Outside, somewhere," Jullup said. "Morven said she'd let her out before she went hunting with Midian."

"I didn't see her when I drove up."

"I'll check the patio. She's probably waiting for me to let her in."

Dwyn didn't know if he would fight or faint if the dog trotted out of Jullup's quarters. An age passed before Jullup appeared in the doorway again. Alone.

Nyssa's car was absent from the parking area. Instead, Tully's diesel idled beside the door. Dwyn took off the raincoat and tossed it in the back seat. He also shed his jacket, and slid it into the floorboard. Illusion or not, he couldn't sit straight in the seat with nine books between him and the leather. He set his sword between himself and Nyssa.

"I didn't plan on running the heater with you in the truck. You could have left your jacket on." Nyssa backed out, looking for Kritha.

It seemed too much to hope that Morven had not played him false. He closed his eyes as the truck lurched through puddles on a road that seemed destined never to dry out.

Nyssa cleared her throat. "Do you know a dwarf called Ehrlik Phaneugh?"

All his fire gathered in his center and huddled there. "I did. What does he want with me?" he added, before he could stop himself.

"You tell me," Nyssa said. "When I went to Whiterock, I expected to be the topic of the special session. Instead, I had to wait while the Seidoche of Nations had his case heard before the necromancers. When it was my turn, they told me he was asking about you—what you were accused of, where you were, the status of your penalty."

He hid his harsh swallow with a soft cough. "What did you tell him?"

"Nothing—I didn't see him. But the council told him the truth. The Southern government reports to Nations when there's no reason why they shouldn't." Nyssa glanced at him. "Is he a friend of yours?"

Dwyn said nothing.

"Did you contact him? Ask him for help? Get your friend Sorcha to ask for you?"

He stared out the window, silent.

"I don't think much of how you repay my kindness—going over my head like this."

"You call this kindness?"

"I said I would speak for you at your hearing!"

"Yeah, speak for me! Speak me right into torment, right into a void cell. Why should I trust you? You've done nothing but hurt me."

"Did you ask him to come?" Nyssa yelled.

The g'hesh tightened viciously around his bones but he would bear it. He had to bear it a little while longer. He might even have to fight through it. "I did not," he gasped.

"Then why is he here?"

Dwyn leaned back against the seat and clamped his lips together.

Nyssa ground out another gear to get up a muddy hill. "When a representative from Nations descends on us without warning, asking questions, the council is not happy. I will have to deal with this dwarf, and send him back to Nations, satisfied. Who is he to you?"

He didn't reply. Years of lies, years of believing the lies, but he still couldn't talk about it. He shuddered.

Nyssa's voice dripped poison. "Well, he's on his way. And when he comes, I will ask him."

Nyssa had her stav with her. Of course, she would need it. She was here to check his work. But seeing it frightened him.

She retrieved it from the back seat while he was busy adjusting his books for comfort. Most necromancers carried a number of canned spells in objects—rings and necklaces being two of the most favored—but weapons were always filled with offensive magic. He'd have to take it out first. Nyssa set off into the pine thicket, yellow parka flapping listlessly about her legs. Dwyn followed, mind churning.

He must be well away from Ironsfork tonight if he hoped to vanish entirely. Where should he go? Ehrlik would expect him to head east, back to his home in Heldasa, and it was his heart's wish to do so, but he couldn't go now. West would be better, but hitch-hiking in this region was a risk he couldn't take, and without a vehicle, he wouldn't get far.

I could take Tully's truck. No one seeing it would question anything. His skin prickled. Oh, God, it was a sign. He touched the hilt of his sword. The rain made it slippery underhand, like a coating of fresh blood.

"Keep up," Nyssa called. "We've three miles to walk, and I'd like to be back before nightfall."

Dwyn followed, burning fitfully in the rain.

He decided to kill her by striking her down with a rock. He con-
structed the murder in his mind, seeing in detail when he bashed
her skull in, and drove his blade between her ribs and through her
heart from the back. She wouldn't be able to look at him then.
Whenever he tried attacking her from the front, taking out her
stav hand first, she always looked, and the hard, blue eyes became
a deep velvety midnight as Riordiin died in front of him again,
and again, and again. Two miles into the journey to the Blackfork
line, Dwyn had killed her so many times he was sick of it.

The drizzle never let up as he climbed the steep scree behind
her. Nyssa used her stav as a walking stick, bracing the tip into
cracks between stones where an ankle would turn over in an
instant if a man or woman wasn't careful.

He kept his head down too, watching his step. The books
banging against his shoulders were heavy, and upset his balance
more than he thought they would. He wished he could soak up
all the courageous truth he'd written in them—his dreams, the
memories of Mn'Hesset through all the centuries that belonged
to him. He wanted to be that warloche, favored by God, born
to kill without hesitation, made to do battle with the dangerous
magic of the underworld and to walk unafraid in the shadows.
He wanted to be anything besides what he was now—a sad,
frightened dwarf with a past too full of memories haunting him,
and a future too full of fear to go forward.

"Are you tired, Dragon?" Nyssa's voice trickled back to Dwyn
as he picked his way through the boulders, blowing clouds of
black smoke. An old landslide, he thought, but the number of
trees growing straight and sturdy at either end of the field made
him wonder. Perhaps it was the broken bones of the mountain
exposed for everyone to see.

Everything looked normal—stone, wind, wood, the ceaseless rain—but *he* felt different, like he was walking over a living,
breathing giant. If the mansion were the heart of the place, this
hill felt like a hand, and he was the bug that would be crushed
when the fist closed around him.

"How much further?" His breath caught sharply in his chest. He was shivering with terror when he should be calm, cultivating the strength he needed for what was bound to be a battle to the death.

"About a half-mile, maybe a little more." Nyssa turned around. "Sit and rest, Dragon. The boundary will still be there if you've done your work properly, won't it?" She bent comfortably over her stav, but Dwyn was nervous enough himself to see that she was equally tense. He quelled the thin veil of flame creeping down his sides, and sat on a rock, shifting as the thorny point dug into his ass.

"Tell me, Dragon, did this necromancer, Ehrlik, introduce you to Riordiin?"

"Does it matter?" Dwyn spied a pebble across the slide. It clattered downhill until it lodged between larger rocks and stopped.

"It does. I must speak for you at Whiterock, much sooner than expected. Your extradition will take precedence if Ehrlik Phaneugh wishes to take you back with him."

"My penalty is not complete—"

"Inconsequential, if Nations has decided to charge you with murder."

"It was an accident." He choked.

"I assume this necromancer's visit means there are further questions Nations wants answered. Perhaps justice will be served, if late, and cold."

Dwyn's angry laugh didn't echo in the damp stillness of the rain. "What were you at Nations, Nyssa Irons? Judge, jury and executioner? They never asked me any questions. Not so much as a where were you." He stood, and all the books shifted, swinging him left.

"Why should they? They knew you would hide behind your exemption." The contempt in her tone made Dwyn want to spit at her. *Good.* Hatred would help.

"Exemption was forced on me, like your damned penalty. I

could not speak for myself."

"If Ehrlik was indeed your friend at some point, then why didn't he speak on your behalf? If he had any faith in you, he would have defended you."

He began to climb slowly toward her. "Are you my inquisitor as well as my jailer?"

"But then again, why would an honorable warloche, bidding for a permanent position at Nations, perjure himself for a Dragon who murders as well as he lies?"

Dwyn reached for his sword. He got as far as the hilt before he froze.

Nyssa held her left hand high in the air. "I should let you try. I'd love to be the one who put an end to you. But I won't. I said I would speak for you, and I will. I won't be in debt to the man who murdered *my* Dragon."

The rain stung his open eyes, frozen, fixed on her gold ring with the gaudy green gemstone. A paralyzer. No mean trick to compress that monstrosity—no wonder the stone was so big. She lowered her hand. He could breathe again.

"What do you mean?"

"You cursed me on the day of your trial," Nyssa said. "You swore you would make me pay for what I did to you. You have no idea. Every day, I wake in the morning, and I wish I had died instead of him. But I lived and saw his killer go free. And to think, I chose you for him."

"What do you mean?" He steamed and smoked fearfully.

"I chose you for Riordiin. I made it happen—a poor boy from Tennessee, a tomb robber, no proper education, no clan, no family, but somehow he wins full scholarship to Nations, complete with a berth in the colony worth a mountain's ransom paid for by the folk of Nations. Did you never wonder why?"

"I went to Nations on my own merit—mine—"

"Your merit was the fire in your blood, Dwyn. You had nothing else to recommend you. I chose you to be Seidwender to him, the one dwarf who truly needed you, and he longed for you, couldn't wait to give you everything for your service. But you betrayed his trust, you murdered him, when all he did was give you his strength, his life, his soul! He loved you before he met you, treated you with the highest honor—"

"You know nothing of his treatment of me!"

The wind turned Nyssa's braids into red ribbons. "I know what they said at your trial, how you hated him, how you chafed under his control. I tell you, Dragon, you had better pray for the forgiveness of your dark God for what you did—no one with a heart could ever excuse you. He gave you everything—his life, his love—"

"You knew him? You loved him?" Fire streamed down Dwyn's shoulders, blackening the rocks at his feet.

"I did."

He spat. "Then I forgive him everything he ever did. I know who ruined him. I know who poisoned his mind, who taught him cruelty. You spoke of prayer. Get on your knees and pray then, necromancer—your guilt is as great as mine!"

Nyssa's face twisted in fury. He waited for the g'hesh to constrict, for her paralyzer to flatten his ribs.

She gripped her stav in both hands. "No," she whispered in a voice barely louder than the rain. "I will deliver you to this warloche, Ehrlik. And then I will speak before the present council at Nations. Oh, yes, I will speak for you. I will tell them the truth of your miserable life and how you repaid his kindness with faithlessness. I will speak—and see you condemned."

She turned her back on him and continued to climb into the boulder field.

CHAPTER TWENTY-FOUR

THE WALL

If today is the day I die, Paloh mhu,
Remember me.
Remember my service.
Remember I gave myself willingly.
I worshipped you with my blood,
I worshipped you with my bone,
My life, my love, my soul.
Remember your Mn'Hesset.

Dwyn lifted his face to the rain. *Mhu Paloh, I ask one thing before I die. I ask redemption for Riordiin. Receive him with honor, for I forgive him. I forgive him everything.*

Courage burned in his blood and raged in his bones as he climbed the hill and stood on the crest beside the necromancer, wheezing, but feeling more alive than he had in days. He gazed into the narrow valley dividing Ironsfork from Blackfork.

A long black wall guarded the land, watchful and purpose driven, unbroken but for a tower of black stone where an ancient rivn once stood. He might have dreamed it, it looked so real. A shimmer of fire glowed deep in the heart of the illusion. Yet he felt no pull on his bones, no indication he was being tasked for the magic.

"I don't have all day." Nyssa's irritated voice drifted up to him. She was picking her careful path through the slippery carpet of dead leaves piled down slope where wind and weather had lodged them.

Neither did he. He bent and grabbed a stone that fit comfortably in his hand.

If today is the day I die, Paloh mhu,
Remember your Mn'Hesset.
Remember my service.
Remember I gave myself willingly,
I worshiped you with my blood,
I worshiped you with my bone,
My life, my love—

Nyssa's scream cut short his prayer.

Dwyn dropped the rock, transfixed. Below him, just short of the wall, Nyssa thrashed around, an obsidian spike protruding from her thigh. Her gray pants flapped open, and a red torrent blasted out of the wound, spraying her face, her chest, the trees around her, painting the bark with livid splotches. She grappled at her leg frantically for a moment, head thrown back, and then she fell forward, shrieking.

Dwyn scrambled the last few feet through the leaves to where she lay panting. Her red face purpled with fury when she saw him, but her lips paled, and her eyes opened wide in terror. For one desperate, horrible second, her acid blue stare pleaded with him, and her mouth twisted, until finally—

"M—meda." Nyssa fainted.

Time crawled. Dwyn stood in the rain for days, hours—maybe a minute. Steam rolled from him like the impending eruption of a geyser as he looked at his enemy lying at that awkward angle.

Both her arms were thrown forward as if trying to claw free of the spike that stabbed through her left leg. Her right splayed out, toe dug into the mud, holding the lower half of her body in the air. Her foot slipped with a sucking sound and she slid down the spike, unconscious, pinned to the ground.

Blood streamed slick and dark along the edge of the knife-like stone. He drew his sword. One stroke and it would be over. He would watch the blood and air gurgle together, and he would turn, clean his blade, make his way back down the rockslide, get in the truck, throw his sodden jacket in the passenger seat, and drive away.

It would be so easy. She might even die if he just left her lying there. She would wake, screaming in agony, and he would be gone. The g'hesh would slide away from him, slipping from his shoulders like his jacket as it thudded on the ground behind him. He knelt beside Nyssa and touched her exposed neck. Her pulse raced beneath his fingers.

She moaned. Her eyes opened slightly, and rolled as she gasped out something incoherent. She jerked and blood spurted across Dwyn's hands as he grasped the spike jutting from the flesh.

"Don't—Dragon!"

A surge of magic ripped through his body and threw him forward on top of Nyssa. Clinging onto the spike, he crashed against her injured leg. She screamed. He lurched and cut his palm on the sharp edge of the stone. His sword touched the inside of her other leg.

She cried out in terror, and hit him over the head with her fist, but he barely felt it. Had she brought the g'hesh to bear, it would have been no more than a sting. Magic burned through him with an intensity he'd never known, never thought possible. Memories flooded him, memories that were not his, but those of that damned Dragon: Captured, enslaved to a mountain he hated, killed, but eternal in the fire, and strong in the bones. Dwyn shook to his foundations as he lived that life in a heartbeat.

He was a child, a captive in Rigah Tarn, and chestnut trees rained pollen so thick he couldn't breathe. Injured, he lay on a bed of sweet-smelling cinnamon ferns, surrounded by an Eseitha hengh, while an old Dragon as bright as summer danced for him, and his broken body hummed in harmony with a powerful prayer for healing. His bones knit together in minutes, whole and sound.

Then he was a young warrior, fighting for his mountain, feeling it his home for the first time. Before him, a goblin army fled down a narrow valley, pursued by his avenging warloche. He stood below his mountain gate, and roared their victory as a new Dragon, strong in his fire. The might he drew from his mountain gave him the power of death to command, and his faith was never stronger.

But he didn't understand it fully, not that young dwarf, not until the old Dragon, bent and white with wisdom, lay on a burning pyre in the Eseitha hengh and clasped the young Dragon's hands in his own as he died. Their fire spoke from bone to bone, and he understood, and he fell on his knees on the crest of the mountain, trembling as his fire and blood flowed into the earth. The old Dragon's hengh crumbled into dust. He wept. Now he truly belonged. He pressed his lips to the softening skin of the mountain, and felt his magic taken like his body, fondled, embraced. Breathless with desire, he drowned in his passion, full with the need to do more, to pour his own magic out, emptying himself to be one with his mountain—one with the land, one with the sky, one with the water, one with the heat of their conjoined heart. And when he had done that, when his promise was made, the stones lay on the earth, his Eseitha stones—clear as glass, bright as tears.

"God under the—" Dwyn couldn't go on.

He *was* the Dragon. And *this* was his mountain.

They rushed into his mind as the Dragon's memories had rushed into his heart. The whole of Ironsfork tumbled into him, floundering angrily in his magic. They were so massive, so beyond the scope of his understanding that he wondered if it weren't the other way around, and he was the one turning helplessly in their current, desperate to paddle to the safety of his own mind.

They were afraid of him. So afraid they planned to kill him to keep him. Their twisted magic was as mangled as their body had been, drawn and quartered so many times that they were scarred from beginning to end. A quarry gouged in their side, not once, but twice. Their folk left, and gone for other mountains—broken, dying, and so very, very alone. They wanted him, they needed him, and they were going to kill him. All along, at every time in his life, in every incarnation, the spike had been for him.

Dwyn cried out, and let go. The strange, frightening magic fled, blazing a trail down the mountain toward the valley, a scarlet snake rippling across the worn, dead landscape, following the length of the wall.

Nyssa had fainted again. The spike withdrew into the ground. Blood fountained from her wound.

"Shit!" Dwyn dropped his sword and pressed both hands over the hole. He would have to burn her to keep her from bleeding out. He didn't know if she would ignite, or if she'd placed protections that would strangle him if he used his fire. That would be like her. But if she had, they shattered when he spoke. "Se arda."

A rush of magic pulsed upward and into him, then into her. Too much. Too strong. He smelled clothes burning, then flesh. He let go with a curse, shaking his hands furiously. But at least she wasn't bleeding now.

He hunkered down in the damp leaves beside Nyssa, staring miserably at his blistered hands. His own fire shouldn't have burned him—that never happened except at recrudescence, when he was at his hottest and most out of control. The rain beat against his back as he wrapped his bare arms around his body, shaken by emotions, desires, and senses he'd never had before.

He tasted his blood, iron-rich, flowing into the earth like a libation to a hungry god. He listened to the trees mutter, surprised in their winter sleep, and they reached out tired roots for the magic seeping down through the ground. All around him the mountain watched, surrounding him with the all too solid wall, awake, suspicious but desperate, holding him hostage now as they had held him under the water and bound him body, blood, and soul to themselves. He knew that with a certainty that made him sure he would doubt his own memory before he would doubt the strange enchantment burning through his mind. Never, not even in the oldest mountains of Appalachia, had he sensed such a fury in the magic of the world. It was as if he'd stood on the surface all his life, never knowing what lay beneath.

He picked up his jacket and balled part of it under Nyssa's head. The pulse in her throat twisted weakly under his touch. Necromancers had huge spleens, and it wasn't unusual for them to lose consciousness until their body released stored blood, but the leaves beneath Nyssa's leg were coated thickly with gore. It might be too much. He'd sat beside Riordiin just like this when the Dragon exhausted himself with bleeding, waiting for him to recover. Sometimes, and he could admit it to himself now, he'd hoped Riordiin would not wake. That would be a peaceful death, one becoming to a great Dragon, instead of the humiliating death that awaited every Dragon in the end—fire in a cramped void cell, waiting for the necromancers to order bloodsmeldt poured over his corpse, like every other dead elemental ever born.

He glanced up at the wall above. It gleamed wetly, like a child coming into the world naked and innocent, but there was nothing innocent about the jagged teeth on the top, or the menacing sense of danger about the foundation. He couldn't go over it. He couldn't go under it. Somewhere there would be a gate, but would it be barred to him?

He crouched, sick and numb. He'd crossed it with Nyssa the

night before without an issue. The sick feeling intensified as he looked at the woman lying in the puddle of blood at his feet. It might be that simple after all—her, and her fucking g'hesh. Nyssa had assumed magical responsibility for him, like the key to a tabah. When the door was forced, it had snapped on her as surely as the library door had smashed his hands. When he'd run from Riordiin, had it been the same? He shut his eyes, remembering his words to Ehrlik. *It was my magic. I don't know how, but it was.*

Nyssa groaned.

He set his hand on her chest. "Don't move."

Her gaze wandered and then drifted onto his face. "You... here. With me?"

"Yes."

"Why?" Her tight lips drew back against her teeth when she shifted and found her pain. "You could have run."

"You don't need to tell me I'm a fool." The hateful vision of the stone growing out of Riordiin's corpse stabbed his memory. Dwyn had been running that night too, running away. A step too close to an ancient land border set in stone by a vengeful Dragon, and Riordiin had paid the price. Dwyn wanted to vomit. *It was my magic. It was. I did it. I murdered him. Whether I meant to or not, it was me.*

Nyssa grabbed his wrist. "We must go back. I need...Nolan."

He shook his head. "Nyssa, I can't carry you. I'm not strong enough."

"I will walk. Help me."

"The moment I try to lift you, warloche, you'll faint. And I'll drop you. You'll bust open and bleed to death."

"I...will...not." Nyssa raised herself on her elbows. She grabbed hold of his muddy jacket; her hand touched the books. She glared at him.

"You help." Her tight whisper contained a touch of arrogance, but when she tried to get up, she slipped, and fell with a frightened cry. She reached for her wound and found his fire

330 R. LEE FRYAR

smoldering over it, holding firm to her skin and exposed muscle. She pulled her fingers away, dripping flame.

"You were bleeding to death."

She shut her eyes. "I won't faint." She pushed his jacket across to him and struggled to rise.

"This is a mistake," he growled, but grabbed the muddy sleeve and slid into it, grunting under the weight. He crouched next to her and she put her left hand on his far shoulder. She threw her other arm around his neck, and locked her hands together. He stood, dragging her up with him.

She didn't faint. She didn't scream. But she sagged against him, and he staggered sideways as she hopped on her right leg, the left one dangling uselessly between them. She screamed, a high, gasping sound.

"Nyssa—" Dwyn tried to lower her down.

"Fuck you!"

He stared up at her, startled.

"Help me," she said, but her voice broke and she whimpered. She ground her teeth as Dwyn stepped forward and she went with him. It took all his strength to struggle up the hill with her, lifting her over fallen logs hidden under leaves and doing his best not to lose his footing on the loose gravel beneath. But it was no easier for her. She was white under her hair by the time he got her to the top. He set her down carefully under a stunted oak tree and doubled over at the edge of the rockslide, panting. "I can't do it," he said, when he could breathe again. "There's no way I can get you down the scree." Nyssa was all muscle, built like a mountain, and she had a good foot on him in height.

"Rest. Then we'll try."

"We're better off here," he said. "They'll be out looking for us soon enough, once it starts getting dark. That won't be long." Rain made it hard to tell the time of day, but it was darker than it had been.

"I'm cold."

"Here." He slumped on the ground next to her, sliding his

sword to one side. He felt nervous letting the fire well up inside of him, afraid he'd be too hot, but nothing felt amiss this time. When he was properly warm, and glowing like a furnace, he put his arm around her and pulled her against him.

Nyssa pressed into his warmth gratefully. "You…never should…" She took a deep breath. "Should never have come here."

"I wanted to leave. It's you who wouldn't let me."

She opened her mouth, as if to argue with him, then groaned. Dwyn sat silent, listening to the wind shiver in the branches above them. He steamed in the darkness, fighting the damp.

Despite his warmth, Nyssa still felt cold, and she quaked against him. She shifted, and he noticed the stain on her pants leaking red, fresh blood.

He sighed. "You're bleeding. I'm going to have to do it again. It's going to hurt pretty bad," he said, setting his warm hand carefully in the mat of blood, clot, and dirt over her wound.

"I know," she said, with disgust.

He branded her good, working his fire down deep into the wound.

She didn't faint. But she cried the whole time. "Meda, meda," she wept, tears pouring down her cheeks. All those times he'd cried for mercy, she hadn't listened, hadn't heeded his pain. He didn't listen either. But he shook when he finished, and he pulled her against him and stroked her hair as if he held Riordiin in his arms, and not Nyssa, his torturer. "You can't walk anymore," he said.

Nyssa didn't argue. She pressed her cheek against his shoulder. He was burning like a bonfire now, but she didn't flinch from him, but held on tightly while her ragged panting slowed as the pain receded and numb shock settled in.

It was my magic. I don't know how, but it was.

All those weeks slaving in the depths of Rivnkyf, falling in love with the magic that had been left to die in that place, bleeding himself dry to restore the library, loving Riordiin so hard he ached when he wasn't touching the man—was there a magic in that he didn't understand? It was the Dragon's mountain, however he hated it, and it had been for generations. Now he was that Dragon.

A vivid picture of himself, twitching on the spike, assaulted him. The loathing and hatred that filled him mingled incongruously with a sense that somehow, that was right and good. The blood dripped gently from his nostrils like the mud drained from the old Dragon's lips. He shuddered. It should have been him. He should have died on that spike at Rivnkyf, and he would have died tonight, but for Nyssa.

"Talk to me," Nyssa's pained voice spoke in his ear. "Please."

"What would you have me say?"

The thread-like beat of her heart weakened under his hands. She lay silent for so long he thought she had fainted again, despite her insistence she would not. "Poem," she whispered.

"You want me to recite for you?"

"Yes."

He launched into *The Siege of Heldasa* without preamble.

Summer weeps the blood of war.
Raven dark the tale I bring.
Tell the bones, the broken bones,
Of mountain lost in crumbled stone,
Heldasa fell, so fall we all.
Songs begun in other tones,
Than ring of sword on riven shield,
No triumph softens sorrow's sting—

Another whisper. "Riordiin. It was like that when he died. Wasn't it?"

Sing the tune, the mourner's tune,
That warloche wrote in bloodstained rune,
The joy in war, the hate of peace—

"Tell me." Nyssa shifted to get closer to Dwyn and the fire crawling down his arms and chest. Dwyn winced as her sharp nails dug into his skin. The sky overhead darkened as evening mixed with the rain. How much longer until Tully or Jullup came looking for them?

"I can't."

"Can't talk to…a friend?"

"*You* are not my friend."

"I said I would speak for you," Nyssa said with effort. "I would see…justice…done."

"It's been done. I deserved everything they gave me."

"No, it wasn't right. Dwyn." She stopped, and drew in a long shuddering breath. "You couldn't—you couldn't have—not…" She trailed off, looking up at him doubtfully.

He remained stubbornly silent.

Her eyes widened.

"It's true. You can't tell me." She closed her eyes. "I chose you…for him…you were better than me. I failed. Go."

"I can't carry you down that rockslide."

"Leave me!"

"If I leave you here, warloche, you're dead."

She made a noise that started as a weak laugh, but she cried at the end. "Then you will…be free." She took a shuddering breath and quieted.

Dwyn eased Nyssa to a sitting position against the trunk of the tree and took off what was left of her raincoat. Great holes gaped where he'd burned it through when he overcame Nyssa's shield against him. He slit it open along the seam, but it wouldn't be enough to cover her completely. He thought of the red coat lying abandoned in the back of the truck, miles away, and useless to him. Surely someone would be out looking for them soon. Three hours to the wall, and he'd been an hour getting her back up the hill at the very least.

Nyssa's eyes opened wearily. "I told you to leave."

"I can't," he said.

Her gaze wandered helplessly over the long patch of jagged boulders and fractured stumps of long dead trees. "Rest," she said and closed her eyes.

Dwyn draped the raincoat over her as the clouds began to shower in earnest.

CHAPTER TWENTY-FIVE

AN UNEASY TRUST

Nyssa slept, or lay in a faint. Dwyn didn't know where one state ended and the other began. When agitation would no longer let him sit inactive beside her, he paced the tree line, returning often to warm her with his body. Sometimes she moaned her thanks. Sometimes she didn't stir.

The woods were as dark as his thoughts, and a melancholy rain drizzled through his memory of a night, not unlike this, when another necromancer's life lay in his hands.

"He asked you, then," Ehrlik said, sitting still and quiet in the bed they shared.

"Yes." Dwyn had been dreading this discussion since he stepped off the private jet that took him to and from Rivnkyf at Riordiin's whim. "He wants me to be his Seidwendr."

"I suppose you fucked him," Ehrlik said, with the barest hint of sarcasm in his voice.

"It happened pretty fast. He surprised me."

"Yes, in other words." Ehrlik sighed.

Dwyn cuddled next to Ehrlik, fists curled against his mentor's bare chest. "There's just this. I can't be his Seidwendr if I'm still yours. I know it's not on the books, and that you'll miss me, but—"

"I won't release you." Ehrlik lay back on the pillows, his face a mask.

"I'll tell him no, then," Dwyn said, but his voice cracked. A week had changed everything. One day he'd been a simple necromancer's Seidoche, overworked and underpaid, looking forward to leaving his assignment. The next day, he was in love and Riordiin meant everything to him. He'd never wanted to say yes to a man so much in his life.

"You want to be with him. You never could hide your feelings from me," Ehrlik said. "But he'll destroy you, Dwyn, like he destroyed his previous Seidwendr. I don't suppose he told you about *that*."

"I read the report myself—a woman, very high on the council, she was the last. He's had no one since she died."

"And you're so eager to die next?"

"A Dragon with a Dragon is a better pairing, theoretically. And there have been dwarves who survived a Seidwendr relationship with a Dragon, if they were sexually active and had a Dragon's blessing—"

"One case, and long ago. You would risk everything on theory and one case out of hundreds. You're a fool, Dwyn." He laughed. "It's one thing I love about you. Fools don't know their own strength, and so they do the impossible where others would fail."

"I need your help. I need your release," Dwyn begged.

"You *do* need my help," Ehrlik agreed. "The council will approve you as Riordiin's Seidwendr, I know. They'll have one less Dragon to care for in his dotage, and Riordiin is wealthy enough to bury you both."

"But if you don't release me from your service, I can't."

"You can't be his Seidwendr, no. But he could be yours."

The rain beating against the skylight in Ehrlik's sumptuous bedroom sounded suddenly loud.

"I'm not a guild-certified necromancer, only a Seidoche." Dwyn hardly trusted his own voice. "It's against the law—"

"Tell me, Dwyn, honestly, how do you find the Northern Dragon? What do you think of his magic? Is he, or is he not, of the illustrious coals of his ancestors, Cheyloche Daffyd and Cheyloche Rivnstone? You know them, Dwyn. You're steeped in their words, their magic, their minds. The truth, now."

Dwyn could never lie. "I find him—lacking."

"Of course you do, Dwyndoche. You are a better necromancer than he is, and you know it. So would he, if he could comprehend it." Ehrlik rose, and poured himself a glass of wine. "He's incendiary already, Dwyn, you might as well say it."

"That doesn't mean he doesn't deserve my help." His body still burned with Riordiin's caresses, his lips tingled with his kisses, and he longed for the bonfire when they made love. Ehrlik might call him beloved, but Ehrlik had never dropped on his knees like Riordiin had, pressing his face against Dwyn's naked thighs, begging him to love him and never leave.

"So, help him," Ehrlik said, sipping his wine. "Tell him you will make the bond with him. I will draw up the terms and swear you have no impediments that would prevent you from joining. If the g'hesh is written with care, there's little chance he'll detect any alteration in the magic—not in his state."

"But if he does find out, if anyone else finds out—"

"Dwyn, if you were his necromancer, and not his stooge of a Seidwendr, could you protect his mind, hold his magic together, and help him survive his last years with grace and dignity? Honest answer. Could you?"

"I think I could." Dwyn said, faintly dizzy. Wonderful, wild landscapes of magic opened up for him as he warmed to the notion, overwhelming him with the pleasure of taking that broken, fractured soul and protecting it.

He half rose from the bed, seizing Ehrlik's hand to kiss it.

"But the council, what will I say when they ask?"

Ehrlik smiled, and pressed a finger against Dwyn's lips. "You can't speak of our bond. We set that in stone long ago, didn't we, and a good thing too. You leave the council to me."

"But I—"

"Dwyn." Ehrlik kissed him. "Don't you trust me?"

He shuddered. Even remembering that memory should have caused his bones to ache and his throat to constrict—more proof that whatever had happened between him and the mountain was rewriting his magic from the bones out.

"Dwyn?"

He turned around. Nyssa's legs moved feebly beneath the raincoat.

"What is it?"

"I'm bleeding again," she whispered.

He pressed his hands over her wound, applying fresh fire. Nyssa didn't even groan—not a good sign.

"I'm sorry," she said.

"Try to stay awake." Dwyn sat down with her and tucked her frigid hands beneath his beard.

"Walk."

"We talked this over an hour ago. You couldn't then, and you can't now. It's late. They'll be looking."

Her shivers lessened as his fire kindled. "I'm thirsty."

"Wouldn't say no to a glass of beer myself—a big tall one— and all the fried cicadas I could eat."

She smiled weakly. "Not hungry."

"I'd eat your share."

No answer. He glanced over at her. Her eyes were rolled back in her head again. He shook her gently. She was limp.

"Hurry up, Tully, damn you." Nyssa could live or die, he wasn't leaving now, even if the g'hesh broke in an instant like glass. The mountain had twisted his words to keep him from ever leaving Ironsfork alive.

He shivered so hard his teeth chattered. Every poem he'd ever memorized from the ancient legends of the Southern Kingdom spoke of mountains as living, breathing things—metaphors, he'd been taught, and he'd certainly written as much in his own translations. A mountain was the sum of the magic of the folk living in it, it had no magic of its own. Yet he'd clearly heard a voice in the lake, and in his dreams the Dragon spoke of his mountain as a man speaks of his mate. He'd felt the urge to take the stones from the old Eseitha hengh, to fill them with magic and brood them in his blood, as the Dragon in his dreams had done.

"No. I heard nothing, saw nothing, felt nothing—" His bones twisted and he gasped. The Dragon's dark thoughts crowded in—his thoughts, Dwyn realized with some uneasiness. He'd long ago accepted that as Mn'Hesset, his memory was less his own than a repository for centuries of magic conducted in the service of the God of the Dead. Elemental fire might be the same. The Dragon had lived on in his flame. His song still echoed in Dwyn's ears, and his own name rang out like a ceaseless dirge: Dwyn, Dwyn, Dwyn. Where the hell had his grandfather come by that name? He wished the old man still lived. He'd shake him good for not telling him where he came from.

A dog barked, far off.

"Kritha." Dwyn eased Nyssa to the ground and stood. He tucked his jacket under her head.

She moaned.

"Someone's coming. Don't move." He flared and walked to the edge of the boulder field. "Kritha!"

More barking. Louder. Closer.

He stumbled and pitched forward, cracking his knees on the jagged rocks. "Kritha! Here, dog! I'm here!"

The barking stopped.

"Fuck!" He wrestled a boulder loose and set it rolling. It clattered down the slope, bouncing a few feet, but stopped well short of causing enough noise to draw attention.

"Kritha!" He squinted, looking for lights in the forest below. The dog barked again, moving east, away from him.

He glanced up at Nyssa lying like a corpse on the hillside. He looked down at the narrow valley where the wall stood, a dark shadow of his own making, crouched in twilight.

Slowly he knelt and kissed the earth.

A small dwarf, brown, and lean as a rat, ran through a sodden field. Rain beat his fire down. He carried the sword of a Southern Dragon strapped across his back, but he looked lost in their drab landscape of water and weed.

They tasted his magic curiously. They sampled his fear when he stood in the water below the stone bridge, knee deep in the bare willows before their door. They admired the way he fought when the necromancer—curse her and her kind!—attacked him in the river.

It had been so long, so very long since magic like his had touched them. Water was all they knew, and that one...there was no hope with that one. The hengh was made for him and others like him, and he had broken it, pulled it down. He didn't listen when they called to him in dreams.

But this one, this young Dragon swaying in the tree, pouring out his blood recklessly for the barest measure of protection, they had hope for him. The passionate ones, those with the ancient lust latent in their bones, they could be made to hear.

They whispered to him as he lay insensible, but the horrible void constrained their speech. They cried to him in dreams, but he fled from them to the realm of the dead, like a necromancer born and bred, and they despaired.

He was too different, mixed of magics that had no business being in union—twisted and evil—a miserable thing that should have died centuries ago when it was conceived and buried.

And yet, he danced.

So they gave him their Eseitha, and he gathered them greedily as any young lover might, bled them full of his toxic fear and hatred, and sowed them vigorously like nettles to wound them. Lust he had in abundance, wicked, furious lust, and they would have killed him for it, taken his magic and eaten it, only…

His mouth moved in the mud with their lament. *"Lonely. We are so lonely. These stones, these trees, these wretched folk. They have each other. We have no one."* The voice that came from him was legion. That great immensity of magic he'd touched with his blood on the spike rushed into him once more.

A million voices shouted, answering him, accusing him, threatening him, pleading with him, as raucous a noise as a haneen full of warring factions, all shouting to make themselves heard. A torrent of anger and pain engulfed him, and he bobbed along in the current, helpless as a leaf in a flood. Yet he was part of it all, and not the least of the voices screaming to be acknowledged, a furious, bright spark, afraid lest the enormous magic extinguish him.

"Help me!" He roared angrily above the sea of voices.

You have not helped us, Dragon. You have poisoned us. You have made us like yourself—a demon of the underworld, a lover of death—and we do not accept you.

"I give you my word, whatever wrong I have done you, I will make it right! I will."

You have given your curse to us.

"I didn't know," he cried. "I didn't know you. I didn't know *of* you."

We should have killed you. Your promises are lies! You do not honor your agreements, Dragon!

Horror filled him as he saw the image of himself, green, bloated, and rotting in the lake. It took all the courage he could find in himself to yell, "But you didn't kill me. And as I live, I will…" He stopped.

Silence. Waiting.

"I—I will honor the promise I made to you. My life. My love. My strength. I don't know what you want of me, or why. There is no one left who can teach me this magic. But I will try. Help me. Kill me if there is no other way, but help me now."

A hum, deep and resonant as a hive of bees, took the place of the silence, as if the voices were joining, coming together to a consensus. When they spoke, they used one voice—deep, bass, and doubtful—his voice.

You would die for us?

"If there was no other way."

You will trust us? You will love us? You will bind your blood to our blood? To our earth? Our air? Our water? Our flame?

"Yes." His nostrils were full of mud and leaves, and he smelled the decay and rot in his magic as he burned and the mountain stirred inside him.

The necromancer's blood belongs to us. She has hurt you, and if your fire is ours, we will avenge you.

"No! She is one of your folk. She is of your...our mountain. And she is...she is my friend." His bones didn't ache. A warmth and a strength that was never his own filled him. A soft voice tickled his ears like a lover's, sweet and tremulous.

Our mountain? Ours?

"Ours."

Dwyn was soiled from head to boots when he rolled over and saw the hill. Every tree was on fire in full leaf: golden, orange, blue and red. The foliage crackled with magic.

"God under the earth!" He'd never done anything like this, not with his fire, not with his necromancy. He stumbled to where Nyssa lay just short of the inferno.

"Dwyn." Nyssa's voice was weak. She touched his muddy beard. "What—"

"I don't know! I don't know!"

The branches swayed overhead, and clouds of embers danced around him. Nyssa cried out. He smelled the rotten-egg stench of hair burning.

Sparks flew as he slid his arms under her body. "I'll get you out of here. I'll carry you."

He groaned as he lifted. She was heavy, and he was too small. He fell to one knee.

"Dwyn!"

"Hang on." He staggered up. He was laboring for breath again when he set Nyssa down clear of the fire. The blaze surged into the wet sky like a beacon.

With a sudden crack, the tree Nyssa had been lying under lost its top to the fire.

"My books!"

"Dwyn!" Nyssa screamed, but he pelted up the hill as fast as a greyhound.

"Shit. Oh, shit. God, no!" He dug frantically through the wreckage.

"Dwyn!"

"No. I won't. I won't lose them. Not now. Not now." They were weeping—crying his name. "Paloh mhu, let me save them!" The heat blistered his forehead. His skin was melting. His hair was burning. He coughed, fighting the smoke.

A shape, hairy and horrible leapt at him. He reached for his sword, but Kritha had him by the belt, pulling him, dragging him away. He kicked her. She yelped.

Morven loomed out of the blackness and grabbed him by his shoulders.

"No, let me go! They're all I have!"

Morven pinned his arms against his back and wrestled him down the hill. Lights moved below like strange, misshapen suns.

Tully's gravelly voice shouted, "Go back! Get help."

"Kritha, stay," Morven ordered. The dog plopped down beside Nyssa.

Tully charged up the hill. Another dwarf was with him, someone thin and wiry—Lokey maybe.

"No." Dwyn fought against Morven's restraint. "They're all I have."

"Nyssa." Tully sank to his knees. He touched Nyssa's wounded leg like he would put it back together if he could only find all the pieces.

It wasn't Lokey after all. It was the goblin, Midian. His braids gleamed beetle-black in the firelight. "We need to make a stretcher. Morven, your jacket. We'll tie the arms together." He was already taking off his coat. Morven let Dwyn go and struggled out of hers.

"No." Dwyn knelt, facing the burning mountain. He covered his face with his hands, and rocked, weeping. "No, no, no…"

"I'll take this end. Tully, help me. Morven, get the other. Dragon!"

"I die! I die here!" He couldn't leave, not with his soul burning on the pyre of his heresy.

Tully yanked Dwyn up by his hair.

Furious, he ignited, reaching for his sword. The g'hesh tightened.

Nyssa gasped. "Don't, Dwyn—don't make me hurt you."

His vision blurred. He stumbled to her side, and set his burned and bloody hand on the edge of the coat, grabbed his corner and lifted. Nyssa's whole body seized. She cried out.

"Honey, honey…" Tully was on his side, at Nyssa's head.

"Hold on," the goblin said.

And so Dwyn did. He turned his back on the ruins of his soul. All he was, all he had ever been, was lost forever.

Nyssa said nothing on the slow, laborious journey down the mountain. Sometimes Dwyn thought she had fainted only to find her eyes fixed on him whenever he glanced her way.

A horrified disbelief gripped him when they reached the end of the boulder field. He was wrong. Everything was fine. It could not have happened. His books were at Ironsfork, safe in the mountain. His soul was safe. In a minute he would wake from this nightmare.

But he didn't. He stumbled through places where sawbriar drew curtains around the corpses of fallen trees, trying to keep pace with Tully. Lights flashed ahead in the distance, blue and red and white against the darkness, illuminating the clearing, scattered vehicles, and giants walking through the woods— human paramedics.

"Tully," Nyssa murmured, "Dwyn. Void."

"I'll put him there."

"No!" Dwyn jerked around, angry and frightened.

Nyssa grabbed Dwyn's hand and squeezed. "Trust me."

"Why?" Breathing hard, he helped Tully lift Nyssa over a ditch.

"Your fire," Nyssa said. "Might be a problem."

"At the hospital?"

She nodded. "When Nolan takes it off it will hurt you."

"I don't care." But Nyssa was right. He'd poured a great deal of his magic into her wounded body, and when Nolan tore the protection away, Dwyn would feel it break loose inside.

"You'll do as she says, Dragon." Tully dripped as he walked, squelching in his boots as his water magic flowed hard and strong.

Nyssa reached again, but didn't touch his hand. "Be all right."

Like hell. Fire curled the pages of his life and his soul was ashes. His heart still beat, but there was an ax through it. The garish lightning of the ambulance flashed, silhouetting Lokey between trucks. He shouted something. Nolan loomed through the winking shadows.

Dwyn stepped fearfully away as a tall woman in medical scrubs ordered him out of the way, and Nyssa was lifted from the makeshift stretcher onto a real one, with Nolan crouched over top of her, his Dragon's protection shielding everyone from Nyssa's leg, glowing like a stick of burning wood.

Dwyn stood well back as they loaded Nyssa into the ambulance. Nolan asked questions in a low voice, and Nyssa replied weakly, but he couldn't hear what they were saying.

"You did this, Dragon," Tully said quietly. "I know you did. If it's the last thing I do, I'll make you pay for it."

The potent hatred of the mountain rushed through him, a fresh influx of complicated emotions belonging to a magic as large and wild as a hurricane. Our mountain. Not Tully's anymore. Dwyn shivered. Wanted or not, it was part of him now.

The doors to the ambulance closed. Lights flashing, it moved off down the road.

Dwyn rode to Ironsfork with Tully, sitting in the passenger seat. Ahead, Morven drove Midian's truck, rocketing over potholes like they weren't there. She would be the first to tell Jullup what had happened. And Jullup would ask Dwyn, the same as Tully, and later Nolan, "What did you do?"

What could he say? *It was my magic. I don't know how, but it was.*

Maybe, he wouldn't talk at all. He would lie in the void room and die like the old Dragon in the mud and let death rot him in disgrace. Kritha leaned over the seat, panting anxiously in his ear. He wished she'd killed him that night in his room.

He was relieved when Tully took him right down to the void room, and Jullup didn't ask him anything. She made the path for him to enter and left with Tully for the hospital.

For the first time since coming to Ironsfork, Dwyn was truly alone. He could die if he wished, thrust his blade into his side, and by the time anyone came, he would be beyond help.

He unstrapped Mh'Arda slowly and gripped the hilt, fingers shaking. With an anguished cry, he threw the sword, still sheathed, across the room. It clattered against the closed door. He lay down on the stone, curled up around the ball of pain in his heart, and wept.

CHAPTER TWENTY-SIX

THE DESOLATION
OF THE DRAGON

When Dwyn first crossed into the void, sudden panic had seized him. Something was wrong with the air. He couldn't breathe. Then he found he could, and the fear was not wholly his own. He couldn't hear the voices anymore, but faces of dwarves long dead beneath mountains in the South stared at him, and he relived their horror as they died in the embrace of their own mountain. His mind was besieged with images—whole mountain ranges on fire, trees burning, bones piled on bones, gates broken and pouring smoke.

He lay awake all night, body burning, mind on fire, waiting for dawn or for the mountain to fall in on him. He knew which one he'd prefer.

Dawn came, and with it, Nolan. The Seidroche's hair trailed in loose ropes over his shoulders; his gray face looked ashen. He slumped on the bench and watched Dwyn finish pissing down the drain.

Dwyn zipped up. "How is she?"

"Lucky." Nolan pulled a thelon out of his pocket and absently combed his mop back into the usual long ponytail he wore.

"Is she home?"

"No. In a few days, perhaps. She lost a lot of blood." Nolan gazed fixedly at Dwyn. "I suppose this is where you tell me it was an accident. You didn't mean to do it. You had no control."

Dwyn left the drain and leaned against the half-wall guarding the bath. "If I said it, you wouldn't believe me."

Nolan stood, eyes flashing dangerously. "No. I wouldn't."

Dwyn cringed. The new magic seemed to crowd into his bones, as if seeking his protection.

"It's time you and I understood each other, warloche," Nolan said. "I knew what you were the moment Nyssa carried you in, ranting about broken promises. You're the worst kind of scum, Dwyn Ardoche, a liar and a murderer. You knew exactly what you were doing, didn't you?"

"I didn't mean to kill Riordiin." Had he known, had he understood, he'd have thrown himself in the way of that spike without hesitation.

"I'm not talking about Riordiin. I'm talking about Nyssa. You meant to kill her."

"Yes." He wouldn't hide it. There was no point.

"Why?"

"You say I'm scum. Isn't that reason enough? You've already condemned me." He turned away from Nolan.

Nolan yanked Dwyn off the floor. "Don't turn your back on me, Dragon!" His breath, smelling of hospital, left a film of spit on Dwyn's skin that sizzled and smoked.

Dwyn hung in the air burning like a blast furnace. "I wanted to escape! Is that so hard for you to understand? I didn't care if I lived or died, as long as I was free!"

Nolan jerked his head in the direction of the sword lying on the floor outside the void. "If you didn't care about death, your deliverance was at hand."

"I don't deserve to die," he said.

Nolan let go of him. "You don't deserve to die?"

Dwyn jerked his shirt front down. "That reward is reserved for better men than I."

Nolan's hackles rose. "You tell me what you did, now, or I will call you guilty of attempted murder and see the necromancer hunting you has the chain he needs to take you away from here."

Dwyn's fire surged chaotically, as directionless as his life, what remained of it. "Nyssa will tell you. Let her condemn me."

"She has refused to press charges."

If the stone had impaled him then, Dwyn couldn't have been more surprised.

"But I'm not so forgiving," Nolan said. "You didn't use your sword to stab her, and it wasn't a stob of wood like she says. That wound was full of magic, from the layers of fire you used to cauterize it to the way you slit her artery, just enough that she would bleed out. It's as perfect as any trained necromancer could do, clean as a scalpel. Do you deny it was your magic?"

He returned Nolan's stare stoically. "I don't deny it."

The silence became so loud even the water trickling endlessly down the drain seemed hushed.

"And yet you saved her life," Nolan mused. "Why?"

"Because she didn't deserve to die, either."

Nolan rubbed his beard thoughtfully, as if making up his mind about something. Finally, he spoke. "Are you ready to go?"

"Is Ehrlik here?" Dwyn barely got the words past the lump of terror in his throat.

"I'm here to take you out of the void. Jullup wanted me to bring you upstairs, but Nyssa insisted you would be more comfortable in your own quarters. I agreed."

"Then—then you aren't going to condemn me either?"

Nolan's expression was inscrutable. "Not today, I think." He held out his hand.

Dwyn got across the boundary with more than his usual fireworks. Nolan didn't notice, or perhaps he didn't care to. He marched down the corridor behind Dwyn, a huge, solemn, frightening presence. Tully's waterfalls were absent from the main cavern and from his doorway, but Dwyn wasn't soothed. The voices inside of him, released from the void, were all speaking at once. A silencer—that was the first thing he'd need to gain a measure of peace.

Nikl's bearlike figure appeared in the doorway. He grabbed Dwyn's hand. "Are you all right? I wanted to come to the void room and stay with you, but Nolan said no."

Nolan smiled. "Take care of him for me, Thunderer. It's food and rest he needs."

"I know what he needs."

Nikl guided Dwyn to the kitchen table. "I'll get you a drink. This is ridiculous. Save someone's life, and they throw you in the void room like a criminal. There's no justice for elementals, none at all. Persimmon brandy," he said, coming back from the counter with a glass. "Best thing in the world for shock."

Dwyn drank the amber liquid, not really tasting it. It should be something stronger. Something lethal.

"God, you look terrible. Do you want a bath, or could you eat something first?"

"I'd take another one of these." He raised his empty glass.

"Only one for you, sweetheart. I don't want you turning into Lokey on me. Then I'll get you cleaned up and put you to bed." He set his hands on Dwyn's dirty legs and kneaded them gently. "I'll get you out of here. I promise."

"Don't promise what you can't give." Dwyn said, blinking tears away.

"I mean it," Nikl said, whispering urgently. "You'll be free."

"What are you talking about?" The tumult of voices in his mind quieted.

"First—I want to ask you, would you go to Norway if I could arrange it? I would join you in a few months, as soon as I find someone to take over the kitchen. I have family there after all."

"You said they gave you indigestion."

"Sure," Nikl said, laughing. "But you'd be there. You're all I need to make me hungry again."

God under the earth. Nikl melted him inside, although the words comforted him less than the hot brandy searing his empty stomach. Still, they were kind words. "I appreciate the thought," he said.

"It's not a thought," Nikl said. "Will you go? Wait for me? I have a brother—a half-brother—at Nations. He thinks he can help. He's a Seidoche on the necromancer's council there. His name is Ehrlik, he said you would remember him—"

Dwyn turned the chair over and landed on the floor. The glass shattered. "You. You called him. It was you!"

Nikl lit up like a summer sky full of heat lightning. "He said he would help."

"Help me to death! Help me to a void cell at Nations!"

"No, you idiot! I told him you were in a bad spot here with this stupid penalty. He said he'd get you out of it. He has friends—powerful friends—what the hell is wrong with you, Dwyn? You're going to burn the mountain down."

He's here to take me all right! Take me back to Nations and throw me under the mountain where the light never shines." Dwyn grabbed the chair, lit it, and held it up, ready to defend himself.

"Dwyn?"

"Get out!" Dwyn blazed. "Get the fuck out of my mountain!"

With a screech, the cat bolted for the safety of the hallway. Nikl ran, taking his thunderstorm with him.

Dwyn cast his silencer. It didn't work as well as he hoped so he drank the rest of the brandy Nikl had brought, and most of a bottle of wine left beside the lonely array of ardchuk. Nikl had called Ehrlik. He should have guessed. Ehrlik's smile. Ehrlik's home country. Ehrlik's temper, Ehrlik's passion, Ehrlik's betrayal. It had all been there, and he'd chosen not to see it.

If there was any mercy in this new hell, he'd die of alcohol poisoning before he had to face the next day. He passed out below his freshly-made bed.

When a noise woke him, Dwyn was stiff and cold. For one moment he thought he was waking up still drunk on the floor of his grandfather's home in Heldasa. Behind him, wrapped in a sheet, the old man lay dead. Bread was laid on the table for his final journey, but all the wine was in Dwyn—it had been the only thing that worked on his grief.

A clatter in the kitchen tumbled him into reality.

"Nikl?"

Someone was thrashing a pan to death with a spoon. Dwyn cracked his eyes open. They broke apart like scales.

Now that his fury had passed, he felt sick inside. Sadness overwhelmed him. He'd lost everything—his soul, his God, the will to die, the will to live. And Nik. He'd lost Nik. He struggled onto his hands and knees.

The din reached a crescendo as Dwyn staggered up. It seemed that the solid floor had turned into a mountain slope. He tumbled down the room and slammed into the wall with a resounding thud.

"Nik?"

The noise ceased.

"Nik!" Dwyn began the uphill climb toward the kitchen but foundered in the attached library when he couldn't navigate the stone table.

"Nik?" He whispered.

No answer. Not even the sound of footsteps.

A half-hour or more plodded past before Dwyn made it into the kitchen. The counter was bare. Nikl had collected his ardchuk. The only sign they'd ever been there was the faint scars that magical fire always left on stone surfaces.

Dwyn hobbled to the refrigerator holding onto the counter

for support. His hands were a mass of blisters—ones he hadn't already burst in his wild merry-go-round-the-room earlier.

The refrigerator was bare. The stacks of frozen food were gone. There had been a bowl with leftover borscht—also gone—but he could still smell it. He followed the aroma to the trashcan. He found the soup, melting down an avalanche of used cat litter.

Dwyn kicked the can furiously, knocking it over, then stumbled to the couch and dropped. He stared hopelessly at the ceiling.

The vision of a tree presented itself, a majestic pine, soaring to the clouds, beset by fire. The needles burned, and flaming cones crackled in the branches. The roots drove through the stone like greedy black claws, pulling death magic from a pile of skulls. The cones fell at his feet, and sprang up, a million tiny flames, closing around his stump like children reaching for his hands. He shuddered.

"Stop it," he said, but he didn't think the mountain heard him. Silencers went both ways.

He winced as another image surfaced—himself, naked, standing in the center of the black monstrosity of his Eseitha hengh. He knelt, pressed his lips to the earth and kissed it. The ground swallowed him whole.

"Paloh…" He couldn't say it. He buried his face in his hands.

"Dwyn?" Lokey looked in anxiously. "I heard you cry out. Are you all right?"

"Do I look like I'm all right?" He sobbed.

Lokey's gaze rested on the overturned trashcan. "He's just angry. He'll get over it."

"He didn't get over it with you, did he?"

"Well, I didn't give him any incentive to. Why don't you come upstairs? I'm not a cook, but I can do toast, and I know a thing or two about hangovers." He helped Dwyn up. "Come on, Dragon. I can't do toast without a toaster."

Lokey parked Dwyn on the couch in the sitting room. After toast, a glass of orange juice, and half a cup of cold coffee, Dwyn fell asleep again. He didn't wake until Morven slammed the door. Startled, he spilled onto the floor.

Morven stalked toward him, beer can in one hand. Her eyes glowed with a wicked yellow light. "You tricked me. I never should have trusted you."

Dwyn used the couch to right himself.

"Lied like a necromancer, huh? What about you, asshole?"

"Morven!" Lokey said, coming up from the music room, "Leave him alone."

She backed away, free hand on her hip. "I thought Mom told you to feed him, not fuck him. Been in his pants already, have you?"

"None of your business. Did you find Nikl for me?"

"He's at Rich Mountain, thundering around the kitchen. Turned about three different shades of green when I told him you wanted to talk." She smirked at Dwyn. "What exactly did you do to him?"

"What did the council decide?" Lokey asked. "Did he say?"

"Why would he tell me anything? He was pissed as hell."

"Did he?"

"He said they condemned it."

Dwyn slumped forward. Jullup's words came back to him. *We will not need you. Whiterock will not want you.*

"And then he told me Nyssa got Rachet and Jack together on the phone and blocked them. Hey!"

Lokey snatched the beer from Morven's hands. "Get another," he snarled, giving it to Dwyn. He sauntered down the stairs back to his music room. "And get him something to eat," he added in a shout that made Dwyn cringe.

"He's your Dragon, not mine. You feed him!" She stomped out of the sitting room.

But she returned shortly carrying a glass bowl full of a nebulous mass of cold pasta and an apple. She handed the bowl to him.

He took it. "Thanks."

"Shut up. I'm not talking to you."

He ate slowly, but the beer he drank in two gulps. His head was pounding.

Morven sat across from him in the recliner with her second beer. She sliced the apple with her pocket knife. "You are Lokey's Dragon now, aren't you?"

"I'm nobody's Dragon," he said.

Nyssa came home two days later in a wheelchair. Her face was purple and blotchy, and she looked tired.

Dwyn stood, setting his paper aside. "Let me help."

"I can manage." She backed up and rolled forward, angling herself to his table. A bulge in her left leg showed where the bandage stretched her pants. "Yes, it hurts," she said, before he asked. "The muscles are torn."

"I'm sorry." He sat down at his writing table. He'd been scribing almost continuously for the past day and a half. It was the only thing that could distract him from the voices that never left him alone.

"So you said." Nyssa touched the finished book of fables he'd bound that morning. "I'm sorry about your books."

"It was my fault."

"Yes. But still, I am sorry."

"Nyssa, I—"

"Don't apologize. I know exactly what you meant to do, Dwyn." Nyssa thumbed through the book. The stiff pages whispered together as she flipped them. "Nolan told me what you said in the void. It surprised me. That's not the way a Seidwendr defends himself. A necromancer, now—prevaricating, hiding every truth—that sounds about right."

Dwyn sucked in his breath.

Nyssa set the book down. "Don't be afraid. I'm not going to tell anyone what you did, and I'm not going to demand you tell me. I don't want the other necromancers to know. But I think I know who talked you into it, and I think I understand why. I will only convict you of what you are guilty of."

"Murder." The word choked him.

"Maybe. But if I condemned you for that, I could never punish you as much as you have punished yourself." She held out a letter. "Open this. I want to see what Nations has in store for you before I say more."

She read over his shoulder. He hated that. But by the end of reading he was grateful when she took the arrest warrant calmly from his burning hand.

"I won't...I can't..."

Nyssa batted out the flames on the edge of the letter. "I'm not going to let him take you."

"If Ehrlik convinces your warloche council I'm a murderer—"

"He won't."

"You don't know how persuasive he can be."

"I know he persuaded you to take this." Nyssa took his left hand in hers and stroked the rune. She sighed. "I wanted to kill you, Dwyn. I wanted you dead for the sake of all that was just in the world. Then you saved my life, and suddenly, I'm not so sure that I haven't been monstrously wrong about everything— Riordiin, you, what happened that night at Rivnkyf—but whatever the truth is, I owe you my life now. Let me pay my debt. Let me defend you."

"What is there to defend?" A film of lava crept down his hand and sizzled on the stone table. "Ehrlik will take me back to Nations and I will die."

"Not if I help you—"

"You don't know Ehrlik."

"And you don't know me." Her bare jaw stuck out stubbornly. "I need you to trust me."

Dwyn slammed the lid on his writing box. "How can I trust you when you, Nolan, and Tully want to send me back to Nations?"

"I promise you, Dwyn, I don't want to do that—not now— and neither does Nolan."

"If I stay—and I'll have to stay—what will happen to me? You gave me six months to complete my penalty. I'll never make that. You'll kill me with that g'hesh in the end. It will eat me alive!"

"The penalty can be amended, and a new g'hesh applied—"

He exploded. "No more g'hesh! I'm sick of them."

Nyssa had that infinitely patient look that probably meant she was losing what little she had. She would tell him he was being foolish, that he should take what she offered and hope she didn't renege.

But she didn't. Instead, she looked down at the table, and folded her hands. "Would it help if you knew? Perhaps so— and I said I would tell you. A long time ago, I fell in love with a Dragon. I found him a singular necromancer—clever, exacting, and a beautiful Dragon. I would have incinerated myself if I thought it would save him. We knew, the council and I, that he would develop the same incendiary state that claimed the Daffyds, and the Rivnstones before them. I accepted the risk," she said, nostrils flaring. "I offered myself as Seidwendr to him. I thought I was strong enough to hold his memory and magic together. It almost killed me."

She paused.

Tentatively, Dwyn touched her hand. His heat pulsed up through her skin.

"I shouldn't have survived. There was only one warloche who ever stood proper Seidwendr for a Dragon and lived. I sought him out for my sickness. He saved my life."

"Nolan," Dwyn said softly. "He was Seidwendr to Cheyloche Rivnstone, wasn't he? The tattoo. Only a Dragon necromancer would have thought of such a thing, and only the bravest of dwarves would ever have dared accept it."

"Yes. When I came back home to Ironsfork, he took care of me, he and Tully both. I'm not whole—I never will be. There are consequences I live with. But when I realized I was dying, before I left Nations, I searched for a young Dragon, someone who could bear Riordiin's fire, and all the harm that came with it. I found one. I had ordered an investigation of the sellers of illegal artifacts in the South. There were deals for suppliers who listed their sources. Among them I found a curiosity—a boy from Tennessee with a penchant for tomb robbing. They told me he was unusually intelligent, he'd taught himself to read and write Dh'Seitha, and he was a Dragon. I wrote the necessary papers needed to bring him to Nations. Then I went home to die."

"And Riordiin gave you the original works by the Northern Dragon himself, Byrd Oxfire, for your sacrifice."

Nyssa smiled. "I wondered how long it would take you to figure that out."

"You aren't quite what I imagined you to be, Dragon's Friend."

"I meant to be a friend to you, too. I left instructions. I gave orders that you were to be educated and live in the colony while you were trained for Riordiin's use, but always to be treated well. You were to be rewarded for your sacrifice, not brought to it like a prisoner with no choice in the matter. I wanted you to be taken care of."

He shuddered and let go of her hand. "Until I died like him? A slow death, losing my mind, trying to hold him together—who were you to make me choose between a dying Dragon or staying in Heldasa to wait for my grandfather to die and leave me homeless? What kind of a fucking choice is that?"

Nyssa shifted uncomfortably in her chair. "I'm sorry. I have caused you much suffering."

Much? How about all of it? His bones creaked and the fresh rush of guilt and anger made him queasy. No, he hadn't known what he was getting into with Riordiin, but neither had she.

"Ehrlik means to take you back to Nations. I can force him to wait the six months, but only because of the challenge I have against your refusal to take exemption. In the meantime, I will extend the working time for your g'hesh to protect you from injury. But there is another way for you to find shelter from extradition, something more permanent." Nyssa took a deep breath. "Become Seidwendr to me."

CHAPTER TWENTY-SEVEN

THE DRAGON
AT BAY

Dwyn ignited when she asked him. The smoke hadn't cleared
yet. Everything he'd told Morven came back to him. *It's a good job*
with the right necromancer, a share in power. You'd be provided for, cared
for, everything you want.

"It's been nine years," Nyssa reminded him. "By law, you may
take a new necromancer, even if your arrangement with Ehrlik
was not entirely legal in the first place."

"I need to think."

"In the meantime, pack your things. You're moving into my
quarters."

He looked up. "Oh, hell. Is this because I didn't say yes?"

Nyssa backed away from the table. "Hardly. Ehrlik could come
to Ironsfork and seek you out. I'd rather you not be disturbed.
As my guest, you will enjoy my privacy as a necromancer. I have
work to do, but Lokey will help you settle in."

Kritha was lying in front of Nyssa's desk when Lokey opened
the library door. Every muscle in Dwyn's body tightened. Kritha

surveyed him with a long, steady look, not unlike Nyssa's serpent stare, then she folded her paws and rested her massive red and white head on her feet.

"You could leave your writing box in here." Lokey unlocked the door that led to Nyssa's quarters. "Nyssa wouldn't mind."

"No thanks." He didn't feel comfortable doing that. Nothing was comfortable about this.

He followed Lokey up the short spiral staircase and through another doorway, past a kitchen, through a sparsely furnished sitting room, and into a narrow hallway.

The minimalist Nation's look persisted in the guest room. The bed was big enough for two, but barely. A simple metal chest for clothing stood alone and aloof on one wall. A chair of white wood hovered ghost-like beside a desk, but such a desk it was—sumptuously, voluptuously walnut—it looked as out of place as he felt. Dwyn set his writing box on it.

"There're extra bedsheets in the chest," Lokey said. "The bath is up the hall, and I'm pretty sure Nyssa doesn't want me telling you this, but the key to her liquor cabinet is in the third kitchen drawer, left side beneath the soup ladle. Simple inlay illusion on it."

"Lokey—stay with me. Please." He stared up at the ceiling.

"You think I didn't feel the same way when I left him? You'll get past it. I did."

Dwyn sobbed a laugh. "I thought I'd be past it already. It wasn't like it should have meant anything—not like we exchanged thelon or something. It's just—he's got this way, this..." He stopped, unsure of what he wanted. Lokey. He wanted Lokey. That would help.

Lokey's blue eyes filled with kindness and pity. "Let me tell you something about Nikl. He does this with everyone, and I mean *everyone*. I wasn't his first. He knows how to hook a man. He wines them, dines them, he calls everyone sweetheart after one fuck. It doesn't mean a thing, but he's worse than a tick when you try to pull him loose. He'll make you pay for it. He

362 R. LEE FRYAR

calls that love. You tell me—is love supposed to be like that?"

Dwyn didn't know. He didn't care. He only knew he needed strong arms holding him and soft words of love whispered in his ear. "Please, stay. I want you."

Lokey ran a thin, smooth hand over Dwyn's forehead. "No, you don't, not really. You just want to fuck to forget him."

"And that's wrong?"

"No. I get that a lot this time of year." Lokey held Dwyn's face in both hands and open-mouth kissed him.

It was over too soon. It was always over too soon.

Dwyn watched Lokey dress, admiring his shining skin, the way the damp sweat of lovemaking turned Lokey's wavy hair into curls that framed a face so divine it hurt. He didn't want him to go, but after what Lokey had said about Nikl, about how possessive he was, Dwyn didn't dare ask him to stay.

He smoldered beneath the cotton sheet, dozing in the lonely afterglow.

You are like me.

Dwyn stood in the library at Rich Mountain. Someone held his hand. He looked down. Una stared up at him. She grabbed him around the waist, screaming, and combusted. All the flesh melted from her bones. He knelt beside her, beating out flames and weeping.

He dug her tomb in the floor of the library until his fingers dripped blood. He carried her bones down into the grave, saving the horrible, charred skull for the last. Her mouth looked like a shark's, baby teeth stacked on top of the adult.

When he looked up, the necromancers of Nations stared down at him. Every man wore Ehrlik's face, and every woman, Nyssa's cold expression of indifference.

"Kill him, while he can still save us," Ehrlik said.

"We do not wish to kill him. Bastard he may be, but he is what we need."

Nyssa replied. "He could not have called the stones if he wasn't able."

"We want his blood."

"We have it. He is already ours.

A stone slab slid over the opening.

Dwyn tucked Una's skull against his body with one hand, and drew his sword with the other. "I am Dwyn, Mn'Hesset to the Paloh Ethean. I belong to myself and to my God. I will not die here!" He stabbed upward, burying his blade to the hilt in stone.

More fire than form, he rose on the wings of a bird.

He sat up, screaming. "I will not die here! I will not!"

A low growl echoed in the hallway. Dwyn landed beside the bed with a thud and grabbed his sword.

Kritha glanced in the open door.

He smoothed the hair on the top of his head flat. "Fuck, dog, I wish you wouldn't do that."

Kritha growled again.

"Dwyn?"

He flinched. "I don't want to talk to you, Nikl."

"Well, I want to talk to you. Come out, will you—Nyssa's damned dog—"

"I can hear you fine from here." He picked up his pants and jerked them on, turning away as Nikl's shadow filled the doorway.

"My brother wants to talk to you."

"Bullshit. I saw the summons."

"That wasn't him," Nikl blustered. "That's the necromancers' council at Nations, and he wants you well clear of it. He told me so!"

"Contempt of a summons gets me extradited, even if your brother wasn't a liar."

"Will you look at me, please?"

Dwyn looked. Nikl's cloud-plump face sagged. His hair looked like he'd braided it without thinking, let alone used a mirror. He wasn't storming, but his face was a dark, miserable gray, and lightning flickered sullenly under his skin. His pants were liberally dusted with flour. Bread day.

"I came to tell you I'm sorry," Nikl said. "I don't know what the hell is wrong about trying to help the man I love, but...I'm sorry."

"I don't need your help."

"You don't know what you need." Nikl took a step forward.

"You think I'm a fool for not believing you had my best interests at heart, is that what you're saying?"

"You think *they* do? You think Lokey does?"

Dwyn tossed his sword on the rumpled bed. The strong odor of his apples and Lokey's cherries hung in the air. He'd done nothing wrong, but a guilty flush burned his cheeks.

"I wanted to save your damned life," Nikl said. "Nyssa and her ilk, they want you dead and you know it. I shouldn't have run out. I should have explained better, maybe, but I was so damned sure you'd want to go with me—Dwyn, I fucking love you. I've never had anyone I could love and not be terrified I'd hurt them with my storms, freeze them in bed, or scare them with my lightning. Do you know how many people I've had to leave because of that? I've never met anyone like you—never had anyone who could love me like you can. Please forgive me."

Dwyn rounded on Nikl in a fury. "You want me to forgive you? Okay. I'll forgive you when you go to your brother, and tell him Dwyn Ardoche says he can take his offer and fuck himself with it!"

"This is the thanks I get for loving you?"

"You don't love me, Nikl. You never did. You used me. You're using me now."

Nikl paled. "What are you talking about?"

"Lokey told me all about you. You've never left anyone. They leave you. And it hurts, doesn't it, because that's all anyone ever does—they leave you because they don't want you, just like your family, just like your mother—"

"You asshole!" Thunder cracked as Nikl lit up the hallway with lightning.

Dwyn blazed on. "—just like Lokey, just like your mate, they
all left when you were most hungry for love, so what did you do?
You went after me because you wanted to get even, prove you
could have anyone you wanted, just like they could—"

"You should talk, I'm gone for half a day and you're in bed
with him—"

"I didn't seduce him to make you jealous!" Dwyn exploded
into flame. Kritha backed up, barking at them both. "I didn't lie
about loving a man to keep him from being loved by someone
else! And I sure as hell didn't pretend I was in love to try to get
him to turn himself in to the person who wants to kill him!"

"Why, I ought to—"

"You want to hit me? Go on! You can't hurt me any worse
than you already have." Dwyn spread his arms out, offering all
of himself as a target.

"Just...just fuck you." Nikl turned and walked away.

A soft, gentle drizzle began to fall in the hallway. Nikl was
raining.

Dwyn sagged to his knees in the doorway, gripping the stone
walls on either side.

Dwyn knew Nikl had cooked the dinner as soon as he tasted it.
The peppercorn tenderloin was perfect. The mushroom risotto
melted on his tongue, and he almost choked on the roll, it was
so soft, fresh, and full of Nikl's scent. He wasn't hungry. But
he knew better than to drink his way through another bottle of
wine without eating something.

"I'm sorry you must get up so early tomorrow," Nyssa said,
"but I felt it best. Rich Mountain was where you took your penalty
g'hesh, so there it must be set again. The fewer folk, the better."

"Yes." He pushed the risotto around his plate listlessly.

"You seem upset."

"I'm just tired."

"Lokey would sleep with you tonight if you think it would help."

He shuddered. "Uh—no, I'm…I'll be fine."

"Then get some sleep. Nolan wouldn't forgive me if I didn't make sure you were well rested. He will be there tomorrow to see to you, given your reaction to g'hesh."

Dwyn left the table gladly. But he didn't sleep. He lay crucified on the bed while the tree in his mind stretched to the sky, through the world, and its roots sucked greedily at the skulls of the dead. The river of voices in his mind babbled, churning and fretting against every constraint he imposed, breaking through when he least expected it.

When Nyssa knocked on his door, Dwyn was already dressed. He waited for her to back out of his doorway before taking the handles of her wheelchair. He needed something to do.

"You're afraid," Nyssa said when he opened the door to the darkness.

"I'd be a fool if I wasn't. You're depending on Rachet for one thing. And Jack, that Christian, wanted rid of me. I doubt he's changed."

"Leave them to me. You do remember how to drive?" Nyssa smirked as he slid awkwardly behind the wheel.

"Oh, that's funny." He pulled out of the parking lot. "I'll bet Ehrlik already knows about this. I don't trust Rachet."

He winced as the horrible Eseitha ring loomed to his right. He glanced at Nyssa, but she didn't look at it or at the dark wall that barred the way to the road beyond. His heart was pounding.

Tree. Hill. Bones. A warning. *Your promise. You will never leave us.*

He hesitated, shut his eyes, pressed down on the accelerator, and drove through the wall. No matter how far away he went, he would never be free, and he knew it.

"This new penalty term—ten years."

"At your hearing Jack said you'd need ten years to make a start."

"I wish he'd said twenty."

At Rich Mountain, Dwyn wrestled Nyssa's wheelchair out of the backseat.

"When will you be walking again?" He grunted as he pulled Nyssa through the doorway backwards.

"I shouldn't even be home yet," Nyssa said. The doors in the hall were closed, but light filtered out of the haneen. A shadow crossed the golden square.

"Jack," Nyssa said with evident relief. "I'm sorry about the hour."

"No need to apologize." Jack glanced warily at Dwyn.

"Where's Rachet?"

"Here."

Dwyn jerked to a stop. Two men had entered the room from the annex.

"Be quiet," Nyssa murmured.

"Don't let me interrupt anything important," Ehrlik said. "You may pretend I'm not here."

Dwyn shivered. Ehrlik's smile looked better on Nikl. Ehrlik was older now; his face had grown thinner. But his gray eyes were still cunning and full of the good humor Dwyn once found charming.

"I didn't expect you at such an early hour, warloche," Nyssa said.

"Rachet was good enough to inform me. I'm perfectly willing to wait until you have finished. I'm sure nothing you do will affect my summons. You risk the contempt of Nations, and I know you would never be so foolish."

"Never. Rachet, if you please."

The note of irritation in Nyssa's voice gratified Dwyn. About time she realized how poisonous the hateful old man was to her, her mountain, and her authority.

Rachet glared defiantly at Dwyn. He hunched next to Jack, strangling his stav with his claws.

Nyssa spoke quietly. "Do you see now? I was right, wasn't I?"

Rachet rumbled angrily. "A Dragon, on my mountain. The world may end."

"Better than the end of cantrev law," Jack muttered, glancing at Ehrlik. "Do you want that?"

"But Jack—a Dragon—" Rachet said. "These are our mountains."

Nyssa's nostrils flared. "Yes, *our* mountains and I intend to keep it that way. Are we agreed?"

"Warloche." Tully's gravelly voice startled Dwyn.

Ehrlik, who had started toward the group of whispering necromancers, stopped. "What is this? I don't think much of you and your conclave, Nyssa, letting elementals wander loose."

"I am the Chieftain of Ironsfork," Tully said. "And you are in the place I need to stand, as witness."

Ehrlik sneered, but stepped back.

Nolan had followed Tully through the doorway. He carried a stav, the first time Dwyn had seen the doctor with a weapon of any kind. It was taller than he was, white ash, and the silver crest looked like a contorted tree.

"With your permission," Nyssa said, glancing at Tully.

"With or without it, you'd have your way."

Nyssa gripped Dwyn's arms by the elbows. "Dwyn Dragon, by these new terms, you will be bound. You will deliver up your entire library to me, written, as your penalty dictates."

Rachet hissed. "He doesn't need to agree to that again."

"I will." Dwyn mingled his magic readily—he'd been bloody since he'd seen Ehrlik come out of the annex.

"You will do this in the new time specified for your penalty, ten years."

"Yes." Ten years would see him free of the time limit imposed on extradition for the trespass. Murder was another matter.

"These terms I accept, as holder of your g'hesh. Do you agree, warloche?"

He looked up, startled. She should have asked him if he was willing to accept *her* terms unless…he stared at her, terrified. He wasn't ready to be her Seidwendr. But she was taking his curse, his penalty, as a g'hesh against herself as his necromancer. God under the earth, he hadn't expected that.

"Yes," he said.

Nyssa screamed, clutched him fiercely and pitched out of the chair, blazing.

"Nyssa!" He went down with her, but without pain. She'd taken it all on herself.

Tully knelt beside him. Between the two of them, they raised her to a sitting position. Nolan hovered above them like a bird over a broken nest.

"Are you all right?" Tully asked.

She let out a smoky gasp. "Yes."

Tully glanced at Nolan.

Nolan grimaced and squatted beside Nyssa, stroking her leg with his stav and muttering.

"Get me up," Nyssa snapped. "I'm not staying down here with that hateful raven watching. Get me up!" She gripped Dwyn's shoulder, and he pulled her upright.

"He is bound," she said to Jack and Rachet. "As am I."

Had she known she would clash so violently with him? Had Nolan warned her? Surely he had. Moved, Dwyn helped her into her chair.

Ehrlik strolled forward. "If you are finished with Dwyn, I want a word with him in private. In the meantime, you will arrange transport. I'd like to take him to Whiterock today."

"The annex is private enough to talk, warloche, if Dwyn is willing," Nyssa said to Ehrlik, "But you aren't taking him—not today, not tomorrow. He is my Seidwendr and does not answer to you anymore, necromancer."

Dwyn swallowed as the familiar noose tightened slowly, seductively in his magic, an old impediment slithering against his new bond. Regardless of how long it had been, his bones would never forget.

"I will listen to you," he said.

The small door to the left of the fire pit opened on a room as cramped and stony as any tomb in Dwyn's dreams. He stood, stiff and sweating, staring across the table at Ehrlik. He opened his mouth to speak first, and then shut it, unsure of what he should say.

"This is no way to greet me, Dwyndoche," Ehrlik said. "Look at you. You've become quite feral in your exile—self-imposed exile—why the hell did you run from me? I swore to protect you."

"I—I was afraid."

"I said I'd take care of you. I risked my career coming here for you. Please, don't scorn my sacrifice, not when I still love you."

He smelled the way Dwyn remembered, of clean rosemary, sharp cedar, and the hint of decomposition Dwyn loved. The urge was too strong. When Ehrlik's arms opened, Dwyn buried his face in Ehrlik's dark beard. He felt every pat on his back the way a beaten dog feels a caress. He wanted to pull away but he couldn't.

Ehrlik kissed his hair. "When I came back and you were gone, I hunted everywhere. All I could think about was you—gone from me, sick somewhere, dying—without me. Oh, Dwyndoche, mh'arda."

A distinct chill of fear tingled down his spine. "Don't call me that."

"That necromancer—what's she done to you, mh'arda? If she's hurt you, I will bring such a case against her—"

"Don't call me that." He jerked free of Ehrlik's embrace.

"Are we not friends? Have I not loved you? Have I not done everything for you?"

Dwyn put the table between himself and Ehrlik. "Nothing you ever did was for me. I understand that now."

"Dwyn, what's wrong with you? You act like I'm here to kill you."

He swallowed. "You're here to take me back to Nations. It's the same thing."

"I am here to get you out of this hellhole, get you cleared of all charges, and then we are going to Norway together, like I promised." Ehrlik smiled.

Dwyn's legs trembled. "I'm not going anywhere with you."

Ehrlik lowered himself into a chair. "I see I'd better sit," he said. "Something *is* wrong with you. Well, I'll hear you out." He was the picture of the rejected friend, disappointed mentor, and wronged lover, and Dwyn loved him so much at that moment, the words he had to say almost strangled him.

"I talked to Sorcha."

Not a flicker of emotion stirred in Ehrlik's metallic eyes as he raised his head. "What are you talking about?"

"You told me Sorcha wouldn't speak for me at my trial. You said she'd abandoned me. That wasn't true. You didn't ask her to speak at the trial at all. You asked her to speak after I'd pled my exemption. They would have charged me with murder."

Ehrlik laughed harshly. "Did you, or did you not read the summons? It's murder they plan to charge you with now and you are quibbling about when I asked for her help? Yes, I asked her to go with me to speak to the necromancers, to plead your innocence, my dear Dragon. In the quiet after the trial, certain ears were ready to hear the truth."

"That's not what Sorcha said."

"Well, I'm very interested in what she said to fool you. She applied for your job in the Haneen after you left. Oh, she didn't tell you? You never could disguise your face, Dwyn. Yes—while your rune was still smoking on your hand. I put my foot down— the board would have confirmed her."

It sounded so truthful. "Sorcha told me why she wouldn't testify and I believe her," he said desperately.

Ehrlik's composure didn't alter, but he shifted, as if his bones ached. "You really think I would have testified to condemn you? I put my reputation on the line, and you are blaming me?"

"I've never blamed you for the rune. That was the price for my sin, and I have paid—for you and for myself. Be done with me."

"You expect me to just let you go? When you need me?" Ehrlik's face darkened. "I never released you when Riordiin wanted you for your own safety! And I certainly won't release you for her. What kind of a necromancer would I be if I did that?"

"The one you always were," Dwyn said. "The one who told the council I hated Riordiin because he abused me and tried to get another witness to confirm it, the one who wanted me condemned for murder, the one who is here to take me back to Nations on the same charge. You lied from the day you met me. I am no longer your Seidwendr, Ehrlik Valkgrim. You have no hold on me."

Ehrlik's hand shot up. Dwyn flinched.

"I am here to take you to Nations and you will come with me," Ehrlik said in a dangerously quiet voice. "Without me, you would already be in a void cell, raving! I saved your life."

"No. I saved yours. But for you, I would have told the truth. I would have told them Riordiin was my Seidwendr, and I was his necromancer. I killed him as his necromancer, and that makes me a murderer whether I meant to be one or not. I'd have died at Nations, but I'd have died clean of my sin. But your career would have been over if I had, wouldn't it? They would have wanted to know who suggested it. Because I loved you, I took the rune. I owe you nothing more."

"You have no idea what all you owe me. You have no idea what kind of trouble you are in, Dwyn. You think that necromancer you just fornicated with can save you?" Ehrlik laughed. "If I hold her and her plague rats in contempt, what do you think she'll do? Wash her hands of you, that's what she'll do. When they drag you back to Nations in void chains, don't expect me to help you."

Ehrlik's derision rang in Dwyn's ears. He wondered that he'd never heard it so clearly before.

"I didn't ask you for help—you or your brother."

"My half-brother, and not the better half. But he at least knows the meaning of loyalty." He stood. "We will meet again soon. You won't be able to hide behind a third-rate necromancer's skirts and her conclave's penalty for long. Then you'll understand what you've thrown away."

"Coalition. Use the right word. It's the South, warloche."

Ehrlik's gnarled hands clenched the table. "You *are* a fool, Dragon."

"And you are no friend, necromancer," Dwyn said. "You never were."

CHAPTER TWENTY-EIGHT

THE DRAGON RISING

Dwyn didn't watch Ehrlik leave the annex. Only when silence descended did he return cautiously to the hall. Nyssa was speaking with Tully and Nolan near the doorway. Everyone else had gone. He sat at the necromancer's table as exhausted as recrudescence usually left him.

Ehrlik was right. If the council meant to charge him with murder, Nyssa couldn't stand in the way, not for long. He thought about the spike, deadly and dark, waiting for him if he tried to cross the border of Ironsfork and leave forever and his stomach lurched.

Nyssa rolled up to the stage. "Well?"

"I wasn't ready." he said. "And it won't work, what's more. You've hurt yourself for no good reason."

"Oh, I have several good reasons," Nyssa said, smiling. "Not the least of which is protecting a man who can't seem to protect himself."

He rose, grumbling. "You tricked me."

"Should that surprise you? I am a necromancer, after all." Her blue eyes gleamed with a hint of Dragon's fire.

"How typical. Now what, warloche?"

"Breakfast, I think," Nyssa said, letting him spin her chair around for her.

"I couldn't eat."

"Fresh air then."

"I have to go where you go, necromancer, and you can't walk with me."

Nyssa chuckled. "You are my Seidwendr, Dwyn. I give you leave to walk wherever you please when you work miracles like you did this morning. I never expected such amazing things: you wise, and my coalition complicit. I warned Rachet that Ehrlik would take you, penalty or no penalty. He didn't believe me. But one thing a southern crow won't abide is a Nations raven sticking his beak in where it's not wanted." She smiled up at him. "Trust me. I will take care of you, Dwyn. I will see justice done."

He didn't trust her—not even the part about walking freely. Only when he watched Tully push her away, with Jack chattering on her right, and Nolan stoically marching on her left, did he believe. He crunched across the gravel in the opposite direction with no clear idea of where he wanted to go—just away. He smoked and steamed as he trudged across the frosted ground, hands in his pockets, sword swaying on his back.

What did Nyssa think she could say when Ehrlik brought his contempt charge to Whiterock? Call Dwyn innocent? He'd been Riordiin's spoken Seidwendr for years. She could no more convince a council he was duped than he could say what he'd really done. He'd killed the man who trusted him, the one he'd sworn on his bones to protect, and whether he meant to kill or not, he was still a murderer. He left the beaten path and headed downhill through the school gardens, jumping from terrace to terrace.

Tree. Hill. Bones. The vision caught him mid-leap and he stumbled.

"Leave me alone," he muttered. "You'll have me soon enough." He stood, looking at the empty building, dark and desolate as he felt.

On the lawn in front of the school, two dwarves were wrestling with a platform bird feeder. Between the empty flower beds, a few cardinals waited attendance on a child throwing fistfuls of birdseed.

"Una! Throw it on the path, for the sake of the earth." The man closest to Dwyn threw back the hood of his sweatshirt. White hair shone in the sunlight.

Dwyn froze. Nikl stared at him for a minute, then turned his back. "Dammit, Cheyloche! Hold it level."

Cheyloche Northslope's bald spot gleamed as he glared at Nikl. "It's you yanking it off center!"

Una missed the garden plot she had been seeding and sprinkled another. When she saw Dwyn, she clamped her fist and raised it.

"Go away, Dragon!" she said in Nikl's voice. "No one wants you." Her hair stood up like a spiky crown.

Nikl spilled the sunflower seeds. He squatted to scoop the black pile into the sack.

"You shouldn't be here," Dwyn said.

"Neither should you." She stuck out her tongue.

"Tell me something I don't know."

Her face took on a conspiratorial look. She beckoned him to bend down.

He didn't. He didn't want a fistful of birdseed in the face.

She whispered, "Rachet's in the library."

"Get Nyssa." Dwyn shoved her aside. He drew his sword and raced down the hill.

He barely heard Nikl call his name as he threw himself against the front door. It catapulted him back. Locked. He jammed his shoulder into it, hand smashed against the handle, hunting for the tabah.

"What is it?" Nikl had followed him up the stairs. Cheyloche Northslope was running up the hill as fast as a dwarf could run. He was all but out of sight at the crest.

Dwyn kicked the door. "It's Rachet, damn him! He'll get into that mess, and all hell will break loose."

Nikl pulled a wad of keys from his pocket and sorted through it. "They let *you* have a key?" Dwyn gasped.

"Yes," Nikl said, scornfully. "The school gardens are mine after all."

"Can't you hurry?" Nyssa had better get there, or Dwyn wouldn't be held responsible if he kneed the old warloche in the stomach, thumped his head for him, and threw him out of the building for criminal dumbassery.

"Can't you go a day without bitching?" Nikl flipped through the ring of keys so quickly he cut himself. His blood welled across the key as the door opened.

Dwyn charged through. "Stay back!"

Nikl said something—it sounded like a curse, but Dwyn didn't hear clearly. He raced into the corridor and tripped over a charred desk. Ruined bookcases and chairs barred his way. Why the hell was this shit still here? He'd said they could dispose of it. He scrambled up, smashed his way through, and headed for the stairs, limping—he'd twisted something when he fell. He scorched his way up the long hall that led to the library.

The boxes disguised in illusions stood untouched where he'd left them. Sunlight flooded the library through the window, but a different kind of light oozed under the storage room door, a sickly blood color, as if the stone were hemorrhaging.

"Rachet?" Dwyn pushed the door open, sword first.

The old warloche's sleeves were rolled up to his armpits. He muttered under his breath as he piled sodden rags of paper and leather on the floor to his left. "Go away, Dragon. You have no place here."

"Put it back, Rachet." He smelled danger—rotten, dank flesh, a reek of underworld magic that didn't belong to the waking world.

"How dare you give me orders, Dragon? And to think, I saved your life." Rachet went on digging while flesh sloughed from his bones. "The warloche from Nations would have taken you, but for me."

Dwyn edged around the puddles of virulent sludge. "If it makes you feel better, I don't hold you responsible. Get your hands out of there, warloche. Don't you see what it's doing to you?" He gagged.

Rachet grinned back at him, a skull with dark hollows for eyes, and broken teeth. "You can't understand what it is to feel your bones breaking for want. You'll never be old. But this man knew—my friend, my most beloved." Rachet caressed a dripping book, placed it to his mouth, and kissed it.

"I know you loved him. Rachet, please. Put it down."

"Oh, 'Rachet, please,' is it? Next, you'll call me warloche and mean it. What does a Dragon know about love? You've never loved."

"I know what it is to lose someone—someone you love more than your life. Put the book back. There's evil here, Rachet."

"A human word—"

"Draug, then, if that means anything to you. You're killing yourself, you're killing this place, and you're killing him."

"*You* are the one killing him." Rachet shook his rotting fist at Dwyn. "You destroyed his work."

"Asa's work decayed long ago. You kept it, Rachet, you loved it, but you did nothing to preserve it. How could you? You didn't know how, but you tried. Believe me, I know what that feels like. Let him go. Leave the dead to God."

Rachet went on digging.

Damn, he was no good at this. Where was Nyssa? She could talk sense into the old man. All he could do was crack Rachet over the head and drag him out. Dwyn crouched, ready to spring.

Rachet raised his free hand. Dwyn's firelight glinted on the barrel of a gun.

"If you attack me, I will kill you."

Fear fought against fury as Dwyn stared at the weapon. Fuck it—let Rachet die if he wanted to. He took a step back.

"Dragon?"

Dwyn jumped. Una stood framed in the doorway, eyes huge.

"Una—get out of here."

"Monster—"

"Go!" Dwyn yelled, backing into the doorway over the top of her.

A gray mass sagged through the ceiling as a heavy, eyeless head crowned through the stone.

Una screamed and grabbed Dwyn. She trembled—not just in her body, but in her thin, weak magic as it sheltered in him, a small, desperate fledgling seeking refuge in a tall tree before a storm. The vision exploded in his mind, furiously bright. Fire gathered in the branches, and he soared skyward on the wings of a bird. Not a bird. A Dragon.

His heart galloped wildly as understanding filled him. It wasn't a vision of the mountain trying to kill him. That was what they saw when they looked at him—their protector, their warrior, their Dragon.

The gun went off.

The impact threw Dwyn backwards. Una's siren scream joined his own as fire erupted from his shattered arm. His sword dropped from his nerveless left hand.

"Una?" Rachet's reedy voice sounded terrified. "Child?"

If the necromancer had killed her—Dwyn's blood-soaked shirt combusted as he struggled to stand, pushing up with his right hand on the floor. Splinters of bone jabbed his raw flesh and his world went misty.

"Child?"

Dwyn had run as fast as he could when the goblins shot him, dripping a trail of fire. December's rain froze him. Blood flowed sluggishly down his shirtfront. He staggered into the house and collapsed.

"Child? What have you done?" His grandfather's face loomed out of the darkness.

"I have loved, grandfather, and I die for it." The story spilled out of him like his blood. She was a goblin. He was a dwarf. But Dh'Morda called to both of

them and he thought—he hoped—if he loved enough, he might belong.
   Hot lead melted into his blood, poisoning him, teaching him the error of his ways.

Dwyn cursed as he stood, sword in one hand, pommel stone pressed against his wound.

"Child?" Rachet knelt beside Una.

"It's me you shot," Dwyn growled.

Rachet's eyes opened as wide as Una's. He babbled something that might have been half-curse, half-apology.

Dwyn didn't hear. "Get out of here. Both of you."

Una buried her face in the sodden fabric of his shirt. "No! I want to stay with you. It's only safe where you are!"

"Get out!" He took a better right-handed grip on the hilt. A wave of dizziness swamped him.

Dwyn lay on the floor alone. His grandfather had gone—to make restitution for him, no doubt. The herbs he'd swallowed for pain inflamed his mind. When the Paloh Ethean appeared, Dwyn blamed the mountain laurel. The God was too beautiful to be anything but an illusion.

   "I have come for you, Mn'Hesset. I've been waiting for you." The God of the Dead stretched out his hand.

   "I don't believe in you. You're not real. I'll blink and you'll be gone."

   "Mn'Hesset, you are mine. You were always mine. You belong to the realm of the dead."

   Dwyn stood, panting, grabbing his wounded shoulder. "I don't believe you! I don't believe in you!"

   "You will." Fingers black as charred stumps and covered with runes red as flame touched Dwyn's wound.

   He fell to the ground, screaming as his wound healed. It still hurt. It would always hurt so he would never forget. "Paloh mhu," he wept.

   Bloody fingers caressed Dwyn's forehead. "You have drunk the dark water. You have eaten the fruit of the dead. Do so now, and never forget."

Dwyn knelt by the black stream, thirsty beyond endurance, and drank. He took the fruit from the orchard and ate. And he remembered when he'd first tasted it, five hundred years before, when the god had torn him from the fire and held him close as a mother might. Sweet yet bitter, he understood the flavor of death. He had never lived without it.

He staggered upright. The top half of his left arm throbbed. Below the elbow he felt nothing. He might have cut it off and not cared in his body. But he sobbed, pouring his pain and hate into his voice like the blood poured from his wound. "I am Dwyn! Mn'Hesset to the Paloh Ethean! Come to me and find your death!"

His first blow missed. He stumbled out of the way as the draugr rolled by, smashing boxes. The putrid mixture of blood, coffee, and confusion escaped in a flood. Dwyn choked on the fumes. The draugr's long arm caught him in the side and threw him on top of the transcription desk. He struck the wall, leaving a blot there like a smashed insect.

The draugr crushed him bodily into the rock. Blood flooded his lungs.

Dwyn lay naked on the ground inside a circle of black stones. Sharp, evil, thorn-like things on a green landscape, they cut the heavens open, bleeding blue on the white clouds, but he was at peace, and completely content, the way he felt only after he made love. His long brown hair stirred as the wind whipped across the bed of grass.

Mh,arda? Do you see us? Do you know us? Do you love us? The voices whispered tenderly.

If this was dying, it was how he wanted to die. He wanted it with his whole heart.

"You know I do," he whispered.

The mountain echoed around him like a drum. Our life. Our love. Our strength.

He went through the wall. One moment he was suffocating under the crushing weight of the draugr, his stomach forced into his chest, drowning in his own blood. The next, he was safe on one side, and the draugr was beating itself against stone on the other. He stood, gagging, gasping for air. His broken arm dangled uselessly, but he was alive and seething with rage. A roar filled his ears as if the entire mountain howled inside him. The pulse of the earth surged beneath his feet, the heartbeat of some great colossus. Fire blossomed from his chest and threw him backwards. It tore him in half. It made him whole. Falling stone showered Dwyn, but he didn't feel it.

He cried out with the voice of the mountain. "I am Dwyn, Dragon of Ironsfork. I belong to myself, to God, and to my mountain. I will not die here!"

He didn't know what he expected. Even so, he was surprised when the mountain fell in on him.

Or perhaps he fell in on the mountain. Fresh fire rippled through his body and pumped through the deep wells of his heart. He'd changed—a sense of purpose filled him, a near-reptilian urge to hunt, to slay, to devour. He snaked into the molten stone around him. He didn't understand what had happened to him, or what he was anymore, but he knew the thing that was poisoning his mountain. Draugr. Only one way to deal with the corruption. Take it apart. Tear it from his body. Scatter it to the water. Throw it to the sky. Feed it to the earth. Consign it to the flames.

With a snarl of fury, he roared through the stone, following the taint deep, deep into the mountain. He lashed at it with talons black as death, and sharp as knives. "I am Dwyn! Dragon of Ironsfork!"

The draugr lost form and slithered away, desperate and bleeding. Dwyn spread himself out, a million flames flooding through the magma, and then he had it by the magic—a cankerous monster in the mountain's flesh, malignant, spreading. It fought, balling up around his beak, but he snapped through the hard skin like a membrane, and thrashed it to death, shredding the magic until it melted and congealed into a puddle of black blood around his claws.

He saw his reflection in the foul pool. He was a monster in flame, tower-ing, winged, and furious. He was tiny, just a child, his infant's skull broken, and blackened to charcoal. His silver teeth were stacked like the mouth of a shark, his eye sockets brimful of fire. He scooped the dark magic up, marveling that he could hold it in his skeletal fingers and gazed into it. The shape of his mountain looked back at him, and he despaired.

It had been too long. Everything was ruined. The mountain lay open before him like a body, gutted for a g'uise, tortured by necromancy. The rot ran too deep. He couldn't undo it. The mountain was as fallen as he, and he could not remake it.

But then, so was he. He was created by necromancy and elemental fire. Renewal must begin somewhere. Maybe it began with him.

He tore off his arm. It came away with little pain, and he stared in surprise at the runes of his books shining ruby-bright on the ends of his dark bones. He'd thought he'd lost his soul on the mountain.

He picked the flesh from the bones, and piled it against the wall. Something else should be there, not that horrible library where decay ran out, saturating the floor. He packed the space full. More liquid squelched out and formed another black pool.

Then there was the spur itself, sagging away into the valley. He braced it with his finger-bones. He laid his long bones on either side of the crumbling mountain and bade it be strong.

Now he hurt. The bleeding stump ached, but deep contentment filled him. He glanced down. It was healing already, coated in the melted stone that had become his body.

He sank down, exhausted. "I will die now and be pleased to die as a Dragon."

The mountain rumbled. "We would not have you dead. We would have you live in us."

"I would rather rest, beloved." He pillowed his head against the mountain's bright heart. "I am so tired and so broken. You said yourself, I was poisonous to you."

The mountain purred around him. "Mh'arda, you are altogether beautiful corruption, like fruit the frost has taken. Live, and be as wine in our blood. You cannot help what you are. Death made you his left hand, and

you will always be his left hand in death, Mn'Hesset. But be ours in life."
"I don't know how. It would break me utterly, and I could never be whole."
"You can be whole. Let us show you. Let us love you."
"Let me rest."
"No."

The library ceiling was a wash of flames and smoke. It blurred beyond a column of golden light that seemed to be part of him. A bright image burned above, something birdlike. Red wings, blackened and clawed at the tips, swooped down. Dwyn yelled in terror as huge, dark eyes stared at him. Rimmed with fire, they spoke of magic beyond anything he imagined he possessed.

He'd seen such things on the walls deep in ancient mansions. The lower halls sunk in darkness contained the pictures of huge creatures soaring over the mountains—but they were pictures on a wall. They could not be real. He'd thought the stories of the Southern Dragons were just that. Only stories.

The Dragon glared at him again. If he had any questions that it wasn't him, they were answered. He half-expected his sarcastic laugh coupled with some snide comment about how bad he looked lying there, crushed to death. He was the Dragon, and the Dragon became him.

The smoke cleared with every sweep of his wings. He tried to trace the magic spinning the illusion from the center of his chest to the sky, but failed. The immensity overwhelmed him. He couldn't tell where he ended and the mountain began. It was all of him. It was none of him. He didn't understand, but he wanted to. He would figure it out the way he unraveled the mysteries of glyph script, a piece at a time, filling in the gaps. This puzzle belonged to him now—him and his mountain. He thrilled at the words. It was his.

The room around him seemed different in some way. He

wanted to see what had happened when he'd dismembered himself to remake the mountain. He tried to sit up.

The Dragon screamed with him—a roar of agony from his soul. He'd only thought his arm was numb. With no grandfather to take out the bullet, the metal had dissolved in the enormous heat of his Dragon's blood. His smashed chest dripped like a broken egg. A section of ribs stuck out at an awkward angle. It moved whenever he gasped for air. The rest of the crushed contour was disturbingly still.

Suddenly, he wasn't an almighty Dragon fighting a war for his mountain. He was a frightened, tiny dwarf, a broken, mutilated wreck. He needed Nolan. Nyssa. Somebody. The pain forced a gargling cry out of him. The Dragon shrieked.

Impressive the illusion might be, but it did him little good. If he'd seen that hovering over a mountain, he'd have legged it the other way as fast as he could run. It might burn out or it might not. He had no control over it. Now *that* was incendiary.

As long as he didn't move and didn't breathe, he wouldn't hurt. He sucked air in a shallow, half-hearted way and surrendered to the darkness.

"Mn'Hesset?"

He knew the voice. "That's not my name. I am Dwyn, Dragon of Ironsfork." He spoke through thick lips, clotted with blood.

"Mn'Hesset. Look at me."

His God was as beautiful now as he had been the first time Dwyn had seen him. He wasn't a tall dwarf, but small, lean and powerful, with phosphorescent golden eyes. His dark bones showed through a mist of skin. It hurt Dwyn in more than his body to turn his back on God, but he did. Shame filled him. "I am not Mn'Hesset. I'm a Dragon. You have the wrong man."

The Paloh Ethean laughed. It sent shivers through Dwyn's body. It was his laugh, or so like, it might have been his. Dark and evil, he'd never been able to change it.

"You are Mn'Hesset—the only one I have ever had, the only one that ever will be. You will remember." The Paloh Ethean bent, and touched his arm.

The exposed bones splintered, split, and remade themselves. The Dragon overhead exploded in a welter of cinders and sparks.

Rain pattered on Dwyn's face. He lay on the floor, surrounded by rubble. A slab of stone entombed much of his broken body. He shifted, and screamed as the pain threatened to twist him in two.

"Nolan! Tully! He's here!"

Dwyn blinked. "Leave me alone."

"Oh, buddy, it's all right. It's going to be all right."

Dwyn tasted the ocean as Nikl kissed him.

CHAPTER TWENTY-NINE

MOUNTAIN MAN

Nikl had found him. Ehrlik would come next to take him away, and Dwyn was helpless.

No—not helpless. The mountain would help him. But he felt weaker than he'd ever been, even after the worst recrudescence. Perhaps it was the price of this new, frightening magic. He had no one to ask. The voices in his head neither confused nor comforted him. No one was there.

Except Nikl. He would pretend Nikl was his friend, not his betrayer, a friend he loved and made love to. He would hold on to that, the way Nikl held his hand. Breathing hurt. His arm hurt. If only everything would just stop hurting.

It's okay. It's all over," Nikl rumbled.

It wasn't, but he didn't speak. All the words he knew were gone. Like the truth of the Dragon's magic, they had scattered and flown to the winds, and one small dwarf could not hope to hold onto them. He closed his eyes.

"Dwyn, stay with me, buddy!"

"Una," he said, wincing. Talking hurt too.

"She got around me before I could grab her. The building

was burning. I got it raining, but I was pissing in the wind until Tully came."

That wasn't what he wanted to hear. He needed to know if Una was safe. She must be, or Nikl would have said something about Rachet carrying out a burned corpse. His stomach lurched.

"Nolan." He wanted so badly to forget. Nolan would have medicine to make him forget.

"He's coming," Nikl said. "Hold on."

Voices echoed, but in Dwyn's ears, not his mind.

"Get the shelf off first."

"He won't stand it."

"I have to get him to the hospital. You'll come with me, Tully. I'll need your help with his fire—"

"They won't allow—"

"Dammit, I say what they will and won't allow, Rachet!" Nolan's long gray ponytail fell forward into Dwyn's face. "Dwyn, I can't take your pain away, not yet. We have to slide this shelf sideways first before we can lift it. You have to tell me when it hurts."

"Shit."

Nolan seemed to take that as acquiescence. He nodded to Tully, standing at the far end of the stone.

"Nikl, stay close. He may need you."

"What the hell am I supposed to do?"

"Breathe into him if he needs it, Thunderer," Nolan snapped. "Now pull."

If felt like they tore what was left of his arm from his body. He screamed, Nikl yelled. Nolan shouted, and then mercifully, there was nothing. Dwyn fell into the darkness.

Dwyn stood in the library at Rivnkyf, but there were no books, no comfortable benches for reading, no soft seidr lamps glowing in the niches between the book cases. He recognized the place only by the massive stone transcription table. Around it, three necromancers stood, dissecting a tiny body.

Dwyn gasped. He didn't want to see this. He turned to leave.

The Paloh Ethean took his arm.

"No. I don't want to remember this!"

"Mn'Hesset, you must know where you came from."

"I know where I came from! When I was born, you took me from your earth beneath the apple trees. You gave me the water of your world, and I ate the food of the dead. I may forget, but I am Mn'Hesset, and I always return to you."

The Paloh Ethean's eyes filled with warm light. "Mn'Hesset, don't be afraid. I will go with you."

Together they approached the table.

Sparsely haired, eyes seamed shut, the child was too young to have ever lived. The thin limbs looked skeletal. The organs, already removed, reposed in quartz jars, suspended in liquids. Dwyn looked away in horror, but not in time to miss one necromancer, taller than the others, tenderly caressing the infant's bald head.

"When the Southern Dragon cursed their mountain, they needed a protector—one who could constrain the fire from eating them all. They made a sacrifice of a stillborn baby to hold the Dragon's fire in his bones forever. You became the greatest of all their warriors, and my Mn'Hesset from birth."

"They could have let me rest." Dwyn rubbed the top of his own head convulsively.

"It was war. They needed a hero."

"But I didn't spare them their curse. They were Dragons all, beginning to end, and all because of me."

"But you protected them, nonetheless. For five centuries their clan survived because of you, Mn'Hesset. You kept them alive long enough to mate even if you could not hold their minds together. And all the while, you served me." The naked teeth of the Paloh Ethean could never smile, but a smile was in his voice. "Not faithfully, no, but I never asked that of you. I wanted a warloche who would always challenge me when he believed it right."

"But I failed them, and now I have failed you," Dwyn said.

An ancient, bent necromancer entered the room. "Chieftain, all is prepared," he said, bowing.

The tall necromancer kissed the baby on the lips, already drawn in a death grimace over the toothless gums. "The Dragon's curse is hard, my son, but you must carry it. Save us, or the Dragon's fire will destroy us all. Hold him in your bones. I love you. Your clan loves you. And your mountain loves you."

The tall necromancer straightened his robes and turned to leave. He stopped and stared hard at Dwyn for a moment as if he could see him. His eyes were too large for his face, spaced wide, and a deep chestnut brown. Dwyn's eyes.

Dwyn backed away, terrified. Fire bloomed around him consuming his skin, his face, and his body. Only his bones remained, black with soot, red with magic.

The Paloh Ethean's soft voice whispered in his ear, "You never failed me." His eyes were burning coals.

Dwyn clawed at his arm. The necromancers were tearing his muscles away and the blackened ends of his bones were on fire with pain. "No," he cried. "Hata! Father, no. You don't know what the Dragon did to me. You don't know what a mountain really is. Please. Don't!"

A hand restrained him. "Dwyn, don't touch."

"Don't leave me here!" He screamed, thrashing. "Don't… leave…"

"Calm down. Come back to us, Dwyn." A cup full of a foul-tasting liquid touched his lips. He gagged, then swallowed before he drowned.

"There, there." A woman touched his cheek.

"Rigah?" He opened his eyes. "Jullup."

Her warm smile penetrated the dark fog of his memories. "You're all right now. You're safe."

His arm felt strangely wet and itchy. His arm. He could feel his arm. He could feel it, all the way to his fingers. He broke down, sobbing. "Will I—"

Jullup stroked his hair. "In time, you'll get the use of it back. Nolan already has a physical therapist lined up for you once you are a little recovered. You've been drugged for most of the last two days."

Dwyn suppressed a groan. Any man—human or dwarf— in Nolan's employ had to be just as demanding as the doctor. Nolan had run him breathless after he'd almost drowned. That reminded him of his chest. He reached with his right hand to feel his ribs.

Jullup patted his hand away. "Leave it alone."

"Where am I?" Instinctively, he pulled the sheets up. There wasn't enough earth above him, and he wanted to hide.

"The hospital."

"It's not allowed," he said, remembering Rachet's words.

"Well, the joint decision of three necromancers and a Seidroche overrides most objections."

Still, he would have been an inferno, not something to have around oxygen and other flammables. Tully must have helped. Yes. He remembered Nolan telling Tully to come, he would be needed. "Where's Nyssa?"

"She went to discuss your case with the necromancers at Whiterock."

He clenched the blankets tightly. "What will she tell them?"

"You'll be three months recovering, that's Nolan's assessment, which should be ample time to decide what to do about the contempt charge Ehrlik Phaneugh lodged."

"What's to deliberate?" he asked, bitterly.

"Quite a lot, as it happens." Jullup smiled. "Do you want to sit up?"

She raised the bed for him in little jerks. His entire left side was swathed in cold, wet bandages that squashed when he moved. Daylight streamed in through the glass. Humans walked around in a parking lot below, breath steaming in the air.

"Better?"

He glanced down at the pale silver tube snaking out of his bandaged chest. "What happened? To the school? To the mountain?" Might as well know the worst. He remembered the way he felt when he'd seen what he'd become and loved it. All that was gone now, replaced by cold, fearful dread of what others might think if they'd seen the Dragon. When they found out it was him.

Jullup pursed her lips enigmatically. "I'm not supposed to talk to you about that. Nyssa planned to be here when you wakened, but there was too much to do."

"I destroyed it. Didn't I?"

"I'd better let Nyssa explain."

"I don't understand."

Jullup laughed softly. "You didn't destroy it. Is that enough?"

"No."

"I can't tell you more. At present, only necromancers are allowed inside."

"Why?"

"Nyssa says the response is natural, given your elemental status, but she believes they will accept it in the end."

"You're speaking in riddles," he said, exasperated.

She patted his hand. "I'm sorry! Nikl may tell you more since he's been on Rich Mountain, but I believe he also has orders to keep his silence. He's at Ironsfork. I sent him to get you some fresh clothes. I told him he needed a shower and a nap, and Lokey drove him home."

Dwyn shifted unhappily. Dh'Morda was ending. Lokey and Nikl must have forgiven each other. They would both forget him, and he would be alone. He deserved it probably, but it still hurt. "Una. What happened to her?" he asked with an effort.

"She's fine—not a burn on her. Rene and Neil had to keep her from running back into the building after you. She says you saved her life."

Either Jullup knew about the gunshot and was reminding him not to speak, or she didn't, but Nolan must. Dwyn detected no dysfunction in his bones from the melted lead, which meant that someone—the Siedroche—had chelated it out of his magic. He didn't feel good by any means, but he wasn't sick. He was tired, and a little dizzy from the drink.

"Jullup...don't leave me."

"Rest. I'm here." She stroked his hair, and he thought again of his mother—the one he never known—and a father who touched the skull of his child and told him to be strong for his family.

The roses in the land of the dead are strong poison and strong medicine. How long Mn'Hesset lay in their shade, nursing his wounds, he did not know. The days passed over him like the moon in the ever-dark sky. The nights rested on him like the dew that fell from the leaves. Insensible, he dreamed his life.

All that remained of the draugr that had chased him from dreams to waking was a hull of empty skin. He remembered killing it, but after that, his memory fragmented. Things he thought he knew, he forgot. Things he forgot returned to haunt him. He wept with sorrow when he did not weep with pain, and his tears frightened him. Never, as far as he knew, had Mn'Hesset wept.

This ground was cold, and he served a cold God. But in dreams he was impossibly young, the Dragon he had once been, and the dwarf he wanted to be. He lingered in them, preferring sleep to waking until the swans came from the river to feed.

Mn'Hesset had never seen them fly. He didn't know they could. But fly they did and descended on him like a flock of vultures, digging at him with webbed feet, pulling at the lips of his healing wounds, tearing him apart in greed and hunger.

Only such an attack could stir the fires burning so low in his breast. He roused, beat them off with his hands, and then with the butt end of his sword. He tore one from his face as it sought to stab his eyes out. He slashed its head off with a single right-handed stroke of his blade. The rest fled, shrieking into the sunrise.

Sunrise. He'd never seen such a thing.

He leaned forward on his sword, blinded by a long band of gold creeping over far distant mountains, wide plains broken with wilderness, countless lakes and rivers, and strange forests. He turned, and stumbled toward his broken mountain, dazzled by daylight, drunk on sadness.

Long ago, a Dragon bound himself through an infant's bones to the necromancy that destroyed him. Trapped in those bones, he'd never thought he'd be free, much less that the curse binding the two parts of his life into one should be broken by a man caught in the curse of his clan—half-necro-mancer, half-Dragon—a bastard in every way. Mn'Hesset no longer knew where he ended and that Dragon began.

But he was alive.

As far as he knew.

Dwyn woke, screaming, thrashing, beating swans off his face. "I am alive! Don't let them kill me!"

Strong hands restrained him. "No one is going to kill you. Not while I'm here." A breath of wind moved through Dwyn's magic like a summer breeze.

Dwyn opened his eyes.

Not dawn here. By the shadows in the corners, it was late afternoon. The face of Nikl emerged out of rose canes and the golden haze breaking over his mountain.

"Why are you here?" he grumbled.

"Well, aren't you a ray of sunshine." Nikl folded his arms over his chest. "You might try to be civil."

Dwyn huffed. He wanted Jullup back, or Nolan, or Nyssa—hell, he'd have settled for Tully. Anyone but Nikl.

"Where's Lokey? Jullup said he went to get my clothes."

"*I* brought your clothes. Lokey had to work today. So did I, ingrate, but I've got my sous chef covering for me."

"You shouldn't have bothered." Dwyn growled.

Nikl snorted. "A little 'thank you, Nik, that was thoughtful of you' would be nice. Or can't you manage it?"

"I'm hurting!"

"Yeah, well, I hurt too, buddy. You hurt me!"

"You're not the one with your arm in a cast. You're not the one with a standing warrant for your arrest. Don't tell me you're hurt. You don't know the meaning of the fucking word. Why the hell did you have to call him? He never would have come if you hadn't told him."

Nikl turned as green as a sky full of tornadoes. "Because of you! I wanted to help you."

Dwyn laughed. It hurt. "Some help," he said, rubbing his chest.

"Yeah, well I didn't know you hated him, okay? Not like I could—you're shut up tighter than my wine cellar when Lokey's around."

"Me? What about you? Let's not talk about my family, Dwyn, they give me indigestion! You could have at least told me your clan name was Valkgrim."

"They don't claim me—"

"He's still your brother, and you've got the same style, let me tell you, grab a man by his cock and make him love you when he's not got the sense to run."

"Like you're any better," Nikl snorted. "One fight, and you're in bed with Lokey before I can even apologize."

"You damned near got me extradited!"

Nikl shoved the chair sideways. Lightning flickered in his hair, and all the lights buzzed. "Okay, you know what? You want me to say I'm sorry? I'm sorry! I shouldn't have done it, I shouldn't have loved you, I shouldn't have cared. You want me to leave? I'll leave. Next time you run into a burning building, I'll step aside and let Lokey run in to save your damned life."

Dwyn's fire surged. "You—you ran in for me?"

Nikl folded his arms over his beard. "Waste of my time, I can see that now. Might have known you'd scorn that, like you scorn everything else. I guess it didn't mean anything, nothing means anything with you—"

"You kissed me in there. I guess you'll tell me that didn't mean anything either?"

"I thought you were dying," Nikl snapped.

"I thought I was dying, too."

Silence settled in the room, falling like the afternoon shadows across the hospital bed. Somewhere in the parking lot, a car alarm went off, shrilling warning until the owner stopped it.

"Dwyn, I didn't come here to fight. I hate fights, and I hate that I want to fight with you. And now you hate me."

Something twisted hard in Dwyn's chest. "I don't hate you."

Nikl ran his fingers through his hair. "You'd be right to. I should never have done what I did with you. But I thought—where was the harm, right? It's Dh'Morda, and all's fair in love and war." He pushed his chair closer to Dwyn's bed. "I didn't think you would care. I didn't think *I* would. But when you ran into that burning building, all I could think about was how I should have gone with you—helped you."

"You'd have been no help to me."

"I could have punched you senseless and dragged you out."

"You said you'd never hit me no matter how angry you got."

Nikl rolled his eyes. "Clearly, I didn't know you were a complete dumbass."

"Thanks a lot, you sure know how to give a compliment—I feel loads better."

"Fuck off."

The square of sunlight, orange now and turning red, fell on Dwyn's wounded arm, warming the aching bones, soothing the miserable place inside his chest where more had been smashed than his ribs. Nikl had come for him. Nikl had run into a burning building to save him, right beneath the open jaws and terrifying eyes of the illusion flying right out of Dwyn's body and into the sky.

His bones bit—no, it wasn't an illusion. But he didn't have the right word for it. Whatever the Southern Dragons had once called it, their word was lost and the meaning with it.

Metaphysical manifestation was more accurate, but Dwyn didn't like to think of himself the same way he thought of a draugr.

It was me. Maybe that was the right word after all. *Me. Dh'Rigahn.*

Dwyn glanced at Nikl, picking at the edges of his thick sweatshirt, storms huddled just out of sight, lightning on the horizon. God under the earth, he could need that man so badly if he let himself.

"Nik," he said softly. "I'm sorry too. I shouldn't have—"

Nikl waved his hand irritably. "You had every right—"

Dwyn reached out and grabbed Nikl's hand with his good one. "No. I didn't. And I think I knew it was wrong when I did it. I just didn't want to admit it to myself."

Nikl squeezed his hand.

Dwyn pulled in a deep breath, feeling a tightness in his chest that had nothing to do with the bandages. "Will you forgive me?"

Nikl pressed his forehead against Dwyn's hand. "Sweetheart, I forgave you the minute I saw you trapped under that bookshelf. Can you forgive me—for Lokey, for Ehrlik, for everything?"

"Yeah. I think I can." He pulled Nikl in right-handed and kissed him on the cheek, or at least that's how it started out, but Nikl moved, hunting Dwyn's mouth, and Dwyn gave it to him, tasting all of Nikl's desire, his desperation, his urgency.

This wasn't love. Love shouldn't be this passionate, this needy, this demanding. Whatever this was, it was broken, as broken as he was—torn open, crushed, bleeding, and like any wounded thing, dangerous. But he could understand that. He moaned softly, deepening their kiss.

It was a long time before he let Nikl leave—breathless, sweating, and grinning, with all his hair standing on end. Then Dwyn settled back on the pillows, watching the sunset give way to nightfall. What he had with Nikl wasn't love—not yet. But he would take a chance on it. Perhaps in time, two broken men might make each other whole again.

When Nyssa came a week later, she was dressed for a winter's day. She shook her keys at him. "Are you ready?"

Dwyn rose from his desk in the hospital room. He'd recently begun to scribe again. It hurt whenever he tried, and he made a sloppy mess whenever he succeeded, but at least it kept the penalty g'hesh from sticking him in the wrists.

"Here to take me back to prison?" He knew he was being released today. He'd been waiting on a ride since nine.

"I'm here to take you *home*," Nyssa said, "but we might go somewhere else first, if you aren't too tired."

She was walking well, he noted with envy. He rose and cleaned his pen clumsily. Nolan had assured him gross movements would come back first, and then he might expect control to return. He stared at the letters on the page and grimaced.

Nyssa looked too.

"Yes, I know it's shit." He tossed his pen back in his box. He had no lack of materials to work with now. Whatever he asked for, he got. His case was stocked with the white paper he favored for ordinary work, and the thicker, cream-colored linen stock for heavier necromancy. He had all the ink he could want, and leather too—beautiful, fawn colored doeskin for binding his finished texts. As if he had the dexterity to use a needle.

"You'll want a coat over your bandages. It's sunny, but very cold."

"Help me, then?" He jerked his head toward the bed where his clothes were folded, ready to take back to Ironsfork. One of the nurses usually helped him dress in the mornings, but today they'd left him to manage on his own. He did well with everything but his fly. He'd tried for twenty minutes before he gave up.

Nyssa eased him into a new camouflage jacket—one Morven had given him, not new, but well-worn, soft, and huge. It fit over his bulked-up arm, but swallowed the rest of him.

They wouldn't let him walk out. Nyssa wheeled him out of

the hospital doors to her car and buckled him in like a baby.

"I'm supposed to do that," he grumbled, flapping hopelessly in his oversized coat.

"I'll let you do it on the way home," Nyssa said.

"We're going to Rich Mountain, then."

"Yes," she said, pulling away. "Don't be worried. The necromancers left a few days ago. No one is waiting for you."

"Do you blame me for being afraid?" He picked at his jacket buttons fretfully.

"This isn't a region where interference from Nations is appreciated. We've been left to fend for ourselves far too long. Besides, I said I would speak for you. And I think I won't be the only one."

"Ehrlik won't stop. Not until he has me again."

"I don't expect him to stop. There will be a hearing six months from the date of your penalty. I'm certain Ehrlik will be there, and he will once again demand your extradition."

"Hell."

Nyssa laughed softly. "Put your mind at rest, Dragon. You have friends now. You have me. You will see."

CHAPTER THIRTY

THE SOUTHERN DRAGON

The doors of the school looked different. They gleamed darkly silver, as if polished. That was all.

Dwyn stared, feeling there should be more, but everything looked disturbingly the same. And yet, it *was* different. Brighter. No. Cleaner. That was the word he wanted.

Only one other car was parked in the lot—Lokey's Corvette. No necromancers' Mercedes with the white logos and tinted windows. He sighed in relief.

"Lokey is here setting up a new computer room. I've asked him to take you back to Ironsfork when you get tired." Nyssa parked, and Dwyn got out, determined to help himself this time.

The hall was empty of the dead leaves and furniture. The countless footprints of coming and going had been scrubbed away. The floor was the same blue-gray sandstone he remembered, but buffed to the deep color of the evening sky when the moon is rising. Where the entry turned into the corridor, a rainbow blossomed on the mirror finish. He hesitated.

"Go on," Nyssa said. "You'll like it."

But he waited for her to join him before he stepped around the corner.

A colorful mural graced the wall, floor to ceiling, stretching the length of the hallway from the entry to the first door on the left, a good ten feet or more. In the four corners, four dwarves held the world in their hands. The scene was of a wide valley surrounded by mountains. He knew the shape of each of them as a lover knew the body of his beloved: Ironsfork, Blackfork, Fourche, Rich Mountain. In the valley, crops grew lush and green beneath the benevolent watch of a Thunderer. An Earthshaker watched over a forest, rich with timber. In the far corner, a Wight fed his blood to the rivers. And in front of him, facing the other three, a Dragon, sword in hand, protected an army marching to war. The face of the Dragon, marred by a single, thin line of smoky quartz, looked out at him like a man divided.

Four birds hovered in the sky above each of the four dwarves: an eagle for the Thunderer, a crow for the Earthshaker, a heron for the Wight, and for the Dragon...Dwyn touched the bird with recognition. It was his Dragon, highly stylized, a lean, vulturine creature with red-rimmed eyes, and long black wings tipped with flame.

"What do you think?" Nyssa spoke softly in his ear.

"I don't know what to think." Had there been a chair in the hall, he'd have sat in it, whether it collapsed or not.

"We believe, the necromancers from Whiterock and I, that this is original to the building, chased out of the stone, like the story walls at Ironsfork. Hardly a room is left that isn't similarly decorated."

"Left?"

"Many rooms changed their shape. Some vanished entirely. Ratchet's old room is gone, and Cheyloche lost most of his classroom to a stairway that wasn't there, but no one is complaining." Nyssa smiled.

He really needed to sit down. "They didn't condemn it?"

"No. It's sound. We've been over the building and under it. There's no trace of weakness anywhere. I've something else to show you, but you can rest when we get there."

Dwyn held his left side with his right hand, laboring as he followed Nyssa up the stairs. These steps were far steeper and narrower than he remembered, and there were more of them. God under the earth. He was heartily sick of feeling like an old man. This poor building was in better shape than he was.

When he reached the hallway in front of the library, he squinted against the light flooding the tunnel. The poorly repaired necromancer's glass had vanished, replaced with stone. Veins of citron, rose quartz, and amethyst flowed through the gray wall, painting gold, red, and purple rivers on the floor. Skylights high above admitted gallons of winter sunshine. Momentarily stunned by beauty, he stared, wondering if he'd been transported to some ancient city of dwarves that had been buried intact, never looted or defiled.

"Mica lined." Nyssa said, pointing at the reflective material in the skylights. "In some of the older parts of Ironsfork, shafts like these bore deeply into the mountain. My father was afraid I would..." She hesitated. "I was quite young, about Una's age, and Tully was afraid I would fall in. So he blocked them. That was before I went to live with my mother at Nantahala, with the Oxfire clan."

"You'd think he'd be proud to call you daughter."

"He has his reasons," Nyssa said quietly. "This is what I wanted to show you. Will it do?" She pushed the library door open.

He walked in, overwhelmed. The dingy storage room was gone. They'd swallowed it up in the new design—no, the old design. Sunlight dumped through additional mirrored shafts in this ceiling, and he thought unhappily of leaks, but the bookshelves were well away from the openings, safe from damp and sunlight alike. They jutted out regularly on ribs from the walls, spaced appropriately to allow for a variety of sizes of books and codices. A wall composed mostly of horizontal stone tubes puzzled him at first.

"Maps," he mused aloud. "For storing maps."

"A bit large, aren't they?" Nyssa said.

"Maps were large. Wars could stretch mountain ranges away, and magic must always be traced." Memories threatened to swallow him—the bready scent of chestnut pollen swirling around him, the tramp of hundreds of feet in his ears, the glint of copper as he led an army to war. *Damn.* He would never get used to this. He swayed, suddenly dizzy.

Nyssa caught him by his right arm. "Do you need to sit down?"

"Yes," he stammered. "I think so."

She led him to the window seat. He shuffled beside her, disoriented and feeling truly old.

"Better?"

"No." He leaned against the window. It had survived his reconstruction, but like everything else, it had been altered. It was taller and wider too, made of a peculiar frosted milky quartz that distorted the view of the valley below. No necromancer alive could build magic on broken bones, but he'd somehow done it. No. The mountain had done it, through him, but that hardly made things better.

Nyssa sat beside him. "You're upset."

"What does this mean?" He waved his hand at the sunlit room in front of him. "What will they do to me because of it?"

Nyssa was quiet for a moment. "That depends."

"On what?"

"On how you explain this."

"I can't explain it to them when I can't explain it to myself." He twisted his right hand around his left, and the incendiary rune seemed to brand him again.

"At first, we all feared this would break. Dragon-made necromancy is inherently unstable. The Rivnstone Dragons are proof of that. Their magic always needed to be maintained:

written magic held together by Seidoche, and the Dragons themselves held together by Seidwendr. No one would trust necromancy forged out of Dragon's fire, no more than they trust Tully's water magic when he uses it in his asphalt."

"Morven told me about that," he said, peeling off his over-sized jacket. Inside the library, it was warm. The warmth came from the stones itself—a Dragon's warmth.

"But this magic isn't unstable. There is fire in it, but the necromancy itself is extraordinarily powerful. Doing something like this should have killed you outright. And it didn't." Nyssa stood, and paced to the nearest bookshelf. She ran a finger over the stone. "When Ehrlik came to Whiterock, yelling extradition and threatening to censure us if we didn't send you with him immediately, the council refused to let you go. Can you imagine why?"

Hope stirred in him for the first time since he'd seen the mural in the hallway. "I hope they don't plan on having their chambers renovated any time soon. I don't think I'm up to it."

Nyssa laughed. "Good, you're getting your edge back. I was beginning to worry I'd have to be nice to you. Can you think of another reason?"

"I can. But they are fools," he said.

"Elected fools. They don't get their position by clan-rite, as they would in the north. Some folk, more foolish than most, are already calling you the next Southern Dragon. I didn't discourage the comparison."

He twisted his hands anxiously in his lap.

"Appearances matter, Dwyn," Nyssa said, softly. "Whether you are, or are not, made of the same fire as that legend, you must seem to be. Do you understand?"

"That only works until they tire of that game. What happens then?"

"By then, I hope I have a better reason for them to stand with you against Nations. But I need time, Dwyn."

"Time?"

"To prove your innocence."

He shut his eyes, frustrated. "I'm not innocent." He held up his left hand painfully. "Riordiin was murdered."

"He was," Nyssa said, "but the man who killed him was not his murderer. I made a vow I would see justice done, and now I will. I will protect you, Dwyn, with everything I am because it's a heinous crime to charge the weapon with the murder."

Dwyn didn't say anything. Tears leaked from beneath his eyelids and stung them open again.

Nyssa was looking down on him, her stern face uncharacteristically softened. "For all his faults, I loved him too," she said. "I can't rest until he is avenged. I swore on my bones I would not." She sighed. "There is one more thing I need to talk to you about. Una is telling everyone that Rachet shot you on purpose. Is that true?"

"He shot me, yes. He wouldn't have minded if he'd killed me."

"He is important to your position here. You need him."

"You say I should call that girl a liar?"

"You know what is said of the debt one warloche owes another."

He ground his teeth. "The truth unspoken, the debt unpaid: this is the treasure one dwarf takes from another and the true measure of his wealth. *Seida.*"

"You could quote me page, paragraph, and exact line, I'm sure. Your silence is powerful."

"Tell me why I need Rachet." He knew where this was going and he hated it, hated it with his whole heart when he thought of Una's trusting teal eyes and her anguished cry. *I am only safe where you are.*

"He is the steward of Rich Mountain. They want to hire you, to make you Seidoche over the school. We must move while the enthusiasm is there."

"I see." Burning fitfully, he stared at the long carpet of light ending in front of the walnut circulation desk, now strategically placed at the front of the library, waiting for him.

He rubbed the bandages under his jacket and his rune glimmered, as fretful as a candle in the wind. "I can't live at Rich Mountain. I must stay at Ironsfork. I belong there." He hesitated, unsure of how to tell her how he felt. The thought had been on his mind almost since he'd woken up in the hospital and found himself glad of Nikl, Nolan, Jullup, Morven, Lokey, and even Tully. And Nyssa—he needed her, as much or more than Rachet. "I wouldn't feel right anywhere else. Also, there is the void room. Inevitably, I will have need of it."

"Unusual to find you thinking so far ahead and with such concern for yourself and others," Nyssa said.

He snorted. "I'm always concerned for myself. But I want something from you, too. Your respect, warloche. I hope I've earned it."

The corner of Nyssa's mouth turned up at one corner. "You thought very seriously about killing me, warloche. Believe me, I respect you."

"I want you to treat me as an independent Seidoche. I belong to you. I belong to your mountain, if you like, but not to anyone else, not unless I wish it. And I want to be paid decently."

"You won't find the salary as lucrative as what you had at Nations."

"Of course not—it's a provincial library, and nothing in it. Yet. But I want to earn something, penalty or no. And I want to be in charge. My library. My rules."

"As long as you abide by the laws set by your guild."

"You think I wouldn't? Do I look like a fool to you?"

"I think I would like you better, warloche, if you could be civil when you're making demands."

He looked away from her. "I can't promise that. I'm used to being the Dragon nobody wants."

"We want you," Nyssa said softly.

He shut his eyes and leaned against the window. "That's going to take some getting used to."

The warmth that was not the sun's doing soaked into his back and his shoulders. He thought of Nyssa's library at Ironsfork, and how he had once yearned for one of his own. This wasn't a thing like what he'd had in mind. The changes his magic had made, while good for the mountain, made him wish he'd done things differently. Where the desk stood, the sun would glare right into his eyes every afternoon. With the storage room gone, he had no place to keep necromantic works away from the children. He'd have to remedy that somehow. And he could already hear the outcry over the need to update the bathrooms and the electrical systems. The magical repairs in those areas would be completely impractical and outdated. Nyssa was right. He needed to sign while the ink was fresh and wedge himself so deeply in this mountain it would be the job of Ehrlik's life to dig him out of it.

"When?" he asked.

"We'll wait until your arm is healed for the teacher's g'hesh," Nyssa said. "But I see no sense in waiting to get you under contract. Would you be up to writing it out for Neil and Tully to sign today?"

"I think so."

"You'll find the proper paper at your desk, and pens and ink as well."

He didn't open his eyes. A breeze ruffled his hair when Nyssa left and shut the door, but he didn't mind. Instinctively he knew he could open it whenever he wanted to leave. For now, he was content to rest and think.

The next Southern Dragon. If they knew what he knew about that Dragon's nature, they wouldn't be so eager to embrace him. He'd torn away his own arm to make the magic that built this place. If it took that kind of sacrifice to restore one building, he didn't want to think about what kind of sacrifice would be needed to rebuild the magic of these mountains.

They wanted that. The image of the tree returned, the tallest thing on a hill, with a mountain nestled firmly beneath its strong roots. Green moss covered the bones that built the mound, and men and women both loved in that mountain, and children were born, and played, and grew in the shade of the great tree. The tranquility of the scene made him smile. And he thought *his* dreams were outrageous.

Extraordinary necromancy, maybe, but he didn't understand it—only enough to know that what had begun with him had not ended. He scratched absently at his bandage and shifted to a more comfortable position. He ought to get up before he fell asleep sitting in the sunshine like a weary dog.

The door opened by stealthy degrees.

"Shut the door, Una." He stretched, and opened his eyes.

Una's pink coat was so dirty he figured she'd rolled down a hill to get there. Her hair bristled with dead grass. She rocked back and forth, heel to toes as she grinned at him. "I was being a mouse," she said.

"You make as much noise as a lizard in the leaves."

She pranced in, frilling like he'd paid her a compliment. "Can you tell me a story? Nikl said you would."

"Nikl can—" He winced. The muscles tightened along his left side unexpectedly. "I'm not sure I'm up to telling stories today."

In answer she held up a wrinkled paper bag. "This is for you. I only ate one of the donuts," she added, when he took it and looked inside.

"And took a bite out of the other one."

"I had to taste them," she said, wide-eyed and innocent. "I wanted to see which was better."

"Yeah, and then you ate it."

"I did not! I saved the best one for you." She hopped up in the window seat next to him.

"Can I see?" She pointed at his bulky arm.

"No," he said, spitting crumbs.

Una leaned back against the window, pouting. "I told everyone Rachet shot you, but no one believes me."

"Yes...about that," he started, but thought better of it. She'd argue with him, and he wasn't in the mood. He left her sitting, got up, and went to the desk. He rolled the chair experimentally across the flagstones. He'd have to ask for a leather mat so he could fireproof it properly. Plastic would melt too easily, and he was prone to hurling bits of ashy paper around when he worked. It wouldn't hurt to go over the entire place with a blessing once he had the blood for it.

"You like stories?"

"Oh, yes." She batted her eyelashes at him.

Little minds like hers were so easy to crack open. He'd threatened Morven with se dwynen, and it gave him a sour taste in his mouth, but it would be easier for Una. He took a sheet of paper from the desk. "Well, quit kicking the wall and I'll tell you one."

He began to write as he recited, slipping into his story voice like a well-worn shirt. "The first thing you need to know about Pekkoh is that Pekkoh is dense, dense as the rock he came from. He was born upside down, and the men of his mountain had to chisel him out of the granite slope. His head was made of rock for weeks before they cracked it all off for him."

He wrote Una's name beside his, and began to work out the details laboriously in slow runic. "He never got any smarter, did Pekkoh. No. He was the same stone-head when he grew up, and that's why they named him Pekkoh. Rock for brains."

When he was done, the shooting would be his secret, and Nyssa's, and Nolan's, all adult dwarves, and Nyssa and Nolan knew how to keep secrets.

"But there's something you need to know about Pekkoh. He has more magic in his stone skull than most warloche have in all the bones of their ancestors. Some folk say Mother Mountain gave him magic because he was too foolish to live without it. Other folk say all fools are full of magic, because like children, they don't know what they can't do. There it is, though. Pekkoh is strong in magic, and it doesn't do to cross him, because Mother Mountain loves him, and she will always look out for him.

"One day, Pekkoh was wandering from mountain to mountain looking for a home, and he came to a place that brewed the best locust ale in all the mountains. Pekkoh had never tasted such wonderful stuff, and he said so. He asked them how they made it.

"The ale-brewer's son thought he would have some fun with Pekkoh. He told Pekkoh if he planted a locust pod, he could grow a beer tree. He gave him a bean and told him how to plant it. Pekkoh did. He planted it on top of his mountain, in the light of a winter moon, and he watered it into the stony soil with a cup of spit."

He sanitized that part slightly. The old stories were always earthy and difficult when it came down to interpreting what they meant.

Una leaned against the window frame, knees drawn up to her soft, furry chin, eyes curiously unfocused as his magic stole into her mind, gently easing the memory of the gunshot away, and all the pain of the disbelief with it. He burned the paper beneath the desk, out of sight, and now out of mind.

"Pekkoh did everything the dwarf told him to do. He dug that seed up every day to see if it had grown."

He had Una giggling by the time Lokey came to the library. The nisse listened from the doorway, and even joined Una in a laugh when Dwyn got to the part where Pekkoh brought down half a goblin mountain clearing out their cesspools.

"In the end, the dwarves were so grateful to Pekkoh—for the goblins never came back to the mountains—they told Pekkoh he could take as much beer as he could carry with him when he left. So Pekkoh picked up their cellar and walked off with it. Sometimes a barrel would slip out and fall, but he was so happy that he didn't care. The ale leaked and got into the ground. And because of that, some mountains in Rigah Tarn have springs so sweet, you can get drunk on their waters."

He let the last gossamer threads of magic drift away in the silence.

"Is that all?" Una said.

"About Pekkoh? No. There are many stories about Pekkoh."

"Tell me another one."

"I think the Dragon's tired," Lokey said, coming to his rescue.

Dwyn let Lokey do the hard work of ushering Una out of the library. She protested all the way up the hall, loudly. If there were more stories, she wanted to hear them all. Now.

"What a brat," Lokey said, laughing when he returned.

Dwyn leaned back in his chair. "Well, she knows what she wants."

"Is this what you want?"

Dwyn stood, and shuffled the unused paper straight before putting it in his desk. "Not all. I want a new storage room, a study table on that wall, and a curtain over that window."

"That's not what I meant." Lokey's gaze rested on the empty paper sack in the window seat.

"I know," Dwyn said, blushing. "But I think you know my answer to that, too."

Lokey smiled. "Can't pretend I didn't expect it. When you were injured, all he would talk about was you."

"When I woke, all I wanted was him," Dwyn said. "Storms and all." He scratched the back of his hand.

Lokey raised his eyebrows. "Sweet springs. Don't think I've heard that version before."

"The dwarves in Rigah Tarn use only local water for making locust beer. They can be quite cagey about their sources—they call them Pekkoh's Springs."

"You ever get drunk drinking from one?"

"Maybe." Dwyn patted the desk with a quick hexn to lock it.

He picked up the paper he'd written his contract on, and folded another sheet of paper over it to protect it. Flecks of ash were all that were left of the magic he'd worked on Una. He scattered them with his foot.

"I'm ready to go home," he said.

CHAPTER THIRTY-ONE

THE BEGINNING

"Today is the day, isn't it."

It wasn't a question and Dwyn didn't answer it. He sat on the stone wall above Nikl's raised beds, legs dangling against the cold concrete. It was the middle of February, a foolish time to plant anything, yet here Nikl was, in dirty sweatshirt and equally dirty sweatpants, digging in his garden, a tray of artichoke plants parked beside his knee.

"They'll freeze," Dwyn said.

"I won't let them," Nikl said. "Do you want me to come?"

"Nyssa won't allow it." Dwyn scratched scabbed wounds under his sling.

"Not now. Tonight. I could take off."

"No." He might be in a world of pain later, but Nikl had taken off much of January to be with him at Ironsfork, taking care of him while he recovered.

"Or I could ask Lokey to stay with you until I get done." Nikl looked up, his cloudy face full of concern.

God under the earth. He'd never get used to this man who could cut him with a look. "No, I'll wait on you."

Nikl smiled and the sun came out from behind the clouds. Dwyn basked in it—that hard-earned light. He'd almost snuffed it out before it could warm him.

Loving Nikl was so different from what he'd expected. He'd hoped they could make a fresh start. Instead, every smile tortured him with Ehrlik's treachery, every passionate embrace burned like Riordiin's fire. He thought the crucible of memory would destroy him.

Instead, it healed him. At the end of every hard-fought battle with his fear, he found Nikl waiting for him to emerge, loving him through the pain, as tender with him as he was with the seedlings he was transplanting today. He needed Nikl, and the more he loved him, the more he understood that Nikl needed him too. He sighed wistfully. One day. One day he would look at the man and see only him.

Nikl stood and wiped the dirt off his hands onto his pants before touching Dwyn's knee. "You'll be fine. Nolan wouldn't allow it if you weren't ready."

"But I'm not fine, Nik. I'm not trained for this. I'm a necromancer's librarian, not a teacher."

"Oh, balderdash. The kids love you already."

"They will love me far less when I have to start giving a grade. I wouldn't pass a one of them at this point. Maybe Una. When she's not interrupting me and everyone else."

Nikl shifted position a foot further down the row, squatted again, and picked up his trowel. "With Nyssa taking care of you, nothing bad is going to happen. Relax."

"I wish this could wait until March."

"It would just be another few weeks to dread it."

"True." Dwyn wiggled down the wall. Nikl had a warm, southwest feel about him lately, which Dwyn understood to be spring coming early to the mountains. Owain Beek, the ancient beekeeper for Rich Mountain, had said as much when he brought in the first swollen buds of the maple tree to Neil, declaring winter was over. No piddly groundhogs for Southern dwarves.

The maple tree never lied. Hence the wind in the southwest.

"So, why do you do it?"

"Do what?"

"Plant those things now."

"So they'll make this year." Nikl settled another seedling home in the ground. "If I plant them any later, they'll never flower."

"You know what really scares me? That I'm going to fall. Break it all over again."

Nikl tamped the soil around the plant tenderly. "You're stronger than you think. Now quit cooling your ass up there and throw me some straw. Mind where you pitch it."

Dwyn grunted, got up, and went to the cart where Nikl had parked a load of fragrant straw. He tore a flake loose and tossed it carefully onto the path near the flowerbeds.

"One more at the far end should do it." Nikl fluffed the straw around his new transplants. "Then you'd better head over."

All the fear that had been simmering since Dwyn had pulled the covers over his head at dawn returned. He dusted the burning straw from his hands. Ashes drifted like snowflakes over the ground.

Nikl grinned. "Go on. You'll be fine."

You'll be fine. He'd gulped the sentiment down at lunch, along with a sedative Nolan had given him, but neither placebo helped.

A warm wind chased him as he walked the long path to the school, whipped around his chest, and gusted hard in his face for an instant before whisking busily away. Nikl would take care of him when the day was over, but it wasn't over yet.

Dragon. A whisper, sensual and soft as Nikl's kiss, drifted through his mind.

With some consternation, Dwyn stopped walking. He didn't need this now, not today, but by now he knew he could never ignore it. He stood still, poised at the crest of the hill overlooking the terraced gardens in front of the school. With Nikl's permission,

Samara's class had planted a flowerbed full of flabby cabbages. Dwyn had one in his library. Una had snapped it off at the base and brought it to him in a paper cup. There were green ones, and red ones, and pink ones too, all bright as summer roses scattered through the riot of colorful pansies, violas, and daffodils.

Dragon. Do you hear us?

He squatted down and tentatively placed his left hand on the tilled earth in one of the beds. "Yes."

We are here. We are with you.

He closed his eyes, shuddering. He wasn't ready for this either, this intimacy that knew no limits and respected no boundaries. They'd picked him open like a bad tabah, undone all his hexn, and lodged inside him, more permanent than any g'hesh. They flowed through his magic in continuous current. His silencer no longer worked. The voices could come in the middle of a story he was telling, they spoke to him when Nikl held him at night, and they intruded on his dreams without warning.

So far, he'd kept his bond with the mountain a secret from everyone. He'd added layers of illusion to his Eseitha hengh, augmenting the commands he'd given the stones in their infancy. Nyssa didn't know what he'd done. Nikl didn't know. He barely knew. But the more he learned, the more incompetent he felt. They wanted so much from him, and he was so small in every way.

Come to us.

"I tried. I've been trying."

Last night he'd stood in the Eseitha hengh beside the lake for hours, naked and terrified. His open wounds had healed, the pins and metal that held his bone together had been removed, but he felt far from ready to be crushed underground, opened up, and explored again. When he finally found the courage to touch the ground, he'd pulled away before the earth could seize him. For the rest of the night, he lay awake next to Nikl, with images of dead and dying dwarves plaguing him as the mountain wove hurt and disappointment out of his fear.

Let us love you.

"You don't understand," he murmured. Thoughts crept in where the mountain could see them. Under the darkness of the lake, he drowned by inches, dragged down by chains until he died, face smashed in the mud beside the old rivn.

In immediate response, a sunny day appeared. The terrifying lake glowed and the little waves rippled innocently in the sunlight. His Eseitha ring glittered. He kissed the earth, and it held him like a lover while he gave himself up completely to the unbearable joy of belonging.

When?

He ran down the hill.

Dwyn expected Nyssa to be waiting for him in the hallway. She was not.

He stopped in the entry, hackles up. "Rachet."

"You're late," Rachet said.

"Nyssa told me after lunch. Here I am," Dwyn retorted. They were equals after today. Dwyn would be the official Seidoche, with the same g'hesh and the same responsibilities as any teacher, just like Rachet, Samara, Cheyloche, and Nyssa.

"We don't have all day. The students will be back, and I want this over with."

Dwyn followed Rachet's bent figure through the empty halls. He wanted it over with too. All the people waiting for him in the library had seen him cower under a g'hesh before, but he was a different man then, a prisoner, not a warloche hoping to become part of the community. He followed Rachet through the door, praying by his God and his mountain he wouldn't be a weeping disgrace in a few minutes.

Nyssa had her hair down, but her weapon was conspicuously absent. She wouldn't take this g'hesh with him. He'd be bound to Tully today. This was no penalty, no crime and punishment. He was a mountain man, contracted by another mountain to work, and he'd answer to his chieftain if he didn't uphold his bargain.

Dwyn flinched when Tully stepped forward. He'd come straight from the quarry, and he smelled of damp earth and dynamite. There was dust in his eyebrows.

"Dwyn, warloche of Ironsfork, are you prepared?" Nyssa said.

As he'd ever be. "Yes."

Nolan watched from the window seat. No doubt he had a pocket full of drugs ready for Dwyn when he collapsed. Jullup sat beside her mate. She gave Dwyn an encouraging smile, and he felt worse than ever. Maybe he should be glad Nikl wasn't there after all.

"Face your chieftain, then," Nyssa said.

Dwyn obeyed. He slipped carefully out of his sling, and laid his left hand in Tully's right. Tully's lips curled in dislike. Dwyn scowled back.

"Today we confirm Dwyn, warloche of Ironsfork, as Seidoche, to be used at Rich Mountain in his capacity. He is agreed to this in contract and we may bind him by g'hesh to service," Nyssa said.

Rachet and Neil stood together, next to the circulation desk. They didn't look happy. Dwyn didn't blame them.

"The oath you take today is the one all of us who teach have taken," Nyssa went on. "You will swear on your blood and bones to fulfill your duties as Seidoche to this mountain, and enter into no contract with any mountain not under the ownership and governance of Tully Irons or his representatives, Neil or myself."

"This I will do." His promise wound through his magic, cold and clammy as lake water.

"You will swear on your blood and bones to fulfill your duties as Seidoche for both children and adults of this mountain, and you will abide by all g'hesh laid on you by your guild."

"This I will do." At Nations, guild g'hesh were applied in batches like this. Sorcha had once carried him off-stage when he collapsed. Underneath his desk he'd tucked a sack full of clean clothes—just in case. He didn't want to ride back to Ironsfork in soiled underwear. Tully's hand tightened, squeezing Dwyn's elbow painfully.

"You will swear on your blood and bones, to regard the folk of Rich Mountain and Ironsfork as your folk, and you will fulfill your duty to your folk, with all your skill and all your strength."

"This I will do."

For a wild, hopeful moment, he thought he'd been spared. Then a violent surge of fire set him ablaze, the g'hesh wrapped him up, and it was not cool like mud, but a heated geyser of molten water, scalding him all up in his magic. The mountain screamed inside him. He yelled and collapsed.

Tully went down with him, lips drawn back in a tense snarl. "Meda," he hissed, boiling over.

"Meda," Dwyn let go. His arm cracked painfully on the hard floor. He balled up, rocking back and forth.

"Lie still," Nolan's voice spoke over the confusion of pained and angry voices. Bitter liquid slipped between Dwyn's teeth.

Beside him, Tully hissed and spit like an angry tea kettle. Jullup held Tully's hand, patting it gently.

"I hate him. I hate him." Tully's eyes were shut tight, and his mouth barely moved.

"Perfectly normal," Nolan said.

Dwyn wasn't sure whether Nolan was talking about his reaction or Tully's confession. He thought it best not to ask. Nyssa touched his forehead, and he grabbed her wrist like a lifeline.

"What's wrong with him? Why does he fall out, cry, and hurt like that?" Neil's voice joined the torrent of noise.

"It's because he's a Dragon." Gently, Nolan helped Nyssa pull Dwyn up.

"Probably it means he won't keep his promises," Rachet said.

Dwyn stumbled up, hanging between Nolan and Nyssa. "Do me a favor, old man," he said, glaring at Rachet. "Don't parade your ignorance of g'hesh in front of another mountain, okay?

They're liable to think we're all as hopelessly backward as you."

Nyssa helped him into his chair. He felt so dizzy he thought he might throw up.

"Enough," she whispered in his ear.

"Keep him the hell away from me."

"You behave yourself."

"I will if he does."

Nyssa left him hunched over his desk, dripping flame. Tully, pale as a mushroom, had to lean on Jullup when he left. Served him right. High time someone else suffered for what they put him through. He had hoped the days of g'hesh burning him to ashes were over.

An image came to him of a long section of bare rock wall sliding down violently into a lake below. Trees and water shivered, and the mountain trembled inside of him. So, he wasn't the only one hurting when a g'hesh was applied to his bones.

He leaned back in the chair, sweating fire, staring at the glossy, quartz-veined ceiling above. Rachet was right. Could he keep his promises when his mountain suffered because of them?

We will help you. We will keep our promise with you. The tree appeared in his mind, but this time he didn't feel so alone. The mountain held him up.

Nyssa brushed his hair back from his forehead. "I told Nolan I'd take you home. I've already cancelled your afternoon class. I thought it might be too much for you."

He roused. He felt like he'd been dreaming awake. "Yes. I want to go home."

"You were brave," she said, patting his shoulder.

"I wasn't going to piss myself in front of Rachet."

"A worthy goal."

"Don't mock me," he grumbled.

Nyssa laughed. "Don't leave yourself so open, then. I was proud of you."

He squinted at her standing in the sunlight beside him. "I collapsed on the floor. You call that brave?"

The smile on her face turned the corners of her mouth in, giving her dimples he didn't know were possible. "But you got up."

She was wrong, of course. He'd done it only because he wasn't about to listen to a necromancer spout nonsense without a fight. But he wouldn't argue with her logic.

He was a Dragon, and he would be brave.

Brave enough to ask Nyssa to drop him off just inside the stone pillars that marked the gates to Ironsfork.

Brave enough to stand in the winter sunshine and wave off her protests until she drove up the mountain without him.

Outside the Eseitha hengh, Dwyn took off his shirt, stripped the shoes from his feet, dropped his pants, and left everything behind in the shadow of the cold, grim knives of stone he'd planted here on this lonely mountain. He drew the cool afternoon air into his lungs and breathed fire out, as he pulled the thelon from the ends of his long braids and let the unruly mass of his hair ripple down past his waist.

Close to the lake, cold would always reign, and weak sunlight made only pale windows between the bars of darkness that surrounded him, but ready or not, he flushed with the fire that forged him. Flame quenched the shadows, bathing the grass red as the welcoming earth quickened beneath his feet. He thrust Mh'Arda deep into the warming soil, and opened his joyful arms to the sky.

He danced.

ACKNOWLEDGEMENTS

Special thanks to Mel and Lynn, who read and gave feedback along the way, and to members of the River Valley Writers' Group, who met Dwyn when they met me and didn't run away screaming.

ABOUT THE AUTHOR

R. Lee Fryar is a writer from the Arkansas River Valley.
When she isn't writing, she can generally be found up a
mountain, out on a river, or in the woods somewhere.
She writes adult fantasy and paranormal romance.

Lightning Source UK Ltd.
Milton Keynes UK
UKHW022110151222
414012UK00016B/451/J